RI

MW00878815

Riding

a

Black Horse

Book 1 of the Night Maiden Series
Dan R. Arman

DEDICATION

To my wife. She's the one who rides the black horse in real life and inspires me every day.

RIDING A BLACK HORSE

Table of Contents

Chapter 1 6

Fall of Year 43 (after the Great Plague) 6

Chapter 2 15

Summer of Year 34 (after the Great Plague) ... 15

Summer of Year 43 (after the Great Plague) ... 16

Chapter 3 28

Spring of Year 43 (after the Great Plague) 28

Chapter 4 40

Spring of Year 43 (after the Great Plague) 40

Chapter 5 48

Spring of Year 43 (after the Great Plague) 48

Chapter 6 61

Spring of Year 43 (after the Great Plague) 61

Chapter 7 74

Spring of Year 43 (after the Great Plague) 74

Chapter 8 83

Spring of Year 43 (after the Great Plague) 83

Chapter 9 88

Spring of Year 43 (after the Great Plague) 88

Chapter 10 97

Spring of Year 43 (after the Great Plague) 97

Chapter 11 107

Spring of Year 43 (after the Great Plague) 107

Chapter 12 117

   Spring of Year 43 (after the Great Plague).....117

Chapter 13 126

   Spring of Year 43 (after the Great Plague).....126

Chapter 14 137

   Spring of Year 43 (after the Great Plague).....137

Chapter 15 148

   Spring of Year 43 (after the Great Plague).....148

Chapter 16 173

   Spring of Year 39 (after the Great Plague).....173

Chapter 17 189

   Fall of Year 43 (after the Great Plague).........189

Chapter 18 200

   Fall of Year 43 (after the Great Plague).........200

Chapter 19 218

   Fall of Year 43 (after the Great Plague).........218

Chapter 20 230

   Fall of Year 43 (after the Great Plague).........230

Chapter 21 256

   Fall of Year 43 (after the Great Plague).........256

Chapter 22 267

   Fall of Year 43 (after the Great Plague).........267

Chapter 23 292

   Fall of Year 43 (after the Great Plague).........292

Chapter 24 299

    Fall of Year 43 (after the Great Plague) 299

Chapter 25 314

    Fall of Year 43 (after the Great Plague) 314

Chapter 26 325

    Fall of Year 43 (after the Great Plague) 325

Chapter 27 345

    Fall of Year 43 (after the Great Plague) 345

Chapter 28 375

    Fall of Year 43 (after the Great Plague) 375

Chapter 29 388

    Summer of Year 42 (after the Great Plague) . 388

Chapter 30 393

    Fall of Year 43 (after the Great Plague) 393

Epilogue 405

    Spring of Year 44 (after the Great Plague).... 405

Chapter 1

Fall of Year 43 (after the Great Plague)

"You know, we're all going to die," Minoru muttered, as he carved his name into the mud with the tip of his spear.

Kamatari banged his friend's shoulder with the shaft of his own. "Now why would you say a stupid thing like that?"

Minoru peered glumly at Kamatari from under his oversized helm. The rust that covered his makeshift armor made him look like a beached crab and his sullen eyes were black against his tawny soot-covered skin.

"Of course, we're going to die," Kamatari continued, kicking at Minoru's thin scratchings with his boot. "Look at us. We've been conscripted into an army led by that Bastard Dauphin of Lutesse. The same bastard who allowed his industrial base to come under siege by an overwhelming enemy force. Now we're the only ones standing in the way of said enemy force having a free and unfettered run of the valley. In a few minutes, we'll be dead and our families will be speaking Fiorese as they mop their masters' floors and clean their toilets. That's our plight. Why do you think I stopped off at the whorehouse in Muckville? We live every day somehow, but I never expect we'll see another morning this time."

"But the Dauphin's soldiers have to be nearby, right? And they've promised to pay us after the battles are over."

Kamatari grunted and adjusted his own pie plate helm and scratched the scraggly patchwork beard. "You should have come with me to the whorehouse."

"Not that whorehouse. That one woman wanted to slit your throat, not sleep with you!"

Before them, the Fiorese had already spotted the Orloinian forces approaching and had ample time to turn their wagon train into fortifications. The opportunity for surprise had been lost as dark slowly began to give way to dawn. The Dauphin's commanders often made a habit of caution and delays. Now the empty plain before them would become a killing ground. "Lord knows how he's done it. But dumb luck eventually runs out."

Just then, a horn sounded, and the ragged bunch of peasant conscripts hastily tried to form a line. Minoru heard the thumping of hooves from behind him and was about to complain about another pompous nobleman awarded a field promotion when he caught sight of the rider. A small woman with short red hair galloped atop a black horse. She bore the banner not of the Dauphin but a strange exotically marked flag with a bird in flight. Even beneath the chain mail and thick leather, Minoru could tell she was a woman of extraordinary beauty. She held her chin high and defiantly but her soft eyes darted uncertainly about her, from the row of motley men to the wall of wagons across the field of battle.

7

"Who's that?" Minoru said. "A woman on the battlefield? Am I hallucinating?"

"If you're hallucinating, then so am I, or we're both already dead and being led to the fields of Elysia with the other dead men walking."

The woman turned her horse abruptly towards the bedraggled rows of Dauphin's men and raised her banner high above her head to gain their attention. But she needn't have done that. The rabble was awed into silence.

"Should we salute her?" Minoru muttered.

"You already are," Kamatari spat back. "With your manhood."

Minoru ignored his friend's coarse jest. Staring up at the wondrous maiden stretching her arms forth atop her glistening black steed, the other man quickly regretted his words. Her figure was slight and girlish but on her bare head she wore her hair short and unkempt like a boy's. Her expression was stern and driven, but her eyes were softened by a look of compassion as she surveyed the carnage on the battlefield. Though her head and face were unprotected, she wore chain mail over a clean white chemise.

After a moment she spun round on her horse and called out to the unwashed masses before her in a calm, resounding voice. "We will win this day. Follow me!"

Then she turned back towards the waiting foe, spurred on her steed and started galloping towards the waiting enemy line.

Minoru turned to his friend. "I don't know who she is," he said in hushed tone. "But I think I want to follow her."

Mesmerized, by what, he was unsure, Kamatari muttered under his breathe. "So do I, Mini... so do I."

Suddenly, a roar rose among the rank and file, and like the swelling of a wave, the mass of soldiers burst into a desperate run towards enemy fortifications. The ragged line of men swept across the no man's land and it was only moments before the report of cannons could be heard from behind the Fiorese lines. Kamatari and Minoru gave each other puzzled looks and then Minoru screamed at the top of his lungs. His voice sounded like a strangled rat but Kamatari raised his pike and the two began running madly after their cohorts. Already, they had fallen far behind the majority of the soldiers and the horse bearing the young maiden. Kamatari was quickly reduced to a waddle under the burden of his impractically burdensome armor.

"This is insanity!" Kamatari screamed.

"I know!" Minoru replied.

The howls of incoming shells could be heard seconds before the ground shook and dozens of men disappeared in an immense cloud of dust and cinder. Then, it happened again, and again. Still, the maiden rode onward and the men followed slavishly towards the enemy lines and their deaths. The exploding shells came at deafening, soul crushing rhythm.

By the time the two men reached within a few hundred yards of the entrenched Fiorese defenders, they could see the flash of muskets and hear the buzz

9

of the miniballs through the roiling air. It wasn't long
before they realized they had caught up with the
forward advance of their line. Already, it had been
picked apart. Men and body parts lay strewn on the
ground amidst craters large enough to lose oxen. A few
were crying for their mothers.

The maiden had dismounted about fifty feet away
from them and had gone to the aid of one of the
soldiers as the Fiorese took pot shots at her. Her bright
white tunic, which had been clean before, was now
streaked with crimson.

"We're doomed!" Minoru said, stumbling to his
knees.

Kamatari, out of breath, gasped and fell beside his
friend. "Shit! Shit! Shit!"

They heard a whistle of an incoming shell and
Minoru whimpered. "It's for us," he said, moments
before a deafening blast picked up the two peasants
and sent them hurtling twenty feet into the air.
Kamatari grabbed his friend by the tunic and clung
blindly to him as they tumbled head over heels. They
landed in a crater nearby. Kamatari felt something snap
inside his back, as Minoru crashed headfirst into his
chest. It was several minutes before either man was
able to speak.

"Minoru," Kamatari said, when he was sure he was
still alive. "Minoru, are you alive? Answer me, you
lazy shit!"

Minoru moaned, but Kamatari could barely hear it,
even though the tiny man's lips were mere inches from
his left ear. The blast must have damaged his ear
drums, he realized. He tried to push Minoru off him,

10

but his friend was limp as a rotten bean and his arms ached from the impact with the ground. On top of that, he wasn't sure if he could feel his legs. Everything below his neck felt dull and throbbing, which made him panicked.

"Mini, get off of me!"

As though finally waking from a deep slumber, Minoru rose slightly and then slumped over. Momentum allowed him to slide off Kamatari's chest plate and come to rest face up beside him.

"We're dead!" Minoru mumbled. "I can see heaven at last."

Kamatari cried out in pain as he tried to hoist himself up by his arms, then fell back onto the ground. His pie plate helmet flopped over his eyes and crushed his nose.

"Why is heaven so dark and grey?" Minoru continued. "My gods, we've gone to the third hell! Our suffering will never end."

Furiously, Kamatari undid the strap of his helmet and tore it off, slapping Minoru across the face as he did so. "We're not dead yet, you moron. We just wish we were. Why do you always do that? I think my back is broken. Shit!"

"We're not dead," Minoru said, with a slight chuckle of realization. "Wait a minute, do you hear that?"

"I'm half deaf from that blast, you idiot. I can hardly hear anything."

"Listen."

Kamatari humored his friend and strained to listen for whatever Minoru expected him to hear through his bruised ears. When the ringing subsided, all that was left was silence. "I don't hear anything," he finally said.

"Exactly."

"Then why—" Kamatari began to say, when it finally struck him what his friend was getting at. Silence. No movement. No bombs or guns. Had the slaughter finally ended? All their cohorts must be dead.

"I have to get up. I have to see."

Minoru willed himself to sit up. He feebly got up on all fours and began to crawl up the side of the crater. Kamatari watched him warily.

"What are you doing?" he said. "If there are snipers waiting, they'll blow your head off. Get back down here. If they think we're dead, maybe they'll leave us alone or just take us as prisoners of war."

"I have to see."

When Minoru reached the lip of the crater, he observed a battlefield transformed. Some of the Orloinian soldiers were climbing the enemy barricades. Others were milling about confusedly. One man, who apparently had an arm blown off, seemed to be searching the ground for something, perhaps his missing limb. Then he crouched and retrieved it from the ground. Dazed, he lifted the bloodied piece of meat to his stump as if he were trying to reattach it somehow. Minoru watched in awe as the man tried to force the dead arm into his tattered sleeve.

Then, he caught sight of the maiden. She had been stooping over another Orloinian when she spotted the armless one as well. She placed a hand gently on the man's shoulder and took the arm from him. The man stared glassy-eyed at her as she carefully reattached the arm to his body. Minoru watched in astonishment as the man began to flex the hand of the reattached arm. The maiden whispered something to the man, and he nodded, picked up a sword with his renewed arm and charged towards the barricades.

The maiden strode towards Minoru, cowering at the edge of the crater. Their eyes met briefly, and the young woman approached him. He could see now that though her clothes had been soaked in blood, she appeared to be unharmed. In fact, she seemed to be surrounded by a glow like a pale moonlight. Instinctively, he slid back down the side of the crater to hide from view of this strange and frightening woman.

"By Gods, she's a witch," Minoru said.

"Who's a witch?" Kamatari grunted. "I can't see a damned thing. What witch?"

"The maiden on the horse," Minoru said. "The one who was leading the charge."

Kamatari grunted again, uncomprehending. Before he had a chance to complain again, however, the maiden appeared at the edge of the crater and he too saw her. She was directly looking at them. She has a vision of beauty, even dressed in the gory rags of war. At this distance, even he could plainly tell she was a girl, not much older than 17. Far too young to be leading men on the battlefield.

"Come with me, men," she said. "You will be safe."

"I can't move, ma'am," Kamatari said, suddenly struck with awe. "My back. I think it's broken."

"It is not. Come. Rise."

13

She waved her hand and Kamatari felt a surge of warmth spring up through his feet, up his back and into his throat and face. He found that he could wiggle his toes and sprang to his feet with surprising ease.

"Come," she said again. "You've no need to be afraid."

Overcoming their apprehension towards the maiden, the two peasant soldiers scrambled out of the crater and surveyed the battlefield.

"What are your names, sirs?" the maiden asked.

"I'm Minoru and he's Kamatari, ma'am," Minoru said.

"Where is the enemy? What happened here?" Kamatari said, looking wearily about the still field and Fiorese battlements, empty but for a few of the Dauphin's men who were now celebrating atop them with hearty cheers.

"Can't you tell?" she said and added a sly smile. "We've won the battle, of course. The Fiorese have fled the field."

Chapter 2

Summer of Year 34 (after the Great Plague)

The first dream Necron had of his daughter was of her as a maiden, riding a black horse. She was traveling with an army: a camp follower. When he awoke, bathed in sweat, he ran straight from the bed to his brother Jon's house. There he found Jon and his other brother Michel and told them the dream and that if it ever happened, he would ask them to drown his daughter. If they refused, he would do it himself. Afterwards, he left his dumbfounded brothers in silence and went back home.

He said nothing to his 8-year-old daughter directly, but told her mother later that evening and she relayed it to her. A father fears for his daughter's virtue, her mother told her when she asked what would cause her father to act so violently. It is more precious than her life in this world. Her mother lamented that she could not have brought her daughter into a better world, where the life of every young child mattered most. But her daughter comforted her mother and said: "Life is just a breath. What we do with that breath is the greatest value."

RIDING A BLACK HORSE

Summer of Year 43 (after the Great Plague)

As a fief of the local demesne, Count Arbor, Kamatari and Minoru toiled in their lord's personal farmland two days a week, in addition to their own farms every other day. In return for their labors, the two peasants received lunch served with fresh bread and a strong ale, which kept their bellies warm against the cold of the afternoon, assuming the count was in a generous mood. If not, they would receive a lunch with watery gruel that retained the flavor of the raw sewage it was born from. But even the warm bread, which was served with the smiles of the buxom serving girls, was meager compensation for the sting of the northern winds against bare flesh and the kick of a heavy iron plow against an already aching shoulder. And it was growing worse every year as the winters grew harsher and the springs and even summers brought no respite from the unremitting cold and the fields turned to slop in the often icy monsoon rains.

One day, as Kamatari examined the stooped rows of emaciated corn and bean plants, he felt the rumble of his empty stomach and finally decided he had enough. He threw down his hoe in anger, only to have the long handle drop loudly and painfully on his foot.

"Gods be damned!" he exclaimed to no one in particular. "First they send us years of drought and heat and now this fucking cold and moisture. Every year, it's the same shit, only different. And these sickly things aren't going to produce enough food to feed a dead gerbil, let alone the village for a year. I've had it. I'm done!"

Minoru had been crouching over his row of beans, picking at the weeds with his fingers. Now he raised his head and shook his head disapprovingly. "What's gotten into you anyways?" he said. "Don't you know they haven't served lunch yet. If you keep whining like that, we won't even get the gruel we're promised and the count's liable to have us locked up."

"Lock me up then. I don't give a shit," Kamatari said. "Better to be cold and asleep indoors than cold and working my ass end off for some lord who's never dirtied his hands a day in his life and tells me how much better he is than me."

"Then go back to your farm and work there. Leave me in peace."

"I would. But shit ain't growing there either."

"Don't I know it."

"Your farm ain't no better."

Minoru's head dropped. "Why is this happening to us? My children go to bed hungry and I have sores on my hand. Every year it takes longer to grow the same amount of food. Did we do something wrong?"

"Like be born?" Kamatari spat. "No, we're doing great. We'll be rich before the season's out."

Minoru tossed a hand full of weeds on the ground and his lip quivered. "There's no need to be mean about it. But what can we can do but farm until we all drop dead of starvation?"

Kamatari scratched his chin and looked up at the sky. The clouds were leaden and barely allowed for a dull light to penetrate the oppressive gloom. "Well,

17

those cutthroats in Vagran or Olivet don't seem to be hurting for eats, and I'm told they've got a little coin in their pocket to boot. It seems the Dauphin will take anyone who can hold a sword or pull a trigger."

"You want to hire yourself out as a sell-sword?" Minoru said. "But you could be killed. You could leave your wife a widow!"

Kamatari pointed to the sodden ground. "And you don't think this will kill us? Between the lack of food, the sickening water and the grippe and the bandits stealing and raping and murdering, we might die anyways. At least, if we're soldiers we can learn to fight so no one will be able to take what's ours and we might enjoy some comfort."

Minoru scrunched his face as though he was pondering a great mystery of the universe. He looked momentarily at his other hand still clenching a fistful of muddy weeds. He threw that wad of plants to the ground and placed his dirty hands at his hips. "How do we sign up?"

"Simple. We take what we can carry and head for the capitol."

"But we have no weapons. And I've never even fired a gun. Why would the Dauphin enlist a pair of unarmed peasants?"

Kamatari looked around hastily. He picked up Minoru's hoe and bent the metal spade at the end under the weight of his boot until it flattened into an extra broad spearhead. "We'll beat our ploughshares into bloody swords," he growled.

Captain Baudrin hefted himself out of bed and onto his leaden feet. The wooden floor was cold as ice against his bare skin and instantly regretted not checking the furnace before retiring the previous night. His head was throbbing from too much mead and ale and he clumsily stumbled towards the bathroom sink, knocking over a spent candle on the bureau next to his bed. The splash of cold water against his face shocked him awake, but then the piercing migraine behind his left eye set in. The migraines usually accompanied bad weather, but these days they worsened as conditions on the battlefront worsened.

He was just thinking how pleasant it might be to creep back into bed and let the day's patrol be damned when a polite knocking could be heard coming from the chamber door. It was a dull thump, but to Baudrin's ears it might as well as been a steam-driven jackhammer.

"Go away, Baldric," Baudrin called, rubbing his temples. "Unless you've got the world's supply of laudanum with you, just pretend I've died for the day and you're in command."

"Sir, she's back."

"Who's back? I don't have the patience or mental capacity for riddles right now."

"The girl from the market. The one who hears voices."

"And why are you telling me this?"

"She claims to have intelligence on the enemy positions."

"Her 'voices' tell her this information?"

"She did not say, but I would assume that's the case, sir."

19

"So? Send her away. Why do I have to be bothered with every emotionally unstable wench with delusions of magical prophecy that wanders through the territory?"

"I would send her away, but—sir, may I come in?"

Grudgingly, Baudrin opened the door. His spindly assistant, dressed as usual in a freshly pressed grey uniform with the house Valcolors epaulettes, awaited him in the hall. He held a clipboard full of papers close against his chest, no doubt with the day's busy agenda scrawled on one. Baudrin ushered him in with a cursory wave of his hand.

"What is so difficult about 'send her away,' Baldric? The concept of sending or the away part?"

"The 'her' part, actually," Baldric said. "She refuses to leave. She—"

"Well, did you ask politely?"

"Yes, sir. She—"

"Did you ask impolitely?"

"Of course, I did. She still refuses. As I was about to say, she insists on seeing you and will not move. She claims that she hasn't eaten in three days and will not eat again until you agree to grant her an audience."

Baudrin sniffed. "You're a strapping young man. Certainly you can handle a hunger-weakened maiden by yourself or command the guards to do it for you."

"I would, sir. However, the girl can't be enticed or forced to leave. I feel that you need to see her and resolve the issue."

Baudrin growled as the searing pain behind his eyes penetrated to the back of his skull and bounced forward. Seeing his master's visible distress, Baldric scampered to the bathroom and emerged with a glass of water and a draught of some sort of medicine. He handed it to Baudrin, who swiped it impatiently and downed the liquid and pills quickly.

"Don't beat around the bush, Baldric. My head can't take the pounding right now. Why should I see this girl again and what assurance do you have that she will be satisfied and get out of our blasted hair?"

"Because, sir, there are over a hundred peasants and townsfolk with her. She's gathered an entourage around her, and they are refusing to let me remove her from the courtyard."

Baudrin flinched. "An insurrection?"

"They seem peaceful. And most of them are your people. They just seem to believe her."

The captain groaned. "And because they are foolish, I must entertain this child."

"That appears to be the case, sir."

"Let me get dressed," the captain said. "Tell her I will see her within the hour and that after she has stated her peace I will expect her and her entourage to clear the courtyard."

Baldric bowed curtly and left. Baudrin struggled into his own grey dress uniform. He was still fit for a man in his early fifties but already he could feel the slow creep of time in his bones and tightness around his middle as he buttoned the waistcoat. He decided to forgo shaving as he had the last several days, preferring to allow the stubble to set in and give his sunken eyes an even more surly appearance.

A few minutes later, after he gave his stomach a moment to settle, he descended a flight of stairs that

led to the Great Room to find the typically sedate
chambers bristling with action as guards, advisors and
even townspeople milled about shelves of books and
tables. It was enough to send his head reeling—even
more than it was. At the center of this whirling mob
stood the maiden, calm and demure, dressed only in
the plain robes of the peasantry. Still, she was fetching,
her raven hair spun into a braid that descended the
length of her back. When the crowd spotted him at the
foot of the stairs, it parted to allow him access to the
maiden, and, as if on cue, she spun to face him.

Baudrin opened his mouth to speak, but was
momentarily stunned by the maiden's serene
expression. "Maiden, and why do you still sully my
door?" he said at last.

"I have been sent for by your Lord to seek you
out," the maiden said. "I am here to save the country."

A single laugh echoed through the chamber, but all
else were silent.

Baudrin guffawed. "You were sent by the
Dauphin? I doubt even he would send a child to
conduct his business."

"No, sir. Your lord king sent me."

The captain eyed her suspiciously. "Careful, girl,
and explain what you mean by that. The Dauphin is
your rightful ruler."

"He is—or will be, once he is made king. I mean,
sir, that his father, the King Rien, sent me."

"King Rien is dead."

"He is," the maiden said dryly. "Nonetheless, he
sent me to come find you with orders that you were to

accompany me to the Dauphin and lead the offensive to expel the Fiorese from the Continent."

"You mean, a dead man told you this."

"He also told me you would not believe."

"You're damn right I don't believe," Baudrin said, seething with anger. "You're the third quack to turn up at my door this month claiming to have some mystical power or another and claiming to have the key to save the Continent from the bloody Fiorese devils. And do you know what they were?"

"Charlatans," the maiden said. "But I tell the truth. I bring word from your late lord and king. He calls upon you from beyond the grave to help me save our kingdom and guide the Dauphin to his destiny."

Baudrin had heard enough. He nodded to Baldric and the guards. "The girl is crazy," he said. "Box her ears and take her back to her father."

Baldric and his two beefy guards looked at each other confused. They seemed hesitant to move against the girl and the group of townsfolk seemed to tense with anticipation. However, the maiden did not wait for the guards to carry out their orders. She walked up to the captain and placed a palm on his forehead. The captain jerked away, but not before he felt a warmth penetrate his scalp and his migraine instantly dissipate. For the first time since he awoke, the haze began to lift from Baudrin's mind, and he studied the maiden's face intently.

"My headache's gone. What—how did you do that?"

The maiden lifted her chin proudly. "It is my gift."

"Your gift? You're a healer?"

"She's a witch!" someone from the crowd shouted, but was silenced by the grumbling of the townspeople.

At last, Baldric and the guards moved towards her as if to haul her off. One of the guards placed a gloved hand on her shoulder, but Baudrin waved him quickly. "Explain by what you mean by gift," he said.

"As I told you when last we met, I hear the voice of your dead lord and master. He instructed me—"

"Yes, yes," Baudrin said impatiently. "But how do you know you are hearing voices from dead people and that this voice, as you say, is that of King Rien?"

"Because he said so," the maiden said matter-of-factly. "Because he tells me things only a king could know."

"Like what?"

The maiden glanced at the crowd and then back at the captain. "Pardon, sir," maiden said. "But do you mind?"

She motioned for Baudrin to come closer. He complied and she leaned into him until her lips almost touched his ear. He could smell the faint aroma of clover and honeydew; it was a mild surprise coming from a peasant girl. He expected her to stink of dung and sweat, like the rest of her kind. In fact, he found her scent almost intoxicating.

"The king told me you would not believe," she whispered close to him. "He bid me tell you that your wife cared for him when he came down with the grippe during his last visit here. He gave her a token of his thanks, a brooch in the shape of his family's flower seal. Does the lady still have his gift?"

24

"Why yes, a lion lily. She wears it almost every day," Baudrin's eyes widened. "But the king's illness was kept a secret. Only myself, my wife and king's physician knew about that incident. How would you…"

"He told me, when he bid me come to you."

Baudrin stepped back and scratched his stubbled chin. He stared deeply into the maiden's pale blue eyes, but he could detect no hint of deception. "Fine," he said after a pause. "Let's just entertain for a moment that you are telling the truth. Why would the spirit of our dead king come to you, a simple maiden?"

"Because I was the only one who would listen."

"Don't be coy with me, girl."

"Forgive me, sir. I am too simple to be coy. I merely meant that speaking to the dead is my gift—and my curse. Truth be told, I do not know why the king chose me over the sages or even his own son."

"And what does he say he wants from you?"

"He wants me to lead the army to victory over the Fiorese and ensure the Dauphin ascends to the throne as is his right."

"You… lead the army?" the captain said, as a few laughs arose from the servants watching from the doors. "Have you ever led men into battle?"

"No, sir."

"Have you ever killed a man in combat?"

"No, sir."

"Have you even held a sword?"

"No, sir."

"Then how could you possibly know that you can lead the Dauphin's army to victory?"

"The king said he would show me the way if I listened to him."

Baudrin folded his arms. "And what martial wisdom did the king's spirit impart to you?"

"That we should launch an offensive to retake the industrial center of Olivet from the Fiorese."

"Olivet is in our hands, girl," Baudrin's averted his eyes from the maiden's unwavering gaze. "One cannot launch an offensive to take something one already holds."

"But we do not hold it. The Fiorese and their allies struck only a few days ago. Yesterday, it fell."

Baudrin shot Baldric a furtive glance. His assistant cleared his throat into his closed fist. "We received word just this morning, sir. I'm sorry. I was going to bring it to your attention when this business was concluded."

"And how do you know about this, girl?"

"The king told me, just as he told me about your wife's brooch."

The captain's eyes narrowed. "But I did not know until just now. And a mere maiden would not be privy to such information unless she had been to Olivet recently or had an informant feeding her from the inside."

"I told you my informant."

"Perhaps," Baudrin said, motioning again for Baldric and his guards to take custody of the maiden. "But perhaps you've told me a fancy tale to go along with a cheap parlor trick. But I'll grant your wish to stay while we sort out the truth."

26

RIDING A BLACK HORSE

The guards laid hands on the maiden, but she did not resist. The crowd seemed restive but made no move to intervene. As Baldric escorted the girl past him, Baudrin whispered into his assistant's ear: "Don't take her to the dungeon. Just take her to the guest quarters and post a guard. That should be sufficient for now."

Chapter 3

Spring of Year 43 (after the Great Plague)

As long as he could remember, Mallory had been a dreamer, which, of course, made him an outcast in polite Fiorese society. He was always more comfortable with a pen in his hand than a gun or sword, so he immediately was doomed to a life of poverty and scorn at birth. However, his father had been a mechanic in the new national navy and he had acquiesced to his family's wishes that he should put aside his aspirations to pursue his "scribblings" seriously, so he studied engineering and found that his dreaming could extend to the designing of gadgets of use to the empire. This pleased his father to no end.

After graduating from school in Oxwell, his parents helped him set up a workshop nearby where he and his wife could settle. Before long, he had settled into a lucrative business servicing the war effort against the Orloinians. Though he disdained making weapons, the design of a new breach-loading musket kept his mind away from the moral questions and on the intellectual challenge of solving another mechanical puzzle.

One late autumn day, Mallory and his wife were strolling across the city square—he on his way to the workshop and she on hers to the marketplace to shop for groceries for the evening's meal. On the six hour, a chime rang out across the square disturbing the resident flock of gulls in the nearby fountain. The birds flew off in a cloud of grey feathers and headed towards the sea.

"And as fast as her time came, she was delivered of a fair child, and well that child was kept and well nourished," Mallory said, sniffing the cold dew on the morning air.

"What was that, dear?" his wife Belle Isolde asked.

"Oh, nothing," Mallory said with a boyish laugh. "Just an old poem I learned as a child. The chiming of the bells reminded me of it."

Of course, the oldest bell mounted in the clock tower of the regional assembly building had been cast more than 100 years ago. It was a tangible link to Mallory, but also the father of city's most famous former resident—the legendary Fiorese dictator and unquestioned ruler Newbold. At the turn of the last century, as it had been for Mallory, it had been rung to summon relatives, friends and neighbors to the induction of the current ruler and again at Mallory's baptism of citizenry before such rituals were outlawed by the government. After the bell ringer finished the peal, he would turn lookout, climbing to the top of the great red sandstone tower. From there, he had a panoramic view over the heart of Fioria. When the engineer was born, knowing who was about had been essential. Those were dangerous times. The freely elected tribunes had either been murdered, executed or were being hunted in the hills while plague stalked the land and killed by the thousands. Hard-faced, hard riding bands of armed men were scouring the shires for

29

'traitors'. This was the world Mallory had been born into—and yet a nursery rhyme prevailed in his mind.

"It's a lovely poem," Belle Isolde said. She walked with a slight limp ever since fell off a horse as a young child. "I thought you might have written it."

Mallory shook his head. "No, you know I haven't put pen to paper since I opened the shop. My parents always frowned upon my literary pursuits. Anyways, there's no money to be made in that, especially since the censors clamped down on publishers."

"I'm not talking about making money, silly," she scolded him playfully. "Not everything is about money."

"Oh?"

"It's about being a whole person," Belle Isolde said. "You know how I love books. I would love to have your skill with words. I would write every day if I were as good as you. I could dream of other worlds and people of other cultures. What they think about and what's in their hearts."

"Careful, dear, such dreams can be dangerous in these times. The national party has eyes and ears everywhere and they don't take too kindly to dreamers. I should know. Anyways, what's important is not what's in other people's hearts, but in our own. I know what's in mine."

He took her hand in his and gave it a gentle tug. They continued across the courtyard until they came to where the roads diverged. Belle Isolde leaned in to him and kissed him softly on the lips. Mallory looked sheepishly about, but it was still relatively quiet and empty.

"Have a good day at work, dear, but don't work too hard."

"I'll try not to stay late."

"Good. I'll take that as a promise and hold you to it. Perhaps after dinner, we can begin our own work to deliver that 'fair child' from your poem," she whispered. An impish smile passed over her lips.

"You are naughty," Mallory grinned, but his face grew hot and he was certain a blush was betraying his attempts to be cool and sultry.

With that, they parted ways. Mallory's shop was a two-story affair about two blocks down the street at the corner of an alley where the young snipes liked to gather to shoot dice and generally make mischief. The front of the building was windowless and, like most newer buildings in the city, was featureless. A large bay door fronted the street and was flanked by a side entrance. The bay door was effective when he needed to test larger equipment or needed to circulate air through the building more freely. Mallory went in through the side door and turned on a few of the gaslights.

In the middle of the workroom stood a large rectangular object that nearly touched the ceiling and was almost as wide as the bay door. The engineer set about removing the tarp he had placed over it the night before. Not even his apprentice was allowed to touch this project much and he was even reticent about reporting his progress on it to members of the government who might demand to see his work. He didn't want to give away too much about its capabilities until he was assured what they truly were

31

and had tested them on his own. However, that was a tricky task given the prying eyes of the chief of engineering corps who delighted in making surprise visits on his engineers to ensure they stayed on their toes and that they were not pilfering materials for their own side projects, which Mallory had often done.

When the tarp was safely removed and tucked away in the corner of the work space, he carefully appraised his creation. It was a vehicle, but more than that it was a metallic beast, crouching upon its treaded wheels and ready to barrel onto a battlefield like a wild boar in heat. The thick metal armor made the vehicle incredibly heavy and it had taken months to forge or scrape together from other machines, but it was virtually impenetrable by musket or cannonball. He had installed a the most powerful steam engine he could find and enhanced it even further so that it could handle a maximum pressure more than 10 percent beyond its original specifications. Two smoke stacks protruded menacingly from the top like bull horns. It was almost complete, but it was unarmed. It was an armored beast with no teeth.

Mallory mounted the vehicle and climbed to the top, where a turret would be mounted. Right now, there was just a circular hole lined with bearings. He had been vague in his sketches about what shape the armament would take, because he was uncertain how much weight the engine could bear after the armor had been applied and tweaked. He could design a cannon that could take down a fortress wall in one shot, but the weight would almost certainly slow the vehicle's mobility to a crawl. Too light a cannon and his superiors would be disappointed with its fighting capability against large targets. Mallory scratched his head as he continued his calculations, then pulled out a tablet from his breast pocket to jot down some figures.

There was a polite knock at the door and then a crack of light crept into the workroom. It was his apprentice Joaquin. He always knocked to alert his master that he was entering but that he was alone. If he had not been alone or if he had been followed by one of the government's spies, he would have knocked loudly on the bay door and waited to give Mallory enough time to return the vehicle to its tarp.

"Good day, sir," Joaquin said, closing the door behind him and locking it. "How does the baby look today?"

"Troubling, as always. But I believe we may be able to test its capabilities tomorrow evening, if the weather cooperates."

"That's good to hear," Joaquin smiled. He was a teenager and eager to please. Yet the young man fumbled nervously at the buttons of his coat.

"What is it, Joaquin?"

The apprentice looked down at his fidgeting fingers and remembered his tell. He smoothed out the front of his jacket as though it mattered and then plunged his hands deeply into his pockets to obscure their jittering from his master. Mallory, unimpressed, climbed down from the back of his contraption and walked over to his flat files to pull out the schematics for it. All the while, Joaquin stood frozen near the door.

"You know something, so spit it out," Mallory eyed him impatiently. "Or get to work. We've got a lot of prep work if this hulk is ever going to move."

Joaquin cleared his throat. "I don't want to alarm you, sir, or put a crimp in your plans to test our new vehicle. However, I heard chatter in the servants quarters that the Supreme Chancellor himself was arriving in Oxwell today."

"Today?"

"Bran Oxley said he overheard two clerks at the tube office about a message from the capitol that said as much."

"Oh, well, if Bran Oxley says it, it must be true," Mallory said, rolling his eyes for effect. "My dear boy, you are quite vulnerable to innuendos and rumor. A scientist must deal only in facts or else your mind will be destroyed by the sheer panic born from speculation."

"Very well, sir," Joaquin removed his overcoat and joined his employer at the draft table. There wasn't more than a decade separating the two men in age, but the apprentice treated him like a full-fledged master.

"Still, we had best assume the worst, that the rumors are true. If so, we can expect a visit to these very premises in the next day or so," the inventor said and sighed. "And we have nothing to show them."

"But we have that, at least," Joaquin said, pointing to the armored vehicle.

"We do, indeed," Mallory said darkly. "It's untested and has no weapons capabilities as yet. If I present this contraption in the state it's in to the

Chancellor's representatives, I'll be laughed out of the profession—or worse."

"But we have the schematics, master. And we have the guns loaned to us by the armory. Surely we could adapt one of them to fit the turret," his assistant pleaded. "At least we can make it look complete enough to impress the Chancellor so he keeps funding us."

Mallory cinched his mouth in disapproval, but said: "I suppose we haven't much choice but to try. I just hate having to rush through a project."

He spread a large roll of vellum blueprint paper across the drafting table and examined it quietly. He knew it by heart but sometimes the act of simply staring at his plans could stir an idea. Besides, he was sure that his assistant needed the visual guide to help him. The designs for the turret were clearly unfinished. Mallory unfurled a few smaller rolls of translucent wax paper and superimposed each on the blank spot where the turret would be.

"What about that one—the ten-pounder?" Joaquin pointed out eagerly. "That has proven destructive power, enough to impress even the Chancellor."

"Yes, of course, it would make a magnificent hole in any enemy fortification but look here," Mallory sighed. "We would be selling this vehicle as a mobile destructive platform, with emphasis on the mobility. If we attempt to mount that on the turret, not only will a team of horses be able to outrun it, but it might not even be able to keep pace with infantry."

"Still, with its range, it might not matter—"

"And look at the length of the barrel. It juts out over 15 feet past the forward visor. All that would need to happen is for them to ask us to drive it down a sizeable incline or crater or across a well-placed field works like a moat or trench and the muzzle will dig into the muck and trapping the vehicle like a bug in amber."

"We could shorten the barrel."

"Compromising accuracy dramatically and reducing the velocity of the projectile. No, the ten-pounder is an excellent artillery piece but impractical for our beast."

Joaquin nodded gloomily. "And I would guess that the five-pounder lacks the punch we would need for a suitable demonstration of firepower."

"You would be correct. Hence our dilemma."

Joaquin dropped his pencil on the table in frustration. "Then we're doomed," he muttered and slumped down over the drawings.

Mallory clapped his assistant on the back. "No, no, we can't give up that easily, son. And being down in the mouth about it won't help. If what we have won't work on our turret, we just have to find something that will."

"But we possess the only working artillery pieces in the district," Joaquin moaned. "Oh, if only we could restore a bit of that old world magic, we'd have a devastating weapon to match with this brilliant vehicle and the war would be won instantly."

Mallory frowned at the young man. "Careful now, son, voicing such thoughts would be considered heresy in these parts nowadays. The old magics are long dead, if they ever existed in the first place. Besides, we are bold men of science. We must trust only that which we can test and prove through empirical evidence. It's not constructive to think about magic."

He waved his hand in the air as if he were dispelling the bad ideas and then cast a sidelong glance at the unfinished vehicle. The inventor tried to imagine what machine of war would mount on that turret.

"I'm sorry, sir. It's just that I was thinking out loud. My parents used to tell me about the Dragon's Breath. It was weightless, but spat out powerful balls of flame and didn't require ammunition, just casks of dragon's blood to fuel. It wasn't deadly, but my granddad served in the infantry and he said it was a scary thing to see on the battlefield."

"An interesting, if curious, family fairy tale, to be sure," Mallory said. Suddenly, as though a spark struck a tinder in his mind and set it ablaze, he had an idea. "Hold on a second, maybe we have been thinking about this problem in completely the wrong direction."

"How so?"

"My boy, you're a genius and you may not know it yet," Mallory said, scurrying to grab a blank sheet of wax paper and a wax pencil.

"Thank you, sir. Does this mean I've graduated to master inventor?"

"Not on your life, but you may have suggested an alternate plan that may save both our skins."

"How's that again?"

"I'd been puzzling over getting artillery on top that thing, for tackling fortifications, but most engagements are between massed groups of infantry and cavalry. That was a mistake, don't you see?"

"Yes, I suppose."

"This beast would be best at taking on moving targets, not fixed ones. Its combination of mobility and armor is what gives it its key advantage. Artillery is nice and we may tackle that another day, but there are other weapons that would be more effective against infantry targets. One in particular may leverage what's already built in to the beast's designs."

"I see your point, sir, but I'm not seeing how that makes me a genius."

"You said it yourself: dragon's breath."

"But you also said yourself that was a fairy tale— and a heretical one at that."

"Of course, I'm not literally saying we try some poppy cocked magical incantation. I'm talking about a flamethrower. The heart of our beast is not unlike your mythical dragons. It harnesses fire in its steam engine. If we could route those flames into the turret, we could mount a flamethrower that would make your dragon's breath seem like a light summer breeze."

Mallory began hastily scribbling across the wax paper, scratching out existing lines in the steam chamber's bulwark and sketching out a crude line to the turret.

"Magnificent!" Joaquin declared. "I can't believe I didn't see that myself."

"I didn't either until we talked about it. That's why we make a good team, my boy. The most wonderful and terrifying things are often hidden in plain view, son. Just remember that," Mallory said. He ripped off a corner of the paper and jotted down a few notes, then handed the ragged slip to his assistant. "We must move quickly though. I'll need a few supplies to make this work. Can you get them for me?"

"Most certainly," Joaquin said with a new bounce in his step. He grabbed his coat and made for the door.

"And another thing," Mallory called after him. "We probably should give our creation a proper name. Any suggestions?"

Joaquin paused at the door and smiled. "Of course, Dragon's Breath."

"Good lad. When all this is over, perhaps we'll try mastering something really important, like flight," Mallory smiled briefly and then dove into his work.

Chapter 4

Spring of Year 43 (after the Great Plague)

The Valley of Colors earned its name from the fiery red blossoms of the draconic trees. In Baudrin's youth, spring had been a time of enchantment, when the hills surrounding Valcolors were set ablaze as the blankets of snow vaporized into memory. Looking at it now, however, the only blazes he could see were the campfires of raiding parties or the fires set by logging settlements as they stripped the mountains of their precious timber. The captain knew he would mourn those lost forests one day, should he live long enough to see the end of the war.

However, Baudrin felt more anxiety than grief as he watched anxiously from the parapet towards the roads leading from Olivet to Valcolors. He had tasked his nephew with reconnoitering at Brewer's Landing, roughly at the midway point to the recently sieged industrial center, and he was seriously overdue. Through his telescope he could scan where the road disappeared into a copse of trees. Twice in the past hour he'd imagined he saw his pointed helmet atop a steed emerging into the clearing, only to be disappointed to find it was just his own harried mind playing tricks on him. Twice, under his breath, he'd sworn to quit the bottle if only for a sign. The warnings of the maiden plagued him.

"Sir," Baldric cleared his throat. The assistant had crept to within a few feet of his captain and he hadn't even noticed nor flinched from his perch, intent as he was at the telescope.

Baudrin glanced briefly in his direction, just long enough to notice a furrowed brow and crumpled piece of paper in his hand. The captain sighed and returned his eye to the eyepiece of the scope where it had been glued for the past hour.

"I suppose you bring news, Baldric?" he said dryly. "And I would guess that that news is that there is no news from Olivet, no contact whatsoever from Lord and Lady Briarwood or their representatives. Am I correct?"

"Yes, sir."

Baudrin sighed and put down the telescope. "I told his mother I'd have him home by mageday," he said glumly.

"Sir?"

"Nothing. Just the idle mumblings of a fool," he said. "How is our young soothsayer doing? Perhaps I should pay her a visit, since it has been several days. Has she given up her sources yet? Is she still making demands?"

"She is as cheerful as ever and her demands grow ever more so each day," Baldric said. "She's resisted interrogation so far, so it's unclear how she could have known about Olivet's capture by the Fiorese. We've gone through her things thoroughly though and found nothing that would contradict her story."

41

"Apart from the fact that it's utterly bunko to believe she's getting orders from a dead king, you mean?"

"I mean, sir, that the factual statements she's made have checked out—where she came from and her itinerary before coming here. I make no statement about her communication with the great beyond."

"But you believe her," Baudrin eyed Baldric suspiciously.

The assistant wrung his hands. "I suppose, sir. I tried not to. I interrogated her sternly and have no reason to believe that she thinks she isn't communicating with our departed king. She truly believes that. There's something about her—I can't place my finger on it—but she seems like someone one ought to trust."

"Most skilled liars will do that. Perhaps she does have magical powers, just not the ones she claims. She's weaving a charm on you, I think. Maybe I should keep my distance so she cannot work her dark powers on me as well."

"Oh sir, I hope not," Baldric said, eyes widening. "And I do apologize if my carelessness has caused me to fall under the thrall of a foul witch or caused you to be compromised in any way. I should rather be flogged."

"Calm down, Baldric. She's probably just a skilled liar. The magic comment was an off-hand joke, and a weak one at that. Magic is just smoke and mirrors the mages used to hoodwink us all for centuries. And where are they now? All fled to some damn mystery island since the Great Plague hit. If magic were real

42

and there were a true God watching over everything, none of that would have happened."

He waved his hand over the landscape. "None of this would be happening now."

Baldric nodded, but gave no indication that he truly understood what his master was saying. He stood mutely waiting for Baudrin to give him some sort of direction.

"Very well, let's go see this maiden and solve her mystery once and for all. Knowing what she knows could give us valuable information. If the Fiorese have Olivet, they will soon be at our doorstep and information will then be at a premium."

Baldric led the way as they descended the tower. The maiden was being housed in a small chamber just a few floors below. A single guard stood post at the heavy wooden door and fumbled with the key to let them in.

The door swung open and the two men entered. The chamber was comfortable, but sparsely decorated, as would befit the guest quarters of a wildlands or border outpost, which presumably it now was since Olivet and all points northwest had fallen into the hands of the Fiorese and their allies. A bed and small desk were crammed against the left wall and a roughhewn wardrobe tilted slovenly against the wall to the right.

The maiden had pulled the chair that accompanied the desk—the only one in the room—across to the portcullis and sat staring at the sky through the opening, her back to the door. She made no attempt to get up and face them. Her only acknowledgement of

Baudrin and Baldric was slight bow of her head as the two men's steps echoed across the flagstone floor. She was still dressed in her simple peasant garb—a brown tunic cinched at the waist with a leather belt and faded sack cloth skirt, frayed at the hem. As the captain approached her, he noticed that she was not sitting on the chair but rather kneeling before it, her head bowed.

"Are you praying, maiden?" Baudrin asked uncomfortably. "You know, you have nothing to fear from me if you simply tell me the truth. That is all that I require from you. The gods will expect no less either."

The maiden was silent.

"Perhaps she has lost her tongue," Baldric said. Baudrin gave him a blank look and then proceeded towards the window. As he approached, he could begin to see the maiden's face framed in the square of light, glistening with tears. When last he looked upon her, her features had been hard and resolute as she addressed the captain. Now, her weeping had softened her and imparted a sort of grace Baudrin had not expected to see in a peasant girl. The sight of it pulled slightly at his heart.

"Madam, we have meant you no harm. I have simply—"

"I'm sorry, captain, and I must apologize for my behavior."

Baudrin nodded. "It's good that you have come to your senses."

"No," the maiden said. She turned to him and suddenly, though gently, cradled his face in her hands. He instinctively jerked backwards, taken by surprise by the maiden's gesture. "I'm sorry that I could not bring you to your senses sooner. Your nephew…"

"My nephew?"

"I heard his screams. I saw him struck down."

"From here?" Baudrin glanced out the window. She could barely have seen the Valley of Colors without a looking glass, let alone a single rider traveling the heavily wooded paths miles away.

"From here," the maiden said, touching her forehead and then her chest. "And here."

"I'm not a man who trusts a woman's heart or imagined feelings."

"You will," the maiden said. "Soon."

"You can't know my heart, girl."

"I know the heart of a man who's suffered through loss and I'm offering you a way to make it right and give your nephew's death a purpose."

"And what way is that?"

"Take me to the Dauphin. Just convince him to grant me an audience. If I am nothing but a liar, he will toss me in his dungeon, and you can still plead your case to raise an army to save your keep. If I am what I claim to be, then I will prove it to the Dauphin, and I will help to save your keep and this entire kingdom."

Baldric nodded. "Her reasoning seems sound."

Baudrin flashed his assistant a cold glare, but he had to admit reasoning was as sound as her mystical visions appeared to be accurate. He bit his lip and turned away from the maiden. "Is that what you really think, Baldric?"

Baldric gave his commander a quizzical look. "I suppose it is. It's not as though any of your previous messengers has made any headway with his royal presence in the past year. With the Fiorese practically at our doorstep, what have we to lose by sending her on to the Dauphin?"

Baudrin shook his head in approval. "Nothing," he said. "But we won't be sending this girl, we'll be taking her instead."

"Sir? I don't catch your meaning."

"I mean that she won't be going alone. I'll be escorting her myself."

"Are you sure that's wise, sir?" Baldric said. "I don't want to bring up the unpleasantness of your nephew's death, but surely now there will be Fiorese scouting parties and bandits sympathetic to them on the roads between here and—"

"And they would no doubt be pleased to serve my head on a platter should they get hold of me," Baudrin growled. "No, you're quite right, Baldric. And leaving the keep under threat of impending attack may not tactically be the best option, but we can't simply wait to be the next domino to fall as the Fiorese sweep the countryside. We will have to make a stand and we will desperately need the Dauphin's arms and support to do so. The girl is right that I could plead my case directly whether she fails or not, and that's clearly something I must do. Besides, I'd like to get a better look at what exactly is happening at court that is causing our presumptive lord to be so tentative and tight-fisted with his resources."

"I see, sir," Baldric said. "It would be enlightening to discover the reason for the Dauphin's indecision in certain matters. But I don't think it's unreasonable to provide you with a small detachment. To ensure your security, of course."

"Of course, you are right to want that. However, a larger party would draw unwanted attention. I feel we need to be more subtle, don't you?" Baudrin turned back to the maiden. "We'll need to stay small and travel under cover. We already have a member who can play a plausible peasant girl. I suppose the two of us won't look as fetching in plain rags as she, but it will have to do."

"The two of us? Just the two of us?" Baldric said in disbelief.

Baudrin put a reassuring hand on his assistant's shoulder. "Just the two of us—for my nephew. No one else must know that we've left the keep. The wider the circle, the greater the risk."

The assistant nodded. "I'll make preparations, sir."

As Baldric left the room, Baudrin turned back to the maiden. She smiled weakly, though her eyes still glistened with tears—of joy or sadness, he could not tell.

"Now, girl—it would seem incredibly rude of me to call you that. What would you have me call you?"

"My childhood friends used to call me Jeanne, but my parents named me Pucelle."

Baudrin smiled broadly. "Pucelle is a beautiful name. Certainly a name befitting a maiden who wishes to honor my nephew's memory."

Chapter 5

Spring of Year 43 (after the Great Plague)

In Minoru's opinion, Olivet was a lot further than the three day's hike Kamatari promised. His feet had worn through the rags on his feet and he could feel every pebble that had pierced his calloused soles, leaving them tender and bleeding. They had taken very few supplies with them, as they didn't want to raise the suspicions of their families or demesne that they were leaving for an extended period. The Valley of Colors was very lovely, even in the dying light, but Minoru could barely enjoy it for the deafening growl of his empty stomach. At last, he could take no more and crouched on a nearby rock along the roadside, resting his cheek against his plowshare weapon and clenched fist.

"What are you doing?" Kamatari growled.

"I'm resting. My feet can't take any more," Minoru whined. "Besides, it's getting dark. We should camp for the night."

"We can't camp here, you fool. We'd be just asking to get robbed by some party of bandits here with our asses sticking out in the road. Olivet's just past this rise. It says so right here on this map. I may not be able to read, but I can tell a picture of a tree from a stick person," Kamatari shook a rag with crude markings in front of his friend's face. "What's the sense in camping out here in the open when there's food and shelter just a few hours march up there."

Minoru looked up the road. The slope seemed even steeper than before. "But I'm hungry now and I can't walk another hour. Can't we stop here for just a little while and have something to eat?"

"You're such a child. Can't you tell it's getting dark? In a few hours, it'll be black as pitch and we won't even be able to see our hands in front of us. We need to get to proper shelter before then," Kamatari said. "Besides, I traded the last of our food for this map back at the last crossroads."

"You did what?" Minoru gasped. His stomach gurgled painfully, and he nearly tumbled to the ground in despair. "But how do you know that map is accurate? We could be days away from anywhere and be food for the vultures before anyone finds us."

"Look," Kamatari said, pointing to a spot on the rag and then towards the ridge. "That's a spotted yarl tree. There's a spotted yarl tree right over there, right where the map says it should."

"But we've passed plenty of spotted yarl trees. How do you know that's the right tree?"

"Because I can read a map, you illiterate buffoon." He rolled the map up and stuffed it in his back pocket. His friend was unmoved by the jab. "You don't think I'm hungry and tired as hell? If you want to stay here and hope, that's fine with me, but I'm moving on."

Minoru said nothing. He adjusted the rags on his bloody feet and sobbed.

"Come on, let's go," Kamatari said. "I didn't mean to call you a buffoon."

"No, I can't go any further," Minoru said. "It was a mistake to leave the demesne. At least I could have died at home with my family and been buried proper instead of being picked over by dogs in the road."

"Come on. You're not dead yet."

"No," Minoru said. "Leave me here."

Kamatari spat in the dirt. "We've been together since we were spring rats in the gutter. And I've been kicking your ass ever since. So, let's go."

Minoru shook his head. He laid down on the rock and let the ploughshare handle drop to the ground. Kamatari made a half-hearted kick at Minoru's shin and missed cleanly, then grunted in defeat.

"Fine, like I said, stay here and mope. Your stomach won't get any fuller just lying there and I'm not going to wait around to tuck you in for your little dirt nap. I'm moving on."

"Then go."

"I will," Kamatari said, pouting. "Don't think I won't."

He took several paces up the road, then turned impatiently. Minoru had not budged from his prone position on the rock, not even to see if his friend had left. Frustrated, Kamatari kicked at the dirt.

"You'll come," he shouted. "When the critters at night start to screech and the hunger eats at you until you can't stand it. And when you do, don't expect I'll hold your place in line with the Dauphin's men."

"Go," Minoru cried feebly over his shoulder.

Kamatari swallowed his anger, cast his friend one last look and then looked towards the ridge. "Fine, be that way, you sorry sack of dung. I can do this on my own."

But even as he said the words, a pang of fear overcame him. He nearly turned and ran back to the rock, but he put one foot in front of the other and then another. Before longing his legs were carrying him up and away from Minoru and past the spotted yarl tree he was no longer certain was the one on the map.

After a few hours, the dim glow of the sun sliding past the horizon gave way to longer and deeper shadows. The howls of some woodland predator could be heard menacingly in the distance. He had to feel with his feet to keep from stumbling off the narrow road. It suddenly seemed to be much too narrow to be the main road heading into Olivet. But pride kept him moving forward.

"Minnie will regret not sticking with me," Kamatari grumbled to himself. "After all the times I put up with his endless whining, and he ditches me because his feet hurt."

He heard a rumble in the distance that drowned out the whistling and moaning of nocturnal wildlife. It sounded like thunder to him, so he wondered if a stormfront was moving in. He could no longer see the clouds in the sky and while he could see a few stars winking above, this was not guarantee that weather wasn't approaching. Kamatari stopped and tasted the wind. It was dry and sweet, not wet and salty as air before a storm usually seemed. Through his years as a farmer, he had become proficient enough in forecasting the weather that the other fiefs often came to him for advice on planting their crops.

"Hmmmph," he said. "Just your imagination."

So, he continued on, but the rumble rose again, this time more distinct. It would crescendo and then fade to a dull roar, but the waves of sound tended to increase in volume the further Kamatari traveled down the road. He began to wonder if a large beast waited for him on the other side of the crest, and the thought made him weaken at the knees.

Kamatari slapped himself. "Now you're thinking like Minnie, you idiot!"

He pushed himself against his own growling belly and fatigue. Several times he tripped over a tree root or stumbled into a pothole, but finally he staggered to the top of the ridge. As soon as he could see to the other side, he fell over gasping.

When he looked up, he began to notice a glow. It framed the silhouette of a large skyline—several towers and perhaps a large keep mounted atop a palisade. Kamatari rubbed his eyes to make sure he wasn't dreaming or hallucinating. He couldn't be sure, but he surmised that the noise was coming from the city. Perhaps they were having a late-night festival.

"I was right! I was right!" he cried, waving his arms frantically in the air. "I'm saved!"

Kamatari got to his feet and began to run on his shaky legs. He stumbled then tumbled and recovered, ignoring the gnashing of the stones against his knees and sting of briars against his elbows. The low rumble grew into thunderous crashing booms. Soon he could see lights flickering and make out the shapes of some roofs. The path itself grew lighter as he neared civilization and his heart filled with joy. He could now see moving shapes—people in uniform! It was probably a sentry unit sent to patrol the outskirts of the city.

"Hey! Over here!" Kamatari shouted in relief. He resumed waving his arms in the air to show that he was unarmed. He suddenly remembered the ploughshare strapped to his back but thought better of ditching it before they could see it was made into a weapon. He was just a simple farmer after all, and from afar he just looked like a simple peasant. He saw some helmeted heads turn by none of them moved towards him, so Kamatari continued walking and flagging them down. Two men nearest him were carrying torches and had their swords drawn. But beyond them Kamatari's eyes were drawn to a crowd unlike the soldiers between them and him. They appeared to be dressed like peasants, like him, in plain woolen cloaks and pants.

"Hey!" he cried out again.

He heard muffled sounds from the crowd. He began to wonder why such a mixed group of people would be wandering outside the city walls at this time of night. If this was an armed patrol, why would they bring civilians? And if a group of revelers were out carousing, why would they come out here?

Before his weary brain could formulate an answer, there was another loud boom. The roof of one of the towers erupted in flame, lighting up the night sky like an enormous torch. Kamatari stopped dead in his tracks, bewildered at what he saw.

"The signal!" he thought he heard one of the peasants call out. Suddenly, a few of the peasants tossed off their cloaks revealing chain mail and

53

swords. They lunged at the guards and several fell to the ground. The remaining guards seemed as surprised as Kamatari was. There was a general shouting among those still in peasant garb and some of them fell to the ground as well. A few looked up at the wall behind them to see a line of sharpshooters with crossbows firing down at them from the battlement.

"What in seven hells?" Kamatari exclaimed.

It was clear no one in the crowd had a ranged weapon to fire back. The men in chain mail and the peasants were dropping one after another as the sharpshooters picked them off. Then, the crowd began to run, like a herd away from the wall. To Kamatari's shock and amazement, they were running towards him. As they approached in their panic, they took no notice of him, but their bodies were so thick in the road that there was barely space between them. Kamatari's brief joy had by this time turned to pure terror as he realizes that he was about to be caught up in a wild human stampede. He looked to his left and right, but the road was walled in by thicket and bramble.

"No! Wait!" he cried out to the crowd in futility.

An arrow whizzed past his ear and stuck into the ground a few feet behind him.

"Don't shoot at me! I'm on your side," Kamatari said. "I mean, I'm on somebody's side. I'm Orloinian!"

But still the crowd stampeded towards him. He cursed under his breath, turned away from the wall and began to run the way he'd came. His shins still sore, he hobbled back up the hill, but the mob was faster. He could almost feel their panicked breathing on the back of his neck and the sensation spurred him on. It didn't matter that the darkness was nearly blinding. His feet fell numbly but deftly over the loose cobble stones. At last, he felt the incline level off. He had reached the summit again. It was downhill from here. Maybe the crowd would lose interest soon. Maybe they'd stop running.

Kamatari's mind went blank. In that moment, his skull crashed into something hard and metallic. A large object, blunt and stiff struck him full in the sternum, knocking the breath from his lungs. Before he knew it, he was prone on his back with the large object crushing on his chest. He clawed feebly at it to push it off him to no avail. The object screeched in pain.

"Minnie?" Kamatari gasped.

"Kamatari, is that you?" Minoru screeched. "Thank the gods, it's you."

"Get off me. I can't breathe."

But Minoru didn't get a chance to roll off his friend when the sound of footfalls and screams came crashing all around them. They heard a dull thud, a gurgle and another crushing weight fell atop Kamatari, still pinned under Minoru's weight. He could not believe his bony friend was so heavy.

"Minnie, get off me!" he croaked.

"I can't. I'm stuck," Minoru said. "I think someone else is here."

"Yeah, there's a whole hoard chasing me."

"What's happening? What did you do?"

"I didn't do anything. The world's gone mad."

"Olivet?"

55

"That's where I came from. When I found it, they were killing each other there," Kamatari said, then cried out in pain as one of the crowd stepped on his wrist in their mad rush in the dark.

Minoru clamped his hand over his friend's mouth to stifle the scream.

"They're killing people? Why?" he whispered.

Kamatari shoved the hand from his mouth. Minoru's hand and breath smelled as foul as fresh cattle dung and he probably hadn't bathed in weeks. "How should I know? I just got here," he rasped.

Kamatari gagged as some warm, sticky liquid dripped onto his face and lips. It tasted strangely metallic and salty. "Minnie, are you bleeding?" he whispered.

Minoru whimpered. "No, but I think someone else is."

"Hold on."

He reached his free hand around what he guessed was Minoru's torso. It felt soft and round, yet firm—a woman's breast. Mortified with embarrassment, he withdrew his hand in expectation that the woman on top of them might slap him for being so forward and rudely groping her. But no blow or cry of outrage came. He reached out for the woman's neck. He felt around a stringy matte of hair and an ear. There was no movement from her. He felt for a pulse, but he could find none. Then his hand brushed against something metallic and sharp, near where the woman's eye or nose should be. It was mounted on a wooden shaft. Kamatari bit his lip to ward off the tide of dread that was washing over him.

56

"Oh gods, no."

"What is it?" Minoru cried.

"Don't panic," Kamatari warned his friend.

"I'm not panicking."

"You will, but don't."

"I won't. Tell me."

"There's a dead body lying on top of us."

Minoru whimpered. This time, it was Kamatari who was shoved a hand in his friend's mouth to stifle him.

"Listen, whoever shot this woman at this distance could shoot us too. Shut up and lay still while I think of a way out of this."

"Why would they kill a woman?"

"I told you, I don't know."

"How do you know she's dead?" Minoru said, straining to look over his shoulder.

"I just fondled a dead woman's boob. Don't ask me how I know," Kamatari growled.

They heard a few other members of the mob thud to the ground and a few more thin whistles as arrows streaked overhead. Kamatari listened as a few men moaned their dying breaths. After a while, the shouting dissipated and only the low thunder of the explosions from Olivet could be heard.

"I think the fighting has stopped. We should go," Minoru said. "But where?"

"How in seven hells should I know. We won't make it to the next city. We don't have enough food and water to sneak off to the next city. And if the Fiorese are this far south, we might encounter the same welcome there," Kamatari groaned. "Oh, hells. You were right. We were better off working the shit at that gods-forsaken demesne. We should never have left that mudpot."

"Don't blame yourself. It was a terrible mudpot and it would have been the death of us," Minoru said. His lip trembled. "I guess it's our lot in—"

Kamatari recovered his friend's mouth with his hand, not because he wanted him to silence him, but because he heard a new sound—hoof beats and wheels against the stones. He heard new voices too.

"They tried to escape this way," they heard one of the voices shout.

"We need to get out of here quick!" Kamatari whispered. "Help me get this woman off your back. Rock yourself to the left and I'll push too."

Minoru shifted his weight.

"No, my left, you idiot!"

"Sorry!"

With a groan, the two men rolled the woman off of them and then Minoru rolled off to the other side of him. "Oh," he cried.

"Shhh," Kamatari said. "What are you whining about now? I'm the one who was almost crushed underneath your bony ass and a corpse."

"I rolled onto something sharp," Minoru said. "Hey, I think it's a sword."

"Some of the mob were carrying those. Be careful with that or you'll hurt yourself."

Kamatari scrambled to one side of the road and then the other. The bramble was still too thick to penetrate. "Give me that sword. Maybe we can cut through this so we can get off this bloody road.

Minoru moved towards his friend, banging him in the ribs with the hilt of the sword as he passed. Kamatari cried out in pain.

"Sorry, I slipped."

Kamatari slid the ploughshare from his back and they both began furiously hacking at the underbrush. In a few moments the bramble had given way enough for them to force themselves into the hedge. Minoru pulled some of the cut branches over them just as the light of some torches reached the spot where they had been laying.

"I thought I saw movement over here," one of the voices said.

"Nah, that bunch ain't movin'," another deeper voice said.

"That can't be all of them," the first voice said. "Where are the rest?"

"Stay on guard!" warned the deeper voice.

Kamatari spied the source of the first voice—a soldier holding a torch in one hand a pike in the other. He crouched momentarily and then flashed his torch from side to side. Minoru gasped as the firelight illuminated the mutilated hedge where he and his friend were hiding. Kamatari quickly clamped a hand over his partner's mouth, stifling a whimper in the nick of time. Thankfully, a curtain of darkness obscured them as the solider turned towards his partner.

"Looks like the rest scampered off into the valley," the soldier called. "Should we pursue?"

"Are you kidding? It's black as pitch out there."

"What if they warn others? The Master Chief will have our hides if the enemy comes back in force."

"You willing to bet your life on that? We're about likely to stumble across a pack wolf as those peasants. Without support, we'd be sitting ducks. I say let 'em run. Let's head back."

"What do we tell the Master Chief?"

"We'll tell him they're all dead. Burn the bodies before they can do a headcount. No one will be the wiser. Come on."

Kamatari heard the two soldiers tromp back towards Olivet. When he was certain they were alone, he pushed away the scratchy brambles and stepped back into the road.

"What are we going to do?" Minoru muttered from the hedge.

Kamatari looked towards the walls of Olivet and the faint glow of the burning city. The growl in his belly, which had subsided during the panic of the mob, flared up again. "Same as before. We'll be making ourselves into soldiers. What choice do we have?" he said. "I'm just not sure whose army we'll be fighting for."

Chapter 6

Spring of Year 43 (after the Great Plague)

Without ceremony, Baudrin, Baldric and the maiden
Pucelle slipped unnoticed on foot through the
gatehouse and out beyond the walls of Valcolors under
the purple cloak of twilight as the cocks first began to
announce the approaching dawn. Just a quarter mile
down the road, they entered one of the keep's auxiliary
stables. There, Baudrin found a drowsy stable boy and
paid him some coin to saddle up three of his best
horses. After Baldric bounded off to the stable owner's
home and returned with enough provisions for the
journey, Baudrin watched the maiden as she fed apples
to an ebony gelding and whispered in his ear.

"If you are done communing with the animal, I'd
like to get underway," he said.

Pucelle did not look at the captain. "His name is
Rienard. And we are asking him to risk his life for us.
It's important for him to understand the dangers he's to
face."

"You're asking a horse for consent?"

"He's a living creature, not a plow or sword."

"Fair enough," Baudrin chuckled dryly. "Do you
intend on informing all of the animals of our covert
mission?"

Pucelle gave him a sharp look. "I leave that to your
discretion, sir."

The captain regarded his own steed, a grey mare with mottled spots on her hindquarters and a yearling's gait. "I think we have an unspoken understanding."

As Baldric passed his master with a satchel of jerky, old bread and dried fruits, he whispered: "My horse has given his consent, sir."

Baudrin grunted. "Let's go."

The captain mounted his horse, but already the maiden was already astride her mount and galloping towards the crossroads, her lustrous dark hair slapping her back as she rode. Baldric's stocky grey shire horse, laden with their packs and the few concealed weapons they dare bring with them, followed close upon her heels. His servant looks small and foolishly awkward atop the immense draft horse, but it helped sell their cover story that they were peasant travelers on a pilgrimage should they encounter enemy forces or bandits along the way. Baudrin donned a simple cowl and tucked his signet ring in a pocket he felt sure had no holes, then spurred his steed to motion.

The captain knew better than to hew to the main roads too closely. The beauty of the valley belied the hidden dangers under the outstretched limbs of its arboreal rulers. Even before the Fiorians and their allies invaded, the gullies and blind curves of the hillside thoroughfares were breeding grounds for all sort of scum who preyed upon pilgrims and farmers traveling to the markets. Before that, during the plague, they waylaid and murdered refugees fleeing the infected cities. Baudrin picked out a route that avoided popular crossroads but were littered with rocks and low-hanging sheets of bramble moss that scratched at the face and caused obnoxious rashes where the tendrils lashed at the skin.

By the time they reached the summit of the first mountain, the sun had reached its peak in the sky and its blazing heat and white light scalded the eyes and sizzled the captain's cheeks. The extremes of temperature at this elevation were bracing even for a native of Valcolors. But the view from on high gave them a strategic vantage point to see the path ahead of them. Unfortunately, it did not look good.

Baldric pointed to some smoke in the direction of Olivet. "Do you think those are enemy campfires, sir?"

Baudrin shook his head. "It may be the enemy, but those fires are too large and uncontrolled. It's like a raiding party went amuck. I fear for the people of Olivet if that is the case."

"The fires appear to be headed in this general direction."

"Yes, the prevailing winds and more plentiful supplies of dry timber are most likely drawing the flames this way," Baudrin glanced at the maiden, who's attention was directed ahead, down the slope of the mountain. "If there's anyone down there, they'll be running to stay ahead of the fire line like rats fleeing a methane-filled sewer. We should keep moving if we don't want to get caught in the fray."

Baldric spurred his horse and the party commenced its descent into the windy path down into the thick scarlet foliage. Surprisingly, it didn't take long for them slip into the deep shade offered by the canopy of trees. Deep in the valley, especially in densest parts of the forest, it was easy to find oneself cloaked in darkness. But Baudrin didn't mind it or the fact that it slowed their travels. It gave them a distinct advantage over any threats they might encounter, so long as they had the element of surprise.

The birds were particularly active in this part of the forest. He could hear them arguing over the muffled clopping of their horses hooves over the blanket of leaves that covered the ground. The thick ground cover, along with the shadows broken by flashes and flickers of brief sunlight, made footing difficult for the horses. They picked their way gingerly over potholes, tree roots and overturned logs. The air was filled with the acrid smell of rotting vegetation mixed with sweet dew and sticky sap.

Pucelle abruptly stopped her horse in front of Baldric's, who reigned in just as his steed nearly collided with hers. "Madam, at least give a warning," his assistant barked in astonishment.

"They've stopped," the maiden said.

"What stopped?" Baldric asked dumbly.

Baudrin listened carefully and felt an ominous still in the air. "The birds. I can no longer hear their chatter."

The captain sidled his horse next to Baldric. As he did so, he noticed a rustle of leaves. What appeared to be piles of leaves on three sides of them rose and formed into man-shaped creatures. Two of them carried swords and three aimed crossbows at the party. All had their faces covered in grime so that their bare heads covered in matted black hair made them seem like shades risen from the dead ground like some sort of golems. The largest of the men, a burly man with unnaturally white teeth that Baudrin presumed was the leader, flashed them a blindingly toothy smile.

"What have we here?" the leader of the golems cried. "Who dares trespass on our mountain and dares walk our roads?"

"We are pilgrims headed for Olivet, if that at all matters to you," Baudrin said, eyeing each of the men as he slowly kept sidling towards Baldric's horse and the hidden satchel of weapons slung over the horse's backside.

"Don't move, peasant," one of the golems with a crossbow warned. "It makes my trigger finger itch when you move. I wouldn't want it to twitch and put a bolt through your heart."

Baudrin raised his hands in surrender. The golem nearest him held a sword. His stance was balanced, like a fighter who'd been trained, not the typical bandit who wielded a sword like a common meat cleaver or axe. He thought he noticed the insignia of the House of Eldritch, known Fiorian sympathizers tattooed on his sword mate's off hand. "I don't mean to make you twitchy, friend. Just let us pass and we'll cause you no harm."

"Cause us no harm, eh?" the Eldritch tattoo man chortled. "He thinks he can cause us harm, does he?"

"No, that's not what I meant to say," the captain bit his lip. He realized that no matter what he said at this point, these ruffians had already decided to kill them. The only thing he could do was distract them and buy for time.

"Then let me tell you what you meant to say, mate," the Eldritch man continued. "You meant to say that you'll get off those horses and surrender all your goods and money to us, as punishment for trespassing in our woods."

The golem nearest Pucelle licked his lips. "And we'll keep the girl too, if you don't mind."

"We'll keep her even if you do mind," the leader exclaimed to loud guffaws from his men.

The maiden stiffened in her saddle. "Not if the girl has anything to say about it, you won't."

The Eldritch man's laugh turned to a sneer and three of the golems approached the maiden on her mount. It was clear they were going to dismount her, by force if necessary. Baldric gave a nervous glance towards Baudrin and the captain nodded subtly back, letting his hands drop to his sides. There was a brief moment of recognition on the assistant's face and then he began to moan loudly and flail his arms. This briefly caused the golems to stop and examine Baldric. He fell backwards off his horse. As he did so, his hand grasped the clasp of the weapons cache and swords, daggers and a miniature crossbow fell to the ground.

With the golems turning towards Baldric, Baudrin freed his lone weapon from his tunic sleeve—a dagger—and let it fly. The blade caught a bowman in the throat, and he fell with a thud in the leaves. He dismounted and dove for the crossbow. Ducking beneath his own horse he sent a bolt into another bowman. The swordsmen ran towards him. He dropped his weapon and grasped the two swords on the ground. It was just in time. Baudrin crossed his own swords to block an overhead blow from the first swordsman and fell backwards, catching the man in the stomach with his feet. The golem's momentum catapulted him over the captain as the second one took a blind stab at his legs.

Baudrin got to his feet quickly and kicked the dagger towards where he heard Baldric still crying on the other side of his horse. The swordsmen stood as well on either side of him. The captain glanced to either side of him. His mind raced as he sized up the competition. His gut told him go left. It was right. The man he rolled was eager to fight. He lunged before his comrade, but Baudrin was ready. He feinted right and then drew his left sword up as he dodged the incoming blow. The blade connected cleanly with the man's ribs and he fell forward with a grunt. The golem on his right who hesitated then lunged. It was a fatal mistake. Baudrin deflected the blow with his right arm. With his left, he swung and caught the man full on the arm. It was not strong enough to sever the limb, but the arm was splattered with blood and the golem was forced to drop his sword in a cry of pain. Baudrin kicked him to the ground. He heard Baldric shout a warning and then felt a breeze whisper by his cheek followed by a sharp thud of a bolt buried itself in a tree trunk behind him.

He spotted the shooter approaching from the rear of his horse. Another bowman took aim at him, but before he got the shot off, Baldric rushed and tackled him. The two tumbled to the ground, sending flurry of leaves in the air. Spotting the bowman who just shot at him trying to reload, Baudrin decided to do the same. He barreled into him, knocking the crossbow from his hands with his left sword and driving the right at the golem's torso. The blade barely missed, tearing a piece of his camouflage from his chest. Their bodies collided and they fell to the ground. His opponent was a lighter man, so Baudrin's weight pinned him to the ground. But his hands were free and clawed blindly at the captain's face. Several blows connected, but Baudrin maintained discipline in spite of the metallic taste of blood in his mouth. He pressed his left forearm against the bowman's Adam's apple. The golem gave a low gurgle. Baudrin's right hand still gripped his sword. He tried to rise up from the bowman's flailing, clawing hands, using the forearm on the man's as leverage. When he finally rose, he poised the sword over the bowman's chest.

"Captain, no!" he heard the maiden scream.

It was too late. His momentum carried his sword arm forward as the golem lunged forward. The sword impaled the man through his sternum and stopped him cold. He felt the bowman shudder and his eyes grow dark. Then he slumped over.

The captain spun round to see Baldric club his opponent across the jaw with a fallen tree branch, knocking the golem prone. Pucelle had dismounted and was racing towards him. When she reached him, she fell to her knees and grasped the dying golem by the arm and rubbed his palm.

"What are you doing, girl?" Baudrin asked, his gaze darting between the prostrate combatants, watching for signs of movement.

"You should not have killed this man," the maiden said.

68

"Oh, I think I should have," Baudrin gave a haughty sigh. "After all, they did try to kill us—and threatened to rape you."

"Look here," Pucelle showed him the man's palm, now scrubbed clean of the caked mud and leaves that made up the golem's camouflage. The flesh was marred by a blood-red raised scar that resembled an X encircled by a snake. It was also strangely ashen and bruised color, as if the body was already beginning to decompose. "This man was branded."

"Yes, well, criminals often are. Your point?"

"If he is a criminal, he was forced to be one. When Fiorese sympathizers would send their scouting party to my parents' village when I was a child, they often rounded up the able-bodied men and branded them with that mark. They told them that if they wished their families to live, they would serve them and then hauled them away. Only the conscripts bear the mark."

"Interesting," Baudrin shrugged. "But unfortunate for this poor wretch. There's nothing to be done for him now."

"Yes, there is," the maiden bowed her head.

"What?"

Pucelle did not answer, but silently whispered to herself. She placed the man's palm over her left breast. Baudrin shook his head in disbelief and looked to Baldric, who simply shrugged and dropped his tree branch. A few moments later, the sword buried in the man's chest began to quiver and vibrate, until it began to shake violently, then dropped to the earth. Astonishingly, as if a demon had been expelled, the bowman's torso lurched forth as the man's lungs filled

69

with air and his eyes suddenly bulged open in horror. Baudrin grabbed the blood-soaked pommel of the fallen sword and pointed the blade at the golem's throat.

The bowman cast a shocked gaze about him and looked down at his own chest in disbelief. He pulled aside his torn cloak and traced his fingers across the bare skin that had just been pierced. The man brushed aside the pooled blood to reveal unblemished skin. "What has happened?"

"I have healed you," Pucelle said simply. "I have given you a second chance at life."

"I—I was dead?" the bowman sputtered.

Pucelle nodded. "More than that, I know why you were with these men and I've released you from your burden."

"Burden?"

The maiden released his hand and showed him hers. On her palm was a distinctive scar of an X encircled by a snake.

"How did I not notice that before?" Baudrin asked.

The bowman looked his palm. His scar was gone. He rubbed the virgin skin and then looked eagerly at the maiden. "How is that possible?"

"It is not a question that is important now," Pucelle said. "The real question is what you will do next with your life since it's been given back to you."

"But you killed me. I was dead. Why—"

"I did, mate. And I can make you dead again," Baudrin growled, placing the tip of his sword under the man's chin. "So choose your next move cautiously."

Pucelle placed a hand on the captain's forearm. "I don't think our friend has any reason to harm us from now on. Do you, friend?"

The bowman glanced nervously at Baudrin and then at the bodies littering the clearing. He shook his emphatically.

"What is your name?"

"Wormy."

"Wormy is a curse, not a name. What is your real name?

"Takashi, ma'am."

"Where did you live before this?"

"Muckville. It's a city far to the north."

"I come from Do'om. My uncles used to travel to your city on trade business. Do you have family in Muckville?"

"A sister and mother. I haven't seen them in almost a year."

"Don't you think they would like to see their brother and son again?"

The man sighed. "I don't know. I've done horrible things. I've killed people. I—I forced myself on a—"

"Go home. Find your sister and mother, Takashi. Above all, do no more wrong," Pucelle said.

The bowman paused. "Yes, ma'am. I'm sorry for what I tried to you and yours."

The man slowly rose and wandered to the edge of the clearing. He stopped only to glance furtively at the maiden. Bewildered, Baudrin watched dumbly as the bowman disappeared into the trees. Then he turned to the maiden.

"What have you just done, girl?" he spat.

71

"What I had to."

"What you did is let loose a criminal with knowledge of our existence and the fact that we are not really peasants but warriors and you—" the captain said. "How did you know how to do that?"

"They came to me when I first heard the voices of the dead king," Pucelle said. "I saved a baby that died from plague flu. It was involuntary but I discovered that I could raise the dead."

"You're a necromancer?"

"If that's what you call it, yes. It is part of my gifts, but one that comes at a heavy price."

"Well, maiden necromancer, let me explain the heavy price you may have just incurred just now," Baudrin said. "Stealth has been the premise of this mission. But the man you just brought back from the dead—the man who was just trying to kill us all a few minutes ago—is going to go back to his fellow bandits to tell them all about us. They will hunt us down and kill us for what we did."

"He won't go back to the bandits."

"You don't know that. He told you what you wanted to hear so that I wouldn't kill him—again."

Pucelle showed Baudrin her freshly branded hand. "He's going home. And when he does, I don't care who he tells about us."

"Then you don't understand the stakes or consequences if we are caught, young lady."

She squeezed the hand into a fist and then released it. As she did, she gave a short cry of pain. The palm was clean and pink with only a few callouses to mark the peasant girl's flesh. She turned and mounted her horse. Baldric gave his captain a quizzical look and then mounted his own.

Baudrin hoisted himself onto his horse's back and ushered it to the front of the party. "I still think it was a mistake," he muttered. "Let's get you to the dauphin without further delay."

Chapter 7

Spring of Year 43 (after the Great Plague)

When Mallory crept into bed from a long day at the workshop, it was late evening. Belle Isolde rolled over sleepily and her eyes opened.

"Mallory, where have you been?" she said. He leaned over and stroked the hair from her forehead. "I held dinner for you, but you didn't come. I began to worry until I got the message from Joaquin."

"I got busy working on a project and lost track of time," he said. "I'm sorry I couldn't get back sooner."

"But the curfew. You should have stayed put at the workshop if you were going to be working so late."

"I couldn't leave you alone all night. Besides, I know my way around the patrols," Mallory kicked off his shoes and slid under the covers beside her. "I've got some important news."

Belle Isolde blinked. "What is it, dear?"

"The project I've been working on," he said. "It's ready for testing."

His wife smiled, caressed his cheek, and leaned in to kiss him, but Mallory pulled back a little. The corners of her mouth turned downward and worry lines creased her forehead and she noticed his rejection. "This is cause for celebration, isn't it? Why do you seem so dejected?" she asked.

"I held off telling you until now. What I'm making is not a steam-powered reaper for the farming

74

communes," Mallory said. "It's a military project. As it turns out, it could be a big one."

"What do you mean? How big?"

"I've built a war machine. It's a vehicle with armor far stronger than anything the Orloinians could ever penetrate," he said. "Originally, I only intended it to be used against fortifications, but there were certain design problems I couldn't overcome. I couldn't mount a powerful enough cannon. I had to change my approach and mount an anti-infantry weapon on board. But it will be terrible weapon. If it works, it will burn people alive with a power much like the dragon's breath of legend. It could kill dozens—maybe even hundreds—at a time, in the most horrifying way imaginable."

Belle Isolde's eyes widened. "Then maybe you should scrap the plans and destroy the prototype. Find another way to satisfy the Chancellor's people. They can't know about the machine yet, do they? The contract you signed was vague in that regard, wasn't it?"

"It was, but they are going to expect something and soon," Mallory said. His voice grew dark. "My apprentice says there's a rumor about that the Chancellor himself is coming for a visit this week."

Her eyes bulged even further. "Oh," was all she could say. She withdrew her hand from his face and stared off into the distance a moment.

"I have to have something to show him for all the money they've given me, to maintain our lives of comfort," he continued. He sat up and folded his arms. "This war is a dirty business and, from what I can make of your brother's letters home, it's not going nearly so well as the government would have us believe. I just wanted to end it quickly. It's dragged on too long and claimed the lives of too many of our countrymen."

"And you think this weapon might provide a tipping point, to bring it to an end and bring Jakob and the other boys home?" Belle Isolde asked.

Mallory nodded. "But I worry now how it might be wielded. It's just that… when I begin to design and build things, I am so focused on the problem at hand that ignore all the consequences these creations entail. I just give myself over to the power of creation. But now I worry about how these weapons of mass destruction could be used to commit terrible acts in the wrong hands."

"And you feel that the Chancellor's hands are the wrong hands?"

"My dear, I'm not sure who the right hands are."

Chancellor Newbold rarely traveled without an entourage. This usually entailed several body guards, a scribe, a body double, personal food taster or chef, a detachment of the imperial guard, and at least one senior advisor. As a matter of practicality, it was difficult to move incognito with such a large party. And yet, by gently mussing his hair and donning a citizen's grey tunic and cloak, Newbold could slip away for and blend into the population—at least for a little while. He liked to do that because he wanted to what the common man thought, not what the echo chamber of his subordinates wanted him to know. He liked to that because he could find out which of the sheep were actually wolves in disguise. Knowest thy enemy and thou will never be a slave, a wise Fiorese statesman once said. Of course, the Chancellor had killed that statesman, but it made the words no less true.

When the imperial party arrived at the Oxwell city limits, Newbold nodded for his body double to take his place in the carriage and then slipped over a low stone wall and into an alley way next to a small tavern. He drew the cowl more tightly over his face as he neared the main street at the front of the building. He needn't have done so, since there were no pictures of the Chancellor circulating about the empire, at least none that weren't idealized depictions of him. Portraits usually smoothed out his crooked nose, filled in the pockmarks left behind by the plague sores and grew out the bald spots that made his formerly luxurious blonde hair look ratty and gnarled.

"Pardon me, sir. Could you spare a coin? I'm trying to put a beer together," a drunk at the edge of the alley called to him.

Newbold surveyed the ragged man. He smiled broadly. A local man to add a little more cover to his disguise. "If you come with me, I'll offer you a little more than just a coin," he told the drunk. The man looked a little surprised and then seemed to give him suspicious eye. "I have some money, but I'm new to these parts and short of friends. You can drink to your heart's content if you accompany me."

The drunk nodded and ushered him around the corner to the entrance of the tavern. It was not a fancy affair, the Leaping Lizard, but it had a little rustic charm that these smaller cities of the empire had, especially those in the more rural districts. And, true to its poorly illustrated sign out front, there was a lizard—a miserable fire gecko—displayed in a glass aquarium to the side of the bar. Newbold limped across the wood floor and lurched onto a stool in the stiff manner he'd learn to adopt when undercover and ordered two ales for the two of him and a bowl of soup for his newly purchased friendship with the town drunk.

As he chatted calmly with the man about weather, he casually scanned the room and the other patrons. It was fairly busy for a workday in early afternoon, but the Chancellor's mission was information, not to bust workers playing hooky from their jobs. At the largest round table behind them there was a party of factory laborers gossiping about the day's events like a coop full of hens scratching at some seed.

"Did you hear that the Chancellor's coming to town?" A burly man with a large facial scar said.

"I've been hearing that for days," A smaller weasel of a man said, downing the rest of his mug and slamming it upon the table. "Doesn't make it any truer than it was last week."

"No, Frankie's right. He was in Midberry two days ago. My wife's cousin messaged her about it. And he'd been in Southberry the day before that. It stands to reason that he might hit here next," a man with a salt-and-pepper beard.

"What could he want here?" weasel said. "Don't he have better things to do?"

"He could be here to inspect the mills," Frankie the scarface said. "The war effort needs steel production to keep it going."

The weasel sniffed. "The war effort needs warm bodies more than cold steel. I doubt the Chancellor would waste his time in the ass end of the empire while his troops were dying on the continent. And if he is here, it's probably not for a reason we'd like."

"Like what?"

"Well, what's that blasted inventor been up to lately? What's his name—Mallory?" weasel said. "My house is just down the street from his workshop and all I've heard is growling noises, like he's been keeping some sort of huge beast pent up in there. Last night, my girls swore they saw a tower of flame come out of the roof of that building."

"That's weird, but what's that got to do with the Chancellor's visit? That spook's been haunting this town since forever. He's harmless," Frankie said.

"Yeah, but where's he been getting his money from to do all that anyways?" said weasel. "And what about the tower of flame? He could burn the whole city down? Don't tell me that quack is harmless."

"Hey, maybe he's keeping a dragon as a pet," salt-and-pepper beard said, giving the weasel a playful jab to his ribs.

"Dragons, my ass," weasel growled. "He's got something mechanical in there—and big. I bet he's a government operative cooking something up for the Chancellor."

"Or maybe he's not a government operative, in which case he's bound to stir up some trouble. Maybe the Chancellor's come to take care of him personally."

Weasel scowled. "That's just nuts. If he were an insurrectionist, the Chancellor'd send an assassin and take care of him quick and quiet-like, not make a great big spectacle of it."

"Well, excuse me, but who made you expert in all government policies?" salt-and-pepper mocked. "Are you an informant?"

"Shut up!"

The Chancellor who had sat side-saddle on his stool to give the appearance that he was fully engaged in conversation with the drunk, turned to face the group at the table fully. "Beg your pardon, but I couldn't help hear you mention a dragon in the city."

The group of workers looked up at the Chancellor in mild surprise. The one named Frankie filled the bowl of his pipe with some sort of herb from a stash in his pocket and eyed the stranger suspiciously.

"What's it to you, friend?" he said.

"Many pardons. I didn't mean to intrude," the Chancellor said. "It's just that I'm new to these parts, having just moved here from Southberry for a day job, and I can tell you that the Chancellor was indeed there just a few days ago for some mysterious purpose none of us could divine."

"You sure talk funny for a day laborer," weasel said.

"The folks in Southberry talk fancy like they've been to university," salt-and-pepper said.

Newbold smiled to deflect the apparent insult. "Precisely why I left Southberry. I never felt like I fit in there. I much prefer the salt-of-the-earth I find here in Northberry," he said. "But I thought dragons were just myths my parents told me to keep me indoors at curfew."

"They are," weasel said. "Total bull dung, and if you ask me."

"Indeed," Newbold purred. "But why would you say there would be dragons at this man's business? Who is this... Mallory, did you say? He seems like an odd sort of fellow if you think he'd be wrangling mythical beasts."

"He's not a beast wrangler. He's an inventor," weasel said. He leaned across the table and lowered his voice to a conspiratorial tone. There was no one near enough to hear anyways besides the Chancellor and the drunk, who was already starting to pass out on his stool. "He's been up to some strange stuff the past few days. He brought in a cow and a few pigs just yesterday. The next thing I know, I see smoke and smell burnt animal flesh. The day before that a tower of flame came right up through the roof. He patched it up but you can still see the burnt roof tiles and charred bits scattered all around."

The Chancellor nodded emphatically. "Certainly a fire hazard. And, if he's smoking meats without a permit, that would be a criminal offense."

"My thoughts exactly," weasel said. "That nut should get what's coming to him."

"Oh, Henry, lay off will you? What's that poor man ever done to you," Frankie moaned. "You're like a starved dog with a ham shank once you get your teeth into someone. Don't go messing in other people's business if they stay out of yours."

"It will be in my business once that nutter's burnt down the entire neighborhood," Henry the weasel growled.

Newbold shrugged. "I think I should like to meet this man. Can you direct me to him?"

"You want to do what?" Frankie said. "I should think you'd want to stay far away from him. Even if he's not doing the things Henry says he is, he's drawing suspicion and with the Chancellor's people possibly swarming the city, you don't want to be anywhere that draws attention to yourself, especially since you're an outsider."

The Chancellor nodded. "A good point and well noted. I will proceed with caution. However, if you can just tell me where he is, I will get out of your collective hair."

The group exchanged looks and then Henry the weasel pointed out directions for the Chancellor.

"Best heed our warning, stranger," Frankie said.

Newbold smiled and tossed a coin on their table. "Much obliged. The next drink is on me, gentlemen."

Chapter 8

Spring of Year 43 (after the Great Plague)

In the darkest corner of the Ocean's Edge Tavern, an old man in filthy grey robes sipped on his bowl of gruel and pretended not to notice the attentions of the shambling figure who entered through the front door. Though the old man was shabby and his grey beard a tangled bramble that doubled a mangy bib for his supper, the man's eyes sparkled as he occasionally eyed the other patrons warily. The other man, cloaked awkwardly in the black robes of the Magical Order of the Seraphim, also conspicuously ignored the attentions paid him by the rest of the patrons. Several glowered at him over their tankards and a few muttered curses about the plague and the disappearance of the clergy. The innkeeper, a sturdy middle-aged woman, instead of offering him a table, kept a healthy distance from the shambling cleric and a keen eye on the intruder as he sauntered around the tables and smiled at each person with a mouth full of crooked teeth. The old man stifled a cough as he passed.

"My, that's a nasty convulsion. May I join you, elder?" the shambling man asked the old man. "It appears that the other tables are... occupied."

The old man did not look up from his bowl but instead took another sip as he dully studied its broth. "If you must," he said at last.

The cleric did not wait for any further invitation, but quickly sat down in the curved booth next to the old man and shuddered. "My gods, but it is damned cold outside today, isn't it?" he said. "It's good to be near a warm hearth right now. It soothes the old bones, does it not, elder?"

"Not for long. The hearth here has run out of fuel," the old man said simply, still keeping his eyes fixed on the gruel.

"Well, then it's fortunate that I've arrived," the man in black said. "Do you believe in the healing power of magic?"

"That's a dangerous question to ask in these parts."

The cleric shrugged. "Why? Because the uneducated rabble such as these don't understand magic? Fear it?"

"And because the uneducated rabble, as you call them, will hang a cleric for simply being alive. You must either be very powerful—or very foolish."

"You are very observant, elder. I knew as soon as I entered this fine establishment that I was near a kindred spirit."

"Did you now?" Another spoonful of gruel dribbled onto the old man's beard. "I wasn't aware I had any kin left."

"You do indeed. And for the right price, I can be of use to a kindred spirit such as you."

A flicker of candlelight caught a glint of gold in the dark man's tooth as he cackled. He withdrew a small orb from his cloak and placed it on the table. The small sphere was made of cloudy glass but seemed to have a faint glow from its core as though as though a dying ember was trapped inside. The old man looked up instinctively for the first time since the cleric arrived and, with cat-like reflexes, clapped a gnarled hand over the orb.

"You know what this is, elder?" the cleric's voice curled into a snarl.

"You clearly do not," the old man gazed intently at the swarthy intruder. He nearly spat in his own soup as he spoke. "To display such an object as though it was to be hocked at market like some cheap bauble. It is sacrilege."

"Times are hard for members of the Order, as you obviously know. What is wrong with helping the old and infirmed-- and make a little coin on the side?"

"You are far too young and stupid to be a member of the Order. I remember the Mages of the Seraphim. Before the Plague."

The cleric growled. "I beg your pardon, old man?"

"How did you come to be dressed in these robes? They clearly do not fit you. From the looks of you, I'd guess you pinched them from an abandoned estate."

The cleric shifted uncomfortably under the old man's icy stare.

"Or, judging by the knife you carry concealed in your left sleeve, perhaps you killed a cleric and took his identity."

"You watch your mouth, old man," the man in black's cheekbones seem to suddenly hollow out and his eyes were hooded in shadows.

"Tell me, did you kill him like a man, face-to-face, or did you wait to spill his blood while he slumbered?"

The cleric's smile returned, only more sinister. "I found him eating cheap gruel in a tavern. Just like I found you. I gutted him like a fish, and no one even noticed. They won't notice you either—or care."

The old man sighed. "You should not have come here. You should leave old men to their gruel in peace."

The man in black cackled. It was a rustling of dry leaves. The knife slipped from the cleric's robe, but it tumbled dumbly from the man's grasp. His throat seized as his hand reached for the orb, still covered by the older man's palm. He tried to pry it free of his belonging, but suddenly the old man's arthritic grip felt like stone, mortared to the table's surface. The younger man clawed futilely at the elder's wrist and sleeve. The eyes which just moments before hid in shadows now bulged and reddened into fiery orbs filled with blood and yellowed puss. Finally, the man in black gasped, his tongue lolling to the side of his mouth, and he slumped forward.

The old man sighed again heavily. He wiped his cheeks, which were now streaked with tears. He slid the orb from his palm into his pocket, passed his hand over the cleric's face to close the younger man's swollen eyelids and then glanced about the room. The other patrons had lost interest in what was happening in the old man's corner and had returned to their meals. He reached into his pocket once more and fished out several coins, which he tossed upon the table. Then, he stroked some crumbs from his beard and slid gingerly from the seat. With stooped shoulders, he limped out the door and into the cold and dark outdoors.

A few moments after the door shut behind him, he heard the waitress scream in terror and he bowed his head in prayer. But it wasn't the scream that occupied his attention. On the wind, he heard a whisper from the north. There was something—or someone—whose power cried out. It was a power he hadn't felt since he was a young man and wore different, darker robes. It was a voice he'd never heard before.

Almost thoughtlessly, he began stumbling into the wind towards the source of the call.

Chapter 9

Spring of Year 43 (after the Great Plague)

After the death of the previous king and the loss of the capitol city to dukedoms sympathetic to Fioria, the Dauphin moved his base of operations to the historic cultural center of Aveon. All who visited the would-be ruler in his presumed seat of power agreed—Aveon had seen better days. Once a spectacle of art and architecture, the towering spires of the Central Embassy of the Order of Seraphim now were broken teeth above the sagging and chapped lip of splintering terra cotta rooftops. The city was surrounded by a defensive wall, half-heartedly fortified and defended by a handful of drowsy, overworked guardsmen.

However, the decay was but an outward manifestation of the rot that had taken hold of the people—both the natives and the transplants from the royal court. In fact, there were hushed whispers that the cause of the disease that seized the once proud and diverse community stemmed from the royal influence of corrupt politicians jockeying for privilege and position as criminals and the poor alike scavenged for scavenged for food and supplies, stripping temples, homesteads and mansions left empty from years of plague and war of their furnishings stone and wood until all that was left of the great city were cavernous husks looming over camps full of meager hovels.

When Baudrin, Baldric and the maiden near the main gate of the city, the captain got cold feet about entering the city directly and redirected them to a roadside tavern of questionable merit in a neighboring village. He bade Baldric stay with Pucelle while he approached alone about arranging an audience.

When he reached the city's main gate, the captain announced himself to the head guard and was escorted promptly to the master of the guard—a man who smelled of expensive whiskey and sported assorted jewelry of somewhat ostentatious taste for a soldier of his station. When he entered the master's office, the man, who went by the name G'rich, smoothed his fine-trimmed beard and eyed Baudrin suspiciously.

"What prompts this rather unusual visit to the capitol, Captain Baudrin?" he asked. "All is well in Valcolors, I trust?"

He pulled a bottle and two tumblers from a drawer behind his desk. He filled both glasses and shoved one across the desk towards the captain. Baudrin looked down at the liquor. It was still morning, early even for him to tip the bottle. But a quick glance at the watchful eye of the master of the guard told him that wisdom would be to play along, so he took a short swig and cradled the tumbler in his palm.

"I have vital information for the Dauphin, and I require an audience."

The master of the guard smiled cagily. "Well, then, you may tell me, and I'll pass it along to the court."

"The Fiorese have captured Olivet."

The master relaxed in his chair and fumbled with a ring. "Yes, we know," he muttered and then sniffed haughtily.

"What?"

"The Dauphin is aware of the fall of Olivet's government and is monitoring the situation."

"Monitoring the situation?!?" Baudrin spat. "Had anyone thought to inform me of the situation? Considering my keep is only on the other side of the valley from this disaster and likely the next target of Fiorese forces, I should have hoped a speedy plan to send reinforcements or at the very least a courier dispatch to alert neighboring friendly forces."

G'rich stared him down coldly. "As you can imagine, the Fiorese, the Orloinian traitor governments and criminal groups are putting a great deal of pressure on all fronts," he said. "The Dauphin simply does not have men to spare to put out every brush fire across the kingdom. Some areas will have to make do until a concerted offensive can be mustered to oust the invader from our lands."

"And when can my keep expect this concerted offensive to arrive at its doors? Would that be before or after the Fiorese burn it to the ground?"

G'rich snatched the glass from his hand and slammed it on the table. "Do you have any other old news that I should pass on to the Dauphin?" he growled.

"None that I can divulge to a lackey like you."

"Then I'm afraid you've wasted a trip and had best get back to your keep in the hinterlands while it still stands."

Baudrin stood and turned to leave. He didn't want to give the master the satisfaction of seeing his frustration. At the door, he paused. "Perhaps I'll just go to the palace steps and take my chances on my own. I'm sure there's a pretty young courtier whose ear I could bend."

The captain heard G'rich cackle. "You yokel, you'll do nothing of the sort."

Baudrin shrugged and gave the door handle a tug. The door opened a few inches before the master's palm slapped against the wood above the iron keyhole plate, slamming the door shut. "I said, you'll do nothing of the sort."

"Was that a threat?" Baudrin turned, partly in surprise at the man's speed and reflexes and partly out of self-defense.

"One does not simply go to the palace and solicit courtiers like common prostitutes," G'rich said. His was less condescending and more guttural now. "The capitol is a complex and dangerous ocean for such small fry as you. Best you run straight along home now."

Unimpressed, Baudrin leaned in until their noses almost touched. "Well, how else am I to deliver my message to the Dauphin if you won't help me."

"What message? Did a shepherd lose a sheep?"

"Mock me if you like, but your elitist attitude will evaporate once the Dauphin learns that you impeded the king's messenger."

"The king's messenger? Are you gone daft from sleeping with farm animals? The king is long dead."

91

"I am aware," the captain said in a mocking tone mimicking G'rich's. "We have been monitoring that 'situation' between naps with the cows. Nevertheless, I am escorting an emissary of the one true lord of this realm."

"You're lying. How could that be?"

"Through magic."

"You're definitely lying then."

"Then let me go and allow me expose myself to the public as the charlatan that I am. I am sure such a bold lie would quickly be revealed and ruin me—unless I had evidence."

Baudrin gave the door another tug, expecting the master of arms let him pass, but instead he leaned harder on the door. G'rich sighed from the exertion and he noticed a vein on his temple begin to pulse. "Let's not be hasty."

With his free hand, G'rich motioned Baudrin back to the guest chair. The captain complied and settled the cushioned seat which was much too soft for his tastes. The master followed suit, pouring them each another drink, his mouth pinched and drawn like his lips had been sewn shut. The captain sniffed the drink and took a light sip. Whatever else G'rich may have lacked in character or competence, he was sure that the master could hold his liquor and he was not about to let him loosen his lips by plying him with mead and grog.

"So, you'll help me get an audience with the Dauphin?" Baudrin asked.

"I did not say that, Captain Baudrin," G'rich said, poking at him with a finger. "As I said, one does not simply stroll into the Dauphin's presence like a commoner ordering a drink at a tavern. There are proper channels that must be traveled, correspondence with proper authorities and propriety that must be maintained."

"And palms that must be greased, I'm assuming."

G'rich cleared his throat angrily. "See, now that's the kind of coarse language that keeps you country folk from any chance of advancement here in the capitol. If you truly seek to serve the Dauphin, you must learn to get along with your betters."

"Does that include getting along with you?"

G'rich's voice lowered to a growl. "Perhaps."

"But I'm a liar, apparently, and one who obviously won't be greasing your palms today."

"No, you're not a liar. Bumpkins like you are too honest and direct and simple to be liars and you seem to be a straighter arrow than most of them. Perhaps you can prove to me you've got something more valuable than a few coins."

"How would I do that?"

"You can tell me what the king's message is or bring this so-called messenger to me."

"Not without an assurance of an audience with the Dauphin."

G'rich smiled. "I can assure that, all in due time. First, tell me the message or where you are keeping the messenger."

"The messenger is safe and nearby. She will not divulge the message to anyone but the Dauphin."

The master's eyes narrowed. "So, you don't know the message?"

93

"I don't know the exact contents of the message, no, but I do know it pertains to the war effort. I assumed that representatives of the Dauphin would be interested in winning this war and gaining any advantage in doing so."

"Then tell me about the messenger. What connection does she have to the king or this magic you claim she brings?"

"She speaks to the dead. She has knowledge from the beyond."

"And how do you know that? She read your tea leaves?"

"She knew about the fall of Olivet before I did."

"We knew about it before you did, and we didn't have to commune with the dead."

"Did you now? When did you learn of it then?"

"Three days ago."

"Really? It took us three days to journey from the other side of the valley. She told me days before that. I had her locked up in my keep for that time."

"Then she must be a spy sent to infiltrate the Dauphin's court."

"I thought that at first, which is why I placed her in custody," Baudrin said. "But use your head, master. Why would a spy concoct such a ludicrous cover story? Why would she come to my keep and for my help instead of heading directly to the capitol?"

"An excellent question—and do you have an answer?"

"From what I've seen, she's a legitimate magic user and she believes she is being sent to help the Dauphin."

"She's a member of the Order then?"

"No. Would that matter?"

G'rich shook his head. "I suppose not. That group of charlatans betrayed and abandoned the king during the plague. I would soon as kill your messenger as a traitor before I'd let her get within a mile of the Dauphin."

"And that would be fair. But she's no charlatan."

The master of arms stood and walked to his shuttered window. "Where is this messenger?"

"She's safe. I haven't risked bringing her into the capitol until I could arrange an audience."

"Fair enough," G'rich. "I can arrange an audience—but not with the Dauphin."

"With whom then?"

G'rich glowered. "Chief Burgundais. He is one of the Dauphin's closest advisors. If he sees fit, he may arrange a meeting with the Dauphin."

Seeing Baudrin's jaw clench, he added: "That's the best I can offer, yokel, unless you have something else to offer me."

The captain nodded. "No, that's fine. Just tell me when and where you expect us."

G'rich retrieved a pen and paper from his desk. He scratched some words on it, then dripped some wax from a candle on the bottom and pressed it with the signet on one of his official rings. "Bring this—and the messenger—to the gate tomorrow morning and my man will escort you to court."

As he placed the paper in Baudrin's hands, he grasped the captain's wrist firmly with his free hand.

"Remember, yokel, I'm sticking my neck out for you. This messenger better not embarrass me."

It was Baudrin's turn to smile. "Trust me, your auspicious career as a glorified door man will remain untarnished by me."

G'rich grunted and then chortled. "You piece of filth. I may grow to like you someday. But it is not this day."

Chapter 10

Spring of Year 43 (after the Great Plague)

In the shadow of the burned ruins of Olivet, Minoru looked ridiculous in his armor and he smelled even worse. He examined Kamatari in his borrowed uniform and began to moan.

"What is it now?" Kamatari said.

"I have a bad feeling about this plan."

Kamatari tucked some excess chainmail under his belt and fumbled to get his sheathed sword fastened to his side. "There's plenty to feel bad about. But we'll feel a lot worse if we don't start acting like proper soldiers and we're found out."

"But they will find us out," Minoru said. "We're not Fiorians. I don't know the first thing about Fiorians, and I can't speak their language. Can you?"

Kamatari whacked his friend angrily with his glove. "I've told you already. If we play it cool we won't have to speak to anyone. We just have to look like Fiorian soldiers so as to not arouse suspicion among the real Fiorians. If we stay out of everyone's way, the chaos of war will do the rest for us and we'll just slip past the enemy lines with no one the wiser."

"And then what?"

"We've come this far and the surest place to go is straight to where the Dauphin's sure to be mustering an army to take back Olivet."

"But won't the Dauphin's people kill us if we show up as Fiorians?"

"We'll ditch the uniforms once we're safe and head for the capitol, of course."

"Oh, that makes sense, I guess."

"Of course, it does. Now stop whining and let's get moving with purpose before anyone begins to suspect."

"My stomach still hurts."

"Eat some more rations we pulled off the dead soldiers."

Minoru looked at the small pouch that latched on at his belt. The leather was still splattered with blood. He prayed that no one would look too closely at the mauled state of their uniforms or get close enough to smell the stink of death that hung over both of them in their borrowed and ill-fitting clothes. He fished out a cracker that didn't appear to be too fouled by the dead man's blood and choked it down. The grumbling in his stomach stilled a bit so that he could at least hear himself think.

"How are we going to get through the enemy lines?" he asked.

"Just follow my lead and keep quiet," Kamatari said. He scratched at the skin around his chin strap and looked about. They were near the main gate to the fortified city and the few buildings outside those walls which hadn't been leveled to the ground bore severe scorch marks and most had lost their thatch or terra cotta roofs. Their gutted faces reminded him of the heads of criminals after they'd seen a guillotine. Next to the nearest dilapidated house, there was a cart left unattended. It was filled with bodies. As they came closer, he could smell the stench of the charred and rotting corpses. Kamatari cast about for a horse or even an oxen or donkey in the nearby stable. In all the chaos of war, someone had to have left something behind they could use. But perhaps the Fiorians had ransacked the useful livestock already. He was about to peer in one of the broken windows of the home for signs of food when they heard activity coming from the gate.

"Hey, you!" Kamatari thought he could make out. It was not Fiorese but a rather thick accented and guttural dialect of his own language. "You by the cart."

"What?" Minoru squeaked, trembling like a frightened mouse. Kamatari elbowed his friend in the ribs to keep him quiet and then turned to face the speaker. Riding up on horseback was a man, an Orloinian, no doubt. He had a sword sheathed at his side and was shouldering a crossbow. He appeared to be a soldier of rank, but in whose army he could not tell. He had heard that some of the northern dukedoms and demesnes had defected to the Fiorian side along with some of the more prominent criminal organizations, but this was the first he'd seen of it in the flesh. Instead of the crest of the king, he sported the insignia of the raven engraved on his left spaulder, which covered the upper portion of his arm. Instinctively at the sight, Kamatari's hand crept towards the knife at his belt.

"You two. What do you think you're doing?"

Kamatari shrugged and thought what he would have said to Count Arbor in the same situation. "We mean no disrespect, sir, but—"

"Just stop loitering about. There'll be time for sitting on your asses later," the officer barked. "Get this cart of rotting corpses off to the pit. This place stinks bad as it is."

Kamatari exchanged a glance with Minoru. Their disguise was working. He gave a clumsy salute and dragged the hesitant Minoru quickly to the cart.

"On it, sir."

"Don't let me catch you napping again, or they'll be hauling you lot off in that cart as well."

The cart was large and too heavy for Kamatari. He grabbed one set of handles and his friend to the set on the other side. They had no idea in which direction the pit was, but Kamatari guessed it was ahead of them. He pushed while his friend pulled.

"It's to the west, you idiots!" the officer shouted.

"Of course, sir," Kamatari bit his lip.

Gingerly they tried to turn the unwieldy cart left. Finally, when they had managed to make the turn, he gave the officer another awkward salute and a nervous smile. The officer scowled and grumbled something that sounded profane. Kamatari could only make out the words "miracle" and "how they had won the battle with so many inbred farmhands in the ranks." But the officer quickly lost interest in them when he spied another group of "loiterers" emerging from the fortress gate. Kamatari watched the officer's back as he galloped away.

When they had shoved the cart far enough so that the house stood in the line of sight between them and the gate, Minoru let go of his handles. The cart lurched to a halt, nearly knocking Kamatari to the ground as he lost his footing on the soot-slickened grass.

"Ouch, Minnie, dammit, what are you doing?"

"They can't see us, can they?"

"What does that matter?"

"We can ditch this awful cart. I'm not lugging a bunch of dead bodies about."

"This cart will add to our cover. No one will dare to question two soldiers hauling a litter of corpses."

"But it's heavy and gross and it stinks. Besides, we don't know where the enemy lines end or where the Dauphin's forces might be."

"Don't you get it? If it stinks, it will repel the suspicious," Kamatari said. "And I have this map that came with the dead man's clothes."

He unfurled a small worn sheepskin with markings on it. As he was functionally illiterate himself, Kamatari had only the foggiest notion of what the markings meant, and though he could locate the major cities, villages and landmarks by the colorful if inaccurate renderings of them he could not exactly pinpoint their location in relation to them. Still, he resolved not to tell Minoru of his incompetence as he pointed to what he believed was the Dauphin's crest next to a smudged building that he took from the legend to mean city.

"We keep going the way we're going and keep a low profile, we'll be alright," Kamatari said. "Just keep your shit together."

Minoru grumbled but grabbed hold of his handle and began pulling. "I wish we were hauling manure. It's far cleaner than this job."

"Keep moving, Minnie."

Minoru sniffed, but the cart lurched into motion. Up ahead was another road that wound through the rolling hills covered in dense swaying grass and grains that hissed loudly as the wind rippled through the tousled beards. Further in the distance was more smoke. This did not appear to be the apocalyptic sort with billowing clouds of soot swirling high in the sky but multitudes of tiny individual wisps that suggested campfires. Kamatari was tempted to veer them away from the camps and look for a side road, but a patrol on horseback sidled up alongside them and dissuaded him from taking any action that might seem suspicious.

They stayed along the road as the patrols passed, keeping their heads down. Aside from a few disgusted looks and grimaces, the soldiers paid little notice of them. They appeared to be more focused on the ridge ahead. As they continued, the road turn to slop, a wide muddy path where the cobblestones were sparse or kicked aside as though massive plows tilled the road haphazardly. Clearly the recent traffic on the road was more than it could handle. Such was the case when armies trampled through the countryside.

The cart suddenly lurched to a halt and the handle caught Kamatari squarely in the sternum this time, just under the breastplate, knocking him to the ground and robbing him of breath.

"A little warning would be nice, Minnie," he gasped as he rubbed his bruised chest.

"There's something happening ahead," Minoru said.

RIDING A BLACK HORSE

Kamatari peered out from behind the cart. The patrol they'd been shadowing joined several others. They had been scattering to flank the road and many had dismounted from their horses. Eventually, they formed up into a sort of line. Beyond them, lay the ridge, a brief spine of rocks and scraggly bushes, but Kamatari couldn't see anything that might've drawn the soldiers' attention.

"Do you hear that?" Minoru asked.

Not only could Kamatari hear a rumble ahead, but through his hands and knees still firmly planted in the rutted mud, he could feel the faint tremors. Something big was heading up the ridge, coming straight for them.

"I have a bad feeling about this," he grumbled under his breath.

A moment later, his feeling turned to terror. Like a wave crashing over a breakwall, a hundred cavalry leapt over the ridge and bore down on the dismounted patrols. They smashed into the lightly armed soldiers with a loud clang. Minoru screamed and ran to the backside of the cart to cower next to Kamatari, who shoved him down so he could keep a watchful eye on the melee.

Much to his relief, he noticed that they wore the tri-petaled giglio flower born by some of the Dauphin's allies. The cavalry proceeded to cut the patrols to ribbons. The few that survived the first wave turned and fled, dropping weapons and freshly looted coins as they ran.

"Are those from the Dauphin?" Minoru cried; his face enveloped in a wondering smile.

"That's right," Kamatari said. "We're saved."

Kamatari's fear gave way to greed as he realized they were in friendly company. He spied several copper pieces and even a silver one shining on one of the overturned cobblestones not more than a few yards away. If he could just reach them, they might be able to buy themselves a nice dinner and clothes that didn't reek of death. For a moment, he took his eyes off the fighting and chaos brewing around him to focus on creeping towards the stray money.

"Kamatari! Look!" Minoru stood and began flailing his arms. "They're racing to save us!"

But as he reached for the coins and felt their cool metal faces on his fingertips, Kamatari looked up to see two of the horsemen bearing down on him. Their expressions—hardened with bloodlust—looked anything but the faces of men who intended to liberate them. Just then, he remembered. They were still wearing their disguises.

"Minnie, no!" Kamatari shouted. "Our uniforms. They think we're the enemy."

Minoru looked down at himself in shock, then began to tear at the straps of his armor with frantic fingers. "Take it off! Take it all off! Hurry!"

In seconds, Minoru had wriggled free of his loose-fitting chest plate and pulled off the tunic with the enemy's insignia and was making quick work of his britches. Kamatari had only moment to weigh his options and since he could think of none, began to follow suit.

By the time the horsemen reached them, they were stripped naked, save for their own peasant loincloths. The lead horseman leveled his crossbow at Kamatari.

"Don't shoot! Don't shoot!" Kamatari pleaded.

"What the hell is this?" the second horsemen said, as both horses slowed from a gallop to a trot.

"Don't shoot us!" Kamatari begged again. "We're not soldiers. We're peasants from Count Arbor's demesne."

"A likely story," the first horseman said, regarding the two friends with an equal mixture of suspicion, revulsion and confusion. "That demesne isn't anywhere near here. Considering I just watched you ditch your house's colors like a bunch of deserters. And what are doing with a cart full of corpses."

"Please, sire, we were just at Olivet. We were trying to escape the enemy. We stole these uniforms from dead guards after they burned it to the ground. The cart is to help us escape notice and not get captured by Fiorians," Minoru said, his lip trembling.

"You were trying to escape notice? We could smell that cart even before we crested the ridge," the first horsemen said. "You must think me a fool to believe such a fish tale—in that get-up."

"Who the hell are these two?" the second horseman said to his partner. "They look like two Fiorian spies to me. Let's use them for target practice and be done with them."

"Of course they're Fiorian agents, but they're deficient, like some sort of retards. Besides, they've obviously surrendered and the code states—"

"Blast the code," the second horseman said, and he aimed his crossbow at Kamatari's head.

"I invoke the code or whatever. We surrender," Kamatari exclaimed. Then he remembered the coins near his hand. He snatched them up and showed them to the horsemen. "Or perhaps you would take some money for your troubles."

"A bribery, eh? Another sign of guilt. Fortunately, today is your lucky day. We will honor the code," the first horseman glared at his partner. "Sergeant, bind these men and take them prisoner. Captain Anville can decide their fate by law, whether they be traitors or deserters."

The second horseman guffawed and then put away his crossbow. With that, Kamatari and Minoru found themselves with their hands bound behind their backs and led away in their underwear by the two horsemen.

Chapter 11

Spring of Year 43 (after the Great Plague)

Mallory held the edge of the tarp and looked nervously at his wife. Belle Isolde waited at the drafting table and watched him as he paced across the workshop. Her eyes twinkled and she smiled, but her voice belied an impatience.

"Well, now, enough with the dramatics. Show me this machine you've constructed. I can't bear the anticipation," she said.

"You won't like it. It's hideous," Mallory warned. "And very unpoetic."

"Poetic or prosaic. It sprang from the mind of my beloved like a child of the gods. I'm sure I'll love it."

"Sure, you say that now, but it's a weapon designed to destroy, not create," Mallory said. "I'm afraid it may the only type of invention the government is interested in these days—or will pay for."

"It burned a hole in your roof, I see," Belle Isolde said. "I think I'm ready for the worst, dear."

Mallory gave the tarp a tug, then hesitated and sighed.

"Sir, perhaps I could assist," his assistant Joaquin offered. He grabbed the tarp from the other end of the Dragon's Breath and pulled.

"No, that's quite alright, lad," Mallory said.

But it was too late. The tarp slid down the side of the vehicle revealing its dark grey scales and horn-like cannon atop its turret. Belle Isolde gasped and covered her open mouth with one gloved hand.

"I know, it's ghastly," Mallory sighed, and his shoulders slumped as he read his wife's expression.

"No, dear, but it's also beautiful," Belle Isolde rushed over to him and embraced him. "It is a truly remarkable thing you've created."

"You haven't even seen it in action yet, ma'am. It can really move fast when it gets a head of steam and it makes a glorious ball of flame," Joaquin said.

"A ball of flame that could be used to kill—a lot of people."

"But it could also protect us all," Belle Isolde said. "And it could bring an end to this infernal war."

Mallory shook his head. "A weapon to end a war. Killing to save lives. It all seems like a lot of doublespeak now that I have time to think on it. I fear that if we fall into this line of thought, we'll be doing the government propagandists' work for them."

"But now your vision is made real, dear. What do you plan to do with it?" his wife ask.

Before he could answer, he heard a knock at the door. Mallory motioned to his assistant and then grabbed an end of the tarp.

"Belle, wait until we have the tarp on and then see who it is," he whispered. "Do not let them in."

Belle Isolde nodded and then went to the door. She waited until the Dragon's Breath was completely shrouded from view. Mallory and Joaquin ducked behind the vehicle out of view of the door. She opened the door a crack and peered into the noonday sun.

"Who is there?" she asked.

"Pardon me, madam. I wasn't expecting such a beautiful young woman in these quarters," came a thick, masculine voice. "I was wondering if I could trouble you for directions."

"Not at all, sir."

"I'm looking for a young man, an inventor of some notoriety in these parts, I'm told. I believe his name is Mallory. Do you know of him?"

"I do," Belle Isolde shifted nervously, though she maintained a polite tone of voice. "May I ask your reason for seeking him out?"

"You may. My name is Sudwell. I am an investor from Southberry. I run several workshops there. You might have heard of Sudwell Toys?"

Belle Isolde shook her head. "No, sir."

"Ah, no little ones, I see. I just assumed by the ring that you were married."

"I am, sir."

"Oh, well, congratulations on your nuptials. Have you been married long?"

Belle Isolde hesitated at this question. She glanced at the spot where Mallory and Joaquin were hidden, listening in. Mallory wondered if he should come to the door and his wife's rescue to be rid of this man. But she recovered quickly and shook him off with a quick flick of the wrist that was still hidden by the door. "I don't mean to be rude, sir, but…"

"Of course, where are my manners? I'm taking up your valuable time and for that I must apologize. But can you direct me to this Mr. Mallory?" the man at the door said. "I have been on a scouting mission seeking out talented minds in these parts. I would very much like to speak with this bright young man and see the accomplishments that seem to have the neighbors twittering."

Mallory bit his lip. His neighbors were simple folk and he knew they found him off-putting and so generally stayed out of his business. That was one of the reasons he had chosen this street to place his workshop in the first place. But his recent experiments had almost assuredly gained him some attention and possibly given them reason to gossip, snoop and pry. Had one of them seen the Dragon's Breath and then carelessly reported to this stranger at the market or had he plied them with drink at the local pub. He also considered the fact that this man claimed to be an investor. His contract with the government did not preclude obtaining outside work so long as it did not compete with the terms of his agreement. Perhaps this investor might provide him with a way out of making weapons and to making devices that would help rather than harm people. He decided at once he must know more about this Sudberry fellow and stepped out of the shadow.

"Dear, who is it?"

Belle Isolde's eyes widened, but when he nodded his assent, she opened the door wider and he could see the dark form of the man framed by the glow of a streetlamp. The man appeared to be wearing a plain cloak that hid most of his face. The cloak was cinched at the neck by a single brass clasp in the shape of a fist. In his right hand, the man held a walking staff capped off at the end by a brass fist similar in style to the clasp. It would be an odd design for someone native to the city, but not for an outsider, possibly someone from the south or capitol.

"Good evening, sir," Mallory said. "What may I do to help you at this late hour?"

"Ah," the man said. The inventor thought he detected a slight twinkle under the hood where the man's eyes ought to be. "Are you the famed Mallory the inventor I am seeking?"

"My name is Mallory, though I don't know about the famed part."

The man tapped his cane on the pavement with a short exclamation. "How fortuitous! I was beginning to think I was lost," he said. "Please forgive my imposition, but as I told the you lady here—"

"Yes, I heard," Mallory said. "Though I am not actively seeking patronage at this time, I would be happy to meet with you during business hours."

"I apologize for the lateness of my visit. I realize my sudden intrusion must seem quite rude," he said. "But I'm afraid my time to your fair city may have to be cut short and I did want to see you before I left."

Mallory shook his head. "Why would you want to hire a man whose work you haven't seen?"

"A very good question, but I can only answer that I trust my intelligence and my gut instincts to do business."

"Your intelligence?"

"If I may be allowed to come in, I'll explain to you where and how I got my information—about a mechanical dragon, perhaps?"

Mallory froze in place at the words. How had he been so clumsy as to allow a total stranger from another city to learn of his most dangerous of inventions? And what did this man hope to gain by approaching him? Blackmail? Extortion? It certainly couldn't be to invest in his business as he claimed.

The inventor stood so motionless he nearly forgot to breathe, until his wife, her hand still firmly on the door handle began to shut the door in the man's face. But Mallory grabbed the door before it could close. He glanced at his wife whose eyes were just as wide as he imagined his own were.

"Come in, sir," Mallory whispered. "It appears we have a lot to discuss."

"Indeed," the man purred. He flashed the white of his teeth as he stepped forward. Mallory moved aside to allow the stranger passage into the workshop, grasping Belle Isolde's arm protectively as he did so. He caught a glimpse as his assistant ducked out of sight behind the Dragon's Breath, still covered by the tarp. However, it was the first thing that drew the stranger's attention.

"And what have we here?"

Belle Isolde became visibly panicked. "Please, sir, we don't want to cause any trouble."

The stranger spun towards the young woman and lowered the hood of his cloak, revealing the face of a handsome, middle-aged man with long straight jet black hair. "Oh, but what trouble could you be in, my dear?" he asked soothingly. "In fact, if I may venture a guess, if I am correct, I could be your best path to stay out of trouble."

Mallory eyed a large wrench propped against the leg of his worktable. He eschewed violence and would rather not harm this gentleman, but whether he realized it or not, his poking and prying was placing him in an awkward position. The inventor already regretted letting him enter the workshop. While facing the stranger, he edged towards the table cautiously, holding his hands behind his back until the heavy tool, with an iron handle as thick as a man's wrist, was directly behind him and almost in reach.

"In what way do you propose to keep me out of trouble," Mallory asked. "You don't even know what type of trouble, if any, I might be in."

The stranger looked up towards the patched part of the workshop ceiling. "You're in whatever sort of trouble that also ignites the rumor that you are keeping a dragon caged in your facility and causes a hole to be burnt in your roof," he said, his hand fingering the brass fist at the top of his cane. "It's the same kind of trouble that every honest tinkerer and ambitious entrepreneur finds himself in these days. Government trouble."

Mallory's own fingers, which had begun to curl around the cool metal of the wrench, relaxed suddenly as he examined the man's face. There was something suddenly very familiar about the man's face, though he could not place it. "Do you work for the government?"

"I am an entrepreneur, sir, as I told your wife, owner of Sudwell Toys, among other interests," the stranger's eyes narrowed as he leveled his gaze at Mallory. "But, in a sense, I suppose we all work for the government. The great father of us all is watching— always—and the claws of his beast stand poised to snatch at all he surveys. Isn't that what they say?"

Mallory stayed silent.

"Well, to be specific, one of my ventures, a black company that I keep off the public books but which the government is very familiar, provides our great nation with supplies and weapons development in support of the war effort," the stranger said. "You see, my being here this week during the Chancellor's visit to Oxwell is no coincidence. I advise his people on new technology acquisitions and I have been charged with bringing in new talent into the fold. If I make a profit while doing so, so much the better."

"My husband already has a government contract," Belle Isolde said. She too had apparently eyeballed a broom in the corner of the room near the rear of the worktable and had stealthily edged her way towards it.

"Ah, a basic, contingent employment contract, no doubt," the stranger said. "Most businesses operate through that kind of business relationship with the government. Low pay and no security beyond the terms of the contract. It's good for them, but not so much for us. What I have to offer is a contract with me. I will pay well, provide you ample security if I can use your work and offer cover so that you don't have to deal directly with government inspectors and their red tape."

"And what do you want in return?" Mallory asked.

"I want your services, of course. I want to make money. Government officials might be stern taskmasters, but they have full coffers," Sudberry said. Then he motioned towards the cloaked Dragon's Breath. "And I would like a peak at whatever you've hidden under that tarp."

114

Mallory glanced back at his wife. She looked furtively back it him but said nothing. Catching the silent exchange, the stranger coughed and cleared his throat. He reached inside his cloak which gave Mallory a start.

"I apologize. I know how this must seem. A strange man comes out of the dark and offers you money and a job for work sight unseen. You have no more evidence to trust me as I have to believe there's anything more than a pile of bricks under that tarp."

Sudberry produced a small notebook and pen from a pocket inside the cloak. He opened the notebook and displayed the contents to Mallory. "Are you familiar with what this is?"

The inventor gasped. "It's a government checkbook with an official seal. How did you come upon this?"

"Though I should not perhaps be telling you this so early in our relationship, it is one of the perks of being a major contractor for His Excellency's government. I would prefer that you not share this information with anyone, but it is proof that my intentions are pure and that I can deliver on what I promise," he said. "Just a word from you, negotiations can begin to have your name placed upon one of these checks and after I see what you have to offer, perhaps a handsome number in reward for your time and assumed brilliance."

Belle Isolde looked from the stranger to her husband. She could probably see the calculations whirling inside his head. She grabbed the broom from behind her and held it defensively against her chest. "Be careful, dear."

The stranger smiled broadly at her. "I believe he is, good lady. Business is not without risk and I believe he is very carefully weighing the risks of doing business against the risks of not doing business with my company," he said. "Though I do admire a woman willing to stand up for her husband. You're a lucky man, Mr. Mallory. Have you decided on my offer or should I have one of my men come for you later?"

Mallory nodded ton his wife with an air of confidence stronger than that he felt in his heart. "I have, Mr. Sudberry," Mallory said. He called for assistant, who appeared timidly from behind the Dragon's breath brandishing the wood handle from one of the lathes like a truncheon. "Go ahead and remove the tarp."

Joaquin hesitated, then dropped the handle and tugged at the edge of the tarp. After several pulls, the drab covering slid from the metal machine and the top-mounted turret was fully revealed and the front armor plating shone dully in the gaslight. Unexpectedly, Mr. Sudberry sighed and stroked his chin as he took in the length and breadth of the mechanical monster before him.

"If this machine performs as magnificently at is appears, I believe this will be a very profitable partnership for the both of us," he said, removing the cap from his pen. "Now, before we begin and you show me all that this marvel of mechanical beauty can do, let me ask: do you have a pot of ink and what number shall I place on this paper for you?"

Chapter 12

Spring of Year 43 (after the Great Plague)

Baudrin thought he had been discreet in setting up his meeting with Chief Burgundais, but the maiden seemed to attract attention and gossip, in spite of being kept safely ensconced in a small tavern away from the bustle of capital life—and prying eyes.

"I thought I told you to keep her in her tavern until it was time to leave," the captain complained to his assistant.

"He did," the maiden said before Baldric could answer. "But I am not a prisoner nor parcel of meat to be bartered at market and so I refused his order."

"That order was to keep you safe," Baudrin growled, as they passed through the city gate and a wall of rapt spectators flanked the street as they passed.

"And I am no child either," Pucelle said, scrunching her face. It was rare for the maiden to show her age, but this expression reminded him that she was just a teenager. "If I wish to meet people and share my gift with them, then I should do so. After all, we are safely within the Dauphin's court and its sphere of control, are we not? What possible dangers are you protecting me from?"

"You are inexperienced and know nothing of how the world works. It would be wise to listen to me from now on. It is precisely the Dauphin's court that poses the danger now," he said, and looked back irritably at Baldric, who scampered behind them, burdened by the packs from all three of their horses. "Baldric, do keep up, will you?"

In spite of the apparent decay, the palace—what was once the domain of the Order of Seraphim—still maintained the pomp and ostentatious display of wealth on the inside. Entering the main antechamber of the fallen temple and embassy, Baudrin noted the ornate tapestries depicting the glorious career of the dead King Rien and the ravages of the plague before him that covered over the frescos of the Order. All traces of magic—statues of the great wizards, imbued artifacts and devices had been removed to where the gods only knew and replaced with suits of armor and a gold-leafed statue of the great king holding his child— the future dauphin—like an offering to the deities or a savior.

On the other side of the room, near the large ornate chamber doors, stood Master of the Guard G'rich and a dour man with a slight hunch that the captain could only assume was Chief Burgundais. The chief was not what Baudrin had expected, not a warrior or general but a withered old magician dressed as a parrot. Wide colored feathers drooped from his comical hat, which failed to distract from his bulging eyes, dry, thin lips and bony neck with its protruding Adam's apple. Burgundais looked at Pucelle like he had just swallowed a lemon and washed it down with broken glass.

"Captain Baudrin, I presume," he croaked. "And is this the girl I've heard so much about?"

118

Pucelle cocked her head. She seemed unimpressed by the noble lord before her. "That depends upon what you've heard about the girl."

The sneer on Burgundais' lips spread further across his face. "I heard that she was an uncouth peasant, and I see those rumors are true," he said. "Let's hope the rest of the rumors are as correct. The outcome of your meeting with the Dauphin will depend upon it."

"Excuse me, sir, but did you say meeting with the Dauphin?" Baudrin asked.

The nobleman sniffed. "I did. The Dauphin as well has heard of the arrival of a magical maiden and, against my better judgment, he has decided to waive protocol and see you immediately."

G'rich gave the captain a look that suggested he was just as flummoxed as he was. He had obviously enjoyed his tiny scrap of power being the gatekeeper between Baudrin and the nobles of the court but now that had been pulled from under his feet by the Dauphin himself.

"This is what you wanted, right?" G'rich said. "A prompt audience with His Majesty."

"Come then," Burgundais motioned them towards the large double doors behind him. "I'm afraid the invitation does not extend to your dog. He'll have to wait here."

Baudrin scowled and Baldric muttered something under his breath. "The name is Baldric and he is my loyal servant. And as I am a loyal servant of His Majesty, so is he."

"And as the invitation only extends to the maiden herself, be thankful that I'm letting you join her in the Dauphin's glorious presence," Burgundais said dryly.

The captain grumbled. Now he remembered why he hated visits from court officials—the way they haughtily looked down their noses at those outside the capitol. It was no wonder the Dauphin was having so much trouble maintaining control of the various dukedoms and demesnes that seemed to be defecting to the Fiorian side every day. As the captain regarded the maiden with her tightly braided hair, simple threadbare clothes but proudly raised chin and wondered briefly whether she really understood the burden that she had taken upon her slender, girlish shoulders.

"Baldric, you better do as the Chief wants," he told his assistant. "Pucelle, are you sure you want to go through with this?"

"I have been since I first heard the voices and my parents were killed," she said.

"Very well. Follow me," Burgundais said. With a flourish of his robes, the nobleman spun round and pushed open the massive double doors with his bony arms.

Baudrin and Pucelle followed him into a grand hall. The ceiling seemed to stretch to the sky. Light shown through the narrow stained-glass windows like a kaleidoscope, flickering and dancing across the crowd of attendants, noble ladies and lawmakers in their polished, tailored suits which flanked a wide red carpet that stretched to the foot of a dais. There, seated on two thrones framed by a tall red curtain, was the Dauphin himself and the queen mother.

RIDING A BLACK HORSE

The captain had never met the Dauphin personally and from a distance His Highness appeared youthful and statuesque in his royal robes. As they approached the royal thrones, Baudrin lowered his head in deference to the Dauphin, but cast glances at the crowd that surrounded them. They were remarkably quiet, all eyes focused on the strange girl at his side with her braids and peasant clothes.

Suddenly, the silence was broken as the crowd erupted in a united gasp. Baudrin felt a panic in his stomach as he sensed the maiden disappear from the corner of his eye. As he walked towards the dais, he whipped his head round only to find that there was no one beside him. Instead there was a gap between two ladies in waiting who had craned their necks to see what was going on behind them. Following their gaze, he spied the retreating form of the maiden, who was diving further into the crowd like a shark carving its way single-mindedly through the waves. And like a school of frightened fish, the lords and ladies parted before her and then just as quickly reformed behind her as thought to swallow her in its mass.

"My gods," Baudrin muttered to himself.

The Dauphin stood up from his throne in apparent alarm. He was still too far away to hear clearly amid the low rumble in the hall, but Chief Burgandais gasped the captain's arm in one clawed hand and attempted to swing him round. Instead of pulling Baudrin towards him, he only managed to drag his face close enough to the captain's ear to whisper harshly: "What is she about? Has your messenger no understanding of decorum in the presence of her lord?"

121

When Baudrin was unable to immediately reply, he hissed. "Well, go fish the girl out and give her a proper spanking—or I will!"

Baudrin nodded and then lunged in the crowd with a flurry of pardons and forgive me's as he bumped into the esteemed guests and court of the Dauphin, each one of whom he imagined could have his head cut off or imprisoned for the slightest touch of their person. He sidled between a large woman with a hand fan and her foppishly dressed husband, but somehow his heel caught on the train of the woman's dress. As he lost balance, he reached out for something to steady himself. Unfortunately, that something was the sleeve of the woman's fine silk dress. To his dismay he felt the stitching of the clothe give and it was all he could do to not allow his entire weight and the fate of his entire career to hang on the balance of seamstress' skill with a thread and the strength of a single handwoven selvage.

"Unhand my wife!" a man cried out behind him. It was not the fop he assumed was the husband. "What do you think you are doing, fool?"

He had time to mutter a slurred "terribly sorry" when he felt the man shove him away from the woman and he toppled over onto the marble floor and sliding between the britches of an astonished nobleman. His nose hit the floor squarely and his nose filled with a chemical smell like chlorine. The crowd of courtiers backed away from the captain's prone body, he assumed, because they were distancing themselves from clumsy oaf on the floor before them. His cheeks flushed with embarrassment.

But then he heard the maiden speak and he lifted his head.

"My lord, I kneel before you as a simple peasant girl," she said. "But I bring tidings of hope from your father, King Rien."

From his sprawled position on the floor, Baudrin cast about for a glimpse of the Dauphin, wondering how he'd descended the dais and made it to the maiden's position in the crowd—and why. But Pucelle was not bowing before His Highness or the Queen Mother. Instead, she knelt before a frail man wearing a simple green wool tunic and a red felt hat arranged in the shape of a rose. His cheeks were sallow and his eyes wide. The captain noted the ill fit of his drab green stockings which looked like they must pinch painfully at the crotch.

Baudrin scrambled to his feet and grabbed Pucelle by the shoulder. "What is the matter with you, girl? That's not the Dauphin. Are you trying to make a fool of me?" he growled at her.

The small man raised a bony arm towards the captain. A smile crossed his thin lips as he regarded the maiden. "No, sir, the girl is right. She has found me. Amongst this throng she has found her one true Dauphin. Quite remarkable."

"But the Dauphin's over there—on the dais," Baudrin said and even as the words tumbled from his lips the truth crept into his mind.

The crowd seemed to look to the man and then at the captain. The man stifled a chuckle and put a hand to his mouth to hide his obvious mirth at the captain's expense. Then, like a dam bursting, he erupted into full throated laughter and crowd around them reciprocated. For several moments, the cavernous hall resounded with guffaws, giggles and chortles of the assembled royal mob.

"Captain Baudrin, is it?" the man said, doffing his hat to reveal a curly mop of red hair. "As you probably have surmised, this has been a test and, strikingly, your messenger has surpassed all expectations. I am the Dauphin."

Baudrin immediately dropped to one and lowered his head. He hoped that his staring at the Dauphin moments ago had not been too overt or offensive. From what he knew of court protocol, it was a direct insult to the royal person to stare at him for longer than three seconds.

"No, captain, I don't think we have to stand on ceremony this time. G'rich has told me your valley has suffered mightily thanks to the Fiorians and their sympathizers," the Dauphin said, but his attention passed back to Pucelle. "Now, child, tell me, what is your name and how did you know it was me in the crowd and not the imposter?"

The maiden's head was raised proudly, too proudly for Baudrin's comfort. "I knew because your father lives inside me and speaks through me. He gave me a vision of you and told me to come before you."

"And why would he do that? Why not speak to me directly from the grave?" the Dauphin smiled slyly. A few, muffled chuckles rose up behind him.

"Because he has foreseen that I rediscovered the magics that can save our kingdom," she said, her voice raising in volume with each word. "He has sent me to

124

bring war upon your enemies and victory against the Fiorians, to place you on your rightful place upon the throne at Lutesse."

The Dauphin's eyes grew dark and pensive. "Then it appears we have much to discuss. Let us adjourn to a more private setting."

Chapter 13

Spring of Year 43 (after the Great Plague)

Captain Anville was unused to winning battles, even light skirmishes such as the one his men had seen the day before, and he hadn't even planned on fighting, his small cavalry unit having stumbled clumsily into the rear guard of a much larger invasion force. Without a prompt response from the capitol bear advice from the Dauphin and his advisors, the commander found himself casting about desperately at intelligence that would explain the size and disposition of the enemy he'd encountered. He had no orders, he thought, but he did have prisoners. Thus, the ragtag collection of Fiorian sympathizers and mercenaries that his corporals presented before him was an awkward and unusual sight. Several guards pushed forth the bound, unarmed men forward with their pikes, but most of them seemed unfazed by the situation they found themselves in. Anville scrubbed his shaggy beard with one hand and pulled his belt up over his belly, hoping the rest was sufficiently obscured by his chain mail shirt.

"Which one of you is the leader?" he asked.

No one spoke. He counted about 20 prisoners, arranged in three ragged rows of seven men standing shoulder to shoulder. All standing save two short figures crouching in the back row. To his surprise, not only were their arms bound behind them, but they were completely naked.

He grabbed one of the guards by the elbow and pointed towards the two cowering naked men. "What in hells is that?"

The guard shook his head blankly. "I didn't capture them myself, sir. But as I understand it, they were pushing around a corpse cart. One of the corporals thought they might be Fiorian spies."

"Really?"

The guard shrugged.

"Bring them forward then."

The guard gingerly nudged forward the two naked men to the front of the line. The other prisoners gave them wide berth. They were both filthy and covered in sores either from malnutrition or hard labor and the captain could smell their foul body odor even from a distance. They stank like death. One stooped with his gaze firmly directed at the ground. He looked thin and wasted, his ribs standing out from the purple blossoms of bruises on his chests like the zombies of old tales. The scant greasy strands of hair that topped his head were pulled back into a tight know, leaving much of his melon-shaped skull exposed to the sunlight. His partner had a slightly stockier frame with thicker hair and scraggly tuft of beard on his chin. The larger man stared dully forward, paying no notice of the captain.

"You think these are spies?"

"That was the corporal's opinion, sir," the guard said. "To me, they are just two naked traitors."

"They look like peasants. The Fiorians must be desperate if they are conscripting scoundrels such as these. What are their names?"

The two naked prisoners said nothing, until the guard poked the smaller one with the butt of his spear. The man yelped and then let out a pitiful whine.

"My name is Kamatari," the big one muttered. "His is Minoru. Not that it matters. The gods hate us anyways."

"The gods hate traitors and so does the Dauphin, so you may be right about that."

"But we serve the Dauphin," Minoru cried, and he stumbled and fell face forward on the ground. He tried to right himself, but with his hands bound behind him, all he was able to do was crawl along on his belly towards Captain Anville.

"Then you will have no problem by offering me a little information, like why Avinian forces are in the area and whether your Fiorian allies are nearby."

Minoru didn't answer but buried his head in the dirt and let out a squeal.

"Leave him alone. He doesn't know anything," Kamatari spat.

"And I suppose you don't either?"

Kamatari fell silent.

"Then what need have I of you?" the captain drawled. He pointed lazily at the guard. "Gut them and throw their bodies in the pit. Maybe that will loosen a few of these other tongues."

The guard shrugged and then flipped his spear so that the sharpened point dipped just below Kamatari's throat.

"No, wait," the peasant gasped, his chest suddenly heaving in panic. "We'll tell you everything."

The guard paused and then looked towards the captain, who already had turned his back towards the prisoners. Anville took a step forward but waited casually for Kamatari to add to his explanation of what he meant by 'everything.'

"I have a map," he finally said after several pauses. "A map of the city Fiorians burned and their plans."

"You don't have a stitch on you. Where would you hide a map?" Anville retorted.

"In my clothes, my pocket," Kamatari looked wildly about as though searching for his missing garments.

"Do we have this man's clothes?"

The guard shrugged again. "Perhaps. I could check with the corporal and his men."

"Please do so. Then have their clothes, map and them brought to my tent at once."

Anville did not look back to make sure his orders were carried out. He would just rather not look again at the two naked vagrant "spies" in his care. He returned to his inspection duties and visited the wounded returning from the field in litters. But it wasn't long before their clothing was retrieved and he could smell their presence behind them, escorted by the guard, prodding them along with the shaft of his spear. Fortunately, by that time, they were near his command tent, a small mobile command center covered by a worn grey tarp and containing a small desk, some stools and a cot for him to sleep on.

The captain ushered the prisoners and their guard through the flap of his tent and then followed them in, careful to avert his gaze and nose from their still naked forms. When they were finally in the tent, he had them seated upon two of the stools.

"Did you find a map?" Anville asked the guard.

The guard handed him a greasy scrap of paper. He examined it. Surprisingly, in spite of its rather crude markings, it showed what clearly had to be the city of Olivet with the crest of Avinois, Fiorian allies since their duke declared the Dauphin's claim on the throne was invalid. There were scratches like X's surrounding the city walls and extending into the Valley of Colors. Alongside them, was the familiar symbol of the Fiorian Empire. Unfortunately, the scratches were obviously rough estimates drawn up in haste for logistics and not meant to indicate strategy should they fall into enemy hands. However, Anville could guess at their meaning: the Avinians' boldness was fueled by military support from the Fiorians and their ultimate goal was control of the valley from one end to the other—where his friend Baudrin commanded a frontier outpost.

The tent flap open and a soldier stepped in. It was Lt. Teuta, his next in command. The soldier glanced at Anville stooped over the map at his desk and then at the two prisoners seated on the stools. The captain noticed Teuta's confused and somewhat pained expression and stood stiffly.

"I'm sorry, sir," Teuta said.

"I'm busy at the moment, lieutenant, as you can see. Can it wait?"

"Yes, I can see. You are obviously busy, ah, entertaining guests. I'll come back when you are, uh, finished."

"Entertaining? These two? Hardly."

"I'm not judging, sir, but I thought you tended to sail on boats with fewer oars."

"What's that supposed to mean? You know I don't—" Anville glanced at the prisoners and blushed. He grabbed a fistful of their clothes and tossed them at the naked men. "Get some clothes on, for gods' sake. And, lieutenant, for your information, I was about to interrogate these men."

"I'm sure you were," Teuta's lips pursed primly. "Again, no judging."

"Just shut the flap and get in here," he barked. "And cut the lip while you're at it. Make yourself useful."

"Very well, sir," Teuta said with a mock salute. "What would you like me to do—bathe them, I hope?"

Minoru and Kamatari snatched up the garments and dressed themselves as quickly as they could. The garments were still stank of blood and bile but at least the outer armor plating had been removed by the guard.

"Now that you're—decent—perhaps you'll be comfortable enough to answer my questions."

"Yes, sir," Minoru said.

"Where are you from?"

"We are from Count Arbor's demesne, sir," he said. "It's south of here. We were scratching out a living as farmers."

"That's a fair distance from where you are now. How did you come to be dressed as soldiers, Fiorian sympathizers, no less?"

The scrawny farmer bawled his fists under his chin and looked as though he was about to burst into tears again. "We're not sympathizers. I don't even know how to sympathize."

"Don't play stupid. Farmers don't simply wander miles away from their demesne into a war zone and play dress up as enemy soldiers. What is your business here?"

"We're not Fiorian. We were starving on our farms. The crops had gone bad and we wanted to get away. Kamatari here heard there was good money to be made if you volunteered to join the Dauphin's army."

"Mercenaries, eh?" the captain spat on the ground in disgust. "I'm still not seeing how this gets you into Avinois armor. I bet they paid better, eh?"

"No! Sir, we want to serve the Dauphin," Minoru said, as Kamatari muttered under his breath that he could care less at this point. "We were trying to get to Olivet to join up there, but, but—"

"Don't waste your breathe, Minnie. He doesn't believe you," Kamatari snarled.

"But I could," Anville said, training his gaze on the smaller prisoner. The one called Minoru was either the worst spy he'd ever encountered or the most convincing actor, he decided. Either way, he looked broken and willing to spill his guts. He held the map in front his face. "Tell me about the markings here. What do they mean and what are your people and the Fiorian

132

scum backing you have planned for the Valley of Colors?"

Minoru took the map in his hands and appeared to be studying the paper studiously, even tracing his finger on some of the bold markings.

"Well?"

Minoru's lip trembled. "I can't read."

"Then what was the—oh, never mind!" Anville snatched the paper from the prisoner's hands and presented it to the other one. "How about you? Want to take a crack at it?"

"We're peasants. Count Arbor never needed his cattle to read so why should we be able to?"

"Then why would you have a map you can't read in your pocket?"

"It came with the uniform."

Teuta stifled a chuckle as the captain closed his fist around the scrap of paper. "So, you're illiterate peasants who decided to risk life and limb to serve the Dauphin and do what—play dress up as the enemy?"

Kamatari looked at Teuta, seemingly distracted by the soldier's slight build and smooth chin.

"We didn't mean to dress up as Fiorians," Minoru mumbled. "We went to Olivet to join the Dauphin's army. But when we got there—"

"When you got there what? Come on, spit it out."

"It was burning. They were killing everyone. My friend and I had to hide under a dead woman, and we switched clothes with some soldiers so no one would notice us."

"Some soldiers just let you take their armor, their clothes?"

133

"They were dead too," Minoru said. "We used the disguises to get away from the city so we wouldn't get killed like the rest and that's when we stumbled into your men. Please, sir, we don't know anything else."

Anville stroked his beard. "Well, that's damned disappointing. I was looking forward to torturing some spies."

"Now, captain," Teuta said sharply.

The captain grunted. "I was only teasing," he said. "The fact of the matter is, I would have had you executed if you were a spy, but we don't stand for torture. We're human beings after all, not Fiorians. Now, what should we do with a couple of peasants like you two?"

"Why don't you ask your wife?" Kamatari said.

Anville stiffened. "My what?"

Kamatari motioned to Teuta. "Your guard here reminds me of my wife—girly lips and fine fingers, but strong enough to wrestle a boar to the ground. Good peasant stock like my wife. I guessed she's yours."

He glanced at Teuta, who had a rather bemused expression on her face, while Anville's face turned red and the whiskers around his mouth bristled as his lips pursed angrily.

"I'm guessing that was supposed to be a secret—a woman serving in the army," Kamatari added sheepishly.

"I was going to let you live," the captain growled. "Now I'm going to have to rethink my entire position on torture."

Teuta removed her helmet, revealing a short thicket of brown hair. Her eyes and lips did seem quite feminine now that the nose-guard was no longer obscuring her face and forehead. She had a square, masculine jaw and strong, muscular neck atop a stocky frame. She reached for Anville's forearm.

"It's alright. Who's going to believe this pair of fools anyways," she said.

"I'd rather not have these fools wagging their tongues about you in any regard," he growled. "If these idiots could see through your disguise, eventually the men will as well."

"The men already have, dear," Teuta said, her eyes softening. "They're just too afraid of you to say anything."

"That's good, for now. Loose tongues could lose you your commission and get me sent to the dungeon," Anville said. He circled the two prisoners like a predator. "I suppose we should rid ourselves of these two, send them back to whatever hole they crawled out of."

Minoru dropped to his knees and hobbled over to the captain, clasping his hands before him. "Please, please, don't send us back to Olivet," he cried. "Or to Count Arbor. He'll have us whipped."

"Maybe you should be whipped. Men who live on their knees deserve such treatment as they get."

Minoru began to whimper again, when the tent flap opened and the guard that had had found their clothes for them stepped in. Reflexively, Teuta returned her helmet to her head and became a man again. "Sir, we have a big problem."

"What is it?"

"Another armed party is headed this way. Much larger."

"How much?"

"At least brigade strength."

"Shit. I should have guessed. If they've burned Olivet, they've come loaded for bear," Anville said. "Until the Dauphin wises up and sends us some reinforcements with real armaments, we'll always be outmanned and outgunned. We best pull up stakes and head for safer ground. You know the drill."

"Aye, sir."

"And as for you two..." Anville said to Minoru and Kamatari.

"They say they want to fight for their Dauphin," Teuta said. "Why not give them a chance?"

"Hmm... why not? We need to get this map to the Dauphin. He needs to know the extent of the Fiorian invasion," Anville said. "I'll put them in your charge. Give them some spears and send them to the line. Keep an eye on them though, and be careful. If nothing else, you could use them as human shields while we make our escape."

"Thank you, sir, thank the gods for you and this chance to make good. We won't disappoint," Minoru grinned wildly.

But Kamatari grunted. "Human shields?"

Minoru looked at his friend. His momentary look of glee fled, and the expression of a whipped dog returned.

Chapter 14

Spring of Year 43 (after the Great Plague)

The band inside the dining carriage played a popular song "The Devil You Know" as Mallory, his wife Belle Isolde and assistant Joaquin rode the elevated train to the capitol. The inventor couldn't help but tap his feet nervously to the catchy tune, but his mind was not on the melody, but on the deal he'd made with the rather odd industrialist who mysteriously and coincidentally happened upon his greatest invention to date on the eve of its biggest test.

Belle Isolde placed a comforting hand on his knee, and it seemed to calm his shakes. He wasn't sure what made him more nervous—the fact that Sudwell had seemed incredibly pleased by the private demonstration of the Dragon's Breath, that he wanted him to relocate his workshop to his facilities in the capitol or the fact that he had access to resources capable of sending a team of engineers and soldiers to scoop up the prototype and spirit it out of Oxwell so efficiently. Mallory couldn't help but glance back periodically towards the rear car of the train. The Dragon's Breath was being towed under its tarp on a pallet car with plainclothes guards posted in the caboose.

"Dear, are you still worried?' his wife asked.

"I'm trying not to. It's too late for that anyways," Mallory said. "The whole visit from the Chancellor that was rumored to happen and then the Sudwell deal. It's left me a little overwhelmed at the moment."

"You know this an engineering marvel," he continued. "I'll have to speak to someone as to why they decided to use an elevated train and how they came upon the ribbing and circular frame. It certainly saves on the weight problem we ran into on the..."

He paused to glance at the other passengers. All were engaged in their own conversations as they ringed the circular dining tables in the middle of the carriage. Nobody seemed to pay heed to the young inventor and his wife in their provincial clothes, plainer than the frilled cuffs and lace trimmed dresses of the southern provinces.

"… Dragon's Breath."

"Dear, don't focus on your anxieties. I'm here for you—and I'm so proud of what you've accomplished," she said.

Mallory smiled at his wife weakly. He removed her hand from his knee and cradled it between his own. The hand was soft and smooth but there was a strength under the skin.

"Thanks," he breathed. "Maybe if we can bring about a quick end to this vile war, we can save more lives in the long run."

"That's a way to look at it," Belle Isolde said brightly.

"It's what I'll keep telling myself—until I believe it."

Mallory peered out the window. The buildings of the capitol city whisked by, progressively growing larger and more mechanical as they journeyed into the heart of the metropolis. Fiori City was by far the largest urban center in Fioria but had only established itself in the past few decades as the Empire recovered from the Plague and flourished under the current regime. Underneath the elevated track, horse-drawn wagons and steam-powered streetcars scurried while above them, the corporate towers and factory spires looked awkwardly top-heavy, connected by skyways and bridges. In the fading light of the sunset, their arched windows glowed an unearthly yellow and above them onion-shaped domes of glass blossomed giant red orchids. They were cathedrals to money and power and monuments to industrial progress.

The track ahead curved to the left and as the bullet-shaped engine with its plume of trailing smoke and glowing embers made the turn, Mallory could see where they were headed. He felt the train begin to brake. The tracks disappeared into the gaping maw of a tall barn-shaped building flanked by flying buttresses and topped by an idealized statue of the Chancellor standing astride the rooftops like a titan. Mallory nudged Belle Isolde and pointed at the strange building. He had never seen anything like it; it sparkled like an enormous gem in the crown of the capitol city.

"It's unbelievable," his wife gasped. "Is that where we'll be staying?"

"I don't know," Mallory fumbled in the breast pocket of his vest for a slip of paper. "The last time I visited the capitol was when my parents took me. I was very little and these buildings—all of this—is all new."

"It's good to see that our taxes are going somewhere."

"Yes," Mallory nodded nervously, glancing about the cabin at the other passengers. "Best not to talk about such things in the presence of strangers."

"Of course," Belle Isolde said. "It's just that things are so overwhelming. Who'd have thought we'd ever even leave our little home in Oxwell? Who'd have imagined that we'd end up in a place so..."

Her voice drifted as she seemed to struggle for a word.

"Modern?" he offered.

Belle Isolde leaned in and whispered. "I was about to say magical, but I suppose that might be unwise given the state's position on magic and persecution of their religious followers."

"That's probably true. However, what they're building here isn't the product of the m-word; it's brainchild of science and technology," he said. "Fioria is building a bold new world on the ashes of the old one. We can only hope that we can help make it a better one."

Belle Isolde gave his hand an enthusiastic squeeze. "We will, dear."

The slip of paper in Mallory's other hand had inscribed upon it in official lettering of the Sudwell Toy Company the name of the hotel they'd be staying and a small sectional map of the city.

"It looks like we're staying just a few blocks from this building. I guess this would be our stop—the Grand Central Terminus," he said. "However, I don't think we have to worry. Sudwell said he'd send a man

140

to pick us up and escort us to our quarters. Once we get settled, you can send a letter to your parents and let them know we've arrived and are safe."

Belle Isolde nodded. As the train, entered the terminus, the cabin was bathed in the glow of the gas lamps that lined the tracks and a broad platform extended on both sides. Finally, the train ground to a halt. Two conductors stood on each side of the cabin and turned the cranks on two curved doors. With a hiss, they slid upward, reveling the platform behind them. The passengers began milling about. Mallory and Belle Isolde collected their carry-on bags from beneath the dining table and joined Joaquin in line as the passengers slowly formed a line and departed the train.

The trio disembarked. It was obvious from the upturned heads and wondrous sighs that mirrored the hiss of steam puffing from the train's brake valves that many of their fellow travelers were also new to the capitol. The glass ceiling arched above them and they could now see that the building was a hollow cavern lined by at least five balcony levels filled with shops where large colored banners and signs hung ostentatiously as if celebrating the arrival of the new visitors.

"Have you ever seen the like?" Mallory asked his wife.

"It's enough to make a girl dizzy."

"It may be the dearth of breathable air at this spot of the fumes from the engine making you light-headed. We'd best get you off this platform," he said, looking about the crowd spilling in all directions. "I wonder

141

where Sudwell's contact is supposed to be. He said he'd meet us here."

"There seem to be some men with signs over there."

Mallory spotted a few men holding up signs between a broad staircase leading up to the second level and a mechanical lift which appeared to be taking a family to the third or fourth level. There were names on the signs and the men, wearing simple workman's clothes and gloves seemed to be scanning the crowd of train passengers furtively. Unfortunately, none of these people carried a sign with their names on it.

"Joaquin, do you see anyone who appears to be looking for us?" Mallory asked his assistant.

Joaquin shook his head.

"Then perhaps you should secure our luggage from the baggage car—and check on our, uh, baby. Belle and I will keep an eye out for Sudwell's man," Mallory said. Joaquin nodded and lunged into the throng of people, heading for the rear of the train. "You don't suppose we got off on the wrong side of the train?"

"Hard to tell," she said. "Perhaps we should go up a level. That way we can see over the train."

"Couldn't hurt to do a little sight-seeing while we wait, either."

Mallory took Belle Isolde's hand in his and they headed towards the grand staircase. The rails glistened with polished brass, just like all the walls around them, which appeared to plated in either a finished copper, brass or silver metal the inventor couldn't quite identify. Amid the buzz of the crowd, he heard shopkeepers shouting about their wares like carnival barkers and he could smell a mix of baking bread, cotton candy and spices mingling with the oil and soot that lingered in the air. The band from the dining car had apparently set up shop on the platform and were playing another round of "The Devil You Know."

A tall, dark form flitted beside them and nearly knocked into the couple as it took them by surprise. It was man riding a unicycle. His face was painted a ghostly white except for his lips which were cherry red. He wore a big, black top hat and matching high-necked shirt and pants. He smiled wildly at them and tipped his hat wordlessly as he passed. Mallory felt Belle Isolde stiffen at the sight of the performer.

"Well, that's… different," he joked weakly.

"Is this the way it's like all the time around here, do you think? Like a party gone wild?"

"A bit wild for my tastes," Mallory put a protective arm around his wife's shoulders and ushered her towards the periphery of the maelstrom where it appeared some of the quieter shops hid in the nook behind the staircase. "Still, I wish I had days to spend just sitting with a notepad sketching all this or, better yet, access the blueprints for this architecture. It's a designer's dream come true."

"What's that?" Belle Isolde pointed to a large man standing on a pedestal.

"I really don't know," Mallory said. The man stared at them, unblinking, with a vacant gaze. It only took a second to realize that it was another statue of the chancellor. Only this was almost life-like, with real clothes, skin that looked pink and soft and hair that was believable. But the eyes were the give-away, light

143

and dull and glassy. They were as unsettling as they were unmoving. Next to the figure was a post with the Sudwell logo, a slot for a coin and a sign that read: "Insert here". Wires and tubes snaked from the base of the post and disappeared under the pedestal.

"Look here," he pointed at the post.

"You don't think this is the 'man' we're supposed to meet?"

Mallory stifled a snort. "No, I don't think so. I think this is some sort of automaton."

"An auto—what?"

"A mechanical man. I've only read about these. Didn't know they could be real."

"What does it do?"

Mallory fished a coin from his pocket and held it in front of his face between his thumb and forefinger. "Let's find out," he said playfully.

He slid the coin in the slot and heard the metal disk rattle inside the mechanisms within the post. After a few seconds, a whirring rumbled emanated from the pedestal as though someone were spooling up a fishing reel. There was a flourish or tiny trumpets and big band song began. The automaton lurched forward a tad, catching Belle Isolde off guard. She scurried behind her husband, grabbing him defensively by the shoulders.

"It's okay," Mallory said, trying to soothe her. "He's not going to leave the pedestal. His legs appear to be bolted down."

"Greetings and welcome to Fiori City, citizens," a man's voice said. Mallory peered around the figure to see where the sound came from. There were a few slits near the feet of the automaton. The inventor deduced that the sound must be coming from there. "What you see around you is a vision—a vision of the future we can build together, so long as we work together and serve the state."

"How can it be speaking? Is it... is it..."

"Magic? No. It's extraordinary science," Mallory said. "A mechanism that can record the human voice and gears that synchronize the movements of the automaton."

"But it's so real. It doesn't look like metal."

The automaton did strike Mallory as incredibly realistic, even though its movements were stiff and jerky and the lips smacked together lazily like a cow chewing its cud.

"I don't recognize the exact material, but the skin must be some sort of flexible cellulose-based matte. They colored it with blush to give it the tone and hue of living flesh."

The automaton jerked its head forward. Its eyes seem to fix on Belle Isolde. "You have come to Fiori City for a better future and I am a symbol of that future, a mechanical marvel among mechanical marvels. But these marvels are nothing without the blood and sweat of you, the citizen, to make the Fiorian Empire great again."

The automaton extended its hand and sparks danced over its fingertips a few seconds while gas torches extended flames about the periphery of the base. Then, with a click, the torches were doused and the automaton returned to its default position, motionless and stiff.

145

"How unnatural," Belle Isolde said, barely able to disguise her uneasiness, yet crept around the automaton like it could leap off the pedestal and attack her at any moment.

Mallory mouthed the words "mechanical marvel." The automaton had used the phrase twice. The inflection of the voice and the way the recording placed emphasis on it reminded the inventor of something. Suddenly, he realized where he had heard it before. He looked carefully at the high cheekbones, the aristocratic chin and regal posture of the figure. There were significant differences in hair and eye color and the addition of a mustache, but a sudden realization crept over him. The automaton was made to look like Sudwell.

"Dear, does this man look familiar?"

"Of course, Mallory, it's the Chancellor. His face is plastered all over the country."

"But he doesn't look like anyone we know, someone we've met?"

"No, not really," Belle Isolde said. "I've never met the leader of our country. And now, I'm a bit afraid too."

"I should say, does his voice sound familiar?"

"What are you getting at?"

"Take away the mustache, age him a bit and change his hair color. Doesn't he remind you of someone?"

Belle Isolde tilted her head and examined the automaton's face more closely. Then she shook her head.

"Here, let's try it again," He placed another coin in the slot and the machine came to whirring life.

"No, dear," she said, backing away. "I don't need to be creeped out any further."

But Mallory ignored her protest. "Look and listen."

She humored him. After a few moments her eyes grew large as she watched the machine man go through his programmed motions. "Is that—"

"Sudwell."

"But how can that be?"

Mallory swallowed. "I don't know," he said gravely. "But a man looking like this automaton, supposedly modeled after the Chancellor appears in Oxwell at our doorstep on the very same day that the Chancellor was rumored to be making a visit."

The inventor felt a chill slide down his spine.

"What could this mean?"

Before he could answer, they heard footfalls behind them. A man wearing a simple suit and bearing a government emblem greeted them.

"Would you happen to be Mallory the inventor?" the man said, adjusting his glasses. "I rather hope so, because I have been searching this entire platform and I am quite out of breath calling for you."

147

Chapter 15

Spring of Year 43 (after the Great Plague)

In her youth, Isabeau had been a lascivious spendthrift. As liberal as she had been with love and her marriage to the king, she had been cautious and stingy with her royal earnings, nipping and tucking her budget to save every copper and cent she could squeeze from it. She would enjoy all the pleasures of the flesh, she thought as a girl, and then have a coffer to guard against her old age and infirmity when lovers stopped calling and the illicit gifts slowed to a trickle. It was a highly logical and practical arrangement.

Now that she had reached middle age and the bulk of her charms had indeed been spent and her handmaidens received more attention from the young stallions of the court than she, Isabeau found the shift in balance in her life uncomfortable. She didn't feel old yet, though the lines on her face and the streaks of grey dulled her otherwise lustrous brown mane and girlish eyes. Gold and the wisdom of age were a cold comfort in bed, especially now that the king, her husband, was dead—and the wealth was being spent propping up her son's claim to the throne in a losing war effort.

Then, the maiden arrived.

"I don't trust her," she told her son, the Dauphin.

"You mean, you don't trust a strange peasant girl with no military training who shows up out of the blue

148

to offer to make me king and save the kingdom and has messages from my dead father, your late husband?" the Dauphin cocked a smile. "Mother, I am shocked."

Isabeau did not care for her son's mocking tone. "I am serious."

"Relax, dear, this girl is no trouble. Regardless of whatever parlor tricks she learned at the feet of some prankster, she can do me no harm. In fact, meeting her was great fun. At best, she's simply mad. At worst, she's—"

"An agent of the Seraphim," said Juvenal, the royal historian, barely looking up from the desk where his quill pen continued to scratch across the parchment.

The Dauphin smile contorted into an expression of mock outrage. "The Seraphim? Are you joking? Have the fumes from your inkpot gone to your head? Or have you wasted so much time staring at the Order relics they left strewn about the palace that you've become enchanted by them?"

There was a low rumble among the advisors collected in the small chamber dominated by a central table. The Dauphin positioned himself at its head next to his mother, but somehow it seemed like the leader of the free peoples of Orloins was somehow the one waiting on the sidelines.

"May I remind His Majesty that was his decision to make this temple your new palace," Chief Burgundais said. "I cannot vouchsafe against any residual magic that may still reside in the structure or artifacts left behind by the order. If I may be so bold, it was unwise to quarter here, let alone relocate our base of operations here. And now you've allowed that girl to poison the court."

"Where would you prefer I take our court and operations, dear Burgundais?" the Dauphin snarled, as his expression hardened. "What have you been doing to ensure our return to Lutesse and ensure my rightful ascendance to the throne? In fact, it's hard to breath in this room for all the hot air spent on no action. According the last report from the battlefront, I should sooner wear a noose than a crown, for all you've done."

The Dauphin leaned back in his chair but Isabeau swept his outstretched legs from the table. "Creating a furor in the court by allowing a peasant girl to play a parlor trick isn't a way to win a war either," she scolded him. "Behaving like a child will only undermine your authority as king."

The Dauphin sniffed. "That's all well for you to say that now, but where were you before, when I agreed to an audience with the maiden?"

"Had I known that would make a spectacle out of this charlatan and then attempt to transform it into a policy statement regarding our handling of the war, I would have stopped you in your tracks," Isabeau said.

"You should listen to your mother," Chief Burgundais said. "You don't want to risk your kingship on a whim."

"On a whim?" the Dauphin stood and paced over to one of the tapestries on the far wall. It depicted his father expelling the Seraphim mages—and the plague—from the continent. It was a fanciful story, one that he was told from the time he was a child. Here

150

was the heroic figure on horseback—quite unlike his frail son—sword raised and a master of his own destiny. Next to the tapestry hung a mirror. In the dim flicker of the gas lamp, the Dauphin recognized his own reflection framed by another painting of his father, seated on the throne, which hung on another wall of the chamber. "May I remind this illustrious court that it was my mother who signed a treaty with Fiorians shortly after the death of her king that made my succession to the throne problematic in the first place. Maybe my problem is that I've been listening to mother for too long. I've been listening to all of you too long."

"What could that possibly mean, my son?" Isabeau said guardedly, but she knew what he meant. The Dauphin's restlessness of late was apparent to all. He had begun to question his generals about why they had taken up a defensive posture and stayed close to the central cities, allowing the Fiorians and their allies a free run of the countryside and he even began to interrogate the exchequer about payments to certain borderland demesnes whose lords were wavering between loyalty to their late king and the practicalities of surviving amidst marauding enemies.

"It means, my mother, that I will do as I please with this maiden," the Dauphin said. "You saw what she did today. She gave people hope, in a matter of minutes. At the very least, I could use her as a recruiting tool to circumvent the dukes and rally the peasants to our cause."

"A recruiting tool?" Burgundais said incredulously. "By making them believe in fairies and false magic?

151

This is precisely what your father fought the Seraphim about, and you want to plunge us into the dark ages of superstition again?"

"Please, Chief, spare me your hyperbole. I am not embracing magic, only using it as a tool to save this kingdom in hour of need."

"A peasant girl won't save your crown," Isabeau said.

"But I don't see how she could lose it for me either, mother," the Dauphin spat back. He cast a glance at the gathered advisors. A few of them were muttering under their breaths, their expressions hooded and gloomy. The Dauphin licked his lips testily. "I'll tell you what I'll do, why don't we give the maiden another test?"

"More spectacle?" Burgundais growled.

"More spectacle, indeed!" the Dauphin replied. "Only this time we'll test her loyalty to the kingdom and the power of her 'magic,' if she truly has any. If she passes the test, then we can decide what to do with her. If she fails we can dump her like garbage for the pigs to slop, back to whatever hovel she came from."

Isabeau folded her arms. "I suppose that you will not leave this matter be until we give into your foolish demands."

"In the interests of time, namely the time we need to spend on more important matters, I suggest we allow the Dauphin his dalliance," Burgundais said. "But just this one."

"How generous of you, Chief," the Dauphin muttered under his breath and then smiled graciously. "See, mummy, everyone can get what they want."

Isabeau grimaced. "Don't call me that. You aren't a child anymore."

But I'm not a king yet either, he thought gloomily to himself, and then turned his mind towards the maiden and the test that would seal her fate at the court.

Several days after their audience with the Dauphin, Baudrin, Baldric and Pucelle found themselves led by armed escort north towards Chinan, a large castle and village along the Garden Plateau River. There was no explanation for their sudden departure, only some mutterings amongst the officers of a "spectacle" or "debacle," Baudrin couldn't tell which. The river wound through some high table land. A garden, as its name would suggest, it had been once. However, years of plague, war and now flooding as damp cold air from the ocean had turned the green farmland and waving seas of grain to sodden swamps and murky fog-filled woods.

By the time they were within a few miles of the castle, a gloomy grey tower surrounded by high walls above which peered the rounded tops of roofless buildings long since abandoned by their wealthy owners, they were greeted by a convoy of the Dauphin's troops. There were about 100 men in all, about a half dozen supply wagons and several cannons hitched behind teams of horses. The leading edge of the convoy had already begun crossing the river at a wide stone bridge that had only just started to show its age from decay and misuse.

Baudrin knew about Chinan, though he'd never been there himself, and he grew suspicious of the

Dauphin, Chief Burgundais and even Master of Arms G'rich's apparent absence. He spurred his horse and caught up with the head of their party, a sullen man by the name of Tremoille. He had only earned his corporal's stripes, but it appeared he was the highest ranking soldier in the convoy.

"Now that we're almost there," Baudrin said as he sidled up next to the corporal. "Can you tell me why we've been spirited off towards Chinan?"

"I cannot, sir," said Tremoile, his voice a low drone as he stared forward into the distance. "I was ordered to bring you and the girl to this bridge and reconnoiter with the caravan you see. I did not question the orders. They came directly from Chief Burgundais."

"Burgundais, I should have known," the captain gritted his teeth against the cold wind. "And it doesn't bother you that you're marching us into enemy territory?"

"As I indicated, sir, I did not question the order. It came directly from Chief Burgundais."

"So, what are your orders once we get there?"

"We are to hold position until new orders arrive."

"New orders? When do you expect them?"

"Chief Burgundais did not say. He only said to wait with the caravan at the bridge until further instructions arrived."

"And it doesn't bother you that every moment we stand around on a bridge in plain view in the middle of enemy territory puts us in more danger?"

"As I indicated, sir, I did not question the order. It came directly from—"

"Chief Burgundais. Got it."

Baudrin cursed under his breath. If the Dauphin's people wanted to get rid of the maiden, there were certainly more polite and effective means than delivering them gift-wrapped to the Fiorians and their sympathizer puppets. The captain could not fathom what else they could be about with this move, especially after Pucelle saw through the Dauphin's trick at the palace. He only hoped that they would all live through the next few hours to find out.

The sun was rising high in the mid-day sky. Baudrin looked back at the maiden, leaning over the shoulder of her horse, whispering in its ear. In that moment, he realized how truly desperate he had been to pin his hopes to a girl that talked to animals. Even if she had supernatural healing powers, how could she be anything more than a battlefield medic or nurse. The Dauphin would need thousands of magic users like her if he intended to change the tide of the war and he was already going let waste the one he had.

A few moments later, a horn sounded. Coming up behind them on the road, was another troop of soldiers. Baudrin felt uneasy until he noticed the Dauphin's colors born aloft by the lead horseman. Like the one that escorted them, it was another lightly armed contingent, only this time, it flanked a litter from which stepped G'Rich and Chief Burgundais. G'Rich was wearing ceremonial armor and well-coiffed head of hair, like he was ready for a military funeral.

Baudrin dismounted and waited until the two royal advisors were in earshot of Tremoile and his mean.

"Chief Burgundais, I'd like to know the purpose behind dragging us all out here to our dooms," he said.

"Our dooms, he says?" Burgundais looked astonished and then smiled sourly. "But a few days ago, you promised this child prodigy would save our lives and the kingdom. Unless you are willing to admit you misled us and the Dauphin, I would think we are quite safe under her protection."

"I am not admitting such a thing."

"Very good. People often lose their heads over much smaller lies."

"Then let me rephrase my question: why are we here?"

"Isn't it obvious?" G'Rich said. "We're here to see if your maiden can make good on her promise or if she is only skilled at parlor tricks."

"How so?"

"She's going to help us recapture Chinan."

Baudrin looked about them incredulously. There were at most only a few hundred soldiers between the three groupings of men. They were ill equipped to carry out a siege of small burrow let alone a fortified castle.

"You expect her to recapture Chinan with that rabble?"

"Of course."

"But Chinan has been in Fiorian hands for over a year."

"Of course, it has. Which makes it a perfect test for the child prodigy," Burgundais said dismissively. "Now, fetch your girl and bid her perform her first miracle in service to her Dauphin."

RIDING A BLACK HORSE

Baudrin grumbled under his breath as he turned obediently and walked towards where Baldric and Pucelle awaited him in the middle of the road. The maiden paused her conversation with the horse and gently stroked its mane, as Baldric offered his own a fistful of oats. The captain grabbed the reins of Pucelle's horse and drew her alongside him.

"As I feared, the Dauphin's test of you is not over," Baudrin said.

Pucelle nodded but didn't meet the captain's gaze.

"They are setting you up for failure," he added.

"They believe so," Pucelle said with a girlish tilt of her head.

"This is serious, Pucelle. Do you understand the peril to my command—my people—if you fail?"

"Do you?" Pucelle said. "The voice of the king has brought me here, has granted me the power to save this kingdom. The peril is not in my failure to impress the Dauphin, but in my failure to use my full gifts to expel the Fiorians and fulfill my promise, whatever it may be."

"But they want you to liberate a city that's been in Fiorian hands for over a year," Baudrin said. "Let me explain the military situation to you. We barely have enough men and material to fend off a patrol from the castle. We aren't prepared to make a proper siege. What can you do with your powers that will change that fact?"

"The voices will tell me when the time is right."

"The voice of the king?"

"Of course."

"Wait, you said voices plural. I thought you were only hearing the king. What other voices are you hearing?"

Pucelle frowned. "You still have doubts about me? After what you've seen?"

"I don't have doubts about what I've seen you do. But I'm starting to have doubts that what I've seen will be enough to keep us alive or out of a Fiorian prison camp in the next few hours."

Baudrin heard Tremoile call from behind. He pivoted to see the men from all three parties begin to cross the bridge together. "I suppose I'll have to table those doubts for now. If we make it through this, we will have to speak again. Baldric, let's get moving."

The captain mounted his horse and led his trio across the bridge and joined the lines of armed soldiers forming on the other side. When the litter bearing the chief and master of arms joined them, the short column of men proceeded down the wide path that parted the woods. Baudrin wondered how long it would take Fiorian sentinels to spot the hodge podge collection of Dauphin's soldiers traipsing down the road like flying their colors as if they were on parade.

It turned out; he didn't have to wonder long. A trio of riders came galloping towards them from the castle and came to an abrupt halt as soon as they came within eyeshot of the Orloinians. At first, they seemed surprised and even one of the horses reared up, nearly throwing its rider to the ground. But after a few brief exchanges between themselves, the three Fiorians took up a defensive posture, blocking the road.

"Halt! Explain yourself!" one of the men called in the common tongue.

Baudrin looked towards the litter where G'Rich and Burgundais sat, chatting and playing cards, seemingly unconcerned by the challenge given by the Fiorian guards. The captain moved closer and called to them.

"They've spotted us," he said.

"Yes, obviously," Burgundais said, playing a card. "I suppose it is time for your maiden to prove her usefulness to the Dauphin's cause."

"But what—"

"Captain Baudrin," Pucelle said from behind. "I could use some paper."

"Paper?" The captain wheeled his horse about. The maiden had dismounted and was leading her horse towards the litter.

"And a quill or pen."

"Why?"

"I need to write a letter."

"You... write?"

Pucelle crossed her arms impatiently. Her eyes were an icy blue. "I brought a man back from death right before your eyes and yet you are surprised a peasant girl can write?"

Baudrin shook his head. "I'm sorry. But why do you need to write a letter? And to whom?"

"I will write to the Fiorians occupying the castle," Pucelle said. "They will leave if they understand what they face."

Baudrin frowned. "They probably already know what they face. If they don't, they'll probably laugh us

159

halfway across the kingdom with their cannons, assuming we live that long."

"They may laugh, at first," she pointed at the two royal members in their litter. "But they won't laugh once proof stares them in the face. To that end, I need the paper and pen."

Baudrin couldn't imagine how a letter was going to make a difference in their situation, since it was obvious they couldn't deliver on any threats. But he returned to the litter and knocked on the door.

"The maiden needs paper," he said.

"Paper? What makes you think we brought paper for your maiden?" G'Rich drawled.

"She needs paper," Baudrin growled. "Or else we're all dead."

Burgundais smirked and fished out some sheets of parchment from a parcel. "Spare us the histrionics, captain."

"And a pen," he reminded them.

Burgundais withdrew a pen and small bottle of ink from his cloak and handed them to him with the parchment. "Don't lose it. That's my favorite pen."

Baudrin grimaced as he thought about snapping the pen in two in front of the chief and his lackey. "Sure."

The captain handed the parchment, ink and pen to the maiden, who found a flat stone at the side of the road upon which she could create a makeshift desk. She opened the ink bottled, dipped the pen and began to write.

"A moment, sir," Pucelle said, when she noticed Baudrin peering over her shoulder. Reluctantly, he backed off, keeping an eye to the Fiorian patrol that

160

appeared to grow more nervous and agitated with each passing moment.

"I'm afraid we may have less than a moment, Pucelle. I'm worried that they might not be inclined to receive mail from a hundred or so armed Orloinians at their doorstep."

The maiden handed him a parchment. "Don't worry. I've kept it short and in terms they will understand."

Baudrin examined the letter. He was surprised by the elegance of the maiden's penmanship but even more so by the directness of her language. It read:

At the Lord King's command,

To the great and formidable Fiorese conquerors and their Orloinian allies who occupy the castle Chinan, Pucelle the Maiden requests of you, in the name of King Rien, my rightful and sovereign Lord, that the Chancellor of Fioria and yourself should make a good firm lasting peace. Fully pardon each other willingly, as the faithful should do; and if it should please you to make war, then go elsewhere. Self-proclaimed prince of Chinan, I pray, beg, and request as humbly as I can that you wage war no longer in the magic kingdom of Orloins, and order your people who are in any towns and fortresses of the holy kingdom to withdraw promptly and without delay. And as for the noble Dauphin, he is ready to make peace with you, saving your honor; if you're not opposed.

And I tell you, in the name of King Rien, my rightful and sovereign Lord, for your well-being and your honor and [which I affirm] upon your lives, that you will never win a battle against the loyal

161

Orloinians, and that all those who have been waging
war in the magic kingdom of Orloins have been
fighting against King Rien, King of this continent and
of all the mystical world, my rightful and sovereign
Lord. And I beg and request of you with clasped hands
to not fight any battles nor wage war against us -
neither yourself, your troops nor subjects; and know
beyond a doubt that despite whatever number of
soldiers you bring against us they will never win. And
there will be tremendous heartbreak from the great
clash and from the blood that will be spilled of those
who come against us.

I commend you to the Great Power and may She
watch over you if it pleases Her, and I pray Her that
She shall establish a good peace.

The captain folded the letter. "It's bold, I'll give
you that," he said. "However, I don't know if this will
save us or make them mad enough to torture us before
they murder us all."

Pucelle laughed and held out her hand. "Then let
me take this letter to the Fiorians and we'll find out."

"Oh no, my dear girl. They won't accept this from
you. I'm afraid they would shoot a peasant on sight.
This has to be delivered by an official of the Dauphin's
government," Baudrin eyed the two in the litter with an
evil grin. "I'd love to send one of those jokers, but
those girls would likely soil themselves rather than go
anywhere near the enemy. I guess that means I'll have
to take it myself."

Baldric trotted up to him on his small horse. "I
must protest, sir. You should not go."

"Then who would you have me send? That stick in the mud Tremoile? He can't change his own diaper without orders."

"No, sir. Send me instead."

"You, Baldric? I can't send you. It wouldn't be appropriate. This is a dangerous mission."

"Precisely why you should send me, sir," Baldric said. "I am charged to be your assistant as such must give up my life to protect yours. Your role here is clear. You must protect the maiden from dangers outside—and from within."

Baudrin's assistant nodded towards the litter. "If you were to be lost, sir, I could not protect Pucelle from those in court who would use and abuse her or discard her like trash. You can. While I don't know if she can save the Dauphin or our kingdom, we've both seen what she can do, that she is special and valuable in some way. She must be safe-guarded, not wantonly sacrificed like this."

Baudrin sighed. "Though it pains me to say it, you do have your moments of clarity, Baldric."

The captain handed his assistant the parchment. They made a makeshift truce flag from a handkerchief and a long stick. Baldric mounted his horse and started to pace towards the Fiorese patrol.

"Be careful, Baldric," Baudrin called to him. "Good assistants are hard to come by these days."

The captain's words rung hollow while G'Rich and Burgundais chuckles echoed in the background. He watched intently as the Fiorians, already on high alert widened their defensive stance across the road. Yet,

163

they must have recognized the white flag Baldric was waving above his head.

After some hesitation and pacing, the center Fiorian patrolman, presumably the commander, raised his own white handkerchief over his head and galloped out to meet Baldric. There was a muffled exchange as the two riders met. The Fiorian shook his head several times and pointed towards their caravan. Baudrin could hear Baldric's replies but was too distant to make out the words.

Finally, the Fiorian nodded and motioned to one of his compatriots. This rider left his position and began to trot towards the castle. Baldric followed his escort, pausing just briefly to look behind him and flash Baudrin a thumbs up.

"Well, that went better than I expected," the captain told Pucelle.

"Have faith, captain," the maiden said. Her face was more creased with worry than satisfaction. "This is only the beginning. The rest will be much harder."

"Can you see the future?"

Pucelle shook her head. "I only know what I must do."

The lead Fiorian motioned to his other comrade and the two began to gallop towards them. Baudrin heard Tremoile bark orders and there was a clatter of footsteps as the Orloinian troops formed lines behind him.

"Tremoile," Baudrin barked at the corporal. "You can relax now. The time for combat is not this moment. If they had wanted to attack us, they would not have done so with just two riders. Also, my assistant would appreciate if did not provoke them to attack and get him killed in the process."

Tremoile said nothing but looked towards the litter for instructions from his masters. Baudrin sighed. "Of course."

"Hail, Orloinians," the lead Fiorian rider called out to them. "Which of you is Captain Baudrin?"

"I am," Baudrin said.

The rider looked young, not more than 20 or so. He wore a plated helm, but the rest of his armor was just a simple leather tunic under which he apparently wore a loose-fitting chainmail shirt. His face was marked by a few plague scars, which took Baudrin aback a little. He had heard from some reports that the Plague had been slow to arrive in Fioria after it had ravaged the Orloinian continent but had lingered much longer. But actually, seeing the pustules that dried and darkened into hardened warts on the young man's face was physical proof.

"You are to order your troops to stand down," he said. "Any provocative action by your people will be considered a violation of the temporary truce and will met by force. We have dozens of artilleries capable of reaching this clearing and annihilating all of you."

"Thanks for informing us," Baudrin said dryly, pausing to glance again at G'Rich and Burgandais who watched from the litter. "I'm not sure all of us were aware of that fact."

The Fiorian arched an eyebrow at this remark. "I will remain here until the conclusion of the meeting between my commander and your manservant."

"And thanks for the company," the captain said. "May I ask your name?"

"You may not."

"Good to know."

They stood in awkward silence for nearly three hours. At least they weren't trying to kill each other. Meanwhile, in the Valley of Colors, Fiorian shock troops could be burning and pillaging their way through villages and his post at Valcolors could be in flames, its people in chains—or dead—like his nephew. It was hard not to want to draw his sword on the Fiorian rider and gut him, but Baldric's safety was his main concern.

As sun reached its zenith and the trees glistened gold against a yellow tinged sky, a cannon fired in the distance, from the battlements of the castle.

"What was that?"

"The meeting with your manservant must have concluded," the Fiorian said. "My commander will be sending his reply his response shortly."

"He'll be sending it along with my assistant, I presume?" Baudrin asked, not satisfied by his equivocal answer.

"I presume that to be the case."

"Then why the fireworks?"

The Fiorian said nothing. So, Baudrin found the spyglass in his pack and scanned the castle and its battlements for movement. He could see a sliver of the gate through the trees, enough to tell that the gate was shut. Above, on the battlements, the muzzles of a dozen cannons bristled. Then, he spied a glint of light reflected from something silver. There was movement

166

of equipment. On the battlement, a wooden-framed structure was positioned between the widest gap in the line of cannons. A large arm mounted atop the structure swung back. In that moment, Baudrin realized what it was.

"Take cover!" he screamed at the Orloinians. "Back off! Back off!"

The men broke ranks and fell back towards the bridge. The captain moved protectively between the maiden and the Fiorians. The two Fiorian riders backed off and quickly took position at the side of the road.

The arm of the trebuchet swung forward and Baudrin spotted a small dark object launch into the air. For a moment, the captain wondered why they would what they considered to be an antiquated weapon when they had so many more devastating pieces of artillery to attack with, but as he tracked the projectile through the air, it began to dawn on him that the projectile was not an incendiary bomb but a large sack. The object spun end over end as it arced high over the treetops and descended towards them. As it neared, Baudrin could see the clothe billowing in the wind and its shape shift wildly as though the contents were struggling inside. There was a loud thud as the sack struck the flat paving stones of the road and skidded to a halt just a few dozen feet in front of the captain and Pucelle.

Baudrin glanced at the maiden. "Were you expecting this sort of response?" he asked.

Pucelle's eyes were saucers but her voice was level and emotionless. "I was afraid this might happen. But it had to be done. The voices told me this was the way."

"Voices?" Baudrin said, aghast. "Like in your head?"

"How else do you think a dead king speaks to me?" Pucelle said. She noticed him move towards the sack to inspect it and placed a hand on his arm. There was a piece of paper pinned to the top of the sack and on it was scrawled 'Our response to your gracious offer.' "You had best let me handle this, captain. You may not like what you find."

"But there could be a bomb or something poison inside. I should examine it or have one of the men or Tremoile open it for you."

"No, it's alright," Pucelle said, leaning over the bag. She took a small knife from her pocket and cut the knot at the top. Then she pulled the cloth down to reveal a pile of shaggy hair. Baudrin could not believe what he saw.

"Baldric! My gods!"

His assistant's face was barely recognizable. His skull was absurdly misshapen from being crushed on the stone and his face was covered in blood and deep purple bruises. His face was frozen in a toothless grin. Pucelle gingerly pulled back the cloth further to reveal a body contorted in an unnatural position, legs and arms all broken and twisted. On his back there was more blood and the tell-tale markings on his tunic of stab wounds.

Baudrin covered his mouth to keep from retching. "How could I have been so stupid? Just like my nephew, I sent him to die when I should have taken the risk myself."

The captained turned on the two Fiorian patrolmen who were beginning to retreat back the castle. "No, you stay!" he screamed, the tears welling in his eyes. "I demand an explanation for this."

The nameless Fiorian rider turned and smiled. "I thought my commander was fairly clear in his response. You should not have come here."

"Then you can stay to hear my rebuttal to this barbaric act!" Baudrin said. He cast his gaze briefly to the two courtiers peering from the litter. "And you can hear it as well."

Baudrin quickly crouched next to where Pucelle kneeled next to Baldric's lifeless form. "Can you revive him, Pucelle? Like how you did the bandit," he said, straining to restraining his voice to a hoarse whisper.

"I will truly try," Pucelle said, placing the palm of her hand over Baldric's flattened forehead. "His injuries are far more severe than the bandit's was."

"But you can save him?"

"You placed your trust in me and I will not fail you—or the Dauphin," Pucelle smiled weakly and then bowed her head and closed her eyes. She placed a hand on his bloody chest, and as she did so, Baudrin strained to see if there was any sign of movement from his assistant's body, but the young man's body was as still and stiff as a statue. The maiden whispered to herself. A faint glow emanated from her fingertips.

Slowly, as his grief swept over him, he realized that Baldric's face looked very much like his nephew's, even in its disfigured state. He stifled a spasm welling up from his chest when it became apparent that it was not only his eyes which were transfixed on the dead body in the road. G'Rich and Burgundais had emerged from his litter and even the Fiorian riders had lingered within earshot to watch the maiden murmur her soundless prayer. The glowing grew and spread across Baldric's body. Suddenly, the maiden gasped and slumped over. The glow from her hands faded and Baldric's body remained cold and stiff. Baudrin's face fell into his hands, so overcome by grief as he was.

Baudrin heard Burgundais sigh. "How unfortunate," he said and then called to the Fiorians. "You there, please convey our sincerest apologies to your master. We shall withdraw our—"

The chief was interrupted by a bloodcurdling scream. Baudrin watched in horror as Baldric's eyes burst open like blood-filled sacs and his broken limbs convulsed and crackled as if the bones were being crushed into powder. The one rib that was jutting through the skin and tunic receded back into the folds of fat and sinews of muscle. His left hand, which had been twisted impossibly outward from his body with its fingers jutting at severe angles at the knuckles began to rotate and the metacarpals straightened. Awkwardly, Baldric sat up, his mouth agape in an expression of agony. His scream subsided to a low ethereal moan.

"Baldric!" Baudrin's mind raced as to what to do for his writhing assistant. He rushed back to his horse and brought back the canteen and scraps of cloth from his pack. He placed the mouth of the canteen to

Baldric's lips and he eagerly drank as though his throat had desiccated like beef jerky. "You're alive."

The assistant looked at Baudrin like a creature possessed. "I died, didn't I?"

"I don't know, Baldric, but the way you are, I don't know how you could have survived."

"The way I—oh, gods," Baldric looked down at his tunic, covered in blood. "The Fiorans who led me to the castle stabbed me in the back. I fell and blacked out. Why am I in a sack? And how did I get here?"

"Baldric, you don't know? They must have stuffed you in the sack and flung you from the battlements with a catapult. You were thrown hundreds of feet into the air."

Baldric feverishly padded himself down, looking for wounds. Except for his leg, which was awkwardly bowed outward, his flesh was pristine under the gory clothes. He took hold of his twisted leg, and to even his own amazement, it snapped back into place with a gentle tug.

"That's all you remember, being stabbed and waking up here?"

"Yes," Baldric replied. "No, wait, no. I saw the maiden's face. She was calling to me."

"Pucelle," Baudrin turned his attention to the maiden, who was lying on the ground. He moved to collect her, but the maiden waved him off, stood up and pointed at the Fiorians, their mouths agape.

"You, there," she said, her voice husky and raw with emotion. "Your master murdered my friend, but as you can see, I brought him back. I can do the same for the rest of the men you see here. I can raise them as quickly as you can kill them. The Dauphin's soldiers will not be stopped by your swords or arrows or cannon. And that is just the beginning of my power. So tell your master what you have seen and that I amend my gracious offer. He must not only vacate Chinan but also surrender all claims south of this bridge. That includes the Valley of Colors. Do you understand what this means?"

The Fiorian commander nodded nervously. His hand gripped the hilt of his sword, but from what Baudrin could tell, it was more out of terror and self-defense than an actual desire to draw his weapon.

"Then go," Pucelle said. "Leave us in peace."

The Fiorians galloped away. Baudrin turned to face Burgundais and G'rich. He read the shocked expressions on their faces. The strip of jerky G'rich had been gnawing on drooped comically from his lip.

"Do you understand what this means?" Baudrin asked them. "Or do you need another demonstration?"

Baldric stood gingerly and groaned. "If it pleases you, sirs, I'd rather not do that again."

Chapter 16

Spring of Year 39 (after the Great Plague)

Pucelle was 13 years old when the Fiorian raiders first arrived in her parents' demesne, driving off all the farmers' cattle and burning the little village of Do'om to the ground. She had been sent to fetch a lamb from the nearby village that her father had bought and was excited to meet her new pet. Thus, she was unaware that the smoke that trailed behind her was not from the hearths of her uncles' homes in the village but the funeral pyres upon which her family's bodies and possessions were being stacked. She was determined not to let her father slaughter that innocent creature, no matter how hungry she became. There were always some vegetables in the garden or an apple to be picked from the tree that could tide them over until the next market.

Though relatively nearby, it was still a long journey taking most of the day. Pucelle had cajoled her father into letting her take the trip herself—her first adult outing on her own. He had relented, but warned her not to dawdle or daydream, which she had obediently agreed to, but now away from the confines of her father's constrictive rules and the borders of her tiny village, she couldn't help but wonder at the endless possibilities that lay before her. The road made traversing the distance worse—a muddy path pitted with filthy puddles and littered with jagged gravel from a local quarry. The girl was wearing a plain smock and her hair was woven into a long braid that hung down her back. To keep herself company and to calm her nerves as she passed a grove of trees or abandoned barn, she listened for the birdsong and tried to whistle along with it. Each bird had its own tune and it changed with the time of day and season.

"Sparrow, have you found your mate?" Pucelle said and gave a cheerful whistle. The sparrow replied with one of its own. Moments later, there was a flurry of bird chatter. "My, you are popular with the girls today. I had best keep my distance then."

Pucelle passed another homestead. It had been a nice building once, with an attached barn and a remains of an aqueduct that brought clean running water to the family that had dwelt there. It seemed to her that peasants of long ago must have lived like lords and ladies, not huddled in damp shacks made of mud and straw like her parents did. Now the homestead was a rotting hulk. Its windows gaped like black soot-covered maws and a sign scrawled in red paint—a crow perched upon a skull—designated it as a plague house. Off limits, even years after the disease had run its course.

A year before, after a heated argument with her father, Pucelle had fled her parents' home and hid for an entire day in one of these plague houses. In the bright liquid shine of the sunlight, it had seemed like a safe refuge from her father's often violent temper, but as the day faded and the shadows grew long, she imagined she could hear strange whispers from empty closets and under the floorboards. Then, she found a body in one of the beds, desiccated and shriveled with a toothy grin of death. She pledged thereafter to obey the wretched warning signs and not enter the forbidden plague houses again, but was secretly pleased that she had looked death in the face and come away unscathed.

As she passed this plague house, however, she paused to take in its desolate beauty. The male sparrow who had been following Pucelle's whistling flitted from one tree to the next until it lighted on the rooftop of the house. Just above it, a wisp of smoke puffed from the chimney. It caught her by surprise, because she had thought she was the only one brave enough or foolish enough to tempt fate by entering the house, let alone light a hearth and possibly bring down the wrath of the authorities.

But if the hearth was lit, there were no lights visible through the glassless windows. It was then that she realized something odd about the smoke—it just hovered in a small cloud a few feet over the mouth of the chimney. She had never seen smoke like that. For a moment, Pucelle had forgotten what had frightened her about her last encounter at a plague house and she drifted towards the ragged fence that encircled the lot to keep intruders from getting too close.

"Sparrow, come down from there. That place is forbidden," she scolded the bird, until it occurred to her that the bird probably had no real reason to fear a magistrate or a human disease, any more than she had to worry about the pox that infected her neighbor's cows. The bird chirped at her and then hopped down to the ledge beneath one of the windows. It seemed to be beckoning her to come closer. "I can't come with you. I'm not allowed. Besides, you won't like what you find there. There're no pretty hens to make music with in that house."

The sparrow ignored her, disappearing into the dark interior of the house. The puff of smoke above the chimney spiraled momentarily and then plunged downward, back into the chimney. Stunned by this turn of events, Pucelle's mind reeled as she tried to imagine what could have tricked her eyes to see smoke seem like it had a mind of its own. She had been told bedtime stories by her mother of powerful mages who could manipulate the elements before the plague had robbed the world of magic. Could this be a tiny piece of magic that somehow lingered from that ancient time? Could she have discovered it hiding in plain sight within this abandoned building?

Her parents' voices rang inside her head, admonishing her to stay to the road, get the lamb from the seller and return straight home, but the pull of the unknown was stronger. Pucelle found a gap under the fence where some burrowing animal had made a hole and crept through the tall grass until she reached the front door, which was already ajar. A board that had been hastily nailed across the threshold was hardly an obstacle at all. As if on cue, a soft breeze caught the door and it creaked open, allowing the soft light of the outdoors to illuminate entry hall and reveal the silhouettes of the sparse furnishings the previous occupants had left behind. From inside, the sparrow's birdsong echoed.

"Pucelle," she thought she heard the bird chirp, and then a flutter of wings before all went silent again.

The girl paused at the doorway and shuddered. Another gust of wind gently shoved her through the entrance. It took a moment for Pucelle's eyes to adjust to the darkness of the room, but once they did, she could see clearly the ash-covered surfaces of a large dining table surrounded by wooden chairs. There were plates and cups laid out as though a family had prepared its last meal and then stepped away, never to return.

The sparrow had perched itself on the mantel just a few feet away from her head on her right. She stepped forward, held out her hand with a crust of bread she kept in her skirt pocket and let out a coo to soothe the bird.

The sparrow snatched the crust from her hand and took wing over the table, out a back window and into the blue square of sky beyond. Involuntarily, she chased after the bird, feeling as though her whole reason for trespassing. She became aware that the people who set the table may not have left the house before the plague had taken them. She did not fancy the idea of discovering anymore dead bodies in her life, but she peered into the fireplace to look for the mysterious smoke. But there was no tinder let alone flames or embers to be found. The stones had been swept clean and scorch marks were only a vague reminder of chilly nights huddled about the hearth and hot family meals of stew or soup from the cast iron cauldron were just a distant memory.

177

"Pucelle," she thought she heard the bird cry. "What are you seeking?"

The words made the girl freeze. Surely a bird could not talk, but she had heard the words clearly and they also resembled the sparrow's chirp. Her father had told her stories about animals who could mimic human voices in order to lure to steal their souls and feast on their remains, but her mother assured her that her father had made the whole story up to make sure she behaved herself. Pucelle understood that her father often lied to her, that something about her stirred a fear inside him. One thing that was clear to her, something—not human—was beckoning her to the window. Not seeing any immediate danger, she calmed her nerves and answered the call.

The window was one of the largest she had ever seen in a home, but the glass had been blown in, possibly by some violent storm. Pucelle tip-toed around the dining room table and across the field of broken glass. The shards were covered in dust yet still so smooth that she could see a thousand little reflections of herself in the little bits of glass.

Pucelle stepped gingerly through the opening in the window and back out into the diffused white light of the open air. It was just bright enough to make her squint, but her eyes quickly adjusted. An unkempt and overgrown garden lay before her. It was a beautiful mess, with roses draped over the mouth of a stone well amid purple flowering sweet grass that swayed in the breeze. Near the back fence, reinforced by a wall of trees behind it, some squash had gone to seed in a pile of compost, its orange trumpet flowers flaring between wooly canopies of the thick, fleshy leaves.

"Sparrow?" Pucelle said and gave a timid whistle.

But the bird was nowhere to be seen—or heard. She assumed that it flew into the trees and to the safety of cover. The garden had a music of its own—the hum of an active beehive in the left corner, some distance away from the well. In spite of the breeze murmuring in her ear and blowing her short dark locks across her ears and against her cheek, the sounds in this little patch of land were crisp and clear. The dripping of water in the well, the buzzing of the bees and the rustling of dry leaves thrilled through her spine. There was something exciting and unusual about this place. And perhaps a little dangerous.

The girl crept over to the well and peered in. It was dark and damp but the rope that had once wrapped about the winch was nothing more than a rotten frayed end and the bucket was bobbing like a cork at the bottom in the inky black water. She was glad she wasn't terribly thirsty anyways, as she was uncertain how long the taint of Plague lingered in the infected food and waters of the land after the people had all died.

"Pucelle," she heard a voice call again. This time it didn't sound like the chirp of a bird but a human voice. "What are you seeking?"

Pucelle heard the leaves on the compost pile rustle and, when she looked up, she saw a tall woman in a simple white dress, the squash flowers braided into her long, flowing hair. She looked very much like her mother, but slightly older. Her carefully manicured

179

hands folded lightly over her stomach and the tendrils of the squash plant encircled her ankles and crept up her skirt. She appeared to have risen from the soil rather than walked there.

"Who are you?" Pucelle asked guardedly. "How do you know my name?"

"You don't know?" the woman asked with a faint smile. "Surely you must have been hoping to find me if you risked coming here."

"I wasn't looking for anyone, so I don't know who you are. I was just following a bird."

"You were following a bird—into this house of death?" the woman said with a hint of a smile. "Then you truly must be brave—or very, very foolish."

Pucelle crossed her arms and pouted. "I am neither."

"You are honest then. But I'm so glad you came, whatever the reason. I was so hoping to see you with my own eyes. I just wish I had happier news to bring you."

The girl backed up a few paces and kept an eye towards the window and also searched the fence line for an easy escape.

"You came here because you heard my song," the woman continued. "Anyone can hear it, but only you could listen to it."

"I don't understand."

"You will," she said. "Are you sure I don't look familiar to you?"

"Maybe," Pucelle answered. "You remind me of my mother."

The woman's smile broadened. "And you remind me of her as well. I am your grandmother, Pucelle."

Pucelle frowned. "That's not true. My mother said my grandmamma died during the Plague."

"Your mother was right. The plague did take my life, but I am also your grandmamma Majie," she said. "I am only able to be here with you now because in this place the boundaries between our two worlds are weak here. Also, because, whether you know it or not, you are attuned to the magic that still lingers in yours."

"If you died, how are you here?"

Majie shuffled her skirt and the vines entangled in it shimmied but remained clung to the fabric as if fused to it. Her bare feet were buried up to the ankle in the dark soil. "I'm here because you need me to be here. And I so want to be here with you, dear. You are entering a dangerous and important time in your life and you need guidance and faith to guard your path."

"I was just going to get a lamb for my father," Pucelle said, pointing to the road beyond the fence. "I don't think there are any bandits on the roads these days and it's only an hour's walk from here."

Majie chuckled. "Oh, dear, you have your father's sense of humor. At least, when he still had a sense of humor."

Pucelle fidgeted. "My father. Right. I have to go. He will be very cross with me if I don't get home before dark," she said. "But you can come with me. I'm sure mother will be very happy to see you after all these years."

The woman grew solemn. "I'm sure she would, dear."

Pucelle noticed a tear tumble from the woman's cheek and drip onto one of the squash leaves.

"You're not coming with me, are you?"

"I can't, child. I'm tied to this place. My body—my real one—turned to dust and bone a long time ago. But, more importantly, you should not leave this place either. It's not safe for you anymore."

"Why?"

"Dear, I don't know how to tell you but to tell you plainly," she said. "Your parents have passed on. They were killed by marauding Fiorians shortly after you left home. I'm so sorry to tell you this."

"What?" Pucelle felt a lump of panic well up in her throat. "I just left them this morning. They're fine. I think it's terrible of you to try to tell me such a lie."

"It's not a lie, dear. If only it were. But they are at peace now. They have passed beyond the veil," Majie cast a furtive glance over her shoulder. "And I'm sure if they could, they would tell you themselves. But now you must stay here. You must not go back to your home in Do'om. The Fiorians will catch you and surely kill you like they did your parents—and your uncles."

"My uncles?" Pucelle gasped. Somehow she knew what the woman who called herself her grandmother was true, but she could not bring herself to accept that her entire extended family had been murdered. "Why would anyone want to kill my family?"

Majie sighed. "There is no answer I can give you that would satisfy you. I can only tell you that you live for a reason and that reason is to make their deaths mean something. Whether by accident or by plan, you were kept safe for a great purpose. You have a great gift that you have not yet realized that can someday save the kingdom and stop the Fiorian invasion. I can help you realize your potential."

But Pucelle couldn't hear what her grandmother was saying. "I can't be here. My family needs me."

"But, dear…"

The girl turned and fled the garden, rushing through the window and out the front door on the other side. In the hours it took her to travel down the road towards Do'om, she would periodically break into a dead run or a sprint, but it felt like her legs were made of lead and wading through quicksand. It seemed like the road stretched forever like in her nightmares, but all she could think of in her numbed mind was getting home.

At last, as the sun began to swell and sink towards the horizon, she reached the outskirts of the village. There were no welcoming signs of the clay and straw rooftops perched among columns of trees because there were no trees to be seen. There were just charred, twisted fingers reaching up from the scorched earth. There was a strange smell lingering in the air that reminded her of cooked meat, but more rancid, and then she saw the funeral pyre in the town square, piled high with burnt corpses.

Pucelle covered her mouth to stifle her scream and ducked behind a stone wall when she noticed movement near the last standing wall of what used to be the town hall. It was Fiorian patrol on foot. They did not appear to be searching for anyone but one of the men was pulling a vegetable cart. He dragged it to the pile of bodies and, to Pucelle's horror, began dumping more corpses on the chest high heap. Even in the dim light she recognized the snow white hair and beard of her uncle Jon as the soldier and one of his comrades dropped the body unceremoniously upon the ground.

Pucelle wanted to scream, she wanted to hurl herself at the men and pound at them with her bare fists, but she could not make her body move from her hiding spot behind the stone fence. Her terror had frozen her in place. Instead, she whimpered and slowly her vision blurred as the flood tears poured down her cheeks.

After about an hour of standing about and murmuring to each other in the dying calm of twilight, the Fiorians finally lost interest in whatever they had been doing and moved off, leaving Pucelle alone in the lengthening shadow of the wall. She didn't know how long she remained they curled up and catatonic, but when she finally stirred, dusk had begun to set in. She crept from her hiding place and made her way towards her parents' home. There was nothing left but the foundation. The animals had all fled or been taken away. She found the spot where her bed had used to be and laid down.

"Mother? Father?" Pucelle said, looking up towards where on the ceiling her mother had painted stars, but seeing instead the real stars in chill of the night. The sky answered with only silence.

This was not her home anymore, she realized. The Fiorians had taken that from her, along with her family, her friends and her neighbors. It was a place of death now, with little to distinguish it from the plague houses. She forced herself to get up from the pile ashes and walk back towards the town square. Without the torches, it was just a matter of muscle memory and stepping careful in the now-alien terrain that surrounded her.

When she reached the pile of burnt bodies, she could smell the stench and feel the residual heat that must have been from fading embers from the pyre hours earlier. She could still make out the white of her uncle's beard and she wanted nothing more than to stroke it like she did when he was still alive.

"Uncle Jon," she whispered. "I'm sorry. If I had gotten back sooner…"

Her mind played out scenarios where didn't dawdle, she got the lamb and quickly returned to before the Fiorians arrived and warned the villagers of their impending doom. Or perhaps she had at least let her father come with her. At least he'd be alive now.

She reached for her uncle's face. Because she could see shine from the glimmering moon reflecting in his vacant eyes he almost seemed alive. Involuntarily, her fingers flinched as they brushed against the stiff bristles of his beard. She felt the dew already forming on the body; the skin was cold and clammy. The body. The thought rebounded her back to the realization that he was quite dead and stiffening with mortis.

Pucelle withdrew her hand and crouched next to her uncle's body. She felt something stir within her. She felt warm, then cold, like the heat was being

185

drawn from her body. She heard someone gasp and her uncle's face stirred. His eyes suddenly fixed on her.

"Pu-Pucelle," her uncle's voice was chilling and uneven. "You sh-should not be… h-here."

"Uncle, is that you?"

"N-no."

"What?" Pucelle swallowed hard. "Who are you then?"

"Too late for your uncle," her uncle's body rasped in a hoarse whisper. "You lack the skill to reach beyond the veil yet. You need to go. They will find you if you stay. You need to go."

"I don't understand."

Against her better judgment she stretched out a hand again towards her uncle's face. As she did so, the body gave a long sigh, a cross been a low moan of pain and a sigh of relief. Her uncle's face disintegrated into dust and quickly the rest of his body faded into the darkness.

"Uncle!" Pucelle gasped.

Out of the corner of her eye, she caught a glimpse of torches approaching from the north side of the village. Could the Fiorians have returned? For a moment, her mind considered the warning that whatever inhabited her uncle's body had given her. She decided she could not stay in the village. She got up and ran blindly towards the road that had led her away from the village earlier that day. Several times she tripped over tree roots or stones and it began to feel like her knees and arms were skinned to the bone, but she continued to scurry down the blackened road with only the moon and stars to light her way. She fought through bitter tears and the burning of her lungs as she ran.

By the time she reached the plague house, it was nearly dawn. The sky was grey, but the sparrows had begun their morning song. She went directly through the front door and out the back window. On the compost pile where she had left her was the figure of her grandmother. She smiled sadly at her and opened her arms in welcome. At the sight of this, Pucelle was overcome with emotion. She ran to Majie and embraced her, burying her face in her leafy skirt.

"I'm so sorry, dear," she said. "I wish I could have spared you the pain. But through pain sometimes we grow. It is an unfortunate but vital fact of life."

"Can you bring them back?"

Majie shook her head. "But you may someday. You have a powerful gift. You have a magic that can restore all—your loved ones, the kingdom, even the world."

"How can I do that? When I touched my uncle, he turned to dust."

Majie held out her hand. There were seeds in her palm. "When you returned to Do'om, did you notice the trees were burned as well?"

"Yes."

"The trees are dead, but the magic within them is not dead. As they burned, they released their seeds. From these, an entirely new forest may grow. When the Plague burned this world, magic died but it sent out its seeds. One of those entered you when you were born. It's just beginning to sprout into a seedling. One day it will grow into a great tree and you will use that

187

tree to produce a great forest. That is why you must stay here with me. Do you understand?"

Pucelle shook her head. "I just want my family and my home back."

"I know, dear. I know," Majie said. She let the seeds tumble from her hand and pulled Pucelle towards her once again. The girl closed her eyes and fell into the folds of her grandmother's dress. It was the first true comfort she had in more than a day and a few minutes later she gave into her body's fatigue and drifted to sleep.

When she awoke hours later, she was alone on the compost pile. Her arms were wrapped around a bundle of dried squash vines.

Chapter 17

Fall of Year 43 (after the Great Plague)

The testing grounds at the Fiorian capitol city was a huge bowl near the presidential palace. Once it held sporting events where, generations ago, crowds watched chariot races and bear fights. Now, it existed only for mandatory parades on government holidays and for shows of Fiorian military strength. Mallory stood in the presidential viewing box along with a vice president of "marketing" for Sudwell Toy Company Fenir Pratt. It had been months since the inventor arrived in the city and nearly as long since his hopes for maintaining control of his inventions had been shattered. He was working for the government directly, and although he had kept to himself the knowledge that he saw through Sudwell's ruse—that he was in fact the president himself—he feared that one there must be a specific reason the president did not wish him to know his real identity, that if he knew Mallory knew about him—he and his wife would be in grave danger.

"Beautiful day for a demonstration, don't you think, Mallory?" Fenir said.

On the field below was not only the original prototype of the Dragon's Breath, but five other copies lined up neatly where the goal line of some ancient sport was situated. They gleamed in the sun as mechanics and drivers scurried about them performing last minute diagnostic checks. He had trained each of the mechanics himself and his assistant Joaquin had devised a simple mockup of the cockpit to train the drivers. Still, Mallory wished he was down there with the machines rather than playing politics with the bureaucrat. He knew he was not good at keeping secrets and it worried him that he might make a mistake that would tip off the parade of government functionaries and company men he'd paraded past as they put him to work on building their superweapon.

"I'm still not sure about the terms of this test, Mr. Pratt," Mallory said. "As the designer, shouldn't I know them?"

Fenir chuckled. The finely waxed mustache under his upturned nose twitched nervously. "To be a suitable test, the experiment must be kept blind. No need to worry though. This is only a demonstration of power for our benevolent government patrons. If things go well—as I'm sure they will—we can expect this machine to go into full production within the month."

"That soon?" Mallory said, feeling a quickening in his pulse. He shot Fenir a weak smile. "But there are still kinks to work out. What if there are problems with the drive train? The drivers and mechanics might need more time to—"

"Time is money, my friend, and while the president is infinite in his wisdom and patience for some things, let me assure you he has little patience for contractors who don't meet their deadlines," Fenir turned his head and pointed to a small scar below his earlobe. "This happened to me the last time I failed to produce on time. I vowed never to let that happen again."

"They whipped you for missing a deadline?"

"Of course. And it was totally justified. I promised a flintlock rifle that could be mass-produced by last winter and hit a target as well as our standard issue crossbows. The rifle was a month late coming out of development and it didn't help that one exploded in the lead engineer's face on demonstration day. Poor bastard died a few days afterward which really put a crimp in my schedule. But I should have seen that coming. Yes, indeed."

Fenir pulled his collar up to hide the scar and then stroked his mustache as he looked out over the field. "Cheer up, my young fellow, you look white as a sheet. Your machine is ready for this, I am certain. Besides, I take the beatings for the failed engineers and projects so you can stay able-bodied and keep working."

Mallory was uncomforted by the man's assurances. There was a short knock at the door to the box and then Sudwell stepped in with a gaggle of government officials wearing plain black suits and slicked hair. They appeared to all look the same. Only Sudwell, who had outfitted himself with a red jacket and the same staff with a brass fist that he always seemed to keep with him.

"And there's the man of the hour," Sudwell boomed, clapping a hand on Mallory's shoulder. His grip almost felt like a vice. "This young man may very well bring an end to this bloody war."

"You're too kind, sir," Mallory demurred but he didn't meet his employer's eyes.

"Gentlemen," Sudwell said, ignoring the inventor's unenthusiastic reply. "Shall we begin our demonstration of the Dragon's Breath."

The lead official adjusted his horn-rimmed glasses and nodded. "By all means, Mr. Sudwell. We are understandably curious to see what this machine can do."

"Outstanding!" Sudwell said with a broad smile. "Mr. Mallory, would you do the honors of explaining the engineering behind your vehicle while Mr. Pratt gives the green light to our men on the field?"

Mallory bowed nervously. He stuttered at first as he explained the design of the Dragon's Breath while Fenir unfurled a green flag and leaned over the ledge of the viewing box, waving it wildly above his head. When the inventor had finished his presentation, he turned to find the Dragon's Breath vehicles lined up in the center of the field. The drivers had entered their cockpits and the mechanics were fleeing the field. At the south end of the field, a line of bowmen stood on a ledge overlooking a large gated entrance. Flanking each side of the gate were guards armed with pikes.

As the gate lifted, Mallory saw a group of ragged men and women stumble onto the field. He didn't recognize the odd clothes they wore—workman's tunics, patched skirts and archaic-looking jackets made from leather or coarse wool—but he guessed they were Orloinians. There were dozens of them, and each appeared to be armed with a primitive wooden sword or spear. Behind them came more Fiorian pikemen. Clearly, they were being forced onto the field by the guards because as soon as they reached the open green they began to meander confusedly and had to be shoved by the flanking pikemen back into order with their fellow countrymen. Some looked towards the walls of the stadium and empty stands for some means to escape. Mallory felt a weight form in his stomach as he began to realize what was about to happen.

"I believe our test subjects are ready to begin—and face the firepower of these mechanical marvels," Sudwell said.

"Sir, may I have a moment before we proceed," Mallory pleaded.

"There will be plenty of time to address questions later," Sudwell replied curtly. His expression was unreadable, but his stare pierced though Mallory and seemed fixed on a point miles beyond him. "In the meantime, let's not keep our esteemed guests—and our test subjects—waiting."

The ersatz businessman turned towards the field and raised a large speaking-trumpet to his lips.

"Gentlemen, you may start your engines," he boomed. A few seconds later, the hissing and squealing of steam valves turning, clack of gears echoed across the bowl of the stadium and then the slow, nearly synchronized, chug of the tanks as they began to lurch forward, slowly at first and hesitantly. The prisoners tensed in fear as they saw the huge mechanical beasts lumber towards them.

"Now, the Orloinian prisoners will serve as a mock army," he said over his shoulder to the collected gang of government officials. Then he placed the cone back his lips and shouted onto the field. "Orloinians, if you wish to win your freedom, you must rush past the metal monsters before you. If you survive, we will grant you your freedom. Fail to attack these beasts and the archers behind you will surely cut you down in your tracks."

The prisoners looked up at the box in bewilderment, then at each other. A small group of them at the rear of the crowd tried to shove back at the pikemen at either side but a volley of arrows from the bowmen in the stands convinced them that their best chance at survival was in front of them, beyond the strange metal beasts that stood in their path.

"Mr. Sudwell, I must protest—"

Sudwell silenced the inventor with a single finger to his lips and another piercing stare. Mallory involuntarily bit his tongue. There was nothing he could do to save the poor souls in the arena. Moreover, if his Dragon's Breath tanks did not perform to expectations, he realized, it could be his soul that might be lost in the next few moments. He had heard stories of officials and occasionally contractors who were 'disappeared' because they disappointed their superiors in government. Now that he knew Sudwell was really Chancellor Newbold, there was no chance that he would really play the role of intermediary or protector if he felt he had no use for Mallory anymore.

"Now watch with what efficiency the Dragon's Breath dispatches its foes," Sudwell told the government officials. Then he smiled at Mallory. "I think you'll agree that our inventor has named his device appropriately."

Mallory cringed. He didn't want to watch the tragedy unfolding on the field, but he couldn't look away. The crowd of Orloinian prisoners hesitantly moved towards the line of tanks at first, then began to trot and finally broke into a panicked run as they saw the gates on the other side of the field open before them. Meanwhile, the Dragon's Breaths gathered speed, leaving trails of black and white smoke behind them.

As man and machine closed the gap between them, the tank gunners leveled their turrets at the scrambling test subjects. Mallory could already see the tongues of flame flickering at the mouths of their guns, like a hungry dog licking its lips at the sight of a fresh meal. The inventor swallowed hard. His breathing became so shallow and quick that his tongue felt parched and thick. He seemed physically unable to move or speak, the anticipation was so great.

The prisoners were sprinting now, and some had dropped their token weapons and were heading for the open gate like Dragon's Breath tanks weren't even there. Mallory could see that they were dividing into two groups, each trying to angle around the lumbering metal beasts bearing down on them. The inventor knew that the tanks were not nimble enough to fully block off their routes, that they had formed their lines too tightly from the start, but it hardly mattered if the cannons did their jobs. At least one would do its job— the prototype—which churned the earth in the center of the line, lagging just slightly behind the others.

"How exciting this is!" Sudwell shouted, as though he were a child watching his wind-up toy soldiers march across tabletop.

As the prisoners attempted to flank the tanks, the gunners adjusted their turrets. They were only 30 feet away, then 20 feet, well within range. Mallory gripped the railing until his knuckles turned white. He couldn't imagine why the gunners weren't firing. He hoped beyond hope for a mechanical failure.

But no sooner than he'd made his wish, the cannons of the two outer tanks fired their cannons. A ball of flame leapt from the mouth of each turret. In an instant the ground round the left flank exploded into an inferno—then the right. Dozens of prisoners disappeared in a flash as two mushroom clouds burst over the field. The remaining prisoners were blown back nearly a hundred feet. Their bodies lay prostrate on the ground. But they weren't dead. A few seconds later, they stirred, terror stricken. Some turned to run back towards the pikemen. Others tried to move laterally to scurry towards the walls on either side.

"Oh, gods," Mallory muttered to himself and then covered his mouth to stop himself from crying out—or vomiting. He knew Sudwell was keeping a watchful eye on him as he spectated the massacre.

The prototype fired its cannon. Another mushroom cloud enveloped the fleeing prisoners in the center. The two interior flank tanks advanced ahead of the line and adjusted their turrets. On the far side, a fourth inferno swallowed the group attempting to reach the wall. A flaming body was flung hundreds of feet into the air before plummeting to the turf with a sickening thud.

The last tank to fire aimed its cannon at the scrambling Orloinians. The muzzle spouted bright orange flames dozens of feet across, but the cannon appeared to fail to shoot its projectile. The flames licked the ground near the backs of the Orloinians as they ran, but the prisoners escaped unharmed. They struck the wall below with such force that Mallory imagined that they must have injured themselves greatly in the impact of flesh on stone. In their panic, several prisoners were climbing on top of their comrades to climb up the wall and gain access to the box where he, Sudwell and the government officials watched. Their eyes were black and wide.

"Mr. Mallory, something seems to have gone wrong with one of the cannons," Sudwell said. His tone was more of bemusement than annoyance. "Still, quite an impressive show, wouldn't you say?"

Mallory's skin felt clammy and he struggled to keep himself calm, even though we felt sure that everyone could see him shaking like a leaf. He clasped his hands together behind his back and attempted a smile to respond to his patron's query. "Sir, perhaps you should summon the guards and have the prisoners taken back to their quarters? Then I can go down to examine the malfunctioning machine myself."

"Won't be necessary."

A nod from Sudwell and Fenir signaled the archers, which had been trailing the mob at a safe distance to circle about in the stands to get a better angle on the survivors. One of the prisoners screamed for help. A rain of arrows descended upon the Orloinians and the bodies collapsed into a heap.

"Gentlemen," Fenir said the officials. "I hope you are suitably impressed by today's demonstration and will recommend this for full production immediately. Now, if you'll step this way, we can discuss what next actions we can take and discuss the details of potential contract."

He ushered the group back through the doors, leaving Mallory alone with Sudwell and his thoughts. The patron seemed to regard with a mixture of puzzlement and concern.

"Mr. Mallory, you look white as a sheet. This is a moment of glory for you. Your dreams become a reality of steel and fire," he said.

"Yes, sir, I am pleased my work has come to fruition," Mallory said, choking back his bile to keep from vomiting.

"Oh, I see," Sudwell said slowly. "You disapprove of the test? Would rather we had used inanimate test dummies instead of these live people?"

"I don't mean to question, sir, but—but what was the point of killing all those people for a controlled test?"

"This wasn't just a test of the devices, son," Sudwell said, placing a hand on Mallory's shoulder. "This was a test of the inventor. If we are going to get the Dragon's Breath onto the battlefield quickly, I need to know that I can send it—and the brains behind it— to the front. And I need you to understand that war is ugly, nasty business."

"To the front?"

"Yes, son, I know the Chancellor very well," he paused ominously. "He'll want to get this in the hands of his army generals as soon as possible. And, while you did a fine job of training these drivers and mechanics, this has to come off without a hitch, which is why, if the contract is approved—which it most certainly will—I will be sending you along as well."

"I am—I am," Mallory tried to process Sudwell's words and come up with a response that would not betray his feelings of utter shock and horror.

"You're overwhelmed, of course, and that's understandable. It's a great responsibility we bear for the glory and survival of our nation," Sudwell said in a mock fatherly tone. "You just have to remember, in order for our civilization to continue and be a beacon of strength to the world, some sacrifices must be made. These filthy Orloinians brought the plague to our land and tried to subjugate us with their fake magic. They must be made to bow or be destroyed. It's the only way. And your machines will save more lives than they will take. After they praise the Chancellor for his victory, your name will be on the lips of every soldier who can come back home to wife and children. Just remember that."

Mallory surveyed the pockmarked field with the strewn remains of charred Orloinian bodies. He would remember something from this day, but it would not be that.

Chapter 18

Fall of Year 43 (after the Great Plague)

In the barracks at Crestfallen Camp, Minoru collapsed on his new bunk. It had been a hard day of fighting— and running—from Fiorian forces. In the bunk next to him, covered in sweat and filth, Kamatari sagged onto the edge of his straw mattress and rested his head wearily against the pike in his hand. The rest of the men were already bedding down or grilling the camp cook for any scraps of food that may have survived the last retreat and not fallen into enemy hands. Kukiyama, or Cookie as he was known, was a short plug of man, resourceful at using whatever was available locally to create a meal that was somewhat edible, had come up short this day. Many soldiers were turned away hungry. Kamatari turned a baleful eye towards the food cart.

"I'm so tired, I can't even care that I'm starving," Minoru moaned. "Why am I always hungry?"

"Same shit, only different," Kamatari muttered.

"Sleeping on the job, boys?" A voice came from as the opening of the tent parted. It was Teuta, Anville's first-in-command. She was dressed in the simple chest armor they had first seen her. Astonishingly, her uniform and hair were almost as unmussed as if she had gone for a short run instead of the forced march across three woods and a marshland, all the while being chased by Fiorian advance divisions. "We've got fortifications to build and you need to earn your keep if you are to stay in the Dauphin's service."

"But, commander, we've been on the run all day," Minoru sighed. "I can't move a muscle."

"And I almost had my head blown off three times," Kamatari added.

Teuta smirked.

"Something tells me you wouldn't miss it if it had been blown off. As for me, I've already been shot once and for real," she pulled down her collar, revealing a bright red slash across her neck where a Fiorian projectile appeared to have grazed her. "Any deeper and might have severed the artery. Then you would not have me to make such a complaint to. And yet, here I am with a shovel and heading out to work on the fortifications. If we don't get them built before sundown, you'd better believe that the Fiorians will be feasting on our flesh by morning. Besides, if we get done before dawn, I'll put in a good word to Cookie for you. I hear he stashed some mutton away and is keeping it for himself."

Teuta lifted two shovels propped along the tent wall and offered to them. Minoru took one reluctantly and Kamatari followed suit. The lieutenant led them to the perimeter. They were atop a hill overlooking a sheep farm. Below them, a frightened old man frantically urged his grazing sheep back towards his hovel, and past him, an old woman, presumably his wife, was laden with two buckets of water from a nearby well as she scampered back home. They realized trouble was coming on the heels of Captain Anville's retreating band, and would not likely leave when they did. There were already three men erecting an earthworks along the ridgeline.

"Shorty, make sure you widen that base," Teuta shouted to the stout one filling bags of soil to stack on the barricades. "If you don't, it'll topple with the first wave of advance cavalry."

Shorty grunted his assent.

"Grab some sacks, boys, and let's get to it," she told Minoru and Kamatari.

Minoru obediently hopped into the deepening trench with Shorty and began filling bags. Kamatari meanwhile followed Teuta and the two of them began hoisting the filled sacks onto the earthworks. The light was growing dim so torches were brought to the site. As they worked, Kamatari watched as the lieutenant undid her breastplate and dropped it to the ground. She rolled up her sleeves to reveal two toned and bronzed arms adorned with tattoos of animals he did not recognize. In the dim light, she almost looked like a woman in spite of her broad muscular shoulders.

Over the last few months, Teuta had gained his respect and Kamatari had to admit to himself that he had grown to even like her a little. She could be hard and curt with her subordinates, but he could respect that, because she was also fair and even motherly at times. Kamatari guessed it was the reason her men had not outed her as a woman. She was a competent soldier and had kept most of them alive despite the stiff odds they faced. Teuta hoisted two sacks on either shoulder, bounded up the wall in a few agile hops and then turned to look down at Kamatari.

"What are you staring at, soldier?"

Kamatari stumbled a bit. "I—I was just admiring how strong you were for a—a—"

"Mind your next words carefully, mister," her pale blue eyes narrowed. "Lest you be using that tongue to clean out the latrines—for a week."

"I just mean that you're strong. Stronger than anyone I've ever met."

Teuta dropped the sacks and gave him a sly smile. "Well, the compliment is appreciated, if coarsely worded. Sometimes I don't know if the captain notices that."

"Oh, he should notice that," Kamatari said and he hoisted two sacks of his own on his tired shoulders and climbed up to deposit them in the row next to Teuta's.

"He's just been busy keeping us all alive until the Dauphin sends us reinforcements."

Kamatari nodded. "You're not from the capitol, are you?"

"No," Teuta continued her work at the base of the wall, the muscles of her biceps rippling as she sliced at the earth with her shovel. "I was born in a village in Boisfonce, south of here."

"Really? I have farm—had a farm—in Arbor."

"Do you have a wife?"

"Yeah," he said.

His thoughts turned to lead when he pictured his wife's face. They had always fought over money and the farm and the lack of children, but was only now that realized how much he missed the growl in her voice and the silhouette of her stout frame against the glow of the hearth. Love had never entered their relationship. They married as soon as they came of

203

age. It was the proper thing to be done in a small Orlonian village and was encouraged by the magistrates to ensure they maintained the stock of cheap peasant labor. And now his wife was alone and childless. But she wouldn't miss him. Probably even hoped he could be declared dead so she could start fresh with a new man. She was young enough. And he wouldn't blame her. He had let his anger and desperation get the best of him when he stormed off. He had been a lousy husband.

"You left her for this?"

Kamatari nodded dumbly.

"Don't look all doom and gloomish, Kamatari," she said matter-of-factly. "I had a spouse—a dumb brute of a blacksmith who beat me nearly as hard as he pounded his anvil. My parents married me off when I was 13. Said it was 'tradition' and the will of the Seraphim or some other bullshit. Anyways, I got out of that stinking village as soon as I could. I had to escape."

"Yeah, I had to escape that shit too."

The lieutenant stacked another sack on the wall. "You and I, we're not slaves. We are soldiers and we serve the Dauphin."

"Yeah," Kamatari muttered. "Hope he starts serving us sometime."

Teuta smiled. "Alright, gloomish, let's go get your pal and see Cookie about some mutton stew."

Just then, Captain Anville came barreling down the hillside. Kamatari expected him to be screaming bloody murder about how shabby the wall looked, but he put up a hand signal for everyone to remain silent.

Teuta immediately recognized what the signal meant and waved at Minoru and the others stationed along the fortifications.

"Torches out now," she called in a hoarse whisper. "Everyone, stay low."

They all doused the torches and ducked behind the wall. In the pitch black, Kamatari could only make out the faint shapes of Teuta and Minoru who crept closer to them. A hush replaced the drone of conversations and dull thuds of the of the dirt sacks. Anville came upon them, slowing from a dead sprint. He couldn't see the commander's face clearly but could tell from the heaving gulps and foul mixture of leather and sweat odors that it was the captain as he placed each of his hands blindly on Teuta and Kamatari's shoulders.

"What is it, Captain?" the lieutenant whispered.

"I spotted a Fiorian patrol headed in this direction. I don't think they see us yet, but they'll be on us soon enough," Anville said.

"Not another attack," Minoru moaned.

"But at least this time we may get the element of surprise on our side," he said. "Now stay quiet and keep your eyes and ears peeled."

Kamatari couldn't imagine what they were expected to see behind a wall and in the growing darkness of its shadow, but he strained to listen past the captain's heavy breathing, the whine of the crickets and the occasional belch of a tree toad. They stood there in relative silence for nearly twenty minutes until the night was suddenly broken by a series sharp cracks. Kamatari had heard the sound before and it made the pit in his empty stomach harden—it was a blast from the Fioroans new weapon, a firestick that could kill from a distance.

"Hold!" Anville called to his men. "It's too far away. I'll go check it out."

"Be careful, captain," Teuta warned. "There could be snipers waiting."

"When have I ever not been careful?" he replied. A dim yellow crescent of teeth framed in a smile was all that was visible of the captain's face before he scrambled to the top of the wall. He kept his body flattened atop the bags. Kamatari heard a few faint screams and then there was another loud crack.

"I can see them," the captain called down. "It looks like a patrol—only about a dozen or so. They've come upon one of the farms down in the valley. Poor bastard. They're probably just looting him for supplies, but he thought he could put up a fight."

"Sir, what do we do?" Teuta whispered up to him.

"We've caught a break. They don't appear to have noticed us, and if we stay dark, they won't until morning. So we lay low for now."

"But we should help that poor farmer," Minoru said. "They'll kill him."

"There could be more of them out there, private," the captain said. "If we give our position away, we could be overrun by dawn."

There was another gunshot and another scream in the distance. This one was distinctly female.

"Sir, with all due respect, I have to agree with Private Minnie for once. It's our duty to protect the Dauphn's people—and these people need our help."

The captain growled. He slid off the wall and back onto the ground between Teuta and Kamatari. "And what about our duty to stay alive so that we can continue to serve the Dauphin and not throw away our lives for some old man and his chickens?"

"I trust, sir, that you are skilled enough to keep us alive no matter if we help this farmer or not," Teuta replied dryly.

After a pause, the captain said: "Very well, you can take a detachment—no more than 20 men—and go see if you can rescue this farmer and his family. But be quiet about it. We don't want to call the whole damned Fiorian army on our heads. And take the meat shields with you."

"The meat shields?" Minoru said.

"That means us, genius," Kamatari barked at his friend. "You volunteered us."

"Gather your weapons and meet us here in five," Teuta said.

She went about gathering her team in the dark. Kamatari and Minoru returned to their tent and gather their weapons—a confiscated Fiorian sword and a wooden pike with an iron tip. When they returned, about 15 men huddled around Teuta.

"We'll go down along the tree line. Stay close and, by the gods, be quiet. We need the element of surprise for this to work. They have at least one firestick amongst them and those can be deadly at a distance— and loud. Bowmen, take the lead," the lieutenant said.

The group scrambled over the wall and crept single-file along the tree line. Minoru seemed to stumble over every rock and tree root along the way and Kamatari was sure that every Fiorian must have heard his scuffling and moaning, but Teuta didn't seem to notice. Her silhouette crouched before him as the glow of the farm's hearth created a halo. When they reached a fence, she signaled them to fan out. Each planted themselves behind a fencepost, except Minoru, who huddled uncomfortably against Kamatari against a millstone half buried in the ground.

"Your knee is on my foot, Minnie," Kamatari growled.

"That's your foot?"

"No, and if lean on it or my bladder any harder you'll find exactly which part I meant."

Teuta shushed them. She pointed to two Fiorians near the barn. They were moving towards the house, but their backs were turned. In front of the door of the little one-room house, the body of the old farmer was lying the mud, face down. Beside him, the old woman knelt, wailing.

The lieutenant pointed to the bowmen to her right and then at the two Fiorians. The men carefully vaulted over the fence, nocked their arrows and aimed. Two arrows whistled through the air and found their marks. The two Fiorians were each struck in backs of the necks. They gurgled and fell to the ground with soft thuds.

"Cover me," Teuta barked to the rest of them.

She placed her sword and crossbow on the ground and then crossed over the fence. She approached the old woman slowly with her arms outstretched and displaying her palms to the woman crouched and weeping over the dead old man.

208

"Ma'am, can you speak?"

The old woman's chest heaved as she sobbed but she didn't look up or acknowledge the lieutenant's presence. Teuta approached each of the Fiorians and examined them. She rummaged through their clothes for something and then turned towards the fence.

"No firesticks or ammo," she called. "Keep your eyes peeled."

Teuta crept closer to the old woman. When she was in reach of her, she placed on the crone's shoulder and leaned over the man's body. Only then, did the old woman look up at her with glazed eyes and wind-hardened faced creased with age.

"I'm sorry. Your husband has passed," Teuta told her. "We come to help. We are still in danger though. Where are the wielders of the firesticks that did this?"

"You brought them here? To our home?" the crone said, pointing to the dead Fiorians.

"They chased us here. I'm sorry about what happened, but there is still time to stop them from doing any more harm."

"They went to the barn, to take our sheep. I told him not to fight, to let them have the sheep but Furuinouka—"

"How many?"

"About six."

"Do you know how many firesticks they have?"

The old woman shook her head. "My granddaughter, she was inside when the men attacked…"

"We'll find her," Teuta said. She waved Kamatari and Minoru over. When they arrived, she told the

209

crone: "These men will take you and your husband inside. Stay there until we give the all clear—and stay quiet."

Teuta motioned for the rest of the soldiers to follow her. About half the men gathered at either side of the barn door facing them while the others split into two groups and crept around the sides of the barn and disappeared at the rear of the barn. The front door was ajar and there were sounds of agitated sheep and clatter of unintelligible shouting from the Fiorians.

The lieutenant caught sight of Minoru and Kamatari dawdling next to the old man and waved them off. Minoru took the hand of the old lady and tried to guide her towards the house.

"Won't you come with us granmama? It's safer indoors," he said trying to feign politeness.

Kamatari grabbed the old man's body under the arms and proceeded to drag it behind Minoru and the crone. The corpse was light like a sack of dried leaves. He could feel the rib cage under the plain tunic. "Why do I always wind up handling the dead bodies," he muttered under his breath.

As Kamatari pulled the corpse through the front door, he watched as Teuta gathered her weapons and slipped through the barn door followed by her men. A moment later, he saw movement along the tree line. At first, he thought Anville had sent reinforcements, but as two men stepped into the clearing, it became obvious they were Fiorian. He bit back a sudden cry of surprise. The men had not seen them. One had a chicken under one arm and the other was carrying a basket of apples. The pillaging Fiorians were facing the house. They were facing him.

Kamatari grabbed the door handle and lunged backwards, trying to drag the body with him as he fell backwards. But the old man's foot caught in the door and it simply shuddered and flew open again. The lead Fiorian shouted something at him. The other Fiorian let go of his chicken, which scurried away, and aimed his firestick. The weapon made a loud crack and a projectile screamed towards Kamatari. He had no time to react. He felt a heavy thud and the impact sent him sprawling with the old man landing atop his chest. This seemed familiar.

"Gods, who's shooting at us?" Minoru cried as the old woman began to howl.

Kamatari was sure he'd been hit. He'd seen the molten ball of lead zoom directly towards his forehead. Yet, except for the ringing of his ears from the blast, he felt unharmed. He looked down at the old man's forehead. There was a new hole in it where the projectile had penetrated. A dark spot on the tawny skull that almost looked like another liver spot.

"Who do you think?" Kamatari yelled. "Help me get this door shut!"

Minoru climbed over Kamatari and the body. He grabbed the door handle and kicked the old man's foot through the threshold. As he slammed the door shut, there was another blast and the wood of the door splintered just over Minoru's head. The projectile blasted a fist-sized hole, whizzed past their heads and buried itself on the opposite wall.

"What in the nine hells kind of weapon is that?" Kamatari exclaimed.

The old woman shrieked and fell to the ground.

"I don't know but this door won't hold out very long. If they keep shooting at it, it'll be sawdust," Minoru said.

"And you'll be a bloody pulp if you stand in front of that door much longer. What are you doing?"

Minoru was peering through the ragged hole on his tiptoes and his teeth were chattering. "There's two of them. They're charging at the door."

"Well, shit."

"We're doomed!"

Kamatari grunted and scratched his head. He knew the basic training Teuta gave him over the last few weeks was insufficient to take on two well-armed, battle-hardened Fiorian soldiers and nor could scrawny Minoru.

"I'm not going to let those assholes kill us—or this old cow," he said. Kamatari looked about for his short sword and then cursed when he realized he'd left it outside when he picked up the old man. He cast about for something sharp and heavy. Propped against the hearth stones was a simple axe. It was short handled but light. Fortunately, what it lacked in heft, it made up for in sharpness. "Get ready to open the door on my signal—and stay out of the way."

"Open the door?" Minoru whimpered.

Kamatari did not wait for his friend's agreement. He pressed himself against the wall to the left of the door, brandishing the axe in his right. Minoru stood dumbfounded with his pike at his side. The old woman cowered at the rear of the room.

"When I give the signal," he growled huskily.

He listened hard for footsteps. He could hear the Fiorians shouting to each other, then dull thuds of boots on the wooden stoop outside.

"Now!"

Minoru open the door. Immediately the head of a Fiorian soldier popped through the opening. He had been charging at the closed door to knock it down. Now his momentum was carrying him careening foreword. Kamatari swung down with his axe as hard as he could. The blade struck the soldier in the back of his exposed neck. The Fiorian gagged and blood gushed from the wound, spraying Kamatari in the face. The soldier collapsed in a heap atop the old man's body.

Minoru yowled, also caught by the spray of blood from the man's neck. Then he stumbled backwards in panic and tripped over his own pike. He slammed flat on his back. The tip of his pike clattered on the ground.

"Minnie!"

Before Kamatari had time to react, the second Fiorian burst through the door. He was carrying the firestick with what looked like a wickedly sharp bayonet at its muzzle. He saw Minoru on the ground and then Kamatari still holding the axe buried in his comrade's neck. He aimed his firestick at Kamatari, and the peasant imagined his life parading in front of him—emptiness.

Then there was a click. No bang.

The Fiorian's eyes widened a bit as he pulled the trigger again—and again. Kamatari realized his opening. He tugged at the axe, but it was too deep. He put a boot on the man's skull to gain leverage and free his weapon, but the Fiorian had already changed tactics—positioning his bayonet to drive it through Kamatari's chest. The peasant kicked hard, and the axe blade emerged, streaked with crimson. But he didn't have time to swing down as the Fiorian was on top of him. All of time seemed to slow and thicken like molasses as he saw the gleaming bayonet close within inches of his breast. He wouldn't be fast enough.

Suddenly, the Fiorian jerked as he charged the bayonet veered away. The soldier continued to charge, plowing straight into Kamatari and knocking him off his feet. It was as though the air had been squeezed from his lungs by a millstone as the two men crashed to the floor. The axe swung downward, but missed the soldier's head completely and only the blunt end struck flesh. The two were face to face with the Fiorian on top and Kamatari could smell the spoiled rations on the Fiorian's breathe. But the breath was only temporary as the man sighed one time and then expired. His grey eyes grew dark and dull. Kamatari was completely covered by the larger man's body and slowly suffocating under his weight. He clawed to get the mountain of flesh off his chest.

He heard his friend moan. "Kama—Kamatari."

"Get this beast off me," he tried to scream, but it only came out as muffled coughs.

Finally, the body was rolled to the side. There was a pike jammed in the soldier's back, right between the shoulder blades. Minoru stood over them, an axe-shaped bruised stamped across his forehead.

"They're dead?" the old woman called from across the room.

"Yes, old cow," Kamatari said, wiping the stinging blood away from his eyes. He spat on the body of the dead Fiorian who tackled him. "They are— not us. Assholes."

Kamatari put down the axe and found a chair to sit down in. His body was numb, and his limbs were shaking. He still could not catch his breath.

"Kamatari, are you okay?"

"Yeah, almost being murdered to death has done wonders for my throbbing headache."

"You had a headache?" Minoru asked, then gingerly touched the swollen spot where the flat of the axe had struck him. "You had a headache?"

"Sorry about that."

Minoru leaned over and picked up the fallen firestick. He examined the weapon and put the muzzle up close to his eye so he could see where the projectiles came from. Just then, Teuta came rushing through the door. Her face was screwed up into a scowl.

"I thought I told you to keep quiet. This not—" she said, but her expression went blank when she noticed the bodies and the two peasants' blood-slicked faces. "Oh shit."

Minoru held out the Fiorian weapon. "Wanna firestick?"

Captain Anville passed a hand over the firestick on his lap as the first morning light crept into the tent.

"You're sure you got them all?" he asked Teuta.

"Yes, sir," she said. "We did a sweep after we cleared the barn and rescued the farmer's granddaughter. There were two we didn't initially account for, but Kamatari and Minoru here, eliminated the threat and secured the weapon."

Anville's eyebrows raised in astonishment as he surveyed the two peasants. "I'm impressed. The meat shields showed some initiative?"

Minoru and Kamatari looked at each other nervously.

"We did what we had to, sir," Kamatari said.

"Aye, but you did well. Been wanting to get my hands on one of these for a while," Anville said. "The Fiorians are getting overconfident with their recent successes—and sloppy."

"But we only recovered a handful of the projectiles the firestick uses," Teuta said. "What should we do with it?"

"We're not letting the Fiorians get it back, that's for damn sure," he said. He scratched his beard and held the firestick up to the light as he inspected intently. "If we stay here for long, they'll get it—from our dead bodies."

"Maybe we could request reinforcements. Maybe if they know we have this weapon, or pleas will be heard finally."

"Doubt it," Anville said. "No, we can't rely on relayed messages to the capitol's emissaries or promises of reinforcements that go up in smoke."

"Then what?" Teuta blinked. "You can't be thinking of disobeying our orders, of leaving these demesnes to the mercy of our enemy?"

"They're already at their mercy. We can't stop them on our own. But this gives us leverage to do what we could not before—go directly to the capitol and plead our case."

"But surely they would have you court-martialed and executed for treason or not respecting the chain of command," Teuta's voice softened and almost seemed feminine. "Char, consider what you are saying."

Minoru looked puzzled and mouthed the word 'Char' at Kamatari. His friend responded by rolling his eyes, shaking his head and folding his arms. He could no longer stay at attention; he was so exhausted. He would curl up in the dirt like a slumbering pig if he wasn't afraid the captain would have him placed in the stockade for the disrespect.

"Leverage," Anville repeated, handing Teuta the firestick. "The Dauphin will have to listen to us if we come bearing one of these. And the host of courtiers and bureaucrats between us and him will part like the sea."

"Then it's decided. When shall we break camp?"

"Give the men a day to rest," he said, casting a glance at Kamatari and Minoru. "Make sure these two get extra portions from the mess today after they've had a good sleep. You boys did well, and you should be rewarded."

Then he frowned. "But make sure they clean up first. They look and smell like a slaughterhouse."

217

Chapter 19

Fall of Year 43 (after the Great Plague)

A month after Baldric's miraculous resurrection, the court at Aveon was still in an uproar. The Dauphin was even more enamored with his little "maiden necromancer" and devoutly believed that she was a conduit to his dead father. He kept her in his quarters until late some evenings attempting to commune with the king's spirit through Pucelle, but the maiden was often evasive on the subject and claimed she could not simply conjure the ghost but that he came to her only when she was alone and her mind was at peace.

Meanwhile, Burgundais and G'Rich had stepped up their tests of her abilities, taking her to cemeteries to see if she could resurrect the long dead and to hospitals to cure wounds. It seemed that the maiden could only resurrect the freshly dead and that her healing powers on the living were limited. But, during a visit to a battlefield where forces skirmished with Fiorian allies near Sullust, she resurrected twelve dead soldiers without even touching them. It seemed her powers, if authentic, were growing along with the population's budding fascination with her.

It seemed to Isabeau that her son and his subjects had gone mad over this girl. The more she watched Pucelle stroll her way into the hearts and imaginations of the people she met, the more convinced she was part of a sinister plot. She passed a group of courtesans in

the grand hallway and pretended deafness to the
hushed whispers and blindness to the guarded glances
between the foppish sycophants. The queen had long
tired of the salacious rumors surrounding her mostly
fictional sexual encounters even though she had
sometimes encouraged them in the past to advance her
own ends. She no longer cared about the vicious
rumors they whispered when they thought she could
not hear. She had enough money to buy them all into
silence if she desired.

At the end of the hall, the seal of the Seraphim was
engraved over the entrance. Though hidden under a
portrait of King Rien, it was a reminder of how much
she resented being stuck here in this miserable den of
the people she blamed for poisoning her late husband's
mind and then vanishing to their island beyond the
open sea. Now, somehow, they were trying to return,
and through the maiden, poison her son with their
perverse magic. She was sure of it.

"Your Highness," Chief Burgundais waved to her.
Inside, she sighed with exasperation, but smiled
broadly as the chief approached and his staff clopped
loudly on the stone floor. "Your highness, the Dauphin
would like to have a word."

"Oh, does he? And what word would my son like
to speak to me today?"

"I did not ask, Your Highness. He simply conveyed
to me his desire to speak with you."

Isabeau allowed her smile to fade. "You, the
Dauphin's chief advisor, did not think to ask why he
would use you like some simple errand boy to fetch his
mother?"

Burgundais cleared his throat awkwardly. "Well, he might have mentioned that he wanted to discuss some military options he was considering to solve the Fiorian problem to the north."

"Ah, did he?" Isabeau purred, tilting her head. "I didn't realize that he still respected my advice these days. It seems like he has sought out the advice of other sources—for many things. In fact, I'm a bit surprised he still has use for your services, Burgundais."

The chief's eyes widened, and his lower lip quivered a bit. "Your highness, you are still regent until the Dauphin ascends the throne and, as such, part of the Seigneury, as am I. Your presence in that capacity is demanded."

"Very well, lead on then."

Burgundais nodded, but eyed her with suspicion before turning on his heel sharply and leading her down the next corridor which dead-ended at the left turret. A set of steep, winding stairs led them upwards several levels, where a landing allowed them to pause and gather their breaths. Whoever the architects of the Seraphim had been who designed this place, they either assumed the mages were in peak physical shape or used magic as their main means of transportation. The building clearly was not designed for comfort or ease of access.

In the war room, under a vaulted ceiling, the Dauphin seated himself atop a tall stool overlooking an enormous diorama of the Orloinian continent. Tiny orange and red trees, neatly manicured and planted amid a crescent of rocks and pebbles represented the

Valley of Colors and the trimmed patches of grass represented the farmlands to its south. Pottery castles and other buildings dotted the doll's landscaping representing the major cities of the continent and the entire table-sized continent was ringed by the roiling waters of a rendered ocean, sloshing against the metal sides of the table as a pump underneath whirred, creating a small whirlpool where the Open Sea would be. From his perch, the Dauphin moved miniature wooden men representing the armies of Orloins and Fioria across the map. It was a toy for children, but one that was determining the lives and deaths of thousands of flesh-and-blood people.

Isabeau frowned. Standing to the left of her son was the maiden. She was dressed in new clothes. Gone was the simple brown peasant dress. She now was adorned with a male page's tunic with a high collar cinched at the throat. It was simple enough to tell that the girl was not putting on airs, but what appalled Isabeau were the blue trousers she sported along with knee-high boots. It was totally unacceptable for any woman to appear to appear before her ruler in anything but a formal gown or proper skirt and blouse.

"Mother, I'm glad you're here. We have important matters to discuss," the Dauphin called to the queen regent.

Isabeau looked about the room. "If this is a military briefing, where are the generals, son?"

"Oh, I sent them with Captain Baudrin to check on the troubles in the Valley of Colors."

"You sent all of your closest military advisors off to that backwater?"

221

"Of course," the Dauphin said. "If we lose both Olivet and Valcolors, we'll be cut off from the agricultural areas to the south. It is absolutely vital that we maintain that access."

"And if we lose this city, we will be forced to flee westward, where we will be surrounded by Fiorian allies," Isabeau scolded him. "There have been bandits and criminals in the Valley of Colors making trouble for supply routes for years. If the Fiorians wish to take the region, they will be simply inheriting the same problem. We can continue to use sea and river routes to the east to keep ourselves supplied, so long as we foster good relations with the Seabards."

Pucelle blinked. "Pardon, mum, but the Seabards are secretly allying themselves with the Fiorians."

Isabeau gave the maiden an icy glare.

"It's true, mother," the Dauphin said. He climbed down from his perch. "There were rumblings the last time Horace Seabard visited that he met with a Fiorian spy before coming here."

"Idle chatter," Isabeau said. Her cheeks began to burn as she felt the anger welling within her. She knew about the meeting, and though Horace had assured her in private that he was impervious to attempts by the enemy to pressure him away from supporting the Dauphin, it was clear that he was also cold and distant towards her the last time they had met—and exchanged affections. "You know that Horace is a close friend of the family. His wife made you a baby blanket with the royal crest on it when you were born, for gods' sake. Betraying you would be like betraying his own son."

"If you'll forgive the intrusion, mum, but while the head of the Seabard demesne may care for His Highness, but not as much as he cares for his own position and family," Pucelle said. She met the queen's gaze directly and did not demure. This was either insolence or brazen stupidity.

"I will not forgive this intrusion," Isabeau said. "Burgundais, why was this girl allowed in the war room?"

Burgundais cleared his throat awkwardly. "The Dauphin insisted that she be present for the deliberations on the coming campaign to the north—"

"There will be no campaign, because I was not consulted first and a quorum of military commanders is not present to approve such an action," Isabeau said. "Burgundais, please escort the maiden from room so that I may have a private discussion with my son."

Burgundais looked to the Dauphin, who nodded. The queen attempted to disguise her shock as she seated herself in her traditional chair near the map. A month ago, such a gesture would never have happened. None at the court would even have dared question one of her commands let alone given even a passing regard for the Dauphin. He was to be king, but she let everyone know for certain where the real power of the throne originated. And it was so hard for a woman, even the wife of the king, to gain the respect and power of a kingdom.

"Come, girl, we have other matters we can discuss while the queen confers with His Majesty," Burgundais told the maiden.

Pucelle bowed her head, but she did not move. "Mum, I understand that you see me only as a peasant girl, not fit for court life. You are right. And I would be satisfied to slop pigs and herd sheep for the rest of my life if that were my destiny. But King Rien has chosen to make me a vessel to ensure your son ascends the throne and saves the kingdom, so that the magic that once made our people prosperous and free may once again return."

Isabeau smoothed out her dress and pretended to be unmoved by the girl's speech. "Very well," she said, primly, not looking Pucelle in the eyes. "It is well that you understand your place in the kingdom. And now, as for place, Burgundais, must I repeat my request that this girl—the vessel—be removed from the room so that I may speak with my son alone?"

"Of course, mum."

Once Pucelle and Burgundais left the room, the Dauphin gave his mother his usual pouty frown. The queen was prepared for the emotional outburst that was to ensue. He was so much like his father, with a volcanic temper whenever he did not get his way. But Isabeau was the unmovable object. She stared down her son with same stone face she gave her husband during his temper tantrums.

"Mother, do not to attempt to lecture me that about your role as regent and my lack of readiness for the crown," the Dauphin said. "Had this war gone as it should, I would have been crowned king by now and you would have no right to lecture me about anything."

"I am your mother and as such will always have the right to lecture you about any subject I desire," she replied.

"I said don't lecture me."

"I did not come here to lecture you."

"Good."

"About my role at least," Isabeau added.

The Dauphin stiffened. "Then what?"

"Your role—as future king," Isabeau said.

Her son folded his arms. "How can we possibly have a discussion about my future as king when you are constantly throwing obstacles in my path that will prevent me from ever being king!"

"What an absurd notion!" the queen gasped. "I of all people in this court am your one true champion. I want you to fulfill your destiny and replace your father as ruler of all Orloins."

The Dauphin snorted. "Then why have more than a third of demesnes on this continent turned traitor? Why do the lords of these lands curse your name and question my legitimacy as rightful? Why is the Valley of Colors—the very heart of our nation—come under siege by the enemy and the loyal subjects like Captain Baudrin resist all the while believing that I will not lift a finger to help them?"

"You cannot help them—and help yourself at the same time."

"But why?"

"Being an adult means making difficult decisions about how to allocate your precious resources," Isabeau sighed. "The truth is that you are in a more precarious situation than you realize. The Fiorians are too strong to attack directly. That is why I have advised our generals to use guerilla tactics to simply slow the progress of the Fiorians while I use diplomatic means and economic pressure against the turncoat demesnes. They turned against us, but they will return to the fold if the conditions are favorable."

"And how will conditions ever change in our favor if I am living in exile and my subjects suffer. At least Pucelle offers hope—and a path to the crown."

"You feel that your path flows through this girl's?"

"Just look at the map, mother."

Isabeau sighed and surveyed the table. "I am not interested in your toys, son."

The Dauphin reached across and lifted the tiny castle that represented Chinan. It had been surrounded by tiny tin soldiers adorned with flags stamped with the royal crest. He held it out before his mother in the palm of his hand.

"We capture Chinan. Then, once we clear that, we can travel up river and retake the throne. It's a plan that's as simple as it is elegant," the Dauphin said. With his other hand he traced the flow of the river up to the miniature gold castle that represented Lutesse, the historic Orloinian capitol of Orloins.

Isabeau scoffed. "That's one of the Fiorians most fortified positions in the north. It's also precisely why we sent the girl there, to see her fail so we could be rid of her."

"But she didn't fail."

"Is Chinan not still in Fiorian hands? And besides her parlor trick with the dead servant, what has she really done? Sent threatening letters to the Fiorians? I

226

can see that they aren't quaking in their boots because of her cutting words. You can lay siege to it for years with the paltry force we sent with her and it would never fall."

"It's called a propaganda war, mother," the Dauphin spat. "As I understand, the Fiorians have been fairly effective at waging one against us. It's about time we turn the table on them for a change. After all, I haven't yet given her an army to lead into battle."

"And you will not. Any attempt to take Chinan with the limited resources we have would be a futile effort."

"But it's not futile—and, with Pucele, our resources—at least in terms of the number of men we can field against the Fiorians will be limitless."

Isabeau glanced at the toy soldiers surrounding the spot where the model castle had been. It was only a division, barely enough to close off supply routes to the city, let alone lay siege to it. "Resurrecting a few men at a time will not win you a battle or the war. At best, she is a glorified field nurse. That is all."

The Dauphin slammed down the model castle angrily. One of the minarets broke loose and clattered to the ground. "If you had spent less time counting your money and more time studying G'Rich's reports you would know that the maiden's powers have grown massively since she arrived here."

"If she is so powerful as you say, and a devoted servant of your late father, why does she not return King Rien to us?"

"She cannot resurrect the long dead, only the recently deceased. I don't know why. But she can

227

bring back dozens—maybe even hundreds at a time now. She doesn't even have to touch them anymore to use her powers. G'Rich and Burgundais confirmed it."

A sudden chill went down Isabeau's spine. "Assuming what you say is true, these poor unfortunate souls who die and return, are they—"

"They appear to be the same as before—only not dead," the Dauphin said. "If you like, I can send for Captain Baudrin's servant and you can speak to him. He's not some golem or mind-blasted zombie."

Isabeau waved him off. She had had enough. "No, that's not necessary. I saw the wretch when they returned from Chinan the first time. And I can see you will be unmoved by my motherly—and wise—advice. My only option is to allow you to have your way until you inevitably fail and come to your senses."

"Thank you, mother," the Dauphin muttered under his breath. "As gracious and magnanimous as ever."

"But you will not risk an entire division on this ill-advised adventure."

Her son nodded reluctantly.

"And the siege must end after one month if no measurable progress is made towards weakening the Fiorians' grasp on the city."

"Very well."

Isabeau smiled. "That's a good boy. Now, run along and take that 'savior' girl to a more appropriate location—and not your chambers."

The Dauphin had gotten what he wanted but his look was a bit downcast and defeated. The queen went to the door and opened it. On the other side, Burgundais stood at attention. He appeared to be smiling and holding an empty glass. The maiden appeared to be meditating at the top of the stairs.

"I presume you heard all that?"

"I did, Your Highness," he said with a slight mocking bow. "My apologies for eavesdropping. I could not help myself."

"Then you know your master will fail at Chinan," Isabeau said and cast a glowered at the back of the maiden's head until the corners of her mouth curled into a half-smile. "No matter how many of our dead she raises, she can't raze the walls of Chinan in one month."

Chapter 20

Fall of Year 43 (after the Great Plague)

Belle Isolde took the news of his departure for Orloins better than he expected. There were no tears, only a resolute "Then, I'm coming with you," and the discussion was over. Sudwell was less thrilled by his wife's demand to accompany him to the front. At first, he flatly rejected it. But when Mallory objected, saying that he would not be able to focus clearly on his work if he was worrying about his wife back home, his supervisor acquiesced, stating that she could come so long as she stayed sequestered from the soldiers and would remain to the rear of any military action. The inventor was fine with that. He had no desire to see Belle Isolde in harm's way any more than he wished to leave her behind.

A week later, they were all packed again and shipped to the port city of Dubris. From there, the departed via a converted freighter that resolutely chugged through the choppy waves of the Strait of Dubris as it belched blackened smoke from its two smokestacks even though it still maintained rigging for a full complement of sails. The rolling and swaying of the ship made Mallory sick to his stomach and not even the sweet smell of the sea breeze at the salt spray on his tongue as he watched his homeland disappear over the horizon could help him feel any better. He stood on the deck of the boat in the frigid air for almost an hour before Belle Isolde finally bundled him up in a thick wool blanket and took him to a bunk below decks where they stayed most of the voyage.

It was the middle of the next day when the crew spotted land—the great continent of Orloins. Mallory had heard stories describing how Orloins was a vast land of varied environs that made his own country seem like a tiny islet bobbing like a cork in the sea, but as they approached the Northerly Peninsula a thing tongue of land that represented the closest point to Fioria, he could see the coastline stretch in every direction. Belle Isolde stood next to him near the prow of the boat, her shawl cast about both their shoulders and her head cradled softly in the crook of his neck.

"So, this is the primitive world we wish to conquer and civilize," Mallory said.

"Look at those trees," his wife breathed. From his angle, he could not see her eyes clearly but was sure they were widened in awe at the strange arboreal castle that rose up on the pinnacle of the peninsula. "They're so big."

Mallory felt his own heart quicken as he took in the sight of gargantuan trees that towered over the coastline. Amidst the branches, the spires of a castle rose. The city of Rune was a feat of engineering to match those he'd seen in his own capitol, cradled amidst the strong central tree of the forest—the World Tree. Certainly, it could not have been made by the same primitive culture he'd been told about in the propaganda.

"I can see at once why the Orloinians believed in magic," Mallory said. "Such structures would seem to defy gravity."

"Be careful, darling, I don't know that we can trust the prying ears and watchful eyes of these sailors," Belle Isolde whispered.

"You're quite right, of course," Mallory said with a pause. "This must be what the captain was jokingly referring to as the 'Ruins of Orloins.' But I don't see how these could be called ruins. This is magnificent. A poor play on words, if you ask me."

"I agree."

Mallory could not see an immediate reason why the castle was built or think of a rational process to explain how it was built. Already forgotten was his brief seasickness and replaced with insatiable curiosity.

Just then, the captain barked the order to disembark from his bullhorn. There was a high whistle and the bosun emerged on deck with a team of sailors. Mallory could feel the boat begin to slow as the crew prepped the rafts on either side. A crane lifted one of the Dragon's Breaths from the hold and onto one of the larger rafts to be transported ashore.

"I guess we should get our things," Mallory said, but Joaquin was already emerging from below decks laden with their luggage and personal effects. He looked like a camel and plodded the deck like a tortoise. "Joaquim, it appears you've read my mind."

Joaquin furrowed his brow and looked about him. He dropped one of the suitcases on the deck with a dull thud. "Sir, did you just accuse me of witchcraft in front of the men?"

"Uh, yes, sorry, no, a poor choice of words, I suppose," Mallory shuffled uncomfortably as he felt eyes suddenly directed at him. "It's just that you appeared right as we were going to come and get the, uh, luggage."

Belle Isolde smiled weakly and patted her husband's cheek. "What Mallory means to say is that your timing is fortuitous, as always."

"Yes, that's it exactly. Thank you, dear."

"Always glad to be of use removing my husband's foot from his own mouth."

"Yes, it does seem to spend quite a lot of time there," he said sheepishly. "Joaquin, let me help you with that luggage."

Mallory picked up the fallen case and relieved his assistant of several more packages. The bosun waved them towards one of the portside boats. They piled aboard with a number of others, crewmembers and passengers, most of them the engineers and drivers of the tanks that had been brought on board the project— employees of Sudwell Industries. Mallory had to admit to himself that he had not made enough of an effort to get know these men, but he felt he had to be guarded when working with them, not to divulge any personal details about himself to them—just keep topics limited to work and the project. It was a relief that he still had Joaquin and his wife to confide in, but he felt like he was struggling inside an emotional straitjacket. All emotions had to be kept bottled or veiled and out of sight. It wasn't something that came natural to the inventor.

"Sir, how long do you think before we get to see some action, do ya think?" one of the drivers asked as he hopped down to join them in the boat—Wittman, the inventor believed his name was. The young man made even Joaquin seem old by comparison with wide red cheeks and a short bulbous nose. "I want to job right in and fry some Orloinian bacon."

Mallory forced a smile. "All in good time, son. Just don't forget that our job is to end this war, not just to kill Orloinians."

"Yeah, but we're going to end this war by killing as many of these turd haulers as we can until they figure out they aren't going to win," Wittman said. "I say let's get to it."

Mallory bit his tongue. "I appreciate your enthusiasm, Mr. Wittman."

"You don't seem all that excited yourself, Mr. Mallory," one of the engineers said.

Mallory said nothing. He just kept his eyes fixed on Belle Isolde, who placed her hand in his. It felt icy cold and they hadn't realized in spite of how warm it had been on dry land, on the wind stung with a bitter chill. He rubbed her hand vigorously to warm it up and then did the same for her other one. His wife smiled gratefully.

"Oh, I get it," Wittman said with a knowing smile. "He wants to get back home so he can start on building a family with his beautiful wife. Well, don't you worry, Mr. Mallory. We'll end this war quick and you and the missus will be banging out little Mallories in no time."

Mallory felt Belle Isolde tense at the salacious talk, but she simply smiled at Wittman. "While I appreciate the sentiment, Mr. Wittman, what I my husband and I 'bang out,' as you so delicately put it, is not a matter of public discussion. And if you plan to ever have children of your own someday, best not to use such coarse language in the presence of ladies."

The school teacher in his wife's voice took the wind out of Wittman's sails. One of the other drivers further rebuked him with an elbow to the ribs. After that, it was another awkward fifteen minutes before the boat finally made shore.

On the beach, the commander at Rune was there to greet them. The man had the tawny complexion of an Orloinian and a sharp nose that reminded him of a bird's beak. His head was crowned by a tall black hat that ended in a point. He wore a red tunic with a fur-lined collar and black breeches. Altogether, from his look alone, Mallory would have assumed he was an accountant, not a military commander. He announced himself as John Farless, lord of the Northern demesne, but the inventor really wasn't clear on what that meant—whether it was a military title, a political one or both.

With little further fanfare, Farless led them to Rune. To Mallory's amazement, as they approached the trees and the castle aloft in its branches, we discovered that the "forest" was actually just one tree that had spread itself over hundreds of acres up and down the peninsula. The inventor could hardly guess at how old such a tree must be, but it dropped thousands of aerial prop roots which had matured into massive trunks. The castle spires grew from the parallel branches, straddling two or three of them like large mushrooms, and the snake-like appendages of the tree seemed to sag under the weight of stone and shingle and glass.

"If you don't mind me asking, your honor, when was this castle built?" Mallory asked Farless.

The lord shrugged, as though the answer to the inventor's question was of no interest. "This structure predates any known records. It was probably built by some ancient culture lost to time. Who knows?"

Mallory was taken aback by the cryptic response. "I was thinking you might know, given that you are ruler of this—demesne—is that what you call it? Surely, the mystery of such a structure would be too compelling not to solve."

"Perhaps your culture is too young to have relics such as these, but there are sites such as these and even stranger strewn about Orloins," Farless said. "Besides, the trivia of history is the realm of the scholars such as yourself, I think, not for leaders such as myself. No, my main concerns are keeping the ruins afloat and out of the hands of the Orloinian rabble."

"Perhaps you are right," Mallory said, but cast a sidelong glance at Joaquin and Belle Isolde who were both clenching their teeth as they listened to the conversation. He already made up his mind that he already strongly disliked this lord for both his arrogance and profound lack of curiosity. He may be an Orloinian by birth, but Mallory had seen a similar sort in Fioria during his brief stay in the capitol. These men were hungry ghosts, always wanting the next thing, not the last thing nor honoring those who laid the ground on which they stood. The inventor would have puzzled over how such men rise to power in the first place had he not been surrounded by the marvels of Rune.

As they passed by the outer trunks, Mallory got a good look at the underside of the castle spires. To his amazement they were made of metal, curved girders that reminded him of the rib cage of some goliath beast. Certainly the ability to cast such materials and raise them to the limbs of the trees was almost beyond the reach of Fiorian technology and certainly out of the reach of what he'd always been told about the Orloinian technology. Near the bottom edges of the spires, there were downspouts, no doubt to carry water from the roof but also could have been used as an effective defense measure should the castle come under siege from below, hot liquid or acid could have been rained down upon would-be attackers.

Along the northern edge of the tree, two of the castle spires appear to have been shattered at their tops and their wall remnants and the tree branches underneath were pockmarked with impact marks that appear to have been caused by cannon fire. To the south of those wrecked towers, Mallory spotted some cranes. They were actually installing what appeared to be a monorail on the underside of the parallel branches. What astonished him the most was that the single train car already installed on the track actually hung down from the rail instead of resting atop it as the rail line they'd taken to the capitol just a few months earlier. Mallory pointed it out to Joaquin, who nodded thoughtfully.

"I see you're building some infrastructure here," Mallory said to the lord, hoping to at least get some information about the castle from him. "Why are they building a rail up in the air like that? Wouldn't it be cheaper to keep it grounded?"

Farless sniffed but did not stop or turn to acknowledge Mallory's question. "You're full of questions, aren't you, Mr. Mallory? The simple answer is that the castle is up in the air and so having the transportation system directly linked to the castle. It's far more secure that way."

"Secure from what?"

"We haven't seen any for a while, but when Fioria first invaded, Orloinian pirates scourged this shore and attempted to undermine our ability to administer this area. Should they attempt to do so again, they will find it difficult to disrupt our supply lines and communications. Now, please come this way. My men will take care of your cargo and luggage."

Farless led them further into the underbelly of the castle. Gas lamps lit the darkened corners of the immense cavern while open sections were bathed in a soft filtered light that Mallory guessed had been channeled through a system of skylights and mirrors to reflect the light through tubes to the underside. The air was cool and damp with a faint smell of peat and decaying leaves. There was flora and fauna too growing on the thick hide of the tree trunks and in crevices. Mushrooms with an iridescent glow attracted tiny clouds of what appeared to be gnat-like insects which apparently fed on the condensation dripping from the fungus shingles.

At the base of one of the larger trunks a lift large enough to fit a dozen or so people was lowered to the forest floor. They stepped onto the lift platform and Mallory examined the mechanism used to operate it. The operator, a squat man in his late thirties, used a crank to operate the pulley mechanism that raised and lowered the platform. It was an effective enough system, but Mallory could tell it was not original entrance to the castle.

"This really is a magnificent castle, Lord Farless," Belle Isolde said. "I don't believe we have anything like it in Fioria."

"I'm sure of that," Farless said simply.

"Oh," she exclaimed with a smile. "You've been to Fioria then?"

Farless grimaced as though he smelled something foul. "I have not."

Belle Isolde's eyes widened. "Then how—"

Mallory gave her hand a squeeze and shook his head. It appeared that Lord Farless was just not a particularly talkative or friendly host. They passed the rest of the ascent in silence until the lift emerged inside the "basement" of the castle. In fact, it was a grand foyer with a tall ceiling and double staircases leading to an arcade not unlike the Grand Central Terminus back in Fioria—only quieter with far fewer people bustling about.

"If you like, I can escort you to your rooms," Farless said.

"That won't be necessary, Lord Farless," Mallory said. "We have orders to head straight to the front and my men are eager to get in the action. We just need you to help with our cargo transport and point us in the right direction."

Farless' sour look lightened, but only slightly. "The front hasn't been anywhere near here for the past several years, Mr. Mallory. I'm afraid you're several days journey from any sort of significant action, unless you count scraps from bandits and various resistance cells. I believe my last communications on the matter placed the main Fiorian and allied armies heading into the Valley Colors."

"Oh," Mallory said. "How far is that?"

"It would be a week's journey from here."

"Well, that's not too bad," Belle Isolde said.

"Or at least it would be just about a week, if the rail system from here to there were complete. Instead, you are looking at about a month's journey, give or take a week, judging how loaded down with cargo you appear to be."

"Oh," his wife said.

"That's okay, really. Our cargo is actually our transport, if need be. We'd appreciate any information you have on the terrain, if possible," Mallory added.

"I'm sure you would," Farless said blandly. "However, the continent is a much larger place than most Fiorians who visit imagine it to be. You will probably want to use my maps to chart your course and that will take time. Then you will need to add provisions for your journey because you will find that what you brought is inadequate to the task. And then you will probably need a guide to help you negotiate the patchwork of minor kingdoms and demesnes that make up the Orloinian political system. You will need to take advantage of my hospitality for all of that."

Mallory was finding it hard to read Farless' expression, whether he was indifferent, annoyed or enraged by their presence in his castle. "Of course, that makes perfect sense. We don't mean to impose, lord, but we are under direct orders from the Chancellor to deliver our equipment to the front. Any help would be appreciated."

"But of course. And any commandment of the supreme leader of our great allies in Fioria will be obeyed. Though my fellow Orloinians may at times give a different impression, we are not all heedless savages. Now, if you will please follow me, the guest rooms are this way. I'm sure the lady would like to freshen up and rest from her long journey."

Bewildered, Malloy, Belle Isolde and Joaquin were led up the large staircase to the second floor and to a series of halls lined with numbered doors which contained a series of private chambers. Farless stopped at three opposing doors—two on the right and one on the left—which had already been opened and waved his hand at each.

"I hope that the accommodations meet with your approval. If they do not, we do not have any other rooms for guests," Farless said.

Joaquin looked beyond the lord at the line of doors that dotted the hallway that seemed to stretch endlessly as far as the eye could see. Then he looked at his two companions and shrugged.

"Thank you," Mallory said, taking a quick peek in each room. "I'm sure they will be fine. I'm not sure why we have three though. Where will my staff be quartered?"

"These three are for you exclusively as dignitaries of the Fiorian Empire. The rest will be housed in servant's quarters below. There are three of you, no?"

"Yes, I see, but we each don't need a room. My wife and I will certainly want to be in the same room. We're married, as you can see," Mallory said, holding up his hand with the ring finger. Belle Isolde held hers up as well so the lord could see.

"Of course," Farless said. "As is the custom in your country, you may share a room. Will your assistant be joining you in the room as well?"

"Uh, no, my assistant Joaquin will be happy to have a room of his own, as will we, thank you," Mallory stuttered, taken aback by the strange turn of the conversation.

"Very well, I'll instruct the maids accordingly. Dinner is at six bells," Farless pointed to a bell pull mechanism on the wall. There was one near each of the doors. "These are tied to a device we call a clock. It is how we keep the time here at the castle."

"Yes, how delightful," Mallory said, hoping to wrap up the conversation with some degree of normalcy. "We also have such modern conveniences in Fioria, but this system is quite clever as well."

"Of course," Farless said and then spun on his heel.

"Could I impose on you for one more favor?"

Farless looked at him blankly.

"Could you make sure that our cargo is not tampered with? We are carrying some very sensitive equipment that could be ruined by the wrong hands."

"My people are discreet, but I will see to it. I will see you again at six bells."

Mallory and Belle Isolde exchanged concerned looks. A few porters passed them in the hall. They carried their luggage into the room and then followed their lord down the hall. When Farless was out of earshot, the inventor, his wife and assistant breathed a sigh of relief.

"What an odd man," Belle Isolde said. "Do you think that all Orloinians are like him?"

"I hope not," Joaquin remarked.

"I don't think so," Mallory said, thinking about the Orloinians he'd watched murdered in the stadium. Their screams echoed in his mind. "People are people. We all have the same needs and desires but we're also informed by our own life experiences unique to each of us."

Belle Isolde found the poster bed and collapsed upon it. "That's wonderful, dear, but that insufferable lord wore me out. I'm much too exhausted for philosophy."

"I agree," Mallory said. "The sea voyage took a lot out of me and Lord Farless did not help. Unfortunately, I tend to be more philosophical the more punch-drunk with fatigue I get."

"When is six bells, do you think? How many bells is it now?" Joaquin asked.

Mallory shrugged. "I would guess six bells is six hours after mid-day, which means we should have about three hours before dinner."

Belle Isolde yawned. "Enough time for me to take a nap, if you don't mind."

"Sounds like a good idea, dear," he said. He looked towards the open door.

"You're not joining me?"

"I'm afraid not. I'm tired, but I'd like to do some exploring first. This place is fascinating, even if its steward is such an odd duck. We may not get another chance to do so," Mallory said. "Care to join me, Joaquin?"

"Of course, master. And, may I add, anyone so strange as Lord Farless must have bats loose in his belfry, literally or figuratively. What do you have in mind?"

"I was thinking we'd snoop about the infrastructure a bit—see what keeps this place afloat. I am curious as to how the ancient people peoples, if Lord Farless is correct, constructed this place and how they keep it stable after all these years. Also, on a more practical note, I'd like to see how viable their monorail system is. Perhaps we can give them some help so we can be on our way."

"Be careful, dear," Belle Isolde called from the bed. "Somehow, I don't think our host would take kindly to you prying into his affairs."

Mallory nodded as he grabbed his kit out of one of the trunks. "If we're caught, we could just say that we are conducting a snap inspection on the Chancellor's behalf—or that we're doing a little fact-finding for

244

Sudwell Industries. Either would do. But we'll try to be discreet anyways, just in case. Have a nice nap, sweetie. We'll be back before you know it. I'll knock three times so you know it's us."

Mallory and Joaquin entered the hallway. The inventor closed the door behind him and made sure it locked. It wasn't difficult for them to find their way back to the main arcade where they entered, but Mallory puzzled at the honeycomb of passageways to decide which way they should go next. But the inventor suspected that interesting parts were well-guarded, and the most interesting parts were hidden in plain sight.

"So, where do we go first, sir?" Joaquin asked.

"It appears this arcade may connect all the spires we could see from the beach. Since we can't go any further down without leaving the castle, why don't we try going up first?" Mallory said.

"But I don't see any stairs going higher than the floor we are on."

"Yes, well, the servants don't appear to have any trouble getting about. I imagine if we follow one of them, we'll come across a lift or some stairs that will grant us access to the loftier reaches of Rune."

A few moments later, they spotted a woman pulling a cart full of laundry. Mallory and Joaquin followed her through a set of swinging doors and into a service area lined with wash basins. The room smelled like the ocean.

"They're pumping in seawater to wash clothes. Note the pipes, Joaquin," Mallory said.

"I hope that's all they use it for," Joaquin said, inspecting the basins with disgust.

"No, I imagine their drinking water comes in through separate plumbing and a different source entirely," the inventor said as he inspected the vaulted ceilings with their intricate yet mysterious carvings with awe. "These Orloinians may be primitive, but I doubt they are foolish. And the ancestors who built this castle were certainly no fools."

The entire room was lit by a combination of light tubes and some lamps that appeared to give of an almost bioluminescent glow, as though they had bottled firebugs in jars. Mallory examined one up close and tapped on the glass. The luminescent liquid inside shimmered as a ripple flowed through the lamp, then it returned to its previously homogenous glow.

"Fascinating. They create light through chemical reaction. It's not bright but oddly soothing," Mallory said.

"Excuse me, sir. This area is off limits to anyone other than personnel," one of the maids who had been pushing a cart through the double doors called. She spoke in broken Fiorian. "May I help you?"

Joaquin stuttered so Mallory cut him off. He fished the company mark that he'd been given when he was hired by Sudwell and showed it to the woman. She stared blankly at the company logo and the inventor guessed she could not read, at least not Fiorian.

"I apologize for our intrusion. We should have announced ourselves. We're inspectors from Fioria reporting back to Chancellor Newbold about operations here at Rune," Mallory said.

"Oh, dear. I see. The lord said there might be officials on that last boat." The maid's eyes grew wide. "Do you need to see my foreman—or Lord Farless? I'm sure one of them could give you a tour of our facilities."

"That won't be necessary. You can just go about your business. We're just here to observe," Mallory lied. He pointed to Joaquin, his mouth still agape. His assistant was clearly undermining the cover story he concocted. "Joaquin, are you taking notes?"

"Uh, yes, sir, of course."

Joaquin quickly fished a notepad and pen from his pockets and began to make scribbling motions on the paper. The maid did not appear to notice that his assistant wasn't good at play acting.

"Well, I'll let you two get back to your business," the maid said, returning to her cart.

"Thank you very much, ma'am. I'll make note of your cooperation in my report, Miss..?"

"Mizouiro," the maid said and gave a quick bow before returning to her work.

"That was good," Joaquin said after he was sure the woman was out of earshot.

"Not as hard as I'd thought," Mallory said, placing the mark back in his pocket. He turned his attention back to the lamps. There were thin pipes that extended out from each along the wall and each eventually ended in a main trunk line that disappeared behind a door right side of the room. "But let's continue to take advantage of our access and learn a bit more, shall we?"

Joaquin pointed to a door to the left. There was a guard posted beside the door, but it did not seem that he had yet noticed them.

"Should we try your trick again and gain access to somewhere really restricted?" Joaquin said, his tone beginning to brim with unjustified hubris and excitement.

The inventor examined the door on the left and then the door on the right. They looked the same in design, but the one on the left bore the scuffs and wear of use. The door on the right, below which the pipe disappeared was painted nearly blend in with the wall. In fact, he would have missed it, partially hidden behind a rack of clothes, had he not been following the trail of the pipes along the wall.

"I think we ought to try a path less traveled, like that door over there," Mallory said.

Joaquin squinted. "That door could be to a supply closet. What would be the point?"

"Because it's not a supply closet. Look more closely. It probably leads to the source of that luminescent fluid that's being pumped into these lamps and I'm very curious to see how that works."

"But what's being guarded would be much more valuable."

"Possibly. Things people value they place under lock and key and maybe place guards on them as well, but things they'd rather keep hidden, they tend to bury in places people are likely to overlook. Come."

Joaquin followed Mallory as he casually approached the door. He occasionally made pointing gestures or tapped on his apprentice's notepad as though he were prompting him to jot something down. Strangely, there was no handle or pull where he would expect one or lock he could pick, and Mallory did not want to draw attention to his ignorance of how the door operated. That would be a clear giveaway that they were counterfeit inspectors.

"I can see why this door is not guarded like the other. Only a staff member who was meant to enter would perceive and know operate the opening mechanism," the inventor said.

"That's a shame," Joaquin said. "Well, it was worth a try. Should we head somewhere else."

Mallory bit his lip. Here was a challenge, perhaps a meaningless one, but he was not going to simply give up.

"Why don't you move that rack over a little and give me some privacy. I might be able to figure this out, given a little time, but I don't want to attract attention to my fidgeting," Mallory said. He traced his finger along the seam of the door. "And keep an eye out in case someone else gets curious about what we're doing."

Joaquin pulled the rack over to obscure his master's lanky frame and stood guard. Mallory's fingers gently pushed against each of the thin wood slats that framed the door. Finally, he felt one give way. He pushed a little harder until his fingers were submerged up to the first knuckle inside the door jam. There was a click and then the door slid aside, revealing a narrow, winding staircase behind.

Mallory poked his head through the portal. The staircase was poorly lit with just a sparse number of the lanterns. The air was also noticeably mustier, as though the area had been sealed for days if not weeks or months.

"Shall we?" Mallory gestured to Joaquin.

His assistant shrugged and followed him up the stairs. The door slid closed behind them. The steps felt slippery and maintaining balance difficult. Mallory felt for a railing as they climbed, but barely felt anything resembling a handhold. Even though they were clearly traveling upwards, the inventor couldn't help feeling that they were descending. It was a curious trick to play on gravity and he found it rather disorienting. Mallory wondered if this was part of the architecture's design, to simply dissuade curious wanderers from penetrating further into the restricted areas of the castle. If so, it was effective, and even Mallory began to question if his insatiable curiosity about this strange place was really worth the effort and risk of getting in trouble. But he marshalled on and after a few more minutes of stumbling up the stone staircase, they arrived at a dead end. The stairs simply ended in a blank, stone-faced wall.

"What in the world?" Joaquin exclaimed.

"Perplexing," Mallory added. "Perhaps they sealed off this area when it became of no use to them or they found they no longer had the expertise to repair the technology held inside. But they are clearly still using something embedded or behind this wall because the pipes lead here. And anyways, why not also brick over the door that led us here and be done with it?"

Mallory felt where the pipe submerged into the stone wall. The pipe was about one fist's width and hummed with the flow of something that felt and sounded like a swarm of bees. What impressed the inventor the most was that the stone was perfectly mated to the pipe; there was no trace of a gap between it and the pipe. It was certainly carved by someone of profound skill. The surrounding stones were not so precisely cut. In the dim light, he could make out grooves between the stones. Each block was about a foot wide and equally as tall. Most were a dusty grey but there were four that seemed a bit brighter and cleaner than the rest.

"I assume someone still needed access to this area. Do you think there is a hidden door in this wall?" Joaquin asked.

"I'm betting on it," Mallory said. He pushed on one of the darker stones. It didn't budge. Then he tried one of the bright stones and felt it yield slightly under pressure. He placed his other hand on another bright stone. The two stones slid backwards an inch and then seized up. He let go and the stones slid back into their original position.

"I think I have it, a secret mechanism similar to the last door."

"How do you know?"

"Clearly the stones are brighter where they've been handled before. The oils in one's hands would retard the growth of fragile microbes that would otherwise discolor the stone. Can you push on those two stones to the left while I push on these other two?"

"Of course," Joaquin said. "What do you think we'll find behind this wall, if anything?"

"I would expect the machine that is generating the power for all those lamps," Mallory said and then smiled. "Or another false wall."

They both pushed on their respective stones. This time they recessed several inches further. Something mechanical deep within the wall sounded, like metal grating on metal. Then the stones parted, revealing a cavernous room with stone floor and a massive crystal dome. The room was brimming with light, so much that they had to squint to make out shapes until their eyes adjusted.

When Mallory could finally penetrate the gauzy haze, he was stunned. In the center of the room on an elevated platform, some sort of large bird or wax model of one was perched in a cage. The creature looked shabby, but magnificent at the same time. It was clear that it once been entirely clad in a blue and green feathers that shimmered down its torso and wings because patches of them still remained. But there were also bare patches where the flesh showed through, and fragments of feathers bloodied and tattered clung to its body. Hundreds of its feathers littered the floor about it amidst heaps of putrid dung. Its beak was bright yellow with a red tip on its sharp hook. From its neck protruded a series of braided tubes which connected through some strange apparatus to a pipe strung out on the floor. This was the pipe that had tracked up the stairs. The tubes glowed the same as the lamps downstairs. Joaquin gasped and pointed at the beast with a shaking finger.

"What is it?" he asked. "Is it… alive?"

"Some sort of bird of prey, I supposed, judging by its claws and beak, but I've never seen such an animal in Fioria, have you?"

"No," his assistant said, then gasped again. "Look, it moved!"

The bird's head, which had been tilted to one side, its eyes closed, began to stir. Its eyelids parted just slightly, revealing pale white iris-less eyes. Its beak opened slowly and silently revealing a red forked tongue. The wings quaked and the tips of its remaining feathers flared a bright red before fading to pale orange.

"It's a living creature," Mallory said in shock. "I could never have imagined... and it's apparently the source of power for all those lamps."

"It looks like it's been mistreated or neglected. If no one comes up here to feed or clean it, how is it still alive?"

Mallory frowned and scratched his chin. He looked about for any other entrances or signs that some caretaker had been up to see to the bird's needs, but from best he could tell, they had come through the only access point and there was not a scrap of food stored anywhere. The bird was the room's only resident. "I can't really say. The bird's metabolism is a factor to consider. There are some lizards that can go months without sustenance. I also don't know what that mechanism it's attached to is doing to it either. Other than pumping some sort of luminescent gas that animal apparently produces, it could be pumping nutrients. However, it does not appear to be having a prosperous life, if one could call that living, and on that point I would agree with you, Joaquin."

"The bird does look absolutely miserable. What should we do? Should we report this to Sudwell or the government? I mean, they're pretty much the same thing, right?"

"What to do? My boy, we don't even understand what we are looking at. There may be nothing we can do for this poor beast," Mallory scoffed. "And what would we tell Sudwell or anyone else, for that matter? That one of our distinguished Orloinian allies is torturing birds in his attic for fuel? If our company—and our own government—doesn't care about massacring several dozen people in the name of a weapons test, why would they care about alleged animal abuse?"

Joaquin stared dejectedly at the bird, which was struggling to rustle its feather again or shivering from the cold and loss of insulation. "So we leave and pretend we never saw this?"

Mallory sighed. "No," he said after a pause. He heard the screams of the dying prisoners in his mind again. "We can never unsee what strange things we've seen today. We tell no one for now but we educate ourselves."

"That means more walks and exploring hidden passages?"

"Of course. And some discreet research and questioning of the staff here, I should think. I think we can easily get back in this room when we like or if need be," Mallory said. "Perhaps we should take our odd host up on his offer of hospitality and get to know

our allies and their relationship with Chancellor
Newbold—I mean, Sudwell—better."

Chapter 21

Fall of Year 43 (after the Great Plague)

The old man traveled from village to village, northward through the heat of the day and black of night, not sure where he was going, only answering a call he'd faintly heard one unseasonably chill, windy night. If it had been a voice, it would have been a scream. But only he was attuned to hear it. And yet it was also an odor, he thought to himself, a power scent that reminded him of the honey tuberoses that only bloomed at night. And yet, in the end, it was really just a pull, like gravity, that tugged on every molecule of his body and soul and caused his aged body and tired limbs to continue moving in roughly the same direction, towards its source.

As he traveled north, the landscape changed from short scrub trees and murky bogs to forests and farmlands. The muted grey colors of the south gave way to bright fall leaves. It occurred to the old man that he had never traveled this far in his life and he suddenly regretted being so provincial.

Like he had done many times since the plague struck and his brethren in the Order of the Seraphim had disappeared without hardly a trace, he stayed away from population centers where long-held anger might still foment towards members of the Order, even a fallen one such as himself. Of course, he reminded himself, it was not he who had fallen, but the Order itself, crippled by corruption and fear at a time when the world needed its saving hand. But it hardly mattered anymore, since he was as cut off from the source of magic as any other mage who dared to stay on the continent. The old man felt that he had fallen, along with the rest, and that's all that mattered. His only source of power now was the strange orb taken from a counterfeit mage back at the Ocean's Edge Tavern months ago. It felt unnaturally heavy in his pocket, where it had remained ever since he'd recovered it from the thief. He was sure it had been a mage's burden before he was murdered and now it was his, until perhaps he was murdered for it. It possessed unspeakable evil that could not be destroyed.

The few people he met did not recognize him as a mage, and so he assumed his disguise was good enough to fool the untrained eyes of peasants unused to the exotic mannerisms and accents of the Order members. Besides, most would not have even been alive during the Plague to recall the atrocities of the Order and the utter neglect of those who should have stood up for the people. Most just took pity on him as an old, feeble man, offering him shelter and whatever food they could afford to offer. The old man accepted their hospitality. It was a relief to not have to suffer the angry curses or distrustful stares of those in the south.

When he came to a crossroads one rainy afternoon, he sought shelter in an abandoned village. It appeared to have been vacant for years. The few homes, shacks and barns that still stood bore the marks of a violent end, most of their rooves and walls charred from fire. In the town center, the ruins of a well still stood.

257

Thirsty, the old man found a stray bucket and some rope and fished out enough liquid to drink. The water was acrid with silt but still potable. As he held the bucket to his lips, he realized he wasn't alone.

"You wouldn't hurt an old man, would you?" he called out to the stranger. He purposefully turned his back towards where he sensed movement. He thought it best to play the part of the feeble old man. "I only stopped for a drink of water and I'll be on my way."

The stranger made no reply, but the old man heard a faint rustle of leaves. Whoever it was, he or she was shifting position. The old man placed the bucket on the lip of the well. He sat down on a rock near the well and surveyed the area. His hand passed over the pocket with the orb. Its increasing weight against his chest made him stoop a bit. He felt the call again, pulling him towards a wrecked farm a quarter mile to the north. The old man struggled to his feet and followed the path, now overgrown with weeds. He did not fail to notice a pile of human remains as he circled the well. His muscles tensed but he kept his focus on listening to the call and the soft footfalls of the stranger behind him.

"I mean you no harm," the old man called again.

The stranger replied with silence so he continued to walk. When he reached the house, he looked inside. It was little more than a burnt husk. The ruins of a peasant's cottage, there was nothing left of the family's furnishings or even walls, just the outline—a memory of where a house might have been. The remains of a hearth where mother and father ate with their children whatever meager food they could stir up from the soil.

RIDING A BLACK HORSE

The old man hobbled over to where the southwest corner of the home had been. He bent down and stirred a finger in the ashes. He felt something soft and round underneath the soot and grasped it with his claw-like hand. As the ash fell from the object, the old man recognized the children's toy—a doll. A girl had lived here.

"Mother? Father?" the old man croaked, and he suddenly felt tears well up in his eyes.

Then, the revelation struck him like a blacksmith's hammer to the face. The call that had pulled him across the continent had come from a small child? She had been here sometime in the past. Had she died along with the villagers or simply moved on when the village was destroyed? The old man searched his feelings for some sense of where or who this girl might be, but his thoughts could not seem to pierce the veil surrounding her. He was cut off, as usual.

The old man let the doll drop to the ground and wiped his cheeks dry with his sleeve. It occurred to him that while meditating, he had lost track of his stalker. He looked about but could detect no sign of movement or sound. Perhaps the stranger accepted his story that he was just an infirmed old man who had lost his way and left him for other interests.

Whatever the case, the old man decided he needed rest and time plan his next moves. Storm clouds brewing on the horizon further convinced him that he needed to camp in the village. The nearby barn had enough of the roof intact to provide shelter from the rain and also a brazier to keep him warm.

By nightfall, he had a fire going and a bed made of straw. He found some sour berries and bitter nuts to make a meagre meal from and washed it down with a cup of the silty water from the well. Outside, the storm clouds blackened the sky and the ground shook from the approaching growl of the thunder. The old man huddled by the fire. He knew it would not be long before the storm would be full-throated and raging overhead.

He heard the timbers creak overhead and felt the orb in his pocket grow heavy again. He struggled to his feet to go check on the fire in the brazier when a faint whistle of an arrow passed by his ear. The projectile zoomed into the darkness and buried itself somewhere in the barn wall some meters away. The old man froze. Somehow the stranger—or perhaps another—had snuck into the barn behind him.

"Is that any way to greet a visitor to your community?" the old man called without turning.

In response, another arrow whizzed at him, this time grazing his left cheek as it passed. The old man did not flinch, but let the blood drip slowly down to his chin.

"I take that as your answer, but as there is nowhere else for me to go until this storm passes, I must beg for your courtesy," the old man said. "Perhaps it was rude of me to intrude on your village. I can see that your people have already had serious trouble with intruders before. However, I can only assure you that I pose no threat to you. Attacking me will only invite more misfortune for you and yours."

The old man sat down and closed his eyes. Whatever would happen to him would happen, but he would not be deterred from meditating and listening to the call that had propelled him on his lengthy quest.

"Why did you come here?" called an angry male voice. "Why did you go to that house?"

"House? To which house do you refer? I went to no house. It seems there are very few houses left standing. Do you know what happened here? Where are all the villagers? Killed? Fled? Chased off by plague, perhaps?"

"I ask the questions, old trickster," the voice hissed.

"Very well, you hold the weapon, after all," the old man sighed. He stayed inside his own thoughts and felt the tug of the call once more amidst the din of thunder. "I cannot fully explain why I came here. My home was destroyed too. And now I wander."

"Liar!"

"Why ask questions if you refuse the answers?"

"Why did you go to that house?"

The old man shrugged. "Again, I must ask to which house you refer? I saw very few homes standing and entered no buildings except this one."

"Don't play stupid! You know which house. The one that this barn belongs to."

A flash of lightning crackled through the gaps in the barn planks and the ground quaked from the proximity of the strike. The old man waited until the ear-splitting howl died to a stony roll.

"You knew the girl, didn't you?"

"What girl?" the man snapped back.

"Now who's playing stupid?" he said wryly. "I found a doll in the ashes. It belonged to someone once."

The stranger was silent. The old man felt droplets of rain rapping against his skull, penetrating the thin matt of hair covering his scalp. In spite of this, he remained still, hands folded in meditation. The call was still telling him to go north. What he felt at the house before was just an echo formed in the magestream as the power—possibly the girl—passed through there last. Such echoes were more common before the plague, but still quite rare even then and usually caused by a trained magic user or attuned person suffering a severe emotional trauma.

"The girl was loved while she lived here," the old man called. "She suffered a terrible loss. Maybe she saw her family die. Then she saw her friends and neighbors perish. Maybe she died too in whatever holocaust descended upon this unfortunate village. But maybe she survived. Maybe she's lost and alone and seeking out someone to save her."

"How do you know this, trickster? No one has lived in this village for years."

"You have. How did you know the girl?"

"I don't know any girl, you old fool."

"Forgive me, I assumed we could help each other. If we have no further business to discuss then you are a nuisance to me and I am an intruder on your land. You should probably just kill me. I am defenseless and it would end my misery," the old man said, but when the stranger did not respond with insult or arrow, he continued. "However, I suspect that if you intended to

262

kill me, you are accurate enough with that weapon to have already accomplished that task. I assume you are a hunter?"

After a moment of silence, the stranger replied.

"A shepherd," he said. "I've killed many wolves to protect my flock, but none as old as you."

"Come into the light, shepherd. Only leave behind your anger. We should face each other as reasonable men."

After an interminably long delay, the man shambled into the light of the fire. The old man glanced at the figure, dressed in rags that made his own soiled robes and tunic seem like royal garments by comparison. He lowered his bow, but kept his distance from the old man.

"Please, sit," the old man said, gesturing to a spot near the brazier opposite him.

The stranger complied, squatting down next to the brazier about 10 feet away from the old man. In the light, he could see the man was young but his skin was weathered and filthy. His bare forearms bore several old scars. They appeared to be from defensive wounds. One eye drooped lower than the others and the lid was swollen like he'd been hit just recently.

"Now, tell me, how do you know the girl who lived in the house I visited?"

"I don't. I lived in Muckville most of my life."

"You seem a bit too pale to be from those parts. Why aren't you there now?"

The man gave him a steely eyed glare, but his lip quivered. "I had family there—a sister and a mother, but I fell in with a bad crowd when I was young. I returned to Muckville recently to find them, to ask them to forgive me for abandoning them. They were... gone. They died in a fire two years ago."

"I'm sorry for your loss," the old man said. He heard a whisper and another tug from the call, but he couldn't quite make out what it was telling him. "But what brought you here? Surely, you had other reasons to stay in Muckville? This is an awful long way from that awful place. Why come to an abandoned wreck of a town like this?"

"I-I don't know. I'm not sure. I just thought I felt something... it made me think of this place after I discovered my family was dead."

The old man's eyebrow arched as he surveyed the stranger. "A place you've never been? Did you hear anything you can't quite explain? Feel a sort of tug at your very soul that made you want to come here?"

"I... I suppose so," the man's eyes widened. "I don't know how to explain it."

"Is your name... Taskashi?"

The man placed an anxious hand on his bow and rose to a crouch.

"How do you know that? Are you a wizard?"

The old man smiled weakly. "I was once, a member of the Order, but my brethren—and my power—has long since abandoned me. I am no threat to anyone who poses no threat to me. I only knew your name because I felt something. Call it... an inspired guess."

"You're one of the Order? I thought they were just a myth, an old swamp hag's tale."

"Oh no, we were very real once," the old man said, feeling a weight lifted from his chest. "But it's been a long time since I've admitted to being one in a very long time."

"Where are they now? Where are the rest of your people?"

The old man looked towards the heavens. "They're out there—somewhere—but not in Orloins anymore. A time ago, before the Great Plague, the Order was formed to help the people of this world. But we became too dogmatic and we stopped practicing our faith. We chased power for the sake of power. We never stopped to question whether we had the right to exist. We clutched our power to our bosoms like a jealous lover. And the tighter we clutched at it, the more it slipped through our fingers—until it was too late—and the power was lost. Or so I thought."

Taskashi relaxed. "I met a young woman in the Valley of Colors. She spared my life and told me to do good in my life. I don't know what that means, but I thought I'd figure it out when I found my sister and mum. Is she one of your Order?"

"No, she is not, to my knowledge. More likely, she is an untrained adept. If the Order still existed, we would have tested her potential to use magic," the old man said. "That young woman lived in the house, did she not?"

"Yes, I think so. She never told me the house. Only that she came from this village. How would I know that?"

"An intriguing question, one for which I might have an answer," the old man leaned forward so that his good eye was fixed on Takashi. "But first, tell me about this young woman in the Valley of Colors."

Chapter 22

Fall of Year 43 (after the Great Plague)

When Baudrin returned to the capitol and learned of
the impending siege of Chinan, he insisted in training
Pucelle to use a lance and sword and practiced with her
and Baldric. The maiden was a good student and
learned quickly but was most interested in learning
how to operate the catapults and trebuchet. She was
even allowed access to the court engineers and
questioned them on the specific designs and
capabilities of the devices. The captain marveled as he
watched her mind at work and puzzled at what she was
planning for her first true military command.

It was only a week later that they found themselves
back on the road, this time with a proper army, on their
way to liberate Chinan. Pucelle had her hair cropped
like a boy's and was given proper armor. She didn't
look any more comfortable in the thick plate mail
G'Rich had selected for her than Baudrin was looking
at her. It was made primarily for ceremonial purposes
anyway so Baldric found a small chain mail shirt and
pair of chausses. The new armor still gave her a
mannish figure, but the captain made a conscious effort
to ignore his own discomfort when he was around her.

When they reached Chinan, the Fiorians were well-
prepared. Instead of a small scouting party, spies
tracked their every move and the garrison's second-in-
command stood atop some sort of mobile battlements

to block the Orloinian forces from even reaching the walls of the city. At least this time, G'Rich and Burgundais were not viewing the action from the comfort of their litter. They were further back, occupying their time with logistics of the supply line.

"I have a bad feeling about this," Baudrin said as he sidled up to the maiden mounted on her ebony steed.

Pucelle simply nodded. "I can understand your reservations, captain. There won't be many good feelings until the Fiorians are vanquished and Chinan is liberated from its captors. But that will come soon."

"Have you even been in a city that's come under siege?"

"No, not in that way," Pucelle said.

"It's a long and cruel process," Baudrin said. "My first campaign involved two sieges of castles less fortified than this. The first took nearly a year. We were able to completely cut off the supply routes and seize virtually half their stored foodstuffs. They ran out of food by winter. And still they did not surrender. By spring, they were so weakened by disease and famine that the people looked like walking skeletons. By the time the enemy had given up hope of reprieve and opened their gates to us, nearly half of the peasants trapped within were dead. But the commandant of the castle had fled the night before to the castle downriver that we also laid siege to—unsuccessfully, I might add. To my knowledge, these commanders have never been made to pay for the horrors they put their people through."

"And now you feel we're going to put the people of Chinan through the same trials?"

"You don't?"

Pucelle stroked her horse's mane. "I believe it can be avoided."

"I'm not sure I see how," Baudrin said, surveying the lines of men following them and the even longer lines of soldiers stretched out before them, under the shadow of Chinan's spires. "Unless you've bought into some half-baked scheme cooked up by Burgundais or the wild optimism of our Dauphin."

"Neither," she said. "I've sent a letter to the commander of this fortress that we plan to end this siege quickly and with minimal loss of life if he cooperates."

The captain's eyes widened. "Another letter? That went smashingly the last time. I hope no one I know I was returned in a body bag over it."

Pucelle wagged a scolding finger at him. "You know I don't want to cause harm to Baldric. I like him very much. He volunteered, after all, and I didn't foresee then that the Fiorians would murder a simple messenger."

"That's where experience can be a harsh schoolmistress," the captain said. "And from experience, we can assume that the Fiorians rejected your generous offer?"

"They did."

"Then what is the plan?"

"I've had the blacksmiths work on something," Pucelle said, "but I'll need some volunteers."

"Are these volunteers likely to face certain death for their troubles?"

"Unfortunately, yes."

"But you'll also be using your gifts to bring them back—the way you did Baldric?"

"Yes," Pucelle sighed.

"That didn't sound like a definitive yes."

"I will bring them back—all of them—but they will still be in danger."

"What sort of danger?"

The maiden pointed at the walls of the castle. "We need to get them in there."

"That's the real trick to a siege, isn't it? It's why we build siege towers, dig tunnels and choke supply lines. It's also why it's so time consuming and costly—and too frequently unsuccessful."

"We need to get in quickly though."

"If your plan is to resurrect a few soldiers in front of the Fiorian commander and then expect him to hand over Chinan without a fuss, then let me suggest that the commandant obviously saw or heard about the man he had brutally beaten and killed returned to life and was quite unimpressed. A few more won't make a difference."

"But where and when they resurrect might make the difference."

"Unless you resurrect a whole detachment practically in the commandant's war room while he's meeting with his officers, I don't..." Baudrin noticed a faint smile pass over the maiden's lips and stopped mid-thought. "How are you going to get the bodies in?"

Pucelle pointed towards several trebuchet that were bringing up the rear of the Orloinian forces, just ahead of the supply caravans.

"You're going to fling the men over the walls? That's insanity. Is this what your voices told you to do?"

"Not exactly. I communed with the king a few days ago. He told me only to lay siege to Chinan and that the Fiorians would leave if we made a show of power. I devised the method of showing my powers to the commandant so that he will not fail to see it."

"He'll see something, all right, but it might not be power."

"When the Fiorians used their catapult to launch Baldric at us and I was able to revive him, it gave me an idea. We could do the same to them."

"But wouldn't you need to be near the men—on the other side of those walls—in order to bring them back?"

"I would."

"Then how will you get into the castle?"

"I will surrender myself to the Fiorians. They will take me inside as their prisoner."

"But they could kill as likely as take you prisoner. You can't resurrect yourself, can you?"

Pucelle shook her head. "My plan hinges upon me surviving long enough to bring back our men on the inside so they can capture the castle. But I suspect they will want to keep me, rather kill me."

"Why is that?"

"Curiosity. They will want to know how I bring back the dead. They will not kill me before they learn how I brought Baldric back to life and only when they realize they cannot use my powers to their own foul ends will they finally kill me."

"That's a foolhardy plan."

"I know. But I must go through with it anyways."

"The voice of the king has told you this?"

Pucelle nodded. "He has not misguided me thus far. Can you help me make this plan work?"

The captain took another long look at the Orloinian and Fiorian forces that were gathering on both sides with the battlements between them. He felt his stomach churn. "As they say, the demons live inside the details, but also the gods as well."

Baudrin spotted Baldric talking alongside two foot soldiers on the line and called him over.

"Did you know that there's a supply carriage just for ale?" Baldric said.

"There's what—never mind that. We have a bigger problem on our hands," Baudrin said. "Pucelle believes we can end this siege quickly if we get some men inside the castle by any means necessary."

"I would agree, sir," Baldric said. "How would we do that?"

"You see the trebuchet?"

"I do."

"Care for another ride?"

Baldric looked downcast. "To be honest, sir, I am not eager to have my parts rearranged again. And if you'd ask me a month ago, I would say that it would be wrong of you to ask me on a mission that is so clearly a no-return situation. But I've learned to trust

Pucelle with my life—and death. I will certainly volunteer for this mission, if required."

Pucelle's eyes softened as she angled her horse towards his and placed a hand on the young man's shoulder. "You know I wouldn't ask if it weren't vital to the mission. I don't want to see you or any of our soldiers hurt."

"War is war, ma'am," Baldric nodded and glanced nervously back at the Orloinion siege engines. "Would I be alive or dead when they fling me over the wall?"

"I want to keep you alive throughout, if possible," Pucelle said. "I don't want anyone to die for me. I would lay down my own life first. I had the blacksmiths create a contraption—a cage—and the trebuchet will toss several of these over the walls. On the other side, I will return you to your living state and you will be able to burst from the cages and take the Fiorians by surprise."

"Well, Baldric, you're handling your imminent death a lot better than I thought but perhaps you needn't worry. The problem we have is getting Pucelle inside the walls alive so she can be near enough to resurrect the infiltration team," Baudrin said. "Certainly, launching Pucelle across the wall with troops is out of the question. I don't like the idea of you surrendering yourself to the Fiorians. We need her alive so that our men will have a shot of surviving the siege."

"How else do you suggest I get in? We could make it look like a frontal assault instead of an outright surrender if you're worried about fooling the Fiorians into letting me into the castle alive."

273

"And risk getting you killed by a bowman or shot down by a cannonball. No, thank you."

Baldric cleared his throat. "Excuse me, sir, but I may have some information regarding your plans."

"What is it, Baldric?" Baudrin asked.

"Well, sir, I was mucking about with some of the soldiers of the line and some of them used to live in this demesne before it fell into Fiorian hands. They were farmers and laborers back then."

"Do they have any information that could help?" the maiden asked.

Baldric scratched his head. "We just need to get Pucelle into the castle, right? No others?"

"Maybe a few others. I'd like to be with her to protect her, of course," Baudrin said. "You have an idea though. Out with it then."

Baldric pointed to the southwest corner of the castle wall. "The best way into any walled city is the same way the rats get in—through the sewers. It's also the way a few of them escaped when the Fiorans first laid siege to Chinan several years ago."

"And these men told you where the sewer entrance is hidden?"

Baldric nodded. Baudrin snapped his fingers. "Then let's go talk to these fine companions of yours. I've got an idea."

If Pucelle looked or felt awkward in the plate armor, the hooded peasant cloak and skirt that she wore over the chain mail did little to make her appear as relaxed as she should. But it would be enough to fool a summary inspection should they be caught on the road. But Baudrin did not plan on them getting caught. He also dressed himself in rough peasant garb as the pike man Baldric introduced him to—a former butcher named Niku—led them on a circuitous route through the forests surrounding Chinan's outskirts to the banks of the river nearly a half mile east of the castle. From there, they walked along the banks of the river unimpeded until they could see the less defended side of the castle walls where the river itself provided a natural defense.

Niku, a short man with stubby legs and a protruding belly that strained the limits of his thick leather armor, pointed to a small portal several feet above the surface of the river. Fortunately, the dry season meant that there was very little effuse through the gated storm sewer outlet, just a slight drizzle at the moment, but even a light rain could change that, the captain knew, since many a fortification would retain some of its collected rainwaters in tanks and expel it only when an unexpected downpour would threaten flooding.

"We'll need some cover to get us across," Baudrin told Niku. "Even with their lookouts occupied with our forces to the south, I think even a couple of would-be peasants would look suspicious if they were caught taking a swim in the river this close to the castle."

"Aye," Niku said. "When my mates and I escaped here years ago, we used the bark of the shag tree as cover. My brother and I made canoes of it when we were little."

The peasant soldier demonstrated by taking a small axe from his belt and hacking at the trunk of one of the trees near the riverbank. In a few minutes, he had peeled a black strip large enough to serve as a tent for all three of them if they needed to camp. Yet it was supple and surprisingly lightweight. Niku tossed the sheet into the water and dove in after it.

"Can you swim, my dear?" Baudrin asked.

"An uncle taught me when I was a child," Pucelle said. "And you?"

Baudrin smiled weakly. "I can dog paddle when my life is under threat. Fortunately, I have not sought many underwater battles."

Niku's head bobbed out of the water and he motioned for them to join them. Baudrin did not fancy dunking himself in the river with his own light armor still under the peasant garments.

"Excuse me," he said and ducked behind a tree to strip off the layers of clothes. As he emerged in his undershirt and pants, he heard a splash. Pucelle was already sliding under the tree bark camouflage, so he joined them, holding his armor and outer clothes above his head. The water was surprisingly chill and murky with sediment. He needn't have worried too much about his lack of swimming prowess since his feet nearly touched the bottom. It was only the other two who struggled to keep their heads above the waves as they drifted with the current towards the castle wall.

When they reached the wall, Niku peered out from under the cover and gave the all-clear sign. He tore a piece from the bark camouflage, rolled it up and stuffed it under his shirt.

"Give me a boost," he said.

The stocky man stepped awkwardly onto Baudrin's shoulders, momentarily pushing the captain's head

underwater as he clumsily tried to gain footing. He felt
the silty brine flood his nostrils and restrained a grunt
as the weight of the soldier forced him to one knee.
The murky water also clouded his vision as he watched
the soldier stretch out against the wall. Niku jerked at
something above his head. The weight on his shoulders
eased up as the soldier himself up into the portal
overhead, allowing him to emerge gasping for air,
thoroughly soaked.

Pucelle smiled a little at the sight of Baudrin. He
was sure he looked like a drowned rat. The maiden
removed a leaf that had adhered itself to his matted,
wet hair. Above them, Niku called out to them and
extended a hand through a gap he had forced under the
iron grate.

"I'll give you a boost next, I suppose," the captain
said.

The maiden nodded. "I'll try not to dunk you," she
said.

Pucelle climbed onto the captain's shoulders as
lightly as a cat. Niku hoisted her up and then the two of
them grabbed each of Baudrin's arms. The captain
pressed his chest as hard as he could against the stone
wall and just barely squeezed under the grate. He
couldn't imagine how Niku had managed to fit his
ample frame through the narrow opening. The tunnel
behind the grate was dark and reeked of rotten eggs.
Each of them crouched on all fours as the rank sewer
water poured past them.

"Well, where to next? I can't see a thing," Baudrin
said.

277

"Hold on, my tinder's wet," Niku said. "The bark should be still dry enough though."

The soldier held out the rolled bark and struck his tinder several times until sparks began to drip onto his makeshift torch. After a few minutes the bark finally lit, and they could see a few feet ahead of them. The tunnel was lined with bricks slick with a kind of slime that Baudrin preferred not to think about.

"That should be enough to get us into the castle," Niku said. "I have to be careful with the fire though. Pockets of nasty gases can snuff the flame and some down here can cause, uh, a bit of an explosion. My wife's second cousin met his fate that way years ago."

"Perfect. Lead on then," Baudrin ordered.

"These tunnels lead directly under the courtyard of the castle. One of the outlets was near my shop. We'll have to be quiet as mice once we get that far lest we get caught," Niku said. "The sound carries down here."

"Noted," the captain said.

"If we get caught, these buggers will kill us," the soldier said. Baudrin thought he detected a glint of fear in his eye. "If they kill us, will the girl bring us back? Like she's going to do for the other men?"

"If they kill you, she will bring you back, I'm sure," Baudrin said. "If they kill me, hopefully she'll bring me back as well. But if they kill her, I doubt any of us will be coming back from the grave."

"Ah," Niku said. "Protect the girl at all costs, then. I guess we're expendable then, eh?"

Baudrin shook his head. "I like to think of it as being reusable. But, yes, protecting Pucelle is our top priority. However, getting through these foul tunnels is also high on my list. So, if you will please, lead on."

Niku grunted. "Good point."

The three infiltrators began their long crawl into the interior of the castle wall in silence. It took nearly an hour for them to traverse the web of tunnels. The slope proved difficult to manage with handholds sparse and covered with slick moss and the disgusting slime that oozed into Baudrin's sleeves and under his fingernails. He imagined it would take weeks to feel clean again. After three wrong turns that led to dead ends, they finally caught glimpse of a shaft of natural sunlight piercing the darkness like a purple and blue dagger through a velvet sheet.

"That should lead to the courtyard," Niku whispered as he snuffed his nearly spent torch in the water. It gave a low his as the tunnel grew dark again.

Baudrin turned to Pucelle. "How close do we need to be to the men as they arrive so you can use your gift?"

Pucelle bit her lip. Her eyes drifted to the shaft of light and then closed her eyes. "For now, I believe if I am at least within eyesight of the men, it should work. I don't want to miss any of them."

"Very well," Baudrin cautiously crept towards the light. A shaft led up to a grate, about ten feet above their heads. Their appeared to be a large pipe jutting from the sidewall just underneath the opening. "I don't suppose either of you packed rope?"

"I did," Niku said, unraveling what had once been his belt hidden under his ample gut into a length of rope about nine feet in length. "If you'll give me another boost I can get climb up there and anchor this."

Baudrin still felt the soreness in his back from the last time he allowed the soldier to climb atop his shoulders. "How about you give me the rope and give me a boost this time? I'll need to scout the location above anyways."

"Fair enough," Niku said, handing him the rope and taking up position with his hands cupped like a stirrup. Baudrin climbed aboard and blindly felt the soft bricks for handholds. Methodically, he lifted himself up until he was standing on Niku's shoulders and then stretched out further for the pipe. His hands were able to curl around the pipe and he lifted himself up. The tip of his left shoe caught on a gap in the mortar and he was able to balance some of his weight on it while his other leg dangled lazily in the air. This also allowed him to let go of the pipe with one hand and reach for the grate. He gave it a light shove and felt the metal give with a light grinding noise.

Baudrin strained to get his head as close to the grate as he could peer through to the outside. In one direction, he saw the curved wood of some wagon wheels parked almost atop the grate. In the opposite direction, he saw a pair of legs, possibly a soldier's, walking away from him at several yards. In the other directions, he could only see cobblestone and what he imagined were the brick faces of a wall or building. He nudged the grate again and it lifted just enough so he could slide it aside. The captain grimaced as the metal ground against metal.

When he had forced enough of a gap, he reached his arm through and grasped the lip of the opening. His fingers felt like they had a solid grip on the metal rim of the opening so he let go of the pipe with his other and swung himself so he could get both hands on the rim to lift himself up. As he moved, he forget his tenuous footing against the brick wall. He felt his shoe slip on the wet moss before he could grasp the rim, leaving him dangling by one hand. The loss of lower stability made his body spin out of control. Disoriented, his hand missed the rim. Instinctively, he grasped the first thing it came to regain stability. Instantly, he regretted his actions. As soon as he gripped the partially opened grate, it slid closed—onto the hand grasping the rim. The iron grate clamped down on his fingers like a vice and he felt the bones smash as a searing pain shot up the arm. Baudrin stifled a moan and held onto the grate in spite of the agony it was causing him.

"Are you alright, sir?" Niku asked in a hoarse whisper.

"No… I am very not…" Baudrin muttered through clenched teeth. He hung on for dear life with his good hand, realizing grimly that if he let go now, he'd probably lose some trapped fingers in the process. "I think I broke my hand."

"Hold steady, captain, and try not to kick so much," Pucelle said.

Baudrin felt hands grab his ankles and a warmth crept through his feet and up through his torso. When he looked down, he saw that the maiden had mounted Niku's shoulders and was trying her best to bear his

281

weight. He took advantage of the momentary reprieve to push up on the grate and release his pinned hand. It felt numb now but now seemed twisted and mashed, somehow fused to the metal rim. He grabbed the rim with his good hand, strained to lift himself up and finally fit his head through the opening so that his eyes were at street level. He glanced about nervously, sure that someone should have heard the moving grate or saw his mangled fingers protruding from the sewers. But all attention appeared to be focused on the wall and parade of Orloinian forces lining up on the other side of the river.

Baudrin quickly lifted himself onto the cobblestone pavement, scurried under the nearby wagon for cover and then searched for a place to hitch his rope. Satisfied that the axle of the wagon would suffice, he tied one end and dropped the other end down the hole. A few seconds later, Pucelle's dark red hair appeared. He grabbed her arm with his good hand and pulled her under the wagon with him. A few seconds after that, Niku's ample frame emerged from the opening and the three of them were squeezed tightly under the wagon. Baudrin reeled in the rope and replaced the grate as quietly as he could. The sky was now a deep violet and the sun was tucked snuggly behind the wall and under the blank of trees.

"Well, that was good timing," Baudrin said. "They should be launching soon. Let's hope that Baldric was successful at convincing enough men to sacrifice themselves for life after death."

Pucelle nodded. "Let me see your hand, captain."

Baudrin had tried to ignore the throbbing in his injured hand. The skin at three knuckles had blossomed with red, blue and purple splotches and the pinky was unbendable, twisted at a ninety-degree angle from the rest of the hand.

"That must have hurt tremendously," the maiden sighed.

"It wasn't great, I'll admit," Baudrin winced as he pulled the pinky into line. "It'll have to be set when we get back, but I'll live."

"I could sense your injury earlier but refrained from healing it," Pucelle said. "Let me finish what I started."

"You can do that? What am I saying? Of course, you can."

Without asking permission, she took his hand and immediately sensation returned. He felt the bones and tendons lock into place. When Pucelle let go, he flexed his fingers. There was no pain.

"My thanks, good Pucelle."

"Try not to get injured again until after we've taken Chinan. I need to keep my focus on the task at hand," Pucelle sniffed.

"Of course."

They waited nearly another hour as the sky grew dark and the torches lining the tower became more frequent and visible. It wasn't long after dusk when they heard the first shouts from the Fiorians atop the gates. The Orloinian catapults had moved into position. Baudrin and Niku each gripped the haft of their daggers as they braced for what was to come. Even the captain himself was not entirely sure how this part of the plan would play out.

Then, he heard a faint whistle. There were bright lights that arced overhead. They arched over the wall and landed on the ground just a hundred feet from their hiding place under the wagon. They were flares. They sizzled on the ground before some panicked Fiorian guards scurried over with buckets of water to put them out. The ballistors, officers who operated the catapults, were taking the measure for the next round, which would presumably include men in cages.

"They're coming," Pucelle whispered.

Seconds later, the scream of several dozen men could be heard, and three large enclosed metal cauldrons struck the ground in the courtyard. One struck the cobblestone road and split open like an egg, scattering bodies like shrapnel from a bomb. The other two struck the soft grass and cratered in the dirt.

Pucelle closed her eyes and bowed her head as if in deep prayer. There was no movement from the remains of the projectile, not even a faint moan to suggest any of them survived. Nervously, Baudrin peered at the bodies littering the courtyard, wondering if he should break cover to check on them for signs of life. No, he realized, if the maiden failed to revive them, he would have given away his position for nothing and Pucelle would fall into the hands of the enemy. He glanced at the other two balls, but there was no movement there either and no sound.

Pucelle placed a hand on his arm, but did not break her meditation. "Wait. They're coming."

"Coming, where? When?"

"Now."

With that, he saw an arm flinch and a form rise slowly. About six Orloinians stood awkwardly, shaking their heads. On the other two balls, doors popped open, swords drawn, more Orloinian soldiers began pouring into the courtyard. The guards who had been dousing the flare looked on in shock as the undead soldiers advanced on them. Then one of them screeched and they fled the field. Shortly, three more balls carrying men struck the ground nearly. The siege had begun.

Before the captain could object, Pucelle emerged from under the wagon. She raced across the courtyard towards where the Orloinians were emerging from their metal cocoons, seemingly half dazed.

"Pucelle! Wait! It's not safe!" Baudrin shouted as her form retreated into the darkness. Then he looked at Niku. "Well, what are we waiting for? We need to keep that maiden from getting herself killed."

He and Niku bolted after Pucelle just as another projectile filled with men struck the wagon they'd been hiding under, shattering into splinters. The great iron bounced and rolled another hundred feet until it struck the wall and split in two. Men tumbled out onto the pavement with loud groans and then sprang awkwardly to their feet as if animated puppets. In the crowd, of revived soldiers, Baudrin recognized the face of his assistant.

"Baldric!" the captain exclaimed. His assistant's face looked ashen in the glow of the flares. "You live."

"Again," Baldric coughed, popped a dislocated shoulder back in place and unsheathed the sword at his side. "I think it was easier this time."

"Good, but you won't get a third try at if we don't find the maiden. She's run off and if she gets herself killed, we're all cooked."

Baldric looked up and pointed towards a staircase leading up to the castle's battlements. "Is that her?"

"How in the nine hells—" Baudrin spotted the maiden leading a thin column of Orloinians up the staircase and onto the battlement. The Fiorian archers, which had been lined up along the battlement seemed stunned as they watched the undead bearing down on them. "Let's go."

The captain, Niku and Baldric raced towards the wall, keeping a wary eye to the sky to watch for more soldier-laden projectiles. They were hard to spot against the black and Baudrin caught sight of one as it crossed the plane of the moon. They ducked as the iron passed just over their heads and crashed into the ground with a thunderous quake that nearly tossed Baudrin onto his stomach.

Above him on the battlements, the captain heard screaming. A body came tumbling from the wall, falling across the stairs ahead of them, and then disappeared into the darkness below. Baudrin's feet found the staircase and he kept running. He hoped the maiden could keep out of any further trouble before he could reach her. At his sides, he kept two daggers poised. When they reached the top of the battlement, Orloinians and Fiorians were entangled in combat.

"Do you see her?" Baudrin called to Baldric.

"There, sir," Baldric pointed to a spot in the middle of the battlement just as a flare shot upwards and bathed the scene in light. Pucelle, wielding the bow of a fallen archer like a staff, had broken away from the other Orlonians and was charging across the battlements. The maiden leaped like a gazelle past several stunned Fiorian bowman. One turned to draw a bead on the girl, but Baudrin's hand was quicker. His dagger struck the back of the man's neck and he crumpled like paper.

"Pucelle!" Baudrin wanted to shout to the maiden, but the word stuck in his throat. His fingers twitched frantically against the haft of his remaining dagger. He broke into a run, dodging past skirmishing soldiers as he struggled to close the gap between him and the maiden. Baudrin watched in awe as the maiden zeroed in on one partially armored figure surrounded by three Fiorian guards. They were dropping their bows and their hands went their belts where they had sheathed short swords. But they seemed to freeze as Pucelle closed the distance.

The moment's hesitation was all she needed. Pucelle swung the bow low and swept two of the guards off their feet. She lunged over their prone bodies and the armored man raised his sword to block her blow. With a flick of his wrist, Baudrin sent his last dagger flying. The blade struck the man in the knee and clattered harmlessly to the ground, but it was enough. His sword missed Pucelle's makeshift staff as it dove under his arm, striking him squarely in the chest. The force sent him sprawling and Pucelle pounced, her bow poised just above the man's throat. The man looked up at her in horror.

"Lord Commander, you are the unlawful tenant of Chinan castle. In the name of King Rien, I twice offered you safe passage if you left this place and its people peacefully. I will only make this offer one last time," Pucelle roared with a strength and passion the captain had not thought within her nature. "Will you yield, sir?"

Baudrin finally arrived at Pucelle's side and Baldric came up panting behind him.

"Is that really the lord commander?" Baudrin asked his assistant.

"Yes, that is the animal who had me murdered and chucked in a sack," Baldric snarled.

Wide-eyed, the Fiorian commander tried to stand but Pucelle shoved him violently down with the bow. "Yes, I yield, whatever you desire. Just get the witch away from me," he screamed.

"Then tell your men to stand down," Pucelle said.

The commander tried to rise again and again the maiden shoved him down with her bow.

"Pucelle," Baudrin said. "The man must stand up in order to stand down."

She glanced at Baudrin. Her eyes were hollowed caves and her hair flickered in the wind like flames licking her shoulders. It was a most horrifying and beautiful sight. When she turned back to the commander, her face softened, and she stepped back so he could get to his feet.

"Captains," the commander bellowed. "Order your men to stand down!"

Baudrin turned and waved to the skirmishing Orloinians who slowly began to step away from the enemy combatants.

"Now, order your men to open the gates so that the rest of our forces may enter the castle," Pucelle said.

"This is madness!" the commander spat, but bowed his head in submission.

"This is liberation," the maiden replied. "Captain Baudrin, take him into custody and make sure that he complies with all our demands. See to it that his men are disarmed, and I will ensure they are properly cared for. No one needs to die for good this night."

The next morning, Baudrin awoke after a brief and fitful nap on the battle-scarred courtyard inside the walls of Chinan. The maiden was already awake and probably had been all night, animated by her victory. She was mingling with the soldiers as the Fiorians were lined up at the gate unarmed, except for their commanders who were safely ensconced in the castle dungeon.

Burgundais spotted the captain before he had a chance to duck behind one of the broken projectiles used the night before. The insides of the iron balls were still smeared with blood and smelled of urine. Not surprising, considering the kind of ride they gave their occupants.

"Captain Baudrin, there you are. I was hoping to offer you congratulations on behalf of the Dauphin for this glorious and astonishingly quick victory," Burgundais said. He was dressed in a rather ostentatious dress armor, usually used for arena combat, not warfare.

"My thanks, your honor," Baudrin said, gritting his teeth. "But it was the maiden's work almost entirely. She acquitted herself with the bravery of a man."

"You are too humble, sir," Burgundais said in a lightly mocking tone.

There was a shout amongst the Orloinian soldiers as the gates rose. A Fiorian flutist began a mournful tune and the defeated army began to march out of Chinan. Baudrin noticed that many of the Orloinian soldiers were shouting Pucelle's name from the battlements and more chimed in from the courtyard. The liberated peasants joined them, looking bewildered and relieved at the same time. Some had taken rags and bedsheets and scrawled crudely some drawings upon them. They waved their rags like battle flags.

"What are the men doing?" Burgundais said. "They've drawn the same childish figure on all those banners."

"I don't know, sir," Baudrin lied. He knew what the image was—and puzzled as to what it meant.

"Well, we should go and congratulate the girl as well," Burgundais said. "She shall have her victory lap today and the Dauphin will have his prize tomorrow."

"Hooray for Pucelle, the maiden who destroys death!" a shout came from the crowd and the cheers rose again. Pucelle seemed to take little notice of the celebrating but appeared to be kneeling with some soldiers who still seemed to be injured. "Hooray for the maiden of the phoenix."

The scene was unbelievable but real, Baudrin thought to himself. The maiden led these men to their deaths and now they were worshipping her. After all, was her victory not a miracle of lost magic and ingenuity? She smashed them to pieces and then returned them from the ashes. No, these men weren't simply returned; they were reborn, like the phoenix, and loyal to her now. They were borne by death into a mystery as glorious as it was dangerous.

Chapter 23

Fall of Year 43 (after the Great Plague)

A Fiorian firestick in the wrong hands is a dangerous weapon—both to the target and its wielder. Kamatari and Minoru watched as Anville's men learned that lesson the hard way, though none of them was seriously injured during their futile sessions to unlock the secrets of the Fiorian weapons. There wasn't much time to investigate the weapons anyways since their scouts were always skirting enemy troop movements and Anville had decided they had to entirely avoid engaging the enemy until they were at a safe distance from the Fiorian invaders.

"Minnie! Kamatari!" Teuta called. "Give me a hand with these wagons."

"Give me a hand, give me a hand, give me a hand," Kamatari grumbled, pulling a hand shovel from the sling across his back. "That's three hands. Don't these people realize I only have two hands to give?"

"You worry about your hands and I'll worry about my legs. I can't feel them anymore," Minoru whined. "When will they give us some horses to ride?"

"When you learn how to ride them without falling off," Kamatari said, giving his friend a quick shove. "Or nearly trampling our commander in the process."

"I told you that wasn't my fault. He just got spooked by a snake in the road."

"A snake, my ass. It was nothing but a coil of rope. You spooked the horse with your infernal whining."

"Boys, let's hurry it up," Teuta called again.

Rains had recently washed out the roads, covering them in a thick layer of muck, in which the wagon wheels had sunk nearly to the axles. From the nearby field, there was a loud report of a firestick and some shouting. Kamatari wedged his shovel under one real wheel of the wagon and Minoru the other and they strained to leverage the cart as Teuta prodded its horse forward.

"Come on, put your backs into it," she chided them.

Kamatari strained hard against the handle of his shovel with his arms and against the wagon with his back. The wagon rocked back and forth and then finally began to gain some traction. As the slick, soft muck yielded beneath Kamatari's feet, he lost his balance and was forced to sit gingerly on the ground, letting his legs sink into the grey slop.

"Pull yourself up, soldier. We have no time to rest."

Kamatari felt a strong hand grasp his collar and pull him up to his feet. He expected Teuta's scowling face but, instead of reprimanding him, her eyes softened, and she patted him on the shoulder. Minoru scampered after the moving wagon and climbed aboard. It was laden with weapons and its armored sides were tall, but the peasant soldier scrambled up the back and reached an arm out to help his friend board the wagon. Teuta meanwhile mounted her own horse and followed after them.

293

From the hedge row, Captain Anville burst through the vegetation. He was carrying one of the firesticks at arm's length and cursing under his breath. The right side of his face was blacked with soot and there were burn marks on his cloak.

"Blast these infernal firesticks!" he screamed. "They must be possessed by some black magic."

"It backfired on you again?" Teuta asked.

Anville simply growled. He slung the weapon to his own horse's side and mounted it.

"Perhaps you should leave them be until we get them to the Dauphin and some alchemists who may be able to operate them safely, while you still have all of your fingers intact."

The captain looked away. "But there's the rub— getting the blasted things to the Dauphin. If we can't figure them out, the Dauphin's men will simply take the weapons, pat us on the head for our troubles and then send us back out here to be cannon fodder. Or worse yet."

Teuta gave him a concerned look. "What makes you think that, sir?"

"I've been looking at the map your two meat shields brought us again," Anville said.

"The meat shields can hear you, sir," Minoru whined.

Teuta waved off the complaining peasant. "The shape of your frown tells me that you found something new that we missed?"

"Think about it," Anville said. "Fiorians and their allies pouring into the Valley of Colors with nary a word of support let alone reinforcements from the

Dauphin. How are they getting through allied territories so easily?"

Teuta tilted her head and stroked her horse's mane thoughtfully. "You believe one of the lords has turned?"

"You're bloody right I do."

"Careful," Teuta smiled weakly. "Depending upon the lord, such speculation could be considered treasonous. Which one, do you think?"

"None other than out good Lord Gouldish."

"Lord Gouldish?" her eyes widened. "Sure, he's a bit of a piss pot, but why would he want to switch sides? None of his demesne had been threatened directly by the Fiorians—until recently."

"That piss pot as you call him has a leaky brain and a thin skin to match. Everyone knows that he was discontent after he pledged his loyalty to the Dauphin upon King Rien's death. He felt the Dauphin was not attentive to his needs as he watched the lands to the north fall under Fiorian thrall. It would be just like him to put a knife in his future king's back. I should have seen it before. His lands are the only ones which have access to the King's Road and the valley. And it hardly seems coincidence that the damned Fiorians have been one step ahead of us for the past seven months."

"His lands are standing between us and the Dauphin, I might remind you."

"Yes, I know," Captain Anville said, scratching his beard. He turned and whistled. More men emerged from the hedgerow and fell in line behind the horses and carts.

"Then why are we still headed in that direction?"

"It would add weeks to our journey to go round Gouldish's demesne," Anville said. "That would strain our supplies."

"Cookie can handle the supply problem. And what's a few extra weeks if we can avoid walking straight into a trap?"

"Gouldish doesn't know that we know it's a trap."

"What does that matter? If we fall into the trap we knew about in the first place anyways, it just means that we're stupid rather than simply ignorant."

"I'm not stupid or ignorant," Minoru protested from the wagon. "What's the difference?"

"Ignorance is simply not knowing a fact that puts us in danger," Teuta said, shooting Anville an angry glance. "Stupid is knowing about the dangers and getting us all killed anyways."

"That proves we're are both stupid and ignorant, dung breath," Kamatari spat at his friend. "We don't even know what this so-called trap is, only that there is one."

"For once, Kamatari, you're making some sense," Teuta said. "Perhaps our good commander should listen to you."

"Listen to the meat shield?" Anville sneered. "Listen to me. Our numbers have thinned since we were sent out. But I've kept us alive after ambush after ambush and I am certain we won't survive a detour into the Wilds. Those stinking marshes may be in allied territory, but they are as rife with hostile sell swords and bandits as the worst of the Valley. No, we need to go directly to the capitol. It's our only hope."

"It's not much of a hope. Do you even have a plan for when we spring Gouldish's trap on ourselves?"

"Springing the trap is the plan."

"So, the plan is to get us killed?" Kamatari asked.

"The plan is to serve the Dauphin, meat shield, the man appointed by the gods to rule, to sacrifice when necessary as true patriots. We are not a band of sell swords."

"We must be patriots," Kamatari spat back. "We ain't being paid and the Dauphin hasn't seen fit to serve you or any of these sacks here. He just takes you louts for granted."

Anville gripped the reins of his horse tightly in his fist. The vein on his forehead pulsed as he stared down the peasant. Minoru grabbed his friend's shoulder and held him down in the wagon.

"The Dauphin's not the only one who's taking us louts for granted right now," Teuta said.

The remark seemed to catch Anville off guard. "Your meaning?"

"You should know my meaning, without it being spoken."

"You dare second guess and hen peck me like a wife? How like a woman you are," Anville growled, but his insult was met with an icy stare. When it became clear Teuta was not impressed, the captain huffed sheepishly then looked down in disgust. "You're right, of course. I should have consulted you."

"I am your first in command."

"You are my first, charged with advising me on all tactical decisions," Anville said. He sidled his horse closer so he could put his arm on Teuta's shoulder. "And you are more."

Teuta grabbed him by the shoulders and pulled the captain closer, nearly dragging him from his horse. "Don't forget that," she whispered.

"Not in front of the men, Teuta," Anville said, squirming away from her grip.

"I know," she said, releasing him. "So, are we continuing this death march into Gouldish's demesne?"

Anville shook his head. "No, we'll find another way."

"The men will thank you for sparing their lives," Teuta said. "Of course, avoiding Gouldish will tip him off that we know he's turned. If he has turned, he'll be sending his hounds after us."

"We'll need a safe place to lay low for a while."

"Any ideas, captain?"

Anville removed the map from his breast pocket and inspected it. "Muckville. It's a dung heap and a den of scum and villainy, but it's just as troublesome for Gouldish to get at as it is for us. Happy?"

"Delighted," Teuta smiled.

"I'm not," Minoru sulked.

"You never are," Kamatari said. He flipped his friend a piece of jerky. "Have a chew and just stay quiet."

Chapter 24

Fall of Year 43 (after the Great Plague)

The library at Rune featured a wide winding staircase that wrapped around the trunk of one of its massive support trees. As Belle Isolde climbed, each stair presented another nook where books were stashed and chain loops hung from some of the recessed shelves that soared towards the skylights above. When she reached the third landing from the bottom, she stopped. As she traced her fingers across the dusty spine of each tome, she puzzled at the collection's apparent lack of organization. The bibliophilistic chaos wouldn't have bothered her so much if she was casually browsing. But she was on a mission for her husband, to find some very specific books.

"Can I help you find something?" Belle Isolde heard a deep voice echo through the shaft.

She looked around but she could not discover who was speaking. The library was empty and still except for the occasional shadow cast by a passing bird. "Hello?"

"I asked if you needed help, not to exchange pleasantries," the voice called again. "What are you seeking, my child?"

"I—I am," Belle Isolde leaned against the spiral handrail and looked down towards the marble floor below. "I am looking for something, that is."

"Then you'll have to find me first," the voice said. "Behind you, girl."

Belle Isolde turned to face the wall of books, but there was no one behind her. She began to wonder if someone was pulling a prank on her. Mallory had once explained the acoustical properties of some buildings in the capitol—the so-called Whispering Galleries—where a noise one made on one side of a space could be clearly heard on another. Mutter a little something into the gallery wall and it can be heard on the other side of the dome. Belle Isolde scanned the row of books at eye level. The leather-bound volumes formed neat rows before her. Suddenly, she noticed a book disappear into the shelf.

Drawing closer, she stood on tiptoes to examine the gap left by the missing book. Dangling from the shelf above the broken net of a cobweb fluttered outward like some ghostly hand towards her face. It occurred to her that was strange. An errant breeze should blow the cobwebs inward, towards the shelf. It was then that she noticed the eyes ogling her from between the books and behind the shelves.

"Oh!" Belle Isolde gasped, stepping backwards spasmodically on her permanently injured right leg and knocking into the railing as she did.

"Careful, young miss. It's a long way to the floor," the voice said. "A very messy accident to clean."

"I'm sorry. I was startled. I didn't see you just now."

"Generally, I am not seen."

Several more books receded into the bookcase revealing a full face of a man. Belle Isolde nearly gasped again as she recognized the beak-like nose and snarled lip of her host.

"Lord Farless!" she said.

"No, I am not Farless. Name's Vade Mecum, but people call me the Book Gnome. I manage this library."

"You're a gnome?"

"Do I look like a gnome, girl?" Mecum's eyebrow arched angrily. A pair of spectacles which had been balanced on his forehead slid nearly down to his eyes.

"I—I just—" Belle Isolde looked closer, but it seemed to her that the man's face looked identical to Lord Farless. "Why—how did you get back there?"

There was a rustle of paper and then Vade Mecum disappeared behind the row of books. All she could see was a faint light peering from the gaps between the volumes before it winked out. Then she heard a faint whirring and the books at her feet began to stir. Belle Isolde crouched down to find the librarian's face. The man appeared to be suspended in a shaft by chains on a little dumbwaiter. Next to him on another dumbwaiter was a stack of books. A small lamp in which one of the many glowing orbs she'd seen around the castle sat perched on his forehead. His attention was absorbed by one of the books he pulled from the shelf. He was reading and scribbling notes on a sheet of parchment as he went.

"For brevity's sake, let me repeat my previous question: can I help you find something?" the librarian asked without looking up.

"Uh, yes, that would be very nice," Belle Isolde replied hesitantly, unsure if she should trust this odd man. "I'm looking for a book."

"Congratulations. You've found 875,674 of them."

"I'm looking for a particular book."

"About?"

Belle Isolde remembered her cover story, should she be challenged about her intentions for seeking information about what her husband and his assistant discovered in the secret room. "Well, I've come from Fioria with my husband and I've had the opportunity to do some bird watching. You have so many unique specimens that we don't have where I'm from. I was wondering if you had any books on ornithology I could peruse."

"Of course, we do."

The librarian returned the books to the shelf and disappeared again with the mechanical whirr of his dumbwaiter.

"Sir, could you tell me where I could find them? Sir?"

There was a moment of silence before Vade Mecum spoke again. "Follow my voice, girl."

Thanks to the echo, the librarian's voice seemed to come from everywhere and nowhere at once. Belle Isolde pulled some books from the shelf at her feet so that she could peer into the shaft. The books were kept from falling into the shaft by a backstop. Behind the backstop, she could make out the movement of the dumbwaiter chains and a glimpse of the receding light from the librarian's lamp. He was heading up. She replaced the books and scampered up the stairs until she reached the next landing, regretting her choice of fishbone corset and long skirt as part of her day's ensemble.

"Are you still there, girl?"

Belle Isolde pulled a book from the shelf and peered through. She caught site of the man's trousers as he leaned in towards the shelves on the other side. Quickly, and with a bit of embarrassment, she returned the book.

"Two shelves up, young miss," Mecum said. "There are two books on native songbirds, two on the flightless unicrow and a volume on the varied species of sparrows that inhabit the peninsula."

"Thank you, sir," she said.

She found a volume labeled Ornithology of Legends, Lore and Prehistory and flipped through its moldy pages. There were illustrations of many winged creatures, but Belle Isolde had no idea if any of the volumes contained the creature her husband described. Though the spoken Orloinian language often seemed primitive and guttural to Fiorian ears, many of the words written in the book were familiar to Belle Isolde. The grammar and syntax were generally the same though the spelling differed on many words. She could at least make out the chapter headings and captions under the etchings clearly. She sat down on the stairs and, from beneath her lace cuff, she withdrew a folded slip of paper. Unfolded, the paper revealed Mallory's drawing of the beast—a large fiery bird with hooked beak and a forked tongue. She compared the drawing with the etchings on each page until she found some likely suspects. There was a bird called the firebrand stickleback kingfisher, which once inhabited the Muck Marshes. It apparently died off as a species shortly after the swamps were drained to establish Muckville, but it was definitely too small to be the bird Mallory saw. A crowned hawk also had a similar shape and beak, but the coloring seemed wrong. It was a dingy brown and only its beak and tail feathers bore any of the red described in her husband's illustration.

Belle Isolde flipped to a section entitled "Arcane Avians of Magickal Origins." The pages of this part were adorned with far more strange creatures than she had ever seen. Some appeared to be serpents with wings, their long bodies coiled around the margins of the pages. Others were flightless terrors with beaks like axes and poisonous curved knives for claws. One bird was tiny and squat like a bumblebee perched on the edge of flower petal as its thin translucent wings stretched out and its pointed nozzle of a beak buried itself in the cradle of the flower. On the last page, though, Belle Isolde was certain she had found her candidate.

With piercing eyes, the last bird soared high above the text with outstretched wings, trailing fire and feather in its wake. Unlike Mallory's sketch of the emaciated, half-dead carcass of an animal, in its full glory the bird sported a full plume of feathers on its head, which perched gracefully on a long ruby neck. At the bottom of the page, the illustrator of the text had drawn what appeared to be a pile of dirt or ashes. Tiny black flecks dotted the page all around the margins. As she read, she became more certain:

RIDING A BLACK HORSE

Phoenix, from antiquity, a fabulous bird associated
with the worship of the sun god. The phoenix was said
to be larger than a bullhead eagle, with brilliant scarlet
and gold plumage and a melodious cry. Only two
phoenices has ever existed at any one time, and it was
very long-lived—no ancient authority gave it a life
span of less than 500 years. As its end approached, the
phoenix fashioned a nest of aromatic boughs and
spices, set it on fire, and was consumed in the flames.
From the pyre miraculously sprang a new phoenix,
which, after embalming its father's ashes in an
indestructible egg, flew with the ashes to Heliotropia,
the mythical City of the Sun, said to exist in a floating
island in the heavens. There it deposited them on the
altar in the temple of the god of the sun. A variant of
the story made the dying phoenix fly to Heliotropia
and immolate itself in the altar fire, from which the
young phoenix then rose. Its blood is said to have had
magickal properties, and was reportedly used by the
Order of the Seraphim as a power source, along with
unhatched eggs, but no confirmation of this exists.
Though associated with the sun, many claim this
fabled bird only hunts at night. Scholars have
disagreed on this point, many pointing to the apparent
contradictions between its supposed nocturnal habits
and connection to a place of eternal sunshine. No
specimens of this bird have been seen since ---.

The date listed was incomprehensible, but she
assumed that it was a reference to a time before the
plague had reset world calendars.

"Young miss, have you found what you are looking
for?" the librarian called.

Belle Isolde fished a pen and inkpot from her handbag and began down scratching notes below her husband's illustration. "Yes, as a matter of fact, I have," she replied. "Thank you very much."

She finished her notetaking and returned her writing implements to the bag and the piece of paper folded back inside her sleeve. When she reached to place the book back on the shelf, the librarian's eyes greeted her from the other side. They were horribly distorted and insectoid thanks to the pair of thick glasses he was now wearing. It was Belle Isolde could do to keep from gasping at the sight of him again.

"You said you were doing some bird watching?" he asked.

"Yes."

"Recently?"

"Of course," Belle Isolde said. "My husband and I just arrived on the continent a few days ago."

"Then you should note that book is about extinct birds and arcane legends. You're about as likely to find a living bird in it as a real book gnome in this library," Mecum said, his voice rising to something that almost sounded like a dry laugh. He shoved several volumes forward on the shelf. "These works are more likely to have what you saw. What, in fact, do you think you saw?"

"I… saw a strange bird, flying over the forest canopy," Belle Isolde said uncertainly. "I just thought since it was flying alone and not part of a flock it must be a rare bird."

"Rare does not mean extinct," the librarian said. "Extinct means there are no living specimens to be seen—in our forest or any other, for that matter."

Belle Isolde blushed and mustered a giggle. "I suppose you're right. It was silly of me, I know."

The librarian grunted. "I thought you Fiorians were better educated than the primitives on the continent. I guess what they say is true," he said.

"And what do they say?"

Mecum's face disappeared momentarily. "Just that for all your technology, your people aren't smarter or better. You Fiorians have just replaced our faith in magic and the gods with the cold religion of science. Without your toys, you'd be just as primitive as we are."

Belle Isolde frowned. The librarian had gone from simply being rude to insulting. "And you determined the veracity of a statement only by my selection of a book?" she said. "We Fiorians practice science because it is founded upon reason and logic. Our minds are disciplined to ferret out flaws in thinking. It is a mistake to judge an entire group of people based on the actions of one member. The would over-generalizing. And it is also over-generalizing to judge that one member by one observed mistake she may or may not have made."

"A fair point, I suppose."

She held out the book, not satisfied that she had made her point in exonerating her intelligence. "And, as a matter of fact, there was a good reason I selected this book. I wished to be thorough in my investigation."

Mecum grunted again. Belle Isolde supposed that was the closest she would get to an apology. "You seem to believe you've found something, at least, since I saw you scribbling something just now," he said. "What bird do you think you witnessed?"

The librarian pointed a bony finger at the book she was holding. He still looked so much like Lord Farless that it seemed to her that she was being interrogated by the man himself. Without hesitation, lest she arouse his suspicion, Belle Isolde opened the book to the back pages and held it up to him.

"A red-tailed nightwing? Legend has it those appear to those who are close to death. The last recorded sighting was by a plague victim," Mecum said. "Are you feeling unwell, young miss?"

"But the story of the bird being a harbinger of death is a legend, as you say," Belle Isolde replied. "That does not preclude the existence of the living creature at the center of that myth."

"It does not confirm it either, but I'll concede your point. There is a kernel of truth in every great myth," he said. Mecum pushed three of the bird books towards her with the tip of his finger. "If you wish to be thorough, young miss, you should also examine these. Let me know if you need anything else."

The librarian withdrew into the shaft and Belle Isolde heard the whir of his pulleys as he and his platform disappeared. Though Mecum might be finished with her and his apparent suspicions satisfied, she realized that she might not be finished with him. She decided to press her luck and press him for more information.

"Sir? Mister Mecum?" Belle Isolde called into the bookcase.

"I am here, young miss," he replied. "Just follow the sound of my voice."

She listened carefully to locate how much higher he might have gone. Then she collected the three other volumes from the shelf and raced up three flights of stairs.

"Mr. Mecum, may I ask you a few more questions?"

"You appear to be in the process of asking anyways."

"I was wondering if you could tell me a little more about another bird I found in the Arcane Avians book. You seem to know something and this text is a little hard to read."

"Very well. Let me see it."

"I—I—uh," Belle Isolde searched the rows of books for movement, a clue as to which ones the librarian's head might be behind. She placed her books down on the stairs and then reached up to remove one of the books from the shelf. As she did so, her knee bumped into several of the volumes tethered by chains to the bookcase. The heavy tomes tumbled over the backstop and swung into the shaft. The librarian gave a cry of pain.

"Young miss!" he shouted. "Will you kindly be careful with my books! They are not toys for your amusement."

"Oh, I'm so sorry, sir," she squealed.

"Pull the books up, please," Mecum growled. "By the chains, if you don't mind. My hands are covered in ink at the moment."

Belle Isolde grabbed the chain of the first book and hoisted it up. When she had returned the last of the fallen books to their shelf, she bent down and parted the books on the bottom one. Mecum's stern face greeted her on the other side. His glasses sat crookedly across his face and the inkpot on a makeshift worktable was overturned and empty. The crotch of his trousers was a puddle of black liquid.

She stifled a giggle and reached into her handbag for a handkerchief. "I really am sorry, Mr. Mecum. I didn't mean for that to happen."

She handed the librarian the handkerchief and he wiped his ink-stained hands on it.

"Well, it doesn't appear that I'll be doing much work until I get a fresh pot of ink—and a fresh pair of trousers," Mecum said gloomily. "Let me see the picture then."

Belle Isolde opened the book to the last page and held it in front of the librarian's face. "It states that it's something called a phoenix."

The dark lines in Mecum's face deepened. "Why do you want to know about that?"

Belle Isolde hesitated before answering. "I just happened upon it in my search for the bird I saw. It just seems so fantastical. Can a creature really transform itself that way?"

"No creature can transform itself from being dead to being alive."

"But you said there is a kernel of truth in every myth," she said. "What is the kernel of truth in this legend, do you think?"

The librarian sighed. "If I had to guess, I would say that it's probably a distorted representation of a real bird better known in the north as a red-winged sea eagle. The bird is known for a peculiar hunting tactic. It deliberately positions itself so that the sun is behind it as it dives for prey," he said, pantomiming with his hand a bird swooping through the air. "The prey that looks up cannot see its killer before it's too late. It was apparently also quite successful in stealing babies from their cradles. Ancient Orloinians likely witnessed this bird descending from the sky with the sun at its back and thought it was on fire, a messenger from the City of the Sun or a child of the Sun God."

Belle Isolde nodded. "And what is this Order of Seraphim?"

"They were—" Mecum's eyelid twitched angrily. "They were a pack of fools who thought they could use parlor tricks to manipulate people and pervert the will of the gods, before the time of the Plague."

"My, they sound awful," Belle Isolde said. "Why have I never heard of them?"

"Because they went into hiding," Mecum said. "They once were the most powerful organization to serve the rightful king of Orloins, but they became corrupted by their power. There are those who believe they were responsible for causing the Plague with dark magic or allowed it to happen or failed to use their magic to stop it."

"People actually believe that magic cause the Great Plague?"

Mecum chuckled. "That's one thing that you Fiorians will never understand or accept."

"What's that?"

"Fiorians only believe in their science and reason, that the universe functions without the aid of gods and that fear of magic was damaging to human life. They reject anything they can't observe or control with their toys."

"That may be true, but science is not a belief system. It's a discipline for understanding how the universe truly works."

"As you say, young miss," Mecum replied. "But Orloinians understand that not everything can be explained or controlled, that faith requires a spiritual apprehension of something greater than self, of even the universe. We believe in these things not because we need proof but because we already know the larger truth behind them."

The librarian gave Belle Isolde a knowing look which made her uncomfortable, so she quickly attempted to deflect. She waved a gloved hand in front of her face as though fanning away a fainting spell. "My, that is far more of an education than I expected when I first came here looking for a bird, Mr. Mecum," she said, selling her innocent charm with a smile. "That red-winged sea eagle you mentioned. Would I find it in this book?"

She held up a volume entitled Illustrated Birds of Prey of the North.

"Of course."

"May I take this with me to show my husband?"

"And this book on the arcane birds too?"

"Yes, but the books must remain on the property," he said, his tone returning to a business-like monotone. "Bring them to me."

Belle Isolde handed him the books and the librarian removed slips of paper from pouches in the backs of each volume.

"Since I don't have ink at the moment to mark these, we'll just say that you may have the books for the duration of your stay at the castle," he said, and handed her back the books. "Leave the other books on the step. I'll take care of them later. You'll return the borrowed books at the desk at the base of the stairs."

"Thank you so much, Mr. Mecum."

"And, young miss, a word of caution."

"Yes?"

"Should you make the remarkable discovery of a living phoenix during your exploits, be careful. They are dangerous birds."

"But you said they weren't—could they hurt me?"

"No, a nonexistent bird cannot hurt you, but the secrets possessed by the myth of one may put you in harm's way. Good day, young miss."

With that, the librarian sped away on his dumbwaiter. Belle Isolde blinked and then thought for a moment about what he could mean. Then, with no answer forthcoming, she clutched the books to her chest and began her descent down the long winding spire.

Chapter 25

Fall of Year 43 (after the Great Plague)

The liberation of Chinan was already a week old, but the city still seemed to be celebrating its newly adopted daughter. As Baudrin approached the maiden's humble quarters in the horse stable nearest the keep, he saw the line of people that stretched out for several city blocks. They'd been standing there for days, each waiting a turn to speak with the Phoenix girl who could destroy death. Nearly all were peasants, most appeared to be afflicted by some ailment or another and quite a few brought with them offerings of chickens, bags of coins, clothes and even a lamb or two. The captain attempted to wade through the crowd, but it was slow going.

Baudrin bumped into an elderly woman, which caused the chicken she clutched to her chest to squawk shrilly and peck at him angrily. The woman gave him a worried look when she noticed the cut of his military uniform.

The captain excused himself. Then, when he realized he couldn't move forward any further through the throng people massed at the stable doors, he turned back to the old woman. "What are you here for, ma'am?"

"My grandson," she said. Beside her a small pale malnourished boy sat. He stared ahead, his pupilless eyes fixed on the sky as his hands worked some small bits of straw into a fine braid. "His parents died in a flood and he was born blind."

"And why did you bring him here?"

The old woman blinked. "Because the maiden can heal him. She can bring back his parents—my son and his wife."

"She can't—" Baudrin stopped himself as he surveyed the crowd of pitiful souls gathered around him. "She can't help everyone today. And I have official business to conduct on behalf of the Dauphin, so I need to see her immediately."

The captain held up the seal of the Dauphin. Several heads turned and though he was sure none of them could recognize an official seal or what it meant, they parted before him and allowed him passage into the stable. Inside, the smell of horse dung and animal odors assaulted his nostrils.

He found Pucelle sitting in one of the unoccupied stalls on a bale of hay. Crouching near her on the ground was a young peasant couple. The man looked old for his age—probably in his mid-thirties. His leather tunic was soiled and patched neatly but obviously with inferior materials and he was missing two fingers of his left hand. His wife looked like a child by comparison, her face framed by a coarse-fabric babushka. In her arms, she cradled a small bundle. Though Baudrin couldn't see what was inside, he could guess, and it made his heart sink.

"Please, can you help us?" the woman pleaded.

Pucelle took the bundle from her and pulled back a bit of the veil to reveal a tiny face with blue lips. The infant looked like a doll with its waxy, frozen skin and sunken eyes.

"How long since she passed?" Pucelle asked.

"Only a few days ago, we swear," the husband said.

Pucelle lightly touched the baby's forehead. As she did so, her eyes flooded with tears.

"There are limits to my power," the maiden said. "I can only those who have very recently passed. I can feel her spirit, but she may be too far gone to retrieve."

The couple exchanged worried looks. "But surely—"

"I will try what I can," Pucelle said. "But I just wanted you to understand it will be difficult and I may not be able to restore your daughter."

The maiden bowed her head and lifted the infant almost to her lips. She whispered almost imperceptibly something Baudrin could not even recognize as a language. Unlike during the battle when she raged, her eyes maintained their normal hue, but the tears began to pour down her cheeks and onto the baby's face. Before long, he noticed liquid streaming down her face was what was changing color this time, from a pale pink to a thick red. Her grip on the infant tightened and her cheeks tensed as her jaw locked as if under some sort of pressure. She was bleeding from the effort to restore the infant's life.

Shocked, Baudrin thought to leap between Pucelle and the couple, wrench the baby from her arms and stop whatever damage she was causing herself. But inexplicably he could not force his limbs to act and simply stood dumbly watching the maiden's lips move soundlessly at a furious pace and the baby lay still in her arms.

Finally, Pucelle gasped and slumped over as though her strings were cut. The child's mother caught the dead infant's body as it fell from the maiden's grasp. Released from his momentary paralysis, Baudrin rushed to Pucelle's side and put a supporting arm around her waist.

"Enough," he said. "I'm sorry for your loss but clearly the maiden cannot help you and it appears her attempt may have caused harmed to herself."

"I'm sorry, sir, we just wanted our daughter back," the husband said. "We didn't know it—"

"I understand," the captain said, not caring about the peasants gathered in the stable. "Now go."

As the man stood and lifted his now weeping wife to her feet, there was a little cough. It came from the bundle. The wife looked down and her expression turned to joy.

"She's alive!" the woman exclaimed. "Look, Samwell, our daughter is breathing."

Pucelle seemed to regain her composure. "Yes, I found her. Your daughter lives again," she said with a sniff. She nudged the captain away so she could sit upright on her own. Baudrin handed her one of his kerchiefs so she could wipe the bloody tears from her face.

"How can we ever repay you?" the man said beaming.

Baudrin glanced at the maiden. She was alert again, but her eyes showed fatigue and her skin was noticeably paler than it had been moments earlier.

"You can repay her by leaving," Baudrin said. He stood and surveyed the crowd around them. "And that goes for the rest of you. The maiden is powerful, but even she has limits and she just reached them today."

"I'm alright," Pucelle breathed and stood unsteadily. "Don't be cruel to them. They just were looking for a little hope."

"Well, I hope that they leave you in peace. It's my job to protect you and safeguard you. And that doesn't just mean from Fiorians," Baudrin said.

The peasants began to file out of the stable slowly. After a few minutes all that were left were the animals and a few hold-outs who seemed reluctant to leave.

"You'd best not do that again," the captain said. "What went wrong?"

"Nothing went wrong. I saved the baby, as you saw."

"But you saved all those soldiers and I didn't even notice you shed a droplet of sweat. Now you're bleeding tears?"

"It's not the number of dead I raise anymore, captain. It's the duration the person's spirit has been separate from her body. The longer the deceased has been gone, the greater the effort to return them."

Baudrin pointed at two farmers holding an urn in the corner watching the maiden with pleading stares. "Did you hear what she said? She can only raise the recently dead. What in nine hells do you expect her to do for your dead grandma's ashes?"

The two farmers looked at each other, then dropped their urn in a corner of the stable and sped off. Soon, the building was empty, except for the few animals it housed.

"I think we need to discourage these people from crowding you every waking hour of the day, and I wish you would accept quarters in the keep where it's safer," Baudrin said.

"I am safe here."

"I beg to differ, Pucelle. You didn't look safe raising that infant just now. And you didn't look safe when you stormed off on your own on the battlements," Baudrin said angrily. "Besides, you have important work to do for the Dauphin. You don't have time to fix every peasant's broken toe and raise everyone's dead aunt or cousin."

"You're right, I don't."

"And another thing, Baldric has told me—wait, what did you say?"

"I said that you're right. I don't have time to fix every peasant's broken toe," Pucelle said. "Though it is my obligation ease whatever suffer, we must continue to press forward. The sooner we restore the rightful heir to the Orloinian throne, the sooner we can repel the Fiorians and make this world a better place for all Orloinians—peasants included."

"Well, I'm glad we agree upon that."

Pucelle went to the stall where Rien was munching on an apple and stroked the horse's muzzle. "I'm sure you have the men and equipment well supplied and ready for a push onward to Lutesse."

Baudrin bit his lip. "Well, that's not exactly where we'll be headed, at least not next."

RIDING A BLACK HORSE

"And why not? Chinan is just a stepping stone so that we can strike at Lutesse. Lutesse is the traditional seat of power of the king of Orloins. We need to retake it if the Dauphin is to gain unchallenged leadership of our people."

The maiden's face was furrowed into a deep frown. It was the first time he'd seen her look so grim since her transformation on the battlements a week ago.

"I understand that," Baudrin said, kicking at some straw with his boot. "But there is the matter of the Valley. The Dauphin still has not sent adequate forces to repel the Fiorians there. If we don't go, it may fall completely. There's also rumors that one of the lords there may have turned on the Dauphin, which would explain why the Fiorians so easily slipped by our forces without notice."

"I don't understand," Pucelle said. "Lutesse should be our main goal. Once we get the Dauphin on the throne, even the demesnes that have been collaborating with the Fiorians will be forced to acknowledge him as the true ruler of Orloins and the Valley would be saved."

"Listen, the Dauphin may be eager to let you off the chain and get him to Lutesse and onto the throne, but he doesn't have full control even of his own court. And the Queen Mother has other ideas, so this is coming from her."

"Are you sure?"

"You've got me, of course. Yet I agree with the Queen Mother on this one though. If we lose the Valley, the Fiorians will be on the doorsteps of over half of the loyal demesnes. We could lose this war if that happens. If the Dauphin's forces had you and your powers, though, the Fiorians could easily be repelled."

"But if we attack Lutesse now, we can legitimize the Dauphin's rule and cut off the Fiorian supply routes to the Valley. The enemy would be forced to retreat."

"But not before they lay waste to Valcolors and all the surrounding demesnes. And how do you know that taking Lutesse would cut off their supply lines. We don't even know how they got into the Valley for sure. Is this information coming the voice of our dead king?"

Pucelle smiled weakly. "It is. But I also studied the maps in the Dauphin's war room. Before their latest push into the Valley, the Fiorians stayed roughly north of the demesnes nearest Lutesse."

"You never cease to surprise," Baudrin said. "But voices or no, you can't possibly know whether the Valley can be saved by putting the Dauphin on the throne. And when we started this journey, you promised to help me save the Valley and my keep and honor my dead nephew, not to mention save all the innocent Orloinians living there. They are your people too, after all."

"My people are all the people of Orloins, not just the people of the Valley," Pucelle said sternly. She leaned against Rien and threw her arms childishly around the horse's neck. "But I have made a promise to you and I intend to keep it. How long do you think it would take to liberate the Valley and return north to lay siege to Lutesse?"

Baudrin shook his head. "I can't say, since our intelligence on Fiorian activity in the region is sketchy at best. But I would say we would not be able to return in force until the spring."

The maiden sighed. "And the element of surprise would be lost. We would not be able take Lutesse as we have Chinan."

"Don't be so sure of that, Pucelle. I'm not sure how an enemy commander would be able to prepare for such—an infiltration—as we used here."

"But it won't be long before the enemy realizes that key to the Dauphin's military success is me—and that I can be killed."

"Then we must endeavor to keep you safe, which was my original purpose for coming here," Baudrin said. "That and to retrieve you for our journey back to the Valley."

Pucelle seemed shocked. "We are ready to move?"

Baudrin nodded.

"But are we leaving a garrison here? I would hate to leave all these people exposed to simply be recaptured by the Fiorians."

"We're leaving a skeleton crew behind, to be sure, but this is a fairly secure base for our forces. Only we'll be entrenched if the Fiorians come this way again. The defenders here should be able to hold out for months, if need be."

The maiden blinked, but said nothing.

"Okay, it's risky. Is that what you are wanting me to say? But it gets riskier the longer we delay," Baudrin said. "Riskier for the people of the Valley—and riskier for us if we continue to cross the Queen

Mother, no matter how enthusiastically the Dauphin appears to support you at the moment."

"Fine, but I'm not going without consulting Rien," she said. The maiden's horse snorted. Pucelle found another apple in her satchel and fed it to the steed.

"By Rien, do you mean the horse or the king?"

Pucelle's eyes narrowed. "Does it really matter to you which?"

"I'm hurt, I really am," Baudrin said, arms folded. "I do believe in your power, girl, and I do believe you when you say are communicating with His Majesty beyond the grave. In fact, I think you may be our only hope of winning this war. It's just your tactical experience that could use some polish. And though King Rien was a capable, just ruler, he lost as many battles as he won. I just don't see how death would have improved his skill in that area and I would question his judgment even if her were alive."

"Then I suppose it is good that you never spent much time at court. You might have lost your head for such questioning," Pucelle said, though there was no sign of threat in her voice. The horse spat a bit of apple on the ground and whinnied. "Rien agrees that I should go with you to liberate the Valley. The Dauphin can wait for his throne a few more weeks."

Baudrin blinked. "I have to ask again: Are you saying the horse approves or the king?"

"The horse," Pucelle said with a smile. "Is that what you're wanting me to say?"

"Fair enough," he said. "Let's mount up and find Baldric. He's with the men."

Pucelle attempted to unsteadily mount Rien, but her strength had not fully returned so the captain helped lift her up. Her tiny frame felt light as air and as fragile as a glass doll. It was yet another reminder to him that she was not just a savior or a weapon, but a girl, still yet a child, like his nephew had been. A warmth flooded his chest.

"Before we go, just remember one thing: I may disagree with you at times, but I will stand by you no matter what, my child. I will never abandon you and I will always try to keep you safe," he said.

Pucelle reached down and touched Baudrin's cheek. "I know. And your loyalty and generosity will always be cherished."

Baudrin mounted his horse and they rode out of the stable, where much of the crowd of peasants still lingered for a glimpse of the maiden. When she appeared, there was a collective gasp and the sea of people parted before her. She waved as they trotted by the wretches and offered words of encouragement to each passerby, promising that she would return to aid them soon, but it was easy to see the disappointment in their eyes—and the pity in hers.

Chapter 26

Fall of Year 43 (after the Great Plague)

It was difficult to distinguish Muckville from the swamp that surrounded it. The original castle had been built by the mad Duke Frydae over a thousand years ago and it took nearly 50 years to complete, but it had sunk into the swamp. His grandson, Duke Sondae of the Muck demesne, consulted the best builders in the land, who told him that the land was too unstable to provide a foundation for a castle. Being a stubborn man like his grandfather, he ignored their counsel and built a second larger castle atop the ruins of his ancestor's. That too sank into the swamp. The land was then passed down to a second cousin of Sondae, Duke Moondae. He too consulted builders for a solution. They suggested draining the swamp, but as workers struggled to dry out the briny marshes that permeated the demesne, they encountered large pockets of toxic gases. Many peasants died when the pockets were breached, and they succumbed to the fumes. Desperate for a solution, Moondae begged the Order of the Seraphim for help.

According to the legend of Muckville's founding, a group of Maesters from the Order used their magics to levitate the duke's castle over the swamp. They planted sacred trees to purify the putrid waters and blessed the crops so they would take root. But a blight laid waste to the sacred trees and beyond a few acres immediately surrounding the castle the crops withered and died. Many peasants fled the demesne for greener pastures. Then, exactly one hundred years after Duke Frydae's disastrous castle sank into the swamp, a festival in honor of the duke's memory got out of hand and a fire that began in Duke Moondae's kitchen raged. Before it could be put out, the fire reached the magical core that held the castle aloft, burning it to a cinder. With its magical protection broken, the castle, it is said, collapsed into swamp and sank. All inside, including the duke and his family, were killed.

The dank, miserable city of Muckville grew like mold over the ruins of the destroyed castle by the descendants of those who found themselves unable to leave the toxic grasp of the swamplands. As Kamatari surveyed the sparse and chaotic arrangement of hovels, whorehouses, saloons and flophouses, the smell of rotten eggs assaulted his nostrils.

"What in nine hells is this place?" he asked.

Teuta smirked at him. "I believe you just answered your own question. Welcome to all nine hells—all in one place."

"Are you sure we wouldn't be better off facing the Fiorians?" Minoru said, peering out of the back of the wagon as some swarthy beggars rushed to greet them. "I think they're less scary than these people."

"What's wrong with them?" Kamatari asked. "These street rats look—purple."

"Put your weapons away, soldiers," Teuta said. "These children won't hurt you. It is said their strange coloring is protection from the gods against the foul airs from the swamp."

"More likely they were cursed by the toxins in the waters in these parts," Captain Anville said.

Kamatari grimaced but sheathed his dagger. A small waif scampered towards the back of the wagon and held out her hands as if she expected something to fall into them. Her skin had a purple sheen from the top of her forehead down to the tips of bare feet. Even the whites of her upturned, pleading eyes were an unnatural shade of violet. He could see ribs were the thin, ragged shift did not cover her body. Kamatari reached into his pocket. As he did so, the girl whimpered and backed away.

"No, it's alright," Kamatari growled. "I'm just trying to give you a cracker, you little beast."

He showed the cracker and the girl's purple eyes widened. She held her hands out eagerly. As soon as he dropped the cracker into her palm, the girl jammed it into her mouth and ran off into an alley, out of sight.

"Hold!"

A swarthy man with stringy hair and wearing loose jacket and trousers blocked the street the short column of Anville's soldiers and wagons. The captain dismounted and ordered his men to stand down. He approached the man with hands raised.

"What brings you to our humble town?" the man said, flashy his yellowed teeth. Unlike the others, his skin was only mottled with pink and purple spots. "I hope you don't intend violence upon the people of this community. This is a place of peace and prosperity, not an armed camp or den for mercenaries."

"We mean no harm. We're looking for safe harbor," Anville replied.

"Then you won't mind if we store your weapons for safe keeping while you're here with us?"

Anville said nothing at first, but he glanced warily at Teuta. "I'm afraid that's not up for negotiation. You see, my men need their weapons. They are soldiers in the service of the Dauphin."

A few men watching from the doorways and windows of the derelict buildings guffawed at the mention of the Dauphin's name. One of the haggard prostitutes who had run out to greet the soldiers with the peasants cackled.

"I hope your brought gold and silver with you, honey! We don't take no Dauphin's promissory notes at our place, sweetie," she screeched to a few hearty chuckles from the crowd.

Anville snorted angrily. He removed a small sack from his saddle bags and also his firestick. "In fact, we do have coin, my friends," he said, dumping the contents of the sack onto the ground. Copper, bronze and silver coins clattered on the broken cobblestones. The peasants and the swarthy mayor licked their lips and edged closer, their eyes locked on the scattered money. Then Anville raised the firestick and aimed it at the nearby bell tower.

"What is that?" the mayor asked.

"Our insurance that you will not take advantage of us." Anville pulled the trigger. The gunshot made nearly everyone leap into the air. The bullet struck the bell and made it ring out across the town square.

The mayor seemed to shrink inside his clothes, but then shrugged. "Then why didn't you say so in the first place? Coins, script, it doesn't matter. Keep your weapons if you like. Please enjoy the hospitality of Muckville. Our people are at your service."

"And if there are any Fiorians in your midst, we'd like to know about it now."

"Of course," the mayor made a cursory bow and then with a sweep of his hand scooped up some of the coins within arm's reach. "But if we had any Fiorians amongst us, you'd know already. They are pale, like yourselves."

Captain Anville turned to Teuta. "Take some men and make a sweep of the village. Have the meat shields go with Cookie and requisition us the supplies we need. They should be up for the task."

"You heard the man," Teuta said the column behind her. "Kamatari, take Minnie and find Cookie. He'll know what supplies we need, but he'll need your help to get them in the wagons."

"Wonderful," Kamatari grumbled.

"And another thing," she said, patting the two peasants on the shoulder. "Stay out of trouble. I don't trust these folk."

"But we don't want trouble," Minoru mumbled.

"Speak for yourself," Kamatari said.

Teuta handed him a pouch from her saddle and leaned towards him. "Don't let our captain's brazen display of wealth fool you," she whispered. "That was all the coin we possessed. The rest is in script and promissory notes."

"We won't spend it all in one place," Kamatari said.

He grabbed his friend and they both hopped off their wagon. Kukiyama was waiting for them at the

329

rear of the convoy, arms folded as he surveyed the contents of his jackwagon.

"If you're looking for an afternoon snack, then, please, let me disappoint you," Cookie said, holding up the last few strips of jerky and half empty sack of flour. "I haven't encountered a decent larder to replenish my stocks in weeks."

Kamatari held out some of the script. "We've been drafted to help you resupply."

Cookie grunted and chuckled, which made his belly shake. "We'll be lucky to find more than an emaciated skunk cabbage in this stink hole. Still, beggars can't be choosers."

The chef sat down and scribbled out a list on some parchment and then handed it to Kamatari. He stared at it blankly, then looked back at Cookie.

"I suppose I should have asked if you can read," the chef said. "Well, can you?"

"No."

"And you?" he asked.

Minoru shook his head. Cookie snatched the list back angrily. He ripped the parchment in two and then handed one half back to Kamatari and the other to his friend.

"Find some storekeepers who can and have them give you the items on these lists. Don't worry about haggling. Since we never seem to stick on one place, we'd best move fast. If you split up, you can cover more ground. I'll be here if you need me."

"You're not coming with us?" Minoru asked.

"No, I've got other shit to do," Cookie barked. "Now get going."

RIDING A BLACK HORSE

Kamatari shrugged. Minoru looked up and down the street at the leaning buildings which squatted about them like old men over a privy hole.

"Where do you think the shops are?" Minnie said.

"How in hells should I know. Just pick one side of the street and I'll take the other."

Minoru whimpered a bit, looked both directions and then wiped his nose. Kamatari, quickly losing patience with his companion, spun his friend to the right, where the remains of the old castle still peered above the ground. Then he gave him a firm push and Minoru was off. Kamatari turned left and went towards where the prostitutes had been leering at them from open windows. One of them, with glossy black hair and firm bosoms, smiled and beckoned him towards her door. Kamatari looked back briefly at Teuta then back at the woman in the window. Then, he looked back at Cookie, who made an obscene gesture towards him. A few moments later, he disappeared into one of the side alleys in search of supplies, the thought of the black-haired woman burning up the back of his mind.

In the boggier areas of the town, makeshift wooden walkways had been erected so that pedestrians didn't sink into the muck, drown in the several quicksand pits or even fall into one of the many sinkholes that appeared, sometimes swallowing entire homes in the process. Minoru walked timidly on the rotted planks and surveyed the businesses. As was to be expected, there was little economic activity that didn't involve alcohol or peddled flesh. He headed towards an alley where the faint aroma of cooking food seemed to whisper past the overpowering stench of bog decay and human waste. Smoke was rising from a chimney in a ramshackle house that had a placard that had a word Minoru couldn't understand, but a crude picture of a pig was enough to convince him that it must be a butchery. In a pen out back, he could see the stock, smaller animals than what he was used to back home and bearing splotches of the strange grayish purple hues that marked the people here, but he hoped the markings were only skin deep.

Minoru crept up the wooden steps towards the door. Just as he reached for the knocker, he noticed movement from the window, which had been left half open to let the smells of cooking to vent. He turned towards it just in time for a violet and grey blur crash into his abdomen nearly sending him sprawling on the ground, but the body that had struck him took a tumble onto the wooden plank. It only took a moment to recognize the waif who had followed their wagon. She held a string of sausages in one hand and several large pieces of salted jerky protruded from her puckered lips and bulging cheeks.

"Little girl, what are you doing?" Minoru asked, offering his hand to the child.

The girl looked at him like he was some sort of mythical creature, her eyes a luminous violet in the shadow of the porch. There were shouts from inside the butchery. Without a word, the girl scampered by Minoru and disappeared into the alley.

The door flew open and a large man burst out of the house brandishing a bloody butcher knife. He plowed into Minoru, but unlike his collision with little girl, the purple and gray bear of man knocked him onto his back. The man took little heed of the prostrate peasant.

"Thief!" he bellowed. "I'll cut you from stem unto stern if ever I lay my hands on you, street rat."

"Sir," Minoru said, finding his voice thin as a whisper in the presence of the giant.

The butcher glanced down at Minoru and snarled: "I'll deal with you later."

Then, he thundered down the creaky steps and into the alley in pursuit of the child thief, screaming obscenities as he went. The door to the house was left wide open. Minoru glanced in the direction that the girl had fled, stood up and then peered into the house.

"Hello?" he called. "I'm looking for supplies for my party. Anyone here?"

The interior of the place was dim and the only sound to reply to Minoru's plea was the faint buzzing of flies. He timidly stepped inside and then covered his nose with a rag from his pocket. Minoru had been in chattel houses. The odor inside was far more foul than it had been from the outside. Strips of meat hung haphazardly from hooks and an old dog lay on the floor gnawing lazily on a large bone. The mutt looked like it had melted onto the floor. The animal was little more than saggy mound of flesh held loosely together by its bony frame. Its purple eyes drifted lazily from its meal to Minoru and its jaw went slack. But after surveying the peasant for a moment, the dog found him less appetizing than the bone and returned its attentions to chewing the gristle on the bone.

In the rear of the room, the face of Zojun, the kitchen god, mounted on the wall above a boiling kettle on the stove. It was not unusual to see an effigy of this god hung near food and he knew that Kamatari's wife hung a paper mask of Zojun in her pantry to watch over their sparsely supplied larder. But this mask, in ornate silver, seemed far more sinister than the depictions of the god Minoru had ever seen before. It had fangs dripping with red blood. From its gaping mouth hung the small figurine of a nude woman, her arms stretched out and neck bare to where one tooth bore into it. Minoru cringed at the sight of the effigy.

"Hello?" he called again.

The dog continued to slobber over his bone, having lost interest in the intruder. Minoru stepped lightly but moved forward, drawn towards the boiling pot and the curious god who stood watch over it. There was still a chance he might find some quality pork to buy and the men had gone several weeks without meat in their diet. Cookie would certainly be delighted by the find.

Minoru picked up the ladle and swirled it around the boiling liquid. There was something strangely metallic and murky about the broth and the smell was vaguely like a mixture of beef in a frying pan and a side of fatty pork on the grill, but it was a bit off. He looked about him again guiltily as he felt the rumble of his stomach at the sight of food and decided to sample a bit of the soup. As he lifted the ladle to his lips, he noticed a bubble rise to the surface, so he assumed it was still quite hot. He blew on the broth and caused ripples across the surface of the soup in the ladle, but the bubble didn't pop. In fact, it grew larger and began to spin. To Minoru's horror, he was staring at the glossy orb of a human eyeball.

The peasant shrieked and dropped the ladle into the boiling pot, splashing the burning liquid on his hand. Flailing about in pain, his hand caught the effigy of the god Zojun and knocked it off the wall and onto his head. The mask split in two. At that moment, the butcher returned from the alley and saw Minoru howling next to the pot, holding broken pieces of the effigy.

"Who said you could come in here?" he growled. "What have you done to Zojun?"

"You eat people!" was all Minoru could think to say.

"We kill people who break things that don't belong to them," the butcher said, menacingly brandishing the biggest cleaver the peasant had ever seen. He looked down at the apathetic down and scolded him. "You worthless mutt. Some guard dog you are."

Without waiting to hear the next word out of the butcher's mouth, Minoru dropped the broken god and bolted towards the door. As he passed near the dog, he tripped over its bone, sending it airborne and straight at the butcher's head. The bone struck him in the temple. The dog, seeing his meal take flight, was suddenly roused into action and leapt at the butcher. The mutt struck his master in the stomach and both tumbled to the ground.

Minoru decided that the momentary distraction was enough to allow him to pass by. He decided to exit the way the girl had—through the window. He dove through the opening. Unfortunately, he did not calculate his size difference and briefly found himself stuck. The butcher angrily reached for him just as he squeezed his narrow torso through the opening and flopped onto the porch like a dead fish. But he quickly sprang to his feet and scampered into the alleyway.

He found himself running the same direction as the little girl had, but in his panic, he quickly became disoriented in the maze of rickety walkways. He turned the next corner, hearing the bellows of the butcher behind him. Dirty laundry and refuse bins created an obstacle course that proved too difficult for Minoru to clumsily maneuver through. A few locals looked angrily out from their windows as he spilled garbage onto the walkway or tore down sheets in his frantic flight from the butcher. He was sure the cleaver-wielding cannibal was close behind him even though he could barely make out his angry shouts.

He turned another corner and found himself back in the red-light district of Muckville. A few of the women there looked at him oddly, perhaps because he had an old sheet wrapped around his head and bits of discarded food stuck all over his trousers.

"What in nine hells are you doing, you zwonk?" Minoru head Kamatari yell. "And why are you covered in dirty laundry and filth?"

"Kamatari," Minoru gasped, tugging at the bit of cloth that was persistently falling across his field of vision. "They eat people here!"

"What are you talking about?"

When he finally freed his sight of the sheet about his head, Minoru noticed that Kamatari was standing on the porch of one of the bordellos looking down

336

upon him. A purple woman with badly smudged make-up and a worn sleeveless blouse was caressing the back of his neck.

"I went to get meat in this house—and—and—they are cooking people parts in a pot," Minoru gasped as he tried to catch his breath.

Kamatari grimaced. "Is this some kind of excuse for why you haven't got any supplies. Did you lose the money they gave you?"

"I'm telling you; I went to get meat at this shop and they're serving human flesh in a pot. They're purple people eaters! It's probably why they're skin is so—queer," Minoru said, but then his face grew long as he noticed his shouting was drawing the unwanted attention of bystanders.

"What you calling queer?" one of the prostitutes said. She flashed a him a toothy smile, a neat row of yellowed jade pearls. "I'll have you know that I was in the capital once and I had the gentlemen lined up at my door for a taste of my purple flesh. Said I was exotic."

"A damn sight prettier than your dung colored ass," the prostitute massaging Kamatari said. "Anyways, we got to be this way, stranger, on account of the werewolves."

"Werewolves?" Minoru said bewildered.

"Yeah, the water's fortified or something with this silver liquid. It keeps the wolves at bay, but it makes our skin all purple," she said.

Kamatari rolled his eyes. "There are no such things as werewolves, deary."

"Yeah, and ya know why?" the prostitute with the smeared make-up said. "We got rid of them all. And

337

our town's been keeping 'em away since before the Plague, you're very welcome."

Kamatari craned his neck in disbelief at the woman. "You've seen one?"

"Well, of course not. How old do you think I am?" she scrunched her nose as if he had passed wind in front of her face. "But the magistrate told us the wolves are gone and as long as we bathe in the silver water, they can't never come back."

"That's daft," Kamatari shoved the woman's hands from his neck.

"Kamatari, what are you doing with these women anyways?" Minoru asked him.

Kamatari shrugged. "I needed a bit of comfort. We've been running our tails off since we left home."

"Oh, you didn't spend the money on—"

"And why not?"

"But you have a wife!"

"I'll never see her again," Kamatari said glumly.

"And you didn't spend the money on them, did you?"

"Again, I ask why not? After all, we're about as likely to find quality food here as in an oliphant's dung heap."

"Oy, you shouldn't be one to judge our cuisine, you smelly little man," a prostitute said.

"So you don't really eat human flesh then? You're not really cannibals?" Minoru asked.

The woman turned towards Minoru and flashed one of her friends a knowing smile. "Well, I can't say we never eat people."

"Wait… what?" Kamatari said, turning in time to see the woman who had given him a massage was now holding a long, jagged knife. "Where did you get that?"

"Wouldn't you like to know?" she said, caressing the folds of her skirt. "But it'll cost you extra."

Minoru heard screams behind him. The cleaver-wielding butcher emerged from a screen of blankets strung across the walkway. When the man's eyes fell on him, the peasant shuddered.

"There he is!" the butcher growled. "He tried to steal from me—and he defiled our god Zojun—and ruined my offering to him."

"You did what?" Kamatari said. "Why would you piss all over Zojun?"

Minoru fretted at his friend's insinuation. "I didn't piss on anything. That's the man who was cooking human flesh in a pot. He came at me with that cleaver. I think he wants to chop me up for stew!"

"I'll chop you up alright, thief! But your stringy white meat ain't even good enough to feed the pigs," the butcher said, closing the distance with Minoru.

"Unless I gut him first for ruining Zojun. Damned outsider!" the woman behind Kamatari screeched.

Minoru looked pleadingly at Kamatari, who glanced at the butcher knife-wielding madman and the prostitute looking dagger, then rolled his eyes. "How do you always drag me into these things?"

Kamatari slapped the prostitute's knife arm aside and leaped over the railing, clumsily slipping off the raised pathway and planting one leg in the boggy muck below before regaining his balance and climbing onto

339

the walkway to join Minoru. He grabbed his friend's arm and muttered something unintelligible as they fled towards Cookie's wagon. The bystanders who noticed them jeered and some shouted in sinister tones to "kill the infidels!" and "gizzards for Zojun's broth!" By the time they reached the town square, the two peasants were being chased by a mob of workmen and prostitutes.

"Where's my supplies?" Kukiyama asked when he caught sight of them scurrying past his station. "Don't tell me you're coming to me empty-handed. I'll use your carcasses for meat if you do."

"Get in line, old man!" Kamatari said, thumbing towards the throng of angry villagers following them. "Where's Captain Anville and Teuta?"

"Shit!" Cookie said as a trace of recognition shaded his face with fear. "What in the nine hells have you boys done? They look like they're ready to skin us alive."

"They will!" Minoru said. "I defiled their crazy Zojun with fangs! And they're cannibals. They'll eat us all."

"What? Never mind. Get on!"

Kukiyama leapt to the reins of his wagon with surprising dexterity as Kamatari and Minoru mounted the back of it. With a crack of leather straps, the wagon lurched forward, but the butcher and his mob continued chase through the village square. When they reached the north side of the plaza, Teuta emerged from one of the side alleys with Captain Anville on horseback.

"Cookie, where are you taking our grub wagon?" Anville asked.

The cook nodded towards Minoru and Kamatari. "The meat shields got mistaken for actual meat. And people here apparently worship Zojun the Cannibal God."

"Ah, son of a dung pile, I should have known," Captain Anville cursed. "When will I ever catch a frigging break?"

Teuta put two fingers in her mouth and emitted a shrill whistle—it was the recall sign. Within seconds, Anville's troops emerged from alleys and houses, wherever they had been sent to patrol or seek out wares. In moments, they were filed into a skirmish line, face to face with the mob that was chasing Minoru, now large enough to nearly fill the town square with a sea of purple.

"Where's the mayor?" Anville asked.

"Right here," the mayor of Muckville called, stepping out from one of the cheap saloons out into the open. "Sounds like one of your men went poking where he oughtn't."

Anville gritted his teeth. "Sounds like you had something for him to poke. Care to explain?"

"I don't need to explain our faith to an outsider— always judging and condemning our beliefs," the mayor said, his frown growing sterner and the lines of his creased ashen face growing longer. "Your man corrupted our incorruptible Zojun and put us all in danger of evil consequences."

"Yeah," interjected the butcher. "He broke his visage and took a piss in the sacred stew!"

"I didn't do any pissing," Minoru whimpered, then looked down at his trousers. "At least not in the stew."

"Quiet, Minnie!" Teuta hissed.

"So the lad peeped your heretical pot full people meat in worship of your frigging heretical god. So what?" Anville said.

The mayor's smile revealed a line of jagged teeth, each filed to a point, and flaming red gums but his eyes hardened into cold, polished stones. "A sacrifice is needed to make amends. So you hand over the heretic who defiled our god and we won't tear your people limb from limb."

The captain snorted haughtily. "He may be a meat shield, but he's my meat shield—and I'll be damned if I'll give him up so you can chop him to bits."

At this Minoru fell back behind Kamatari, clutching his friend's hand fervently.

"Besides, I have this, remember?" Anville held up the firestick in plain sight of the mob. "You saw what it did to that bell. Want to see what it'll do to a man's skull?"

"It no longer matters what Fiorian toy can do. Your man must die to keep us safe," the mayor said. "If you try to stop us, we'll kill you all. Zojun must be appeased or the werewolves will return."

"You're off your nut—all of you," Captain Anville growled. "You're paranoid about the damned werewolves. Where have you been while the damned Fiorians have been terrorizing the countryside and slaughtering your fellow Orloinians by the thousands? Where have you been while my men have died trying to keep you people safe."

"The same place you and yours have been for generations," the mayor shot back. "Taking care of ourselves and staying true to Zojun, who gives us strength. We will not kneel before your Dauphin and his witch mother. And we sure as hell won't kneel to the unbelievers who destroy our god—or their boom-boom tubes."

Teuta grabbed Anville's arm and gave him a concerned look. "I don't think it would be wise to get in a brawl with these people. There are too many of them."

Without looking at his lieutenant, he shouted at the mayor. "Very well, we'll leave your stinkhole swamp in peace. But you're not touching any of my men."

The crowd roared in anger. The mayor hopped onto the pedestal of what used to be a fountain so that he could be as elevated to eye level with the captain. "Then I'm afraid you and your men won't be leaving at all."

Anville's jaw stiffened. "You don't threaten me, mayor."

The captain shrugged off Teuta, took aim with the firestick and before the mayor had time to leap down from his perch, a crack shattered the air. The mayor's skull was nearly split in two as the miniball struck him squarely between the eyes. His body dropped to the pavement with a dull thud and the blood gurgled over the cobblestones.

"Anyone else want to threaten me?" Anville screamed.

But none of the people of Muckville were listening. His play to scare off the crowd by its leader had

343

obviously backfired. The butcher bellowed and a roar went up amongst the crowd. The people were rabid with rage and lost all sense of reason. The mob surged forward, brandishing knives, farm implements and sharp tools. Anville's men on horseback readied their bows and looked towards Anville for direction. Teuta drew her sword, while Minoru dove under a basket in the wagon.

Kamatari checked himself for his daggers. Realizing he had forgotten them, he cursed. "Well, this is some pretty shit we're in now, Minnie," he muttered.

The crowd began to gain momentum and speed. Several arrows shot into the mass of purple bodies and several stumbled and fell, but it was obvious that the sea of people would reach them before the bowmen could finish enough off to make a difference. Then as the crowd came within arm's length of Anville's men, a hollow horn sounded in the distance.

As if awoken from a nightmare, the people of Muckville stalled en masse and stared blankly at each other. Then, the horn sounded again, more clearly this time. The crowd turned and parted, seemingly in confusion.

"What in the nine hells is that about?" Anville said, struggling to reload his firestick.

"Look," Teuta said, pointing to one of the main roads leading to some foothills to the west. "Fiorians, and they're headed this way."

"Out of the dung heap and into privy, it seems," Kamatari said glumly.

Chapter 27

Fall of Year 43 (after the Great Plague)

"I should have listened to you," Baudrin said, as he surveyed the devastation at Olivet. "Now all is lost in the valley and the Dauphin is no closer to his seat on the throne."

"No, you were right. I owed you and your nephew after you placed so much faith in me," Pucelle said, her face buried in the ebony mane of her horse Rien. "We needed to at least try for their sakes."

The bodies of the dead were still in piles near the damaged castle walls. Even the ravens had abandoned the rotting carrion and already one could see the discolored, boated flesh begin to show signs of decomposition. The odor was overpowering. Nearby were half-dug pits. It was as though the Fiorians, have claimed their prize, grew bored with it and moved on, leaving their gruesome work only partially finished.

"I suppose there's nothing you can do for these poor wretched souls," Baudrin said.

Pucelle shook her head and wiped the tears from her eyes. "Too far gone."

"Shame," Baudrin could only say. "I suppose this means they must have already moved on to Valcolors. Gods be damned!"

Baldric, who had gone on ahead of them, returned and dismounted. "Perhaps not, sir. Scouts are saying that the main body of the Fiorians encountered a small detachment of Orloinians near here. They appear to have veered off towards the west."

Baudrin's assistant handed him a ragged cloth. On it was emblazoned a red anvil and hammer and above it the Dauphin's crest.

"Anville? What could he be doing roaming about these parts?"

"Someone you know?" Pucelle asked.

"We trained together when I was still a private in the king's army," Baudrin said. "But the last message I received from him was over a year ago. He was supposed to be harassing the Fiorians along the border in the Eastern Demesnes. He must be in deep trouble if he's fled all the way to the valley. I can't even imagine why Lord Ghouldish would have allowed him to stray from his sight."

"Do you think he's alright?" Pucelle said.

"His detachment was a light one, built for speed, hit-and-run operations. I seriously doubt he could fend off a serious Fiorian incursion on his own," Baudrin said gravely. "But he's a scrapper and a stubborn bastard. If there were a way to survive, he would have found it."

"Then maybe we can make something of our detour, after all," Pucelle said. "Perhaps we should pursue the Fiorians. Find out if we provide your Captain Anville some assistance. Baldric, do the scouts have a clear idea of how long ago they went in pursuit of the captain as his brave men?"

"I'm sure I could ask," Baldric said.

346

"Then do so," Baudrin said. "And send a messenger party to Valcolors. I want to be sure our home is not in immediate danger. There's always the chance the Fiorians split their forces in order to sow confusion."

"Will do."

Baldric hopped onto his horse and sped off. Baudrin signaled his men to follow the trail of destruction left behind by the Fiorians, but he kept a few workers behind to finish what the enemy had started. The dead needed buried and the ground consecrated to ease the lost souls' passage to the afterlife. Pucelle knelt beside the fresh graves and performed what had become a common ritual to the commander—speaking to the dead. He could never make out the words in her whispers. They always sounded like a foreign tongue to him. But they felt soothing to him and he was sure that the spirits—if they were capable of listening—would take comfort in them.

After a few hours, the Orloinian forces resumed their march. By nightfall, they climbed the eastern edge of the valley and bunked in the shadow of the great shadows of the draconic trees.

The next morning, after word from Baldric's messengers caught up with them that all was clear at Valcolors, they marched on. The enemy, it seemed, was headed towards the marshes and the only major city—if one could call it that-- in the vicinity was Muckville.

"If they're headed to Muckville, hopefully Anville has the sense to just let them have it," Baudrin said

347

dryly to himself. "There's nothing there worth dying for."

As they traveled, the late fall foliage of the valley gave way to rolling farmlands and then to scrawny groves of skeletal shrubs hunched over swales and murky ponds. The land was flatter here, but paths were narrow and treacherous as they wound through bogs and cauldrons of quicksand that threatened to swallow horse and rider whole. There were, in fact, signs that such a fate befell a few Fiorians who carelessly wandered too far from their corps. But they had been inexplicably abandoned by their brethren to die anonymously in the mire.

"The Fiorians are a strange lot, sir," Baldric said as he passed his commander.

"They are indeed."

By early evening of that day, they could see the dying embers of Muckville against the violet sky. Baudrin signaled for his men to hold up and make camp. His scouts had not reported back yet on whether they had made contact with the enemy, but they had to be close, and he did not relish the idea of entering Muckville in the middle of the night unannounced. He knew little about the people here, but had heard the residents of Muckville were a strange and secretive sort who were as suspicious of strangers as they were dependent upon them for currency.

The last scouts returned sooner than Baudrin had expected. They brought him news he'd been expecting—but dreading. The Fiorians were attacking Muckville. It was going to be too dark to take action against the enemy, so he set up patrols between the camp and Muckville, so that in case the Fiorians caught wind of the Orloinians to their rear they wouldn't attempt a sneak attack. The captain hoped that whoever was fighting the Fiorians, whether it was Anville or the citizens of Muckville, wouldn't be entirely slaughtered by morning, but the night was eerily quiet and he was sure that they were close enough to hear at least the faint rumblings of cannon and the massed screams of the dying and their killers.

He was about to send for Pucelle, but the maiden was standing at his tent flap as soon as the thought crossed his mind. She clutched a coarse wool shawl around her shoulders but was still shivering.

"I feel death in the air," she said.

"Here?"

"No. But nearby."

"Muckville," Baudrin said. "The scouts have located the Fiorians. They appear to be engaged in an attack on the city. We don't how many or who they're fighting, but we'll set up camp until the morning until I have a full report."

"They may not have that time," she said.

"I know," Baudrin said. "But attacking in the dark we could easily lose the enemy in the fog of war and fall prey just like the poor wretches in Muckville."

Pucelle nodded. "I understand, of course."

"But you have an idea of how we can help?" Baudrin asked, smiling wryly as he thought about the assault on Chinan. "I'm afraid we've not brought any of those cages of death we used before and not nearly enough catapults to launch them."

Pucelle cocked her head as if she were listening to a voice over her left shoulder. "We don't need the catapults to save your friend and his people—or the soldiers."

"Then what would we need?"

"Just me."

Baudrin shook his head. "I sense a plan that will place us both in grave danger."

"No, just me."

The captain sat down and looked at his maps. He sighed. "You know we've gone over this before. You can't go gallivanting off on your own without protection. You are the Dauphin's main asset at this point. It's become clear to me that he cannot win this war without you. If you were to be killed or captured, the consequences would be catastrophic. I'm sorry, but I can't risk losing you—even to save a friend."

Pucelle found a seat next to his small desk. "I notice you haven't called me girl in a while."

"No, I don't think you are anymore," Baudrin forced a smile. "You have proven to me you are far wiser, more confident than you appear. Far wiser than any of those fools in the Dauphin's court, to be certain. It was folly of me to be duped by appearances anyways. I can see why the other peasants place such faith in you. Your heart is pure and your thoughts are clear, even when they don't make sense to me."

"Tell me more about your friend."

"He's a loyal king's man, and he's stood true to lord of his demesne for as long as I've known him. Incredibly unlucky though. We were both involved in King Rien's assault on a fortress along the northern

RIDING A BLACK HORSE

coast. At that time, it was the only foothold the
Fiorians had on the continent. We each led a platoon in
a pincer maneuver against their forward fortifications.
Splitting our forces was always risky business but if
we had timed it properly, the Fiorians could not have
held out. My platoon crossed a wooded plain east of
the Fiorians and Anville's party was to cross a river to
the west. Unfortunately, it had rained buckets for
weeks before the operation and reports that the river
was safe to cross proved to be woefully inaccurate.
The river was swollen and flooding. It took hours for
Anville to get his men across. I tried my best to distract
the Fiorians and keep them busy, but by the time he
arrived, all surprise had been lost and my men had
been exhausted. I had to retire from the field, but my
messenger was killed before he could reach him to call
of the attack. He launched and his platoon was nearly
massacred.

However, the lord commander of the offensive
didn't take kindly to Anville's misfortune. He had him
court-martialed for negligence, and though he was
eventually found to not be at fault for our failure to
destroy the Fiorian fortifications, it was several years
before he was able to earn another command of his
own. He's a good man and a loyal friend."

Baudrin looked down at his maps. As he thought of
Anville lying dead on the battlefield or in a ditch just a
few miles away and his own inability to help him,
anger swelled in him. He swatted the papers from his
desk. Pucelle placed a hand on his forearm to stay his
hand.

"It would be a shame to allow such a good friend to throw his life away when we could come to his aid," she said. "And to win this war we will need all the friends we can muster."

"What do you mean?"

"I fight not only to get the Dauphin on the throne. The Dauphin is the means to King Rien's end, but he is not the end itself. The king wants freedom for all his people—freedom from fear, from tyranny, freedom from want. Hope."

Baudrin nodded. "You'll want to keep those ideas to yourself when you are around court. The Dauphin may lose interest if he thinks your orbit doesn't revolve around him, the Queen Mother, who's already threatened you, will take you for a revolutionary, and the rest of the inner circle seem to eschew idealism in favor of cynicism."

"You're right. I should save my idealism for the battlefield," Pucelle stood. "To that point, will you accompany me to Muckville, or should I go alone?"

"After what I just told you, you're still going to defy my orders?" Baudrin growled.

"Yes, but you forget. If I can simply get close enough to the allied forces, I can save each and every one of those men, including your friend," Pucelle said. "And if you're worried about protecting me, I'll take Baldric with me. He's been through the resurrection process before. Or send the entire army. I can keep them safe, no matter what enemy we face."

"You are confident in your gift," Baudrin said. "But it's my experience that too much it can quickly turn into arrogance. The gods have instructed me well the consequences of arrogant behavior."

"You have faith in me. Have a little more in yourself."

Pucelle's words seemed less scolding than gently chiding. Baudrin sighed and stood. "Since your mind will not be turned from this course, I suppose I must find more faith as you suggest. But we will only take a small party—you, Baldric and myself. Stealth will keep us safe and perhaps you can reserve your strength for Anville's men."

"Very well."

"Best get your armor. I won't be putting you in harm's way without at least some protection."

While, Pucelle raced to don her armor, Baudrin summoned Baldric and they headed into the black on horseback, using the moon to guide them into thick of the swamps surrounding Muckville. It was difficult for the horses to maintain their footing on the softened soil. In the boggier areas, quicksand threatened to suck in creatures that slipped into the gullies and ravines. In the dark, the claws of dead branches lashed at their faces and Baudrin took sharp blow to the cheek from a thorny arm of a bramblebush. The captain felt the warm blood drip down his chin but said nothing. They proceeded in silence.

After an hour, they could see fires and hear the shouting of men and screams of women. They came to a short ridge that overlooked a barren expanse adjacent to Muckville. A flash from a cannon muzzle could be seen from the opposite ridge as it fired in the distance.

Baudrin counted three breaths between the flash and the roar of the cannon.

"That must be the Fiorians on that ridge, about half a mile's distance," the captain whispered. "Then our people must be on the plain or in the city. Can you sense anything?"

"I sense death," Pucelle said, her eyes black and empty like pools of oil.

"Yes, I know that, dear," Baudrin snapped. "But I mean something more specific, like where those poor souls might be dying out there, particularly ours."

"I'm not a scout, captain," the maiden said. "And the souls of the dying I sense are not on this physical plain—if you'll forgive the pun."

"If he had a choice, Anville would probably stay close to the city and fight street-by-street, especially if her outnumbered and outgunned. However, if he were to avoid endangering the civilian population or if he had no other choice, he'd take to the plain. But why would they be shooting at each other in the dark? I can't make out but a few torches down there. It must be mass confusion out there, and the plain would be nothing but a killing field if the Fiorians have command of that ridge."

Baldric circled his horse round a large clump of bramble bushes. "Look, sir, I see a mass near the town."

Baudrin came up alongside his assistant and peered into the darkness. A large group of shadows were swarming out from Muckville proper and spilling onto the field. The ghostly bodies were backlit by torches. A few figures appeared to be on horseback, their taller shadows looming over the smaller ones.

"I assume Captain Anville must be among them, sir," Baldric said. "But it looks like a disorganized rabble. Do you think he is leading a revolt from amongst the peasantry?"

"If he's desperate enough," Baudrin said. But something didn't feel right about his friend leading a bunch of untrained commoners into a field of certain death. "But look at how the mass of people staggers and stalls. It's as though they are all drunk—or there's no one in charge at all down there."

"You don't think—maybe Captain Anville is dead. Perhaps his men a fleeing in panic?"

"No."

"Then what— you think they're brawling with the common folk of Muckville?"

Baudrin frowned. That was, in fact, what the inebriated dance of shadows on the ground below suggested to him. But not just a brawl. A pitched battle and neither side seemed to have the upper hand. But clearly if it was Anville's men and the townspeople who were the combatants, they were headed for disaster should the Fiorians and their powerful artillery draw a bead on them out on the open plain, even in the dark.

"Baldric, head back to camp. Rouse the men and carefully bring them the way we came," Baudrin said. "And keep them low. We don't want to rouse Fiorian suspicions that we are here until it is too late."

"Aye, sir."

355

Baldric's horse trotted off into the black. Pucelle, on her black steed, stood on a promontory and the girl appeared to be reaching out toward the plain with her hand.

"Can you do anything from here?" he asked.

Pucelle shook her head. "Just a little closer. I can feel them, but I can't help them from here."

Baudrin sighed. "How much closer?"

The maiden smiled, but her eyes were still unsettlingly dark. "Much closer."

"Then, go, quickly," Baudrin said. "I will follow."

Pucelle spurred her horse and the steed bolted down the side of the ridge and disappeared into the night. The speed at which she moved surprised him, and he immediately knew he could not keep pace with her. He just hoped the maiden would not fall into an enemy trap—or a pit of quicksand. Above him, a bright star flickered momentarily, and he was distracted. He had never noticed that star. A second later, he realized to his horror why it had flickered—mortar shot had been fired from the Fiorian side. There was a brief whistle, not time enough to even dismount. Then a loud crack, and man and horse disappeared in a cloud of smoke. The captain never consciously felt the concussion caused by the exploding mortar. It took several minutes for Baudrin to realize his horse had been knocked out from under him—or he from it—and now he was lying on the ground—blind and dumb.

Pucelle galloped straight for the mass of shadows, sensing the carnage of both warrior and civilian. She could not determine the source of the animosity between the two parties, only that it was primal and fearsome. She heard the voice of King Rien urging her on, a cross between a babbling brook and the roar of a dragon.

As she drew closer she felt the pull of the souls against her own, as if they were fleeing the battlefield as soon as their bodies had expired, and clawing at the maiden's soul as they passed. She forced them back and then soothed them with a prayer like a song. Moments later she encountered her first fallen soldier, draped across a fence line, his neck pierced by one of its posts. She beckoned to it and the body reanimated, gingerly prying itself from the fence post. The blood streamed for just a moment as the arteries mended and the tissue knitted itself back together. The man gasped and opened his eyes for the first time since death. He locked eyes with hers and a look of shock and horror melted into joy.

"Good sir, can you tell me what is happening here?" she asked.

The man placed a hand to his throat, unsure at first if he could speak. "The towns folk. They tried to kill us. Claimed we defiled their cannibal god. Then the Fiorians attacked. From the north ridge. The captain tried to get us out. Head for the south ridge. But we're cut off."

"What do you need to do? What were you trying to do just now?"

"Trying to warn them," the man choked. "The captain was killed. We lost the lieutenant. Needed to warn the others who got turned around in the fight. They're lining up in the plains, I think. I think I saw them as I—I was dead, wasn't I?"

Pucelle nodded. "You are safe now. Go back and find your lieutenant. Keep the townsfolk from attacking us from the rear. Report back to me when you do. I will save your comrades in the plain."

The soldier nodded and attempted to stand.

"Your name, sir?"

"Corporal Fujiki," he looked at the young woman aghast, as if she were on fire. "You're just a girl. I can't thank you enough, but how—"

"My name is Pucelle, and there'll be time enough to explain later, once we are all safe. Now go."

The corporal stumbled into the dark. Pucelle followed the sound of explosions to the east. Between the two ridges, the faint glow of a new morning cast a pale halo over the foggy swamps. But the cannon fire was becoming more intense. She knew she had to act quickly. She spurred her horse on and listened to the whispers guiding her towards the throng of men that were gathering in harm's way. As she drew closer to the Orloinian forces, she remembered the cloth one of the peasants of Chinan had given her, with the symbol of the phoenix emblazoned on it. It's bright white color would be visible even in the dimness of the dawn. She spotted the long handle of a discarded pitchfork or shovel sticking out of the mud, so she stopped and lifted in from the muck. The fork had one bent tine and there were traces of blood on the handle. Pucelle wiped them off, tied the flag as best she could to fashion and makeshift standard and then remounted Rien.

A mortar shell whistled overhead and exploded just over a few dozen yards behind her. The blast was deafening. But Pucelle calmed her mind and focused

on her breathing and continued to let the voices guide.
Step lightly, they seem to say, now charge forth. Rien
seemed to understand the maiden's orders as soon as
she heard them, because the horse suddenly lunged
forward and galloped towards the ragged line of
Orloinions that appeared to materialize from the fog in
front of her.

She found a gap in their lines and urged Rien
ahead, holding her phoenix standard high above her
head. At first, the soldiers did not notice her, but when
she managed to get ahead of them, several looked up in
apparent shock and pointed her out to her comrades.
For a moment, there was a hush on the battlefield. The
men were huddled and filthy from the mud and dust
stirred up by rain of artillery fire. She could tell many
were simple peasants conscripted or hired into the
Dauphin's service. Pucelle surveyed the Fiorian
barricades hastily drawn up on the northern ridge.
Their defenses were formidable, but she could make
the men behind her unstoppable.

"We will win this day. Follow me!" she tried to
shout as she spun her horse round towards the enemy,
but her cry was cut off by another explosion. But it
didn't matter because she seemed to have their
attention. She waved her banner and galloped towards
the teeth of the enemy artillery. The maiden did not
look back. She hoped that the voices were right—the
men were following close behind.

Incoming shells howled overhead seconds before
the ground shook behind her. She could feel the
screams of bodies and souls being torn apart and
reached out to them to mend them as soon as they fell.

359

Time began to slow as the life force ebb from her and the world became as crisp and sweet as a fresh apple.

"Push forward, my child," she heard King Rien say. The words—and hail of hissing miniballs—singed her ears. "They will follow. Push forward."

A shell exploded mere yards in front of her horse, causing the animal to buck. She was thrown from her saddle and fell onto her back in the mud. The voices went dark for a moment. In their place was a high-pitched ringing and the world began to spin as she sensed the casualties mounting.

"Calm your mind, Pucelle," she told herself. "Focus on one thing, and then the next. Then, all will begin to fall into place. Have faith in the strength given to you and Maijie's guidance."

The maiden felt the rush of blood through her own body and then the ringing subsided. She shut out the noise of battle and reached out with her thoughts for the voices. She heard only one. It was a cry of pain coming from one of the newly formed craters near her. Pucelle stumbled to her feet and lurched towards the source of the cry.

On her way there, she tripped over a man. He was still unconscious. His face was so covered with soot and dirt he looked like a clay statue. She placed a hand on his neck and checked his vitals. He was still alive. His eyes flickered open.

"You're alright. Let's keep moving. Your comrades need you," she told him.

When she looked up from the clay man, the dust from the explosions had cleared enough and she spotted the one who had cried out. He was a younger man and already on his feet, but he looked confused as he cradled his left arm in his right. She made her way towards him, blotting out all the other sounds but the man's silent cry for help.

As she neared him, the Orloinian soldier continued to work at his injured arm and shoulder, and the arm hung limply, covered in soot and blood. To her horror, she realized the limb had been torn completely from his body and, in shock, he was numbly trying to push the dead arm back onto his stump.

"Let me help," she told him, gently embracing him. He pulled back in surprise at first. His eyes were dilated and uncomprehending what the maiden was attempting. But she repeated her soft plea and the man nodded and loosened his grip on the severed limb. It was wet with blood and so was the soldier's tunic. It was clear that he was losing too much and she felt his life force slipping away. She tilted her head and listened for the voices again. They came on like the rushing of the wind.

"Tell my wife, tell her..." the soldier moaned, but he was already starting to lose his balance.

"You can tell her yourself when I am done."

Pucelle worked quickly. She felt warmth move from her torso to her fingertips and into the arm. She held it against the man's stump and pressed the two pieces of flesh together. The meat and bone yielded like fresh clay. The sinews and skin began to knit together and soon the soldier was whole again. He fell into her arms briefly and then his eyes widened as he looked into hers. He raised his reattached hand in disbelief and flexed his fingers.

361

"How?" he asked.

"Just keep moving. Everything will be fine," she reassured him.

He didn't question her, but searched the ground for his sword and resumed his charge towards the Fiorian battle line. Meanwhile, her horse Rien had wandered towards another crater, from she heard some unintelligible shouts and moans. There were two distinct voices. At least one of the men was seriously so she headed towards the crater. She could feel the power building up inside her and, with it, her confidence. She was now a conduit and her life force was flowing freely from her fingertips to all the dead and dying Orlonians. They were rising, one at a time, then dozens and resuming the assault in earnest. Through their eyes, she could see the stunned faces of Fiorians as her resurrected soldiers closed on them, cloaked in their own entrails and brandishing weapons soaked in their own blood. It was as horrendous as it was glorious.

"Minoru, are you alive? Answer me, you lazy shit!" she heard a voice cry out from the crater.

"We're dead! I can see heaven at last," a second, thinner voice replied.

"We're not dead yet, you moron. We just wish we were. Why do you always do that? I think my back is broken. Shit!" the first man cried and then gagged in a spasm of what sounded like agony. Pucelle felt the pain as if it were her own.

There were a few more muffled cries and, as she approached, she spotted a pair of eyes peered out at her from the edge of the crater. A child-like man wearing a pie-plate helmet and sooty rags stared in awe she walked towards him. When she looked down into the base of the crater, she saw the other man, a stocky man with a poorly hewn beard, lying on his back. They were clearly conscripts, but they reminded her of the farmers from her hometown.

"Come with me, men," she said to them. "You will be safe."

"I can't move, ma'am," the stocky man said. His surly expression dissolved in her presence. "My back. I think it's broken."

"It is not. Come. Rise."

The stocky man looked down at his feet. One toe stuck out from his mangled boot. He wiggled it and gasped as he saw it move. Pucelle smiled at him as he awkwardly sprang to his feet and checked himself as though to make sure all his body parts were still attached.

"What are your names, sirs?" the maiden asked.

"I'm Minoru and he's Kamatari, ma'am," Minoru said.

"Where is the enemy? What happened here?" Kamatari said. Pucelle did not even look to know the answer that question. The Fiorese battlements were already emptied of defenders, who were fleeing in disarray and the Dauphin's resurrected men were already celebrating atop them with hearty cheers.

"Can't you tell?" she said and added a sly smile. "We've won the battle, of course. The Fiorese have fled the field."

The man with the scraggly beard blinked. "Maybe we are dead, Minnie," he said. "I just saw half our men

363

get blown to bits. They ought to be fertilizing the marshes right now. And my back was busted. How'd you fix it?"

"I have a very special gift, sir."

"You keep calling us sirs. Are you blind, woman?" Kamatari barked at her. "We're just a pair of muck farmers from down south."

"Then you are the best of people, sirs, deserving the highest respect for your toils and service."

Kamatari grunted. "What's this gift you talk about?"

"It allows me to bring back the recently dead and heal some wounds. I can reach beyond the veil of this world and speak to those souls we've lost."

"I don't know what any of that means," Minoru said. "But it sounds nice. I bet Captain Anville will want to know about that."

"Anville's dead, Minnie. I saw him fall," Kamatari said.

"Captain Anville?" Pucelle said. "Is he here?"

Minoru frowned. "We left him in Muckville. The people there were trying kill me," he said. His eyes widened. "Oh no, what about Teuta?"

"Can you take me to him? My companion is a friend and is searching for him. If he has passed on, I can help," Pucelle said, sifting through her senses among the Orloinian and Fiorian souls that she was still trying to reconnect with their repaired bodies.

Minoru looked towards Muckville. "I think he's still there."

"Teuta was still fighting the villagers over his body," Kamatari said. "We were separated though. The

364

captain had ordered us to march out of the city. Those Muckville creeps just pretended to back down when the Fiorians showed up. They attacked as soon as our backs were turned."

"Can you take me to him?"

Minoru whimpered, but his friend nodded.

"Don't mind him," Kamatari said. "They just want to sacrifice him to their god and eat him alive. They won't be happy to see us again."

"Leave the people of Muckville to me. If you could lead me to the captain, I would be in your debt, sirs."

Kamatari smiled at his friend. "I like the sound of that. Can we ride your horse?"

"If it pleases Rien to allow you to do so, I would not object."

Pucelle called to her horse, retrieved her fallen banner and mounted him. The steed waited patiently as Kamatari struggled to lift himself on his back. Minoru wrung his hands as he watched, seemingly unsure if he should join them.

"Come on already, Minnie," Kamatari shouted. "This woman obviously can help Teuta and the captain and we owe it to them to do what we can. It was your mutton head that broke their little god and fouled up their soup."

Minoru sulked but relented. "It wasn't my mutton head that broke Zojun. It was my clumsy hands," he muttered as he joined his friend and the maiden atop Rien. "Anyways, how can you foul a soup made from people. It was foul enough already."

The horse trotted towards Muckville. Smoke rose from a dozen spots surrounding the town square and it appeared that the entire city was still rioting. Amidst the sounds of screams, they began to smell a faint odor that disturbed Pucelle and spooked Rien. She had smelled something similar when she had returned to find her hometown and all its people burned. It was the smell of cooking flesh.

"There!" Kamatari cried. "They have Teuta. She's alive!"

Amidst a group of purple-hued rioters in the middle of the town square, were several Orloinian soldiers. They apparently had been taken prisoner. Their hands were bound behind them and their armor stripped. Their faces were bedraggled, smeared with mud and blood. To Pucelle's surprise, one of the men was not a man at all. The apparent woman, with short hair like the maiden's, only a tad lighter, struggled violently against her bonds and was being held down by two of her captors. Her tunic had been torn to the waist along the seam on one side. Pucelle imagined she had been pretending to be a man, judging by the men's clothes, but had been exposed either in the fight or after she was captured. Pucelle felt her terror and agony as one of the captors clubbed her over the head with a short, blunt stick. She fell down but for a moment she was free of their grasp. Teuta propelled her body forward on her stomach. She was not struggling to get away, but to get to something held between two other purple men.

In horror, the maiden discerned that it was a person she was trying to reach. The people of Muckville were taking the dead and captive soldiers to a hastily built campfire, over which they erected a large spit. The

366

figure of a man was already dangling from the spit and a one of the larger men was carving at it with a butcher knife.

"Oh no, Captain Anville," Minoru cried. "They're going to make soup of him!"

Just then, Captain Baudrin rode up alongside Rien. "There you are! I've been looking all over the battlefield for—"

The captain's words were choked off by the sight of his former comrade trussed up while the butcher extracted his entrails as though he were removing a chain of bloody sausage links from the dead man's abdomen.

"You'd best dismount, sirs. What I'm about to do might be unpleasant," Pucelle heard herself say. She felt a darkness overtake her as she surveyed the gory scene. Something else was assuming control of her. The voices told her it was alright, so she tried not to resist.

Kamatari muttered something incomprehensible and Minoru stared blankly at the back of the maiden's head. Her body seemed to stiffen.

"You need to dismount now!" Pucelle said. She pivoted in the saddle to face the two peasants. They gasped in horror as they looked into her eyes and saw only two black empty abysses. Kamatari lurched backwards in surprise and his movement caused both he and Minoru to tumble off the horse's rump and onto the cobblestones.

Pucelle grabbed her banner and leapt from her horse, swinging downward as she did. The butcher looked up just as the pole caught him full in the face, shattering his jaw. She then swung the staff in a wide arc around her, causing the shocked guards to back off. Baudrin saw his opening and drew his sword. He ran at the two guards holding Teuta down and struck the first across the neck and shoulder. The second raised his dagger but as he stooped over Teuta, the lieutenant kicked him solidly between the legs. The man groaned and the captain quickly disarmed the untrained thug, kicking him aside.

"Release these men," Pucelle hissed. Her voice boomed with an almost otherworldly quality, like an angel singing while dragging an iron grate. "Don't force me to kill you."

The guards seemed frozen, their expressions blank, but they gave no ground and gave no sign that they were afraid. Two of them held swords at the ready. Baudrin realized that they were measuring up the maiden, trying to figure out what she was and if they could risk attacking her.

"Pucelle, help Anville. I'll deal with this scum," Baudrin said.

The maiden nodded, but she turned her attention to Teuta, who, still bound struggled to her feet. Her eyes were locked on Anville's body on the spit. Pucelle caught her as she desperately rushed at the fire.

"No, you don't have to," Pucelle told her. She began to regain control of herself. "It will be alright. He's not gone yet."

Teuta's body quaked in her grief as she tried to shove past the maiden. Pucelle removed the banner from her staff and placed it about the lieutenant's shoulders, allowing her to regain some modesty. She then retrieved a bucket near the fountain, filled it and doused the fire pit.

"Teuta, is it? Teuta, can you hear me?" Pucelle asked the woman. The lieutenant sighed and her eyes flickered with recognition. "You can help me. You can help him. Come."

"What are you doing, Pucelle?" Baudrin said, and then he noticed one of the guards twitch. The captain snarled. "Give me a reason to gut you like my friend there."

"I am easing his return."

The maiden led Teuta to the body and placed her hand on Anville's abdomen where the butcher had split it open and unraveled his innards.

"When I begin, you will want to push these parts back into his belly, gently, so he feels less discomfort."

"Begin what?" Teuta choked.

"You will know."

Pucelle, as she had done many times before, closed her eyes and focused on her breathing. This time, she placed a hand on the lieutenant's shoulder. She felt the warmth leave her and she let it pass through Teuta's frame and into Anville's body. As commanded, Teuta began to feed the intestines and liver that spilled out of the captain back in to the cavity as the wound slowly knitted itself together as though a surgeon's invisible needle. As soon as the entrails were safely back in, Pucelle allowed the cavity to seal itself with new skin. Anville's lungs filled with air and his head lurched forward, eyes bulging in horror until he saw Teuta's face. She began sobbing.

"Teuta, I thought I'd lost you," he breathed.

"Lost me?" Teuta cried, burying her face in his newly repaired chest. "I thought I'd lost everything."

Anville tugged at his bonds. "Wait, why am I tied up?"

"The people here tried to make a meal of you, Rock," Baudrin said.

"Baudrin, is that you?"

Pucelle drew a dagger from her belt and handed it to Teuta. Then she turned on the cannibal cultists of Muckville. Their tentativeness gave way to fear as they muttered amongst themselves. More of them appeared in the plaza from side streets. Most were peasants armed with pitchforks and hand axes. From them emerged a swarthy man with greasy hair. He carried a mayor's staff and his face was covered in blood. He flashed his rotting, yellowed teeth in anger.

"What have you done, girl?" the mayor cried. "How have you defied our god Zojun?"

"I have defied nothing, other than defying the barbaric practices of you and your people," Pucelle snapped back.

"These men and their commander ruined our sacrifice. Unless we make amends with Zojun, the werewolves will return and kill us all, just as they did during the Plague," the mayor hissed. "These people need to be sacrificed."

Pucelle shook her head. "No one needs to be sacrificed. I don't know of these werewolves you speak of, but I know of a higher power that will protect you all without the need for blood to be spilled."

"And what would that be, witch," the mayor cackled. "Your traveling show tricks?"

370

"No. Real magic. Born of compassion," the maiden said. She motioned to the man she had struck with her staff. He was still cradling his broken jaw, moaning in pain. With the flick of her wrist, the bones mended and the mandible snapped into place. The man gave her a shocked look and then shouted to his comrades that he was healed. This caused the mayor's lip to twitch and his sneer dissolve.

"Furthermore, if you meet my demands, I will raise any of your citizens who may have been killed in the conflict and heal the wounded," she said.

"Demands? What demands?"

"First, you must allow the Dauphin's men safe passage to conduct military operations against our common enemy, the Fiorians—no interference," Pucelle said, looking intensely at the mayor. She felt the darkness stir once more as the little man shrank from her like the coward he was, but forced it back into the recesses of her mind. She had to maintain control of her reason and her heart. "Second, you will end this barbaric practice of human sacrifice—now and forever."

"But what of the werewolves?" the mayor pleaded. "Zojun has kept us safe for generations."

Ignoring the man's question, Pucelle continued, looking outward into the gathered crowd. "Third, you will no longer worship Zojun or any other false gods. You have been lied to and hoodwinked by men who have kept you sick and depraved and forced you to believe in perversions. You don't have to live like this, in squalor."

371

"We can't do that," the mayor protested. "We don't know that this witch isn't serving the werewolves. What would you have worship instead, witch, or shall go blind and faithless into the night?"

"Do you wish to see your loved ones again?" Pucelle said, pointing to Teuta. "Just as this woman has been reunited with her captain?"

There was a murmur in the crowd. The mayor looked nervously about him. He appeared to realize he had lost control of his mob.

"From now on, you will worship one true god, the god of the sun and of the phoenix. She shall protect you and keep you warm as she has me," As she said this, she reached out for the souls of Muckville and guided them back to their bodies. Several of the dead strewn over the bloodied cobblestones in the plaza were roused from their death slumbers and the crowd gave a collective gasp. "Now go home in peace. Your families await you."

After a few moments, the crowd began to disperse. The mayor frantically cast about to the various prostitutes and workers, but it seemed that the people of Muckville had lost their stomach for a fight. Pucelle helped Baudrin, Minoru and Kamatari free Anville's men from their bonds, while Teuta helped Anville gingerly dismount the spit. As soon as he could stand, the captain threw his arms around her and kissed her deeply on the mouth.

"By the gods, I've been wanting to do that for weeks," Anville said. "Court marshals be damned. All the while I was dying, all I could think was what a shame that I'd never be able to hold you in my arms again."

"We've been over this before. Your command in the military would be over if you acknowledged a relationship with me," Teuta said, and the tears began to flow again. "You are my commander."

"And you command my heart. That is more important."

Teuta lovingly patted his beard and then turned to face Pucelle, who had returned to comfort Rien with a carrot from her satchel. She was still wrapped in the phoenix banner the maiden had given her. "Ma'am, you've done more for me than a sister, and yet you are stranger to me. Who are you and how can I repay you?"

"Her name is Pucelle," Baudrin said, giving his old friend a wink. "Rock, I see you've had as much luck at collecting female traveling companions who aspire to be warriors as I have."

"You owe me nothing, lieutenant," Pucelle said with a smile. "Though I like the sound of the word sister. I never had one."

"Perhaps sisters in arms," Anville chortled. "I too owe you both a great debt. Baudrin, it seems your sense of timing has improved since last we fought together. I hope you brought some men. You're just in time for a good fight with a Fiorian army that's been hounding us for months."

"Not anymore. Your people took care of them."

"What? The entire bloody Fiorian invasion force?" Anville's eyes bulged.

"With a little help from Pucelle."

"The last I saw of them, the Fiorians were fleeing in terror. Seeing their enemies rise from the dead en masse was too much for them, just as it had been in Chinan," Pucelle said.

"And you got these people to stop worshipping a cannibal god," Baudrin said. "But surely you don't think they're going to give up their faith just because you waved your hand and performed one miracle, do you?"

"No, but faith is a powerful weapon in the right hands," Pucelle said. "And it will guide them to the truth eventually."

"I know you had special gifts, but I didn't take you for a religious zealot," Baudrin said. "Remember, be careful how much of that you share with our Dauphin."

Captain Anville clapped his hands.

"Glorious!" the captain grinned. "But, by gads, I missed all the fighting—and the winning!"

"There are more ways to win than on the battlefield, dear," Teuta took Anville in her arms and kissed him for a full minute. Afterwards, she spat and smiled sheepishly. "If we're to do that regularly, you'll need to shave."

Chapter 28

Fall of Year 43 (after the Great Plague)

Mallory and Belle Isolde's spacious guest room at Rune was beginning to look more like a laboratory than living quarters. The inventor had ordered some of the equipment they packed for the journey to Orloins be brought directly to the room, while Joaquin had smuggled in test tubes, pipets and even a small laboratory burner. The once spacious bedroom and its canopied bed was now cramped amongst the crates, barrels and makeshift tables that Mallory had constructed to conduct his experiments. The room had to be constantly monitored, either by Joaquin or his wife, lest the prying eyes of Lord Farless, his people or members of his own team begin to suspect what he was up to.

"What is it you are up to, dear?" Belle Isolde curled an arm around her husband's waist and leaned into him. "The natives are getting restless, and I don't mean just Farless. I overheard talk amongst the team that they are most displeased with your delays. I'm afraid that one of them might a message back to the Chancellor's people."

Mallory removed a small vial of bioluminescent liquid from the burner and examined it carefully through a pair of his work spectacles. The glasses had many lenses that flared out from the frame that could be rotated in front of his eyes to increase magnification. The liquid he had smuggled in by bleeding one of the lamps in an empty hallway. Somehow, even under the intense heat of the burner, the vial and its contents were still cool to the touch.

"I know of the risks, Belle," Mallory said. "But I don't know when we'll pass this way again and I don't know when I'll have the chance to study this creature again. I doubt if anyone in Fioria—even the Chancellor himself—is aware of this phoenix or its significance to the Orloinians as a cultural symbol and a power source. If I can present something about this, it might take the government's mind off of slaughtering Orloinians and conquering these people and onto designing technologies for peace and prosperity for all peoples."

Belle Isolde rested her chin on his shoulder. "I understand, dear, and I do want to help that poor, suffering beast as much as we can. But at what risk? And, be honest, my sweet, do you really think you can divert the Chancellor's bloodthirsty desire for conquest with another gadget? Don't you think that's just a bit... wishful?"

"Are you saying I'm naïve?"

"No, dear, but I don't think we can stall for much more time. We've been here for almost two weeks."

"Just a few more days and I might have something."

"And then you'll do what?"

Mallory paused, then took off his glasses and set them on the crate. He turned off the burner and replaced the vial in its cradle. "You do have a point, my dear."

376

"I know I do," she said. "Besides, we've refused maid service since we got here and it's starting to smell a little rank cooped up in this room, don't you think?"

There was a knock at the door, three short raps. It was Joaquin. Belle Isolde opened the door to allow the assistant to come in and then closed the door quickly behind him. Joaquin was wearing a light blue jacket, wool breaches and the inventor noted the wet leaf stuck to the young's man boot.

"You have something for me, Joaquin?" Mallory asked.

"Only news," his assistant replied. "Lord Farless claims that he has completed the rail system and wants to test the steam engine. He's requesting your assistance."

Mallory sighed. "I'm not about to hand over my engine schematics for the Dragon's Breath. I think he suspects the nature of what we've brought with us. I hope Wittman and his men are keeping a tight guard on the prototypes. I don't trust Lord Farless. He has prying eyes."

"Unlike yours, of course, dear, which have stolen into the recesses of his secrets and are performing experiments on purloined phoenix blood," Belle Isolde chided her husband.

Mallory sniffed. "This is about scientific inquiry. And ethical concerns. Farless is just being nosy. He didn't seem to regard us as anything more than an inconvenience when we first arrived."

"What should we do?"

"I suppose it's time for me to face facts," Mallory said. "I'll go see what Farless wants and oversee this new rail system of theirs, but we need to be prepared to move. Joaquin, could you remain here and help Belle pack up our things?"

His assistant nodded, but Belle Isolde withdrew from her husband and he heard a slight humph that he knew to be her signal that he had done something wrong. When he turned from his work to face her, her hands were positioned firmly on her hips. It was only then that he noticed that she was wearing a simple brown jacket and matching skirt that was slit along one side, under which she usually wore a pair of warm breaches. She was clearly dressed for the outdoors.

"If it's all the same to you, Mallory, I'd rather accompany you when you go see Farless. I think Joaquin can handle the packing."

"You want to spend more time with Lord Farless?"

"I want to show you that I'm not crazy—that there are two Farless' out there, or that he's parading as two different people."

Mallory grabbed his pen and notebook from the bed. After a brief consideration, he decided to pocket the vial of phoenix blood rather than leave it with Joaquin. "I don't think you are crazy, dear. But that idea sounds crazy."

"As crazy as these Orloinians chaining a large extinct bird and draining its blood as fuel oil?"

Mallory looked at Joaquin who shrugged and went into the cupboard to find the couple's trunks. "I suppose you have me at a disadvantage there, dear," he said. "Well, let's go find out what Farless wants—and maybe his doppelganger."

Belle Isolde grabbed the copy of Ornithology of Legends, Lore and Prehistory she had borrowed, stuffed it into her handbag. Then, they strolled hand-in-hand down the long hallway, down to the grand foyer and then out onto a platform that flanked the newly constructed rail system. On the rails crouched a steam engine, less sophisticated than Mallory's Dragon's Breath and not as sleek as the rails of the Fiorian capital, but compact and nimble-looking, like an arboreal squirrel dangling precariously from a branch and stretching out for a nut.

Lord Farless, dressed in a simple waistcoat, was waiting for them on the platform. He appeared to be ordering about some porters and engineers, who were loading some coal into the trolley behind it and water for the boiler through a crane operated from the platform.

"Lord Farless," Mallory said. "I hear your rail system is about to come online. This must be a great day for you and your people."

Farless shrugged. His pointed hat tipped slightly as he cocked his head the other way. "Contrary to your propaganda about the knuckle dragging barbarians on the continent, we Orloinians are a people capable of great accomplishments. This is just one of many."

Mallory glanced at his wife. Their host was as expressionless and opaque as ever. Dining with the man over the past several weeks had been excruciatingly awkward, but Farless had insisted upon it, even after Belle Isolde had feigned illness to avoid it.

"Still, I suppose it would have taken us a bit longer to complete the project had you not decided to linger and offer your assistance. It was fortunate that Fioria would send us one of its best steam engineers just as we were advancing a project of our own."

"Yes, indeed," Mallory hummed sheepishly as he noted the suspicious tone of the lord's voice. "The Chancellor is as wise as he is generous."

"So they say."

"Lord Farless," Belle Isolde interjected, holding out the book from her handbag. "I've been meaning to thank you for loaning me your books. They've been a great help to me."

"What books, Mrs. Mallory?" Farless lifted one well-manicured finger to his chin, as he watched the porters scramble.

"It's just Belle Isolde, if you don't mind," she replied, shrugging off Mallory's worried look. "And it was the books on birds you recommended. From the library."

"I don't seem to recall…"

"Oh, that's right," Belle Isolde chuckled politely. "It was Mr. Mecum that recommended the books. My mistake. He's quite a good librarian. A peculiar fellow though."

The mention of Vade Mecum's name made Farless snap to attention. "What books, Mrs. Mallory?"

Belle Isolde held out the book in her hand for the lord to see, open to the page with the phoenix. "A book on birds of legend and lore. It was quite a fascinating and imaginative book. . This one in particular piqued my curiosity. It made me wonder whether some of these birds ever existed—or maybe still exist, even today."

Farless grunted. "Even Orloinians don't believe in fairy tales. We learned that the hard way during the Great Plague."

"Then you don't agree with Vade Mecum," Belle Isolde pressed him.

"Agree with what?"

"That this phoenix bird does really exist and might be secreted away in one of your many forests."

The lord frowned and Mallory cleared his throat awkwardly. "Mecum does not believe that," he said. "And he would never spout such nonsense to a guest. I shall have to have words with him."

Belle Isolde's eyes widened. "I'm so sorry, Lord Farless. I don't mean to make trouble for you or Mr. Mecum. It was just idle curiosity."

"There was nothing idle about it," Farless said. "But you do have an air of foolishness about you."

"Now see here," Mallory said. The hair on the back of his neck bristled at the tone of the man's cutting remarks against his wife. "There's no call to—"

The steam engine whistle gave a loud screech like a barn owl. The engineer onboard waved at Lord Farless. It was the signal that the engine was primed and ready to go.

"Ah, lovely," Farless said. "That means that the engine's maiden voyage is about to commence and that you and your people can be on your way."

"That is wonderful, but I was hoping—"

381

Before Mallory could get another word in edgewise, he noticed movement coming from the castle's bay doors.

"And there they are," the lord chirped, almost sounding pleased.

Through the open gate doors, more porters, along with the rest of Mallory's team emerged, tugging on chains attached to a series of cars, atop which the hooded forms of the inventor's Dragon's Breaths had been loaded.

"Wait, why is my equipment being loaded onto this train? You haven't tested the length of the rail yet, have you?"

"When you first arrived, you told me that you wished to get to the front as expeditiously as possible. I am only fulfilling your wishes," Farless' expression remained blank but there was an icy edge to his voice.

"But you're risking equipment vital to the war effort," Mallory protested. "At least let me and my team inspect the track and pilot a test run with only the engine."

"Not necessary."

"It will be necessary if the track design fails and you will need to explain to the Chancellor himself how the empire's equipment is lying wrecked at the base of one of your trees."

"That will not be necessary either. I've already sent messengers to your chancellor and his emissaries have informed me that you are to delay no further."

"When did he do that?"

"Just this morning," Farless said. "He also seemed rather concerned that you had not sent your last weekly report back to the company. He asked me to inquire about that."

"I was working on that, but as I sent in my first communique, I would update headquarters once we settled the matter of transportation off the peninsula."

"Well, now, it seems that has been sorted. You can be on your way immediately."

"Sir," Belle Isolde said. Her eyebrows were knitted in an angry cross. "The Fiorian Empire and your kingdom are allies. You cannot simply kick the representatives of your allies out into the cold. There are protocols to be observed. You signed a treaty, an agreement of cooperation between our two peoples. That is why there is no Fiorian garrison here."

Mallory waved his wife off, sensing Farless' mouth tightening at the mention of the word garrison. But it was too late.

"There is no need for a garrison here because your government and its previous representatives understood the strategic importance of allowing Rune its autonomy," the lord hissed. "But I suppose that's a fact that you and your husband will learn sooner or later."

Several guards marched onto the platform. Between two of them was Joaquin, looking a bit scuffed up and being dragged by his heels.

"Joaquin!" Mallory said. The guards dropped him like a sack of potatoes. The inventor turned angrily upon Lord Farless. "What have you done to my assistant? You have no right to abuse an official of the Fiorian—"

"He was reported being seen snooping in a restricted area," Lord Farless' voice called. But to Mallory's confusion, Farless' lips were not moving, and the voice did seem to be coming from the direction of Mallory's team assembled by the Dragon's Breaths.

"Where?" he asked, dumfounded.

"In the laundry," Farless' voice seem to speak again. Farless' actual mouth remained closed, his lips barely shaping an imperceptible smile at the corners. "And he apparently wasn't washing clothes."

"Maybe he was there to get towels," the inventor said dully, his attention fixed on how the lord was pulling off his ventriloquist act.

Mallory felt Belle Isolde's hand tap urgently on his shoulder. When he turned, she pointed to a figure that had appeared behind Joaquin. It was Lord Farless—except not. The man had the same eyes and thin jawline, but his hair was thinner on top and he wore a well-trimmed beard that came to a point just below his Adam's apple. He was dressed in military garb, with a red sash over his grey uniform and Fiorian pips at the collar.

"Or maybe he was there to spy on our operations," the Farless look-a-like said. "Our so-called allies."

Mallory's jaw dropped as his eyes darted between the apparent twin Farlesses. Belle Isolde's expression communicated silently a mixture of panic and a wry "I told you so" demeanor.

"Fortunately for you, Rune's agreement with the Fiorian Empire precludes imprisonment of its citizens," the first Lord Farless said. "But we can strongly incentivize both your departure and cooperation. So we will send you, your manservant and your team on your way to the front where you will no doubt attempt to murder many of our fellow countrymen, but we will keep a... security... from you to ensure you will not cause us trouble in the future."

"Look," Mallory said. "I apologize for being a poor guest. We overstepped our bounds, I know, but you may not seize any of my equipment. It belongs to the Sudwell Enterprises and, by extension, the Fiorian government."

"I don't wish to seize your toys. I can't imagine what I would use them for even if I discovered what they were," Farley said. "However, I can use information. Though I can't keep you, your curious bookworm of a wife may be useful to me and ensure your silence about whatever it is you think you discovered about our operations."

Belle Isolde stepped between her husband and Farless. "This bookworm wife has no interest of being useful to you, sir."

"A shame," Farless sneered. "But I don't recall soliciting your opinion—and I have no more use for your husband's either. Mr. Wittman, I believe you are next in charge of this expedition, are you not?"

Wittman, stone-faced with shock, looked at Mallory and then at Farless. "I am," he said. "But what is the meaning of all this? Why are there two of you?"

"Never mind that," Farless said. "I understand that you and your group, unlike Mr. Mallory here, are eager to get to the front. Your impediments have been removed. I expect you to take Mr. Mallory, whatever equipment and depart at once. Mrs. Mallory will be staying with us for the time being."

"This is an outrage," Mallory said, stabbing a finger at Farless. "You have assaulted one of my people and now you want to illegally detain my wife? You can't do that."

"File whatever formal legal protest you would like, Mr. Mallory. I will inform both the Fiorian government and Sudwell Industries what has transpired here as well," Farless pointed to his guards and the towers where Mallory now spied archers peering from their perches. "As you can see, I very much can do what I please. To subjugate this land, the Fiorians need me as much as I need them-- and they need me far more than they need you, let me assure you. I just received a report that the fortress of Chinan has fallen to forces allied with the Dauphin. So your nosiness and dallying may have cost your nation an important foothold on the continent."

Mallory could no longer contain his anger. He lunged at Lord Farless, but Wittman and Belle Isolde grabbed each arm to restrain him.

"Hey, do you want to end up like your assistant?" Wittman said. "We'd best do what he says."

"I'll be alright, dear," Belle Isolde added, but her eyes were already filled with tears. "I can't go to the front with you anyways and I'm sure Lord Farless will promise that no harm will come to me."

"Your wife is correct," Farless said. "No harm will come to her. Your servant may also stay, and we will ensure he receives medical treatment for his injuries."

"Belle," Mallory could not think of words as he stared into his wife's forlorn face. "I promised you better than this."

She nodded. "The world conspires to give us something else."

They were allowed a brief kiss before the guards dragged him away and loaded him onto the train. He was tossed into a seat and stood over by a guard. He scrambled towards the window like a child and pressed his face against the cold glass. As the train began to lurch forward, his view of the Rune, the castle in the trees, was his assistant, still a bloody heap of bruises on the platform, and his wife flanked by two guards, her palm extended out to him. The vial of phoenix blood pressed hard against his chest.

Chapter 29

Summer of Year 42 (after the Great Plague)

Pucelle's hoe hit a rock. She lifted the blade and struck again. The blade found the edge, but the roots of ragweeds encircled the stone and ran deeper. She would need to work around the edges and cut through the roots to free the rock and remove it from the garden. She lifted the hoe and swung down harder. Again, the dull thud of metal on stone. The shaft of the hoe vibrated with the blow, sending a sharp pain through her palm and wrist. In frustration, she dropped the hoe and it fell on the tender stalks of some barberry plants, flattening two of the plants and scattering half-ripened berries across the dirt.

"Bother!" she cursed at herself.

She gingerly tried to prop the damaged plants up with wooden stakes and gathered the fallen berries, but she was still sore at hitting the rock. She tossed the hoe to the side and tore at the ragweed roots with her fingers. It was tedious work and the rubbery roots tenaciously maintained their death grip on the stone. Pucelle grunted as she struggled to burrow a hand under the rock. Finally, exhausted and bloodied from scratching at the knotted roots and dirt, she fell back on her haunches and wept bitterly. A light breeze caressed the back of her neck.

"Breathe," her grandmother whispered. "Just breathe."

Pucelle closed her eyes and inhaled. Though her hands still throbbed, her frustration subsided.

"You have a lot of anger in you, child," the shade said.

"The weeds are choking the plants. If I don't get rid of them, there'll be no harvest this season," Pucelle said. "Every year, it gets harder."

"I know it does," Majie said. "But I don't think you're referring to the gardening."

"Isn't it supposed to be easier? They've been gone three summers now."

"Loss is never easy, sparrow. But your family and I need you to let us go. You can't hold on to the past and embrace your future at the same time."

"But why can't I talk to them? Like I talk to you?"

"You don't need to speak with them. And you need me only enough to help with your training."

"But I'm sitting here crying about some broken barberries for no reason. I absolutely need my parents," Pucelle wiped the tears from her cheeks, but only managed smudging dirt across her face. "I'm a wreck half the time. And a poor gardener the rest of the time."

"You are neither, sparrow. You are far stronger than you believe."

"I can't do this alone."

"You are never really alone."

The maiden looked up at the shade with her reddened eyes. "And you are not my real grandmamma."

Her grandmother smiled, as though Pucelle had just paid her a compliment. "You're right, of course. I'm not."

"Then who—or what—are you?"

The shade sighed. "It's time you know."

Her grandmother's features dissolved in a cloud of pollen. The shape slowly grew until it stood well over six feet tall. The form hardened, solidified and its edges became sharpened and angular. Before she knew it, Pucelle was kneeling before a large man wearing a fine cape over a soldier's breastplate. The man's face seemed youthful, but the beard was greyed at the tips and his hairline receded from the temples. A crown adorned the top of the man's head.

"Are you a king?" she asked.

The shade laughed. "This form once was the king, sparrow. I ruled all of Orloins, though imperfectly, as King Rien."

"You were King Rien, the father of the Dauphin?"

"I was, but I am so much more than that. And so are you."

"I am the daughter of some dead peasants who doesn't have a home."

"You are a daughter of magic," the king said, but then he shrugged. "Magic works in mysterious ways."

"What do you want from me?"

The shade leaned over and lifted Pucelle up. At first, she wanted to resist, but the figure that once took the form of her grandmother still felt like her. There was a gentleness in its touch that soothed her.

"What do I want from you, your majesty. I told you that you have anger inside you."

RIDING A BLACK HORSE

"I'm sorry, your majesty. I'll learn not to be angry. I don't want to be."

"No, don't be sorry. I can use that anger."

Pucelle's eyes narrowed. "How?"

"Uncontrolled rage is like a wildfire in a dry wood. It destroys everything and develops a mind of its own. A mind and a power that can turn on its creator. That's not the kind of anger I'm talking about," the king said. "But anger under control can also forge a sword or power a furnace."

"How do you control anger?"

The king seemed to bristle at the question. He reached down into the hole that Pucelle had made and effortlessly drew the rock from the tangle of roots and tossed it aside. "This rock caused you harm. It seemed to anger you with its stubbornness. Do you wish to avenge yourself upon it?"

The maiden laughed in spite of herself. "No, of course not. A rock can't mean me harm. Anyways, I wasn't angry at the rock."

"Really? Then you were angry at the men who killed your family then? Do you seek vengeance against them? And the rock was simply in your way?"

"No."

"Why not?"

Pucelle looked down. "Because vengeance won't bring back my family, your majesty. It won't make me any less alone than I am right now."

The king let out a sigh of relief. The leaves began to rustle around Pucelle as though the breath the shade cast had caused a stiff breeze. "You are indeed wise for a sparrow. What if I told you that you could bring back many families to those who have lost?"

Pucelle blinked, but said nothing.

"Well then," the shade said after a moment of silence. "I was expecting a more enthusiastic response for your king."

"Tell me what I must do."

Chapter 30

Fall of Year 43 (after the Great Plague)

Takashi joined the old man as a traveling companion and accompanied him to the Valley of Colors. But as they neared the Southern Fork, where the roads split, one descending into the dale where the Marron River flowed, the former thief seemed to grow anxious. He constantly scratched at his palm and looked over his shoulder, back to the south where the farmlands lay.

"You're nervous."

"No, sir."

"You're making me nervous."

"I'm sorry, sir."

"Don't be. I need to rest anyways."

The old man found a large rock to sit down on and stretch his legs to work out the arthritic pain in his knees. Nearby the river roiled as it tumbled down the rapids and into the valley below and the sparrows chattered angrily in the tree branches above his head. The old man inhaled deeply and took in the scent of the fall leaves. He closed his eyes and focused. Was the call on the wafting on the breeze? No, it was tumbling in the current. It was splashing against the rocks. It was seeping into the soil and being soaked up by the roots of the draconic trees. He envisioned it spreading up the trunk to the branches and expiring through the leaves. By the time he opened his eyes, he was uncertain where the call was directing them. It was all around them. Yet the orb in his pocket felt no heavier than it had in the destroyed village of Do'om.

"You say you encountered the maiden here in the valley?" he asked.

"Yeah, she was with two other blokes—soldiers, I think."

"A peasant girl with soldiers. Do you think you would remember where you encountered them?"

Takashi swallowed hard. "I think so."

"You must take me there," he waved a gnarled finger in the air. "I'm getting a mixed signal here."

"Like at the plague house."

The old man shook his head. "No, the call I heard there was clear. She spent significant time there, it's clear. The emotions were conflicted, dark and full of sadness. This is conflicted in another sort of way."

"How?"

The old man looked up and watched as the sparrows twittered away at the two intruders. There were several of them and some were squawking at him while several made jabbing moves at each other with their tiny beaks. One with a dull brown body and orange-tinted beak but no color on her wings, most likely an immature female, lifted one scrawny leg and defecated as she did so. The old man bowed his head just as the incoming feces splashed against the back of his cowl.

"The conflict is not in the place," the old man said. "It's within me."

"Please, sir, we should be on the move. It's not safe out in the open. There are bandits prowling the forests, looking for easy prey."

394

The old man grunted. Old and frail as he was, he would make no easy prey for bandits, he wanted to tell Takashi, but he held his tongue. His companion's worries were well-founded, and he was aware of the lawless reputation the valley had acquired since the Fiorian invasion. Any confrontation here in the open would not be advantageous and would be a distraction from his main goal. He balled his fists and struggled to concentrate but clarity would not come. Under his breath, the old man cursed his age and the Order for abandoning him. Not the first time since the Plague he had done so.

"Let us be off then. Into the valley. You lead the way," he said, rising stiffly.

"Down into the valley? Perhaps it would be better to take the high road."

"Do you think the you think the young woman took the high road?"

"No," Takashi said, his shoulders slumped.

"Then I must go where she went. I must make sense of what is happening?"

"But what will you do when you find her?"

The old man removed his cowl and shook off the excrement as best he could. "I do not know, but my faith in the calling of magic will guide me," he said. "I will know what to do when action is needed. All that I do know is that I need to find the young woman. She is the source of the call. You'll hear it more often, if you learn to listen."

"I'm not sure I want to anymore."

"As if you had a choice," the old man said with a scowl. He spotted a fallen tree branch that was just the right size and straight enough to make a walking stick. He lifted it and picked off the extra twigs. "Magic keeps its own counsel on whom it selects to receive its call. The Order spent a millennium attempting to reason with it, control it, but it never worked. It's a mystery not for mortal men to know. If it selects you, you must obey and make something of it, or it will leave you in the gutter where it found you. Now, I believe you were about to take me into the valley."

Takashi still hesitated. His droopy eye twitched.

"I might die soon, so you won't have to be burdened with my old carcass for long. Come on, shepherd, let's face the wolves together," the old man grunted, licked his finger and held it to the wind. Today, it was blowing northerly and heading into the valley along river's edge it would be at their backs. The old man did not wait for Takashi, but trudged on alongside the river towards the valley. After several minutes of walking, the old man heard Takashi let out a muffled curse and a flurry of footsteps as his traveling companion scampered up behind him.

They walked for hours, Takashi reluctantly leading the way. For the time being, the old man was content to follow him. The danger of the Valley of Colors was easy to miss, masked by the bed of crimson leaves over which stood guard as sentries the trees and the halos of light that almost seeped into the shadows and darker hollows of the forest. It had been a long time since the old man had been in the valley. The southern territories of Orloins where he had spent his younger years had less vegetation and colder winters than the north on average, but the warm ocean currents manipulated by the Order when it was still a functioning organization kept climate more temperate and calm than moodier northern demesnes. Or so he was told. During the Plague and even before the disappearance of the Order, the weather fluctuated almost as much as in the north. The old man wondered whether Vice Elder Pluto's exaggerated his power to control phenomena that were actually the result of natural processes.

Takashi stopped.

"What's wrong, shepherd?" the old man asked. At first, he didn't notice anything amiss, so intent he was on listening for the clarion of the call. Then he noticed the lack of another sound—the voice of the forest. The birds and squirrels were hushed and only occasionally he could hear the rustling of leaves.

"There," he whispered. Takashi pointed to the trunk of a nearby tree. The old man moved closer to it. Etched in the trunk was a simple shape in the form of a snake. It was low to the ground and easy to miss for those not looking for it. He leaned over and traced the symbol with his finger. It had been carved quickly and would have been easy to miss if Takashi's eagle eyes had not been searching for it.

"A gang symbol. What does it mean?"

"We're entering Black Cobra territory. They're expanding their reach. This mark is fresh, a sign to any other gangs to stay out," Takashi said, scratching the stubble under his neck as his eyes darted from side to side. "We should turn back."

The old man rested on his walking stick and peered beyond the tree to the clearing ahead. "But the place where you met the young woman is in Black Cobra territory, is it not?"

"It is, but when we ambushed the maiden we were at the extreme edge of our territory. This mark is miles away from that spot," Takashi said. "I'm not willing to spend more than a few hours in their domain. If they find me without my mark, there's no telling what they might do."

"They would kill you," the old man said dryly. "That's what they would do."

"I have no wish to die—again."

"I have no wish to die for the first time. And yet I know it will happen to me sooner more likely than later," the old man said. He began to hike towards the clearing. "For a man who's cheated death, you lack the courage I would expect. The maiden raised you for a reason. You should not let her down."

"It's a trap."

"Then let's spring the trap."

"Do you think that's smart?"

"I think it's necessary to get where I need to go."

"Then you're insane."

By the time Takashi caught up with the old man, he was already standing in the middle of the clearing. A shard of light penetrated the canopy and he chose to stand framed in the ray. It seemed suitably dramatic. He surveyed the area for movement. It was unnaturally quiet. He was certain that any bandits near the area clearly had seen him by now. Takashi skulked behind one of the trees and watched as the old man felt inside his pocket for the orb. It was cold in the palm of his hand. He muttered some words to himself that he'd never spoken since he forsook the Order, ancient words he still hoped had some meaning. Then he took his makeshift staff and slammed it hard against the earth.

Suddenly, there was a cracking high up in the branches. Several cracks followed by a muffled cry. A body tumbled through several levels of branches and thudded on the leaf-bedded ground, followed by a small branch, which struck him square on the head. It was a man, squatty and gnarled like the trees in which he'd obviously been perching. Slung over his shoulder was a bow. His quiver of arrows had spilled out over the ground as soon as he landed. The old man advanced on the prone man and stuck the butt of his staff in his face just as he groaned and lifted it to see his would-be prey standing over him.

"Are there others?" the old man asked, fixing the bandit with a steely gaze.

The bandit simply gurgled, but his eyes widened in surprise, apparently calculating how he'd lost his footing and fell so clumsily to the ground. The old man decided not to wait for a coherent response and banged his staff one more time on the ground. Two more thuds followed, and two more short, stocky men lay prone in the clearing. The old man released the orb in his pocket.

"Now then, that's more like it," the old man said, amid the groans of the fallen men. "I have questions and I hope you'll have answers to them."

The bandit at the old man's feet slowly lifted his face, half-caked in wet leaves, and croaked. "What are you? And what makes you think I would tell you anything?"

"Your survival instincts, I would assume," the old man sniffed. "I have a friend who has a bow trained on us as we speak."

"You lie, old man."

"I am incapable of lying," the old man said. "Besides, I find the truth to be an uglier and more sinister weapon than deception."

He called to Takashi. The three bandits looked at each other in confusion then scrambled to unsheathe daggers and find cover. But after a few moments of silence, the men began to regain their confidence. They began to advance on the old man.

"Then it seems like your friend has left you in the lurch, mate," the first man growled.

"No, not left," Takashi called. His voice sounded strained. The old man turned to find his companion emerging from behind the tree, a knife held to his throat. Another man was standing behind him, holding Takashi in a crushing headlock. "I told you it was a trap."

The old man snarled and reached for the orb in his pocket. Its stored magic was weakening, he could tell, but he hoped it had enough left for at least one more spell today. Quietly, he cursed at his own carelessness.

"Ah ah, old stone," the man who held Takashi said. His face was more scar than face. "Better keep your hands where's we can see them or I might lose my nerve and slit his throat."

The old man's eyes narrowed. "Slit his throat and you won't find out what I have in my pocket."

400

"I don't need to see it to know it's no weapon's gonna hurt me," he said, but his tightening grip on Takashi suggested he was still wary of what the old man could do. "Spitter, Asp, Garters, relieve this ancient farter of the contents of his pockets."

The three bandits grumbled and advanced on the old man. One stretched his hand towards the hand that was still buried in his pocket firmly gripping the orb. His eyes drifted towards Takashi the hostage and widened.

"Wormy, is that you?" he asked.

"What's left of him," Takashi replied.

"Where you been? After we found Fang and Tail's carcasses, we wondered if we'd find you gutted and hanging from a tree."

The man holding Takashi glanced at Garters and then craned his neck to see his hostage's face more clearly. He sniffed, then grinned and slackened his grip. "That is you, Wormy. I should have recognized your foul smell from the first," he said. "What happened to you?"

"I met a girl," Takashi replied.

Garters chortled. "Must been one pretty piece to make you go quiet so long. Tell me, Wormy, this girl the reason why several of our boys are fertilizing the trees right now," he said, and then snarled. "Old man, do you have anything to do with that?"

"No."

The old man locked eyes with Takashi for just a moment. But his companion seemed to recognize the wordless message he was sending. He used the moment's distraction to slip free of his captor and with his left hand the blade that every gang member kept holstered at their thighs. Takashi held the knife to the man's throat. The old man swung his staff Garter's midsection, sending the thug sprawling once more on the ground. Spitter and Asp, who were still several paces away from the fray took up a defensive posture at the edges of the clearing.

At first, the gang leader seemed shocked at the sudden reversal of fortune. Then, he chuckled. "Well, look at you. Wormy, did this girl give you a spine? All ballsy and brave. Does she make you feel like a man?"

"She showed me I was still a man," Takashi said. He bared his right arm up to the elbow and showed his former master and showed him the unblemished flesh of his forearm.

"Where's your mark?"

"The girl removed it."

"A girl?"

"She gave me my life back, Cobra. I was dead and she raised me. She has magic, like in the old times," Takashi said. "She made me promise not to steal and murder anymore. I intend to keep that promise."

"Well, good for you. And good for her," Cobra said. "But where did you pick up the fossil? Is this some sort of a joke."

"The fossil seeks the girl. And the fossil can do more than shake a few ruffians out of a tree. So perhaps it would be best if you listen to the fossil when he says that he was once a member of the Order of the Seraphim."

Cobra's grin diminished. "That's not a very good joke. The Order is an old hag's tale told to make

402

children eat their vegetables and keep honest folk from claiming what's rightfully theirs. Your kind's magic is dead, old one."

"Then explain my missing mark, Cobra. And how do you explain this?" Takashi pulled back the collar of his shirt to expose his neck to the gang leader. "Do you see the scar where you cut me when you stole me from my home?"

Cobra grunted.

"It's gone like the mark you put on me," Takashi continued. "The girl took it away when she brought me back from the dead. She has real power. This man, he knows what it means. The stories about magic are all true—and it's coming back to Orloins. The girl can help free us."

"Free us? From what?"

"You chose to ally yourself with the Fiorians," the old man said. "You chose unwisely. The reason that magic would return to this land is to restore the Order and purge the land of these invaders."

"I ain't seen this girl. But I've seen what the Fiorians can do. They have the power in the Valley now. Your faith in your magic is misplaced."

The old man smiled inside as he noticed a slight tremor in gang leader's lip. "Really? Well then, we must surrender ourselves at once so that you may take us to your masters for a reward. I'm sure they would pay a handsome price to learn about their enemy's new weapon."

The old man stepped towards Cobra and tapped the man on his chest with the tip of his staff. "Since you say they control the Valley, they must not be far from here," the old man continued. The gang leader's lip twitched again. "Oh, but perhaps they aren't so close as you might hope. I suspect that perhaps you lost touch with your Fiorian friends recently. Have they abandoned you? You see, I have seen what Fiorians can do as well, many years ago when I was sent as part of a mission by the Order to civilize those barbarians. If they were here—now, in the valley—they would conquer Olivet to the north and Valcolors to the south and be swarming this place as we speak. There are no other defenses this deep in the continent. And yet, the journey here was uneventful until we stumbled upon you. And I suspect a rival gang is far closer, waiting for their opportunity to reclaim their turf from you once your back is turned."

"What do you want, ancient one?" Cobra hissed.

"It's not what I want," the old man said. "It's the choice you need to make. You can try to kill us—and likely die. Or you can join us and share in what's to come."

"What's to come?"

"This," the old man drew the orb from his pocket. It was as heavy as a lead cannonball, but he held in his trembling hand for the gang to see. It was glowing a faint blue. He concentrated on the call and prayed that it had one more charge. The ground shook for a moment and then the forest came alive. Birds circled overhead and the cries of a stag and howls of several wolves echoed across the valley. "Magic is real and will return. The girl will save us all—or destroy us."

Epilogue

Spring of Year 44 (after the Great Plague)

Queen Mother Isabeau surveyed the crowds that had gathered to the line the streets of D'Orloins to watch their new sovereign crowned king of Orloins. It was a day a long time in the making—one that she at times worried would never come. Now that it was here she looked on it with dread and foreboding.

She lifted the hem of her heavy gown and picked up her pace. The Dauphin was strolling gleefully alongside his trophy, the miraculous maiden responsible for the sudden string of victories against the Fiorians, and her two pet peasants, Kamatari and Minoru. From behind, Pucelle looked angelic and glowing, in spite of her plain, unadorned hair and simple dress. By comparison, the fineries worn by Isabeau along with her carefully painted make-up and expensive jewelry made her look whorish and haggard. She resented it and she resented the way her son ogled the maiden. It was the same doting look mirrored in the masses. She had cast a spell on them, and all were entranced. They could have crowned a potato king of Orloins so long as the Night Maiden was present to give her divine blessing. Their cheering was deafening the queen mother.

She pushed aside Chief Burgundais who hiccupped a protest and reached her son by the time they climbed the steps leading to the chapel of Ange Foenix, where

405

the Order of the Seraphim had presided over the coronation of every Orloinian king until the Great Plague wiped them all out. She grabbed her son by the elbow and forced him to the side as soon as he crossed the threshold. There was a darkened corner in the foyer where they were unseen by the crowd outside and the host of courtiers inside.

"Mother, what is the matter with you?" the Dauphin protested. "Are you trying to tear my arm off? I might need that to rule Orloins someday soon."

"I'll have none of your lip today, boy," Isabeau spat. "You may be getting a crown on your head, but you'll be getting a crowning as well if you don't listen to your mother."

"I should think you'd be pleased today. After all, it's what you've always wanted since father died."

"I want you to have the throne, but I also want you to have real power to rule," she said. "But you haven't earned the right to lead a country yet. Today, you just won some jewelry."

"I don't know if you're going deaf or if you have cotton stuffed in your ears, but there's a throng out there cheering for me. And there's thousands more flocking in from the countryside as we speak. I think that's proof that I've earned something today."

"Foolish child, they're not cheering for you. They're cheering for their new idol. The girl is the one they will follow," Isabeau hissed, glancing briefly at where Pucelle paused at the great doors, attended by Captain Baudrin, his manservant, and the nose-picking peasants who stood in awe of the glass ceiling of the chapel. "And why shouldn't they. She has the real power. And should she decide to, she could easily turn that throng against you—and snatch that toy crown from you."

The Dauphin guffawed. "Why should ever want to do that? As you've told me countless times, she's just a girl. And she's committed to serving me," he said with a snort. "So what if they cheer for her today. I control her and her gift. I have the real power, mother. They'll cheer for me once I am king."

"You self-deluded brat. Sometimes I regret the day I ever let you suckle at my breast."

"I regret that as well sometimes. And I'm sure there are many ambitious courtiers who now regret they did the same."

Instinctively, she slapped the Dauphin. The loud crack of her hand against his cheek echoed throughout the foyer. Her rapier-like fingernails left three long red scratches across his face, from his eye to the corner of his mouth. At first, he appeared shocked, but then a sly smile surfaced.

"You need not join us for the coronation, mother," he said. "After all, you've survived worse scandals."

The Dauphin spun around and strolled towards the maiden and her entourage. Ostentatiously, he draped an arm around Pucelle's shoulders and leaned in to whisper something in her ear. The last Isabeau saw of her son as the mammoth doors creaked shut, locking the queen mother in the solitude of the foyer, was his backside and finger poised over his shoulder in some sort of gesture. It was obscene and unkingly.

ABOUT THE AUTHOR

A long time ago, in a galaxy not so far away, Dan R. Arman decided he wanted to tell stories. Stories about other worlds populated by interesting characters, because he thought these people and worlds would help him reflect on the world he was living in, its beauty, horrors and absurdity. While he was starting to pursue this dream, he began teaching English Composition at Stark State College in Ohio. For several years, he worked as a newspaper reporter, an editor and now teaches literature and writing at an online high school. He holds a master's degree in English literature and rhetoric from Kent State University. He currently lives in Akron, OH with his wife and two cats. Riding a Black Horse is his third novel.

Made in the USA
Monee, IL
26 February 2023

28763028R00239